When mentally challenged Janie Braxton arrives at the emergency room, she doesn't remember the rape and beating that sent her there. Nor does she understand why the spirit of an ancient Indian chief talks to her. But as gang criminals chase her two little girls through the streets of St. Louis, her rage builds to an inferno that threatens the Indian chief's plot to realign the cosmos.

I0565407

VIRGIN BLOOD

Richard Stooker

In Dreams Extreme Press

ISBN-13: 978-0692235416

ISBN-10: 0692235418

Cover art and graphics by Derek Murphy

Published by In Dreams Extreme Press.

http://www.InDreamsExtreme.com/

DEDICATION

First of all to my mother Virginia Stooker who deserves—finally—a book dedication after encouraging her son who wanted to be a writer.

To the paid and volunteer staff of all shelters protecting anyone from spousal/partner violence.

And to T.B., who'll never read it.

ACKNOWLEDGEMENTS

I want to extend my heartfelt thanks to following people for their role in helping me to make VIRGIN BLOOD as good as possible:

1. The paid and volunteer staff at the Cahokia Mounds United Nations Heritage Site in Illinois. They are studying, preserving and presenting the artifacts and culture of the pre-Columbian civilization I have chosen to call "The Great People." In the centuries before climatic changes and, possibly, smallpox brought by Spanish explorers destroyed them, they made the St. Louis metropolitan area the largest city north of the Aztec center in now-Mexico City. They also built the largest structure in the world—the great Temple Mound—which is even bigger than the pyramids of Egypt—out of dirt. If you ever visit St Louis, be sure to drop by its United Nations Heritage Site.

2. Elizabeth E., a nurse who is afraid if I use her entire name she'll be deluged with requests for assistance. She graciously pointed out many medical blunders I made.

3. Rennie Browne, for accepting VIRGIN BLOOD as an Editorial Department client even though she was busy with many other projects.

4. Dave King, then-Vice President of The Editorial Department. Back when I thought VIRGIN BLOOD WAS 99.99% perfect, he pointed out the many problems I had been too close to it to see. Dave, thank you for your diligence.

5. To the creators of the special, horrific typefaces I've used—Cramps (pOPdOG fONTS), Castle Dracustein (Chad Savage), and Creepsville (Tony O'Farrell). And dafont.com.

All remaining errors or lapses are my responsibility.

CHAPTER ONE

I

Holy Virgin Mother of God Medical Center

Whirling as fast as her heart thumped, the cold red light whipped Janie.

She lay on the bed inside the ambulance with a needle stuck in her arm, already hooked up to a glass bottle with blood food in it. The side of her head felt like a pumpkin. The loud siren screeched to a halt and doctors in orange uniforms carried her off. Everything looked so funny she wanted to laugh, but she could only croak. Far away, voices babbled.

"Coming through! Out of the way!"

"This the girl? Number Two's ready."

A loudspeaker blared. "Trauma Team to Number Two. Stat! Trauma Team to Number Two. Stat!"

1

Janie was in a hospital. She was stupid, but she knew about hospitals. She liked nurses because they smiled and talked nice to her.

They slid her onto a cot that rolled on the floor, and then men and women in hospital uniforms surrounded her. Many hands worked on Janie's body. They held doctor tools against her chest and all over her body. Fingers grabbed her wrists. A damp washcloth wiped the blood from her face. Small plastic blew air into her nose that made her feel dizzy. A TV-like machine next to her beeped when her heart beat. The boss doctor pulled on rubber gloves. They always made Janie think of condoms. Michael didn't like rubbers. That's why Shontell was born.

Strong fingers pressed against the big side of Janie's head, just like her mother taught her to squeeze cantaloupes so she didn't buy a rotten one. Janie felt proud of herself for remembering that. Maybe she was stupid, but she never bought a bad cantaloupe.

"Get skull and c-spine and head CT without contrast," he said. "And all the lab work—HBG and HCT, type and cross match for two units of blood. Electrolytes and arterial blood gas. I want x-rays, and call the neurosurgeon NOW."

A nurse cut off Janie's shirt with a pair of big scissors. "She doesn't have any pants on. Where're her pants?"

A nurse with long blond hair who was so beautiful she looked like an angel said, "You think the guy raped her pulled her pants back on before he ran away?"

"Shut up and cut that sleeve so I can wrap the blood pressure cuff around her arm," a man nurse said. "The cops'll want her clothing for evidence."

2

"Can the chatter," the bossy doctor said. "And drape her before she freezes to death."

"My God, she's so small," a black woman with a kind face said. "Like a little girl."

"My thirteen year old daughter is bigger than her," an older woman said.

A black nurse leaned over Janie and pulled up one of her eyelids. "How're you doing, honey?"

Janie wanted to tell the nice lady she was doing fine, but her tongue and lips wouldn't move.

"Say something, sugar. Come on, talk to me. What's your name? Can you tell me that, baby? Do you know where you are? Do you know what time it is?"

Janie stared into those deep black eyes but couldn't make any words come out of her mouth.

"She can't be oriented at all," the nice nurse said. "You hear me, don't you, honey?" she asked Janie. "But you just can't talk back."

A bright light shined into Janie's eyes.

"Left eye is dilated to four millimeters with sluggish contraction."

The angel nurse looked up Janie's nose. "Both nostrils clear, no sign of drainage." Then into her ears. "Tympanic membranes clear. Right ear is clear. Left one has bloody discharge."

The bossy doctor listened to Janie's lungs with the stethoscope. "Lungs clear to auscultation."

The nice nurse grabbed Janie's hand and tried to wrap Janie's fingers around two of hers. "Can you hold on? See how hard you can squeeze my fingers. Come on, honey, make them hurt."

She lowered Janie's hand. "No response."

A man nurse placed his palm flat against the bottom of Janie's bare foot. "Can you push my hand away?"

After a moment he said, "No response."

The doctor hit her knee with a hard rubber hammer. "Weaker than normal reflexes." He ran the plastic tip of his pen up and down the bottoms of both bare feet, making her toes curl slightly. "Only a small Babinski reflex, especially in the right foot. She's totally unresponsive."

As he spoke, the angel nurse was sliding a little plastic tube inside the hole where Janie went pee pee. The beauty of her long, wavy blond hair made Janie feel good.

Janie

The voice calling her sounded as if it was from far away, under the ground. It sounded like Daddy, but Daddy didn't come to visit her when she was in the hospital. Not anymore.

"Her breathing's irregular now," the angel nurse said. "She's pausing at the end of each inhalation."

"Another early symptom of hematoma. What're her vital signs?"

"Pulse rate over 100 and climbing."

"Blood pressure 75 over 40 and dropping. I think we're losing her."

"Louise, take orifice swab samples to the lab immediately. I want the blood work back here five minutes ago. What's her temperature?"

"Still 97.9."

"BP holding at 80."

"Pulse just over 100."

Janie

4

That voice again. It could be Uncle Tommy, but Uncle Tommy never came to see her in the hospital. She hadn't seen Uncle Tommy since she left home. Anyway, Uncle Tommy was dead. Mommy told Janie Uncle Tommy had a heart attack, back when Shontell was just a baby.

Janie

Go away. She wanted to look at the pretty angel nurse again, and the doctor standing in front of her head. He was handsome and sexy even if he did have a bossy voice.

"Looks like somebody tried to split her skull open with a baseball bat," he said. "What happened? Anybody know?"

"The cops found her in a vacant building," the angel nurse said. "Joe told me she was unconscious at the scene. We were the closest ER with Level One Trauma Care."

"Aren't we always?" the man nurse said. "And it's only Thursday night."

"It's spring."

"Do we have a history on her?" the doctor asked.

"The cops found a Medicaid card in her pants pocket," the angel said. "Cerise thinks she's been here before. Will's called down to Records for a file."

"She's been someplace before," the older nurse said. "Look at all these scars. Up and down her legs, on her belly—I bet there's more on her back."

"You win," Angel said. "She looks like she's been flogged with a lash."

"That's a belt buckle or I'm crazy."

"Get her under the x-rays before that hematoma kills her," the doctor said.

Janie

Now the voice sounded like Michael, but that couldn't be right either. Michael was in jail, had been ever since he was arrested for robbing and beating up that old woman who lived down the street. He wasn't supposed to get out for a long time, until at least next year.

The doctor and nurses placed her on a big table and fastened foam pads around her neck and head. They stretched a thick bib over her from throat to knees, then left the room. She heard a brief humming. They returned and moved her around to a different position.

Janie knew they were taking special pictures of her head bones. She dimly remembered doctors showing her funny-looking black and white photographs. She went to the hospital a lot because she was so stupid and clumsy. When she was a little girl a bad man burned her leg with a hot clothes iron. Lots of times bad men on the street jumped her. Once a bad man pushed her down the basement stairs at Michael's house and she had to wear a cast on her left arm for a long time and it made her itch like poison ivy.

The nice nurse shone a light into Janie's eyes again.

"Her left pupil's blown. Now it's seven millimeters."

The doctor placed Janie's hands on her stomach, then shocked Janie by suddenly reaching out and pinching one of her nipples! Why didn't that hurt?

"Decortate response to noxious pressure." the doctor said. "She's a 3 on the Glasgow Coma Scale for sure."

"Respiration up to 24."

"We need that CAT scan, stat. Prepare for emergency burr hole procedures. After we've drained the hematoma we'll install a drain and monitor to measure her intercranial pressure."

Janie

The voice was louder now, more insistent, like Mommy calling her for supper.

They placed her on another table, stuck her head in a big machine and tied her down with straps. She didn't understand. She wanted to leave. She didn't like hospitals.

Janie

Now it sounded like a woman's voice. Maybe Mommy was yelling at her again. Maybe Odelia was screaming at her about something. When Odelia did that, Janie sat inside the back of her head and turned her off, just like a TV. She learned to do that when she was little and Mommy and Daddy fussed at her so much she could hardly stand it. She knew she was a bad girl and too stupid to do things right even when she tried. She just couldn't listen to them all the time.

Janie

She didn't want to listen to this voice either. It wasn't a pleasant voice. It wasn't that nice nurse asking her name or Marilyn calling her. She wouldn't pay any attention to it.

Janie grew chilly cold as a strange gray mist filled the room like smoke. Her flesh and bones felt heavy, thick, uncomfortable, like rock. She stood up to escape the weight, and suddenly she could hear and see everything more clearly, even her body still lying on the table.

She watched the beautiful nurse who looked like an angel cover her head and face with white cloths and place doctor tools out on a shiny tray by her head. Now all Janie could see of herself was that big, bald knot on her head. It looked like a pink baseball.

Another doctor was in talking to the first one. He was hold-

7

ing up weird pictures. "She has a parietal fracture with significant bony depression extending inferiorly from the anterior aspect of the temporal bone's squamous portion. CAT scan indicates tearing of the meningeal artery, so she does have an epidural hematoma. She also has uncal herniation with a ten millimeter mid-line shift to the left. If we don't hurry, she's taking a permanent trip to gaga land."

Janie watched the second doctor drill a hole in the side of her head. She wondered why that didn't hurt, then remembered that in the hospital they always put you to sleep before they cut on you.

Except she wasn't asleep, unless she was dreaming. But she felt wide awake. How could she look at the doctor and nurses and even at her own body just like watching a hospital movie on TV?

"Janie."

There it was again. Calling her. Wanting her.

It sounded different now. Still from below the ground, but somehow not so far away. It was the doctors and nurses who sounded like they were speaking through a bad telephone connection, even though they were right there in the same room with Janie.

She watched as the gadget in her head pulled bloody water out of her skull.

How did all that get inside her brain? What happened to her? Something about Dewie. She tried to think, but she never could think very good. Things she planned never worked out right and everybody always laughed at her.

But what was it about Dewie?

She didn't like Dewie even though he was Michael's younger brother. She didn't like how Dewie looked at her. Michael didn't like Dewie either. Michael told her that Dewie was a bug-eyed weasel, even if he was his brother.

Michael was nice. He talked soft to Janie, stroked her back and ran his fingers through her hair. At night, in bed, he held her pressed close against him. Janie missed that. Of course, lots of nights he hadn't come home until late, or not at all, but when he was there he gave her lots of loving. And when he wasn't, Janie at least had his bed to sleep in.

Now, since Michael went to jail, Janie didn't get nothing. Odelia'd kicked her out of Michael's room and Janie was lucky if she could lay down on the big, lumpy gray couch in the front room.

But what happened to make her go into the hospital?

"Janie. Janiiiiiiiiiieeeeeeeeee."

Janie wouldn't say anything. If that was Dewie, she didn't want to talk to him.

"BP up to 90," the angel nurse said. "Pulse rate down to 85. Temperature 98.1. She's stabilizing."

"Left pupil dilation has decreased nearly two millimeters. It's sluggish, but it's reacting."

"Intercranial pressure should be near normal limits by now," the first doctor said. "Have that cop go through the rape procedure as fast as he can. After we patch her together she goes into the neurological intensive care unit. We need her hooked up to an ICP monitor for baseline readings. Order the EEG. I want it ASAP."

"Janie."

Oh no, who could that be now? Nobody Janie could think of came to visit her when she was in the hospital, except Michael, maybe. But he was in jail. She kept forgetting that. Besides, when Mommy and Daddy used to come see her it was always when she was in a bed in a room, not being worked on by the doctors and nurses. Nobody saw her then. People in the hospital sometimes asked her how she got hurt and why she had so many scars. Because she was so dumb, Janie always told them.

Not a genius like the real smart kids who made straight `A's in school or even a normal kid like Mommy and Daddy kept saying they wished she was. But stupid. Once she ate a whole bottle of aspirin. She was so stupid, she didn't care what anybody thought.

"Janie."

Why wouldn't he go away and stop pestering her? She was busy. The nice nurse and the angel were taking her back to the first room. Janie saw a young, fat policeman in the waiting area. He was drinking coffee and flirting with the nurse behind the desk.

"Janie."

Janie looked down. A long way past her feet, below the basement, she saw a ghost who looked like an Indian. He held a big, green stone hammer. He also had on a big headdress of white feathers and a skirt made out of woven grass that did not make him look like a girl because he was an Indian. But he wasn't like the Indians in cowboy movies. He had bright red circles on his cheeks. Janie thought that was his war paint, then she realized they were tattoos. He must be a real strange Indian. Janie knew lots of men, and some women, who put tattoos on their bodies, but nobody she knew had big tattoos on their faces.

"Pull me up to PeopleLand, Janie. I long to see Elder Brother Sun again. I long to live in flesh again. I will again be king."

What was he talking about?

"Once I was the absolute ruler of your land, but I have been trapped here in Dirtworld for twelve cycles of the sacred fifty-two years. It is time for me to reign again. It is time for your people to worship Elder Brother Sun and obey his younger brother. Your people need my wisdom, my guidance and my strength. I long to feel the warmth of Elder Brother again."

Janie didn't understand. The Indian made her think of Dewie, and she didn't want to do that. She turned her attention back to the hospital.

The fat policeman was opening a big plastic pouch and talking to the nice nurse and the angel.

"I don't have any other officers available to help me," he said. "So I hope at least one of you ladies will stay here and observe. It's standard procedure to have a woman present." His face reddened and his voice choked with embarrassment. "I'm sure you understand. So there's no suspicion on me of doing anything wrong."

"Go head on, Jerry," the nice nurse said. "We'll stick around and make sure you behave yourself. Looks to me like this baby done been abused enough already."

Janie watched the policeman comb through her sex hairs, cut some off, clip some hairs from the top of her head, take cotton swab samples from her mouth, pussy and asshole, and put everything into sealed envelopes. He also scraped under her fingernails. The nice nurse pricked Janie's finger and drew blood for him.

"Associated injuries?" Jerry the policeman asked.

"Some vaginal lacerations and bleeding. We're going to disinfect and sew her up as soon as you're done. It'll all be in the report."

"How soon do you think before she can tell us anything?"

The two women looked at each other. The angel said, "The prognosis is very poor, especially if she doesn't regain consciousness by tomorrow. You guys going to catch the motherfucker did this?"

Jerry was packing up the rape kit. He sealed it shut and returned the Bic pen to his shirt pocket. "I hope so. Just in case, we're putting her under protective custody, so nobody can find out she's here. I wonder what she was doing way up north in that neighborhood anyway? Helluva thing."

The doctor sewed up the skin on the side of Janie's head and the inside of her pussy. The nurses swabbed her with smelly goo and taped white bandages on her.

The doctor said, "With a ten percent chance of developing seizures, her side rails must stay up at all times, and keep an airway at the head of the bed. I'm ordering a prophylactic anticonvulsant dose for her IV. Dilantin. Point 2 normal saline solution."

"Janie," the Indian ghost said. "Your sacrifice will break me free of Grandmother Earth's embrace. You must die so I can live again."

Janie shivered. She felt like when she had to get out of bed in February after the gas company turned the heat off or she played in wind packed snowdrifts behind the house in Eureka when she was a little girl.

That was the Indian. He was under the ground, cold—and dead.

As a man wheeled her down the hall to another room in the hospital, she suddenly knew. Something real bad happened to her. Like the time she was in South St. Louis late at night with Solange, only even worser.

She remembered now Dewie told her to meet him at that abandoned house on the corner in ten minutes. Of course Janie had said no. She was stupid, not crazy. Then Dewie told her he had a special message for her from Michael. He couldn't tell her in the house, because Michael didn't want Odelia to find out. Janie knew that Michael didn't trust Odelia even if she was his mother and didn't like Odelia being all up in his business. If Dewie told Janie in the house, even late at night, then Yolanda or Tiffany would find out and go to Odelia. Janie knew that was right, so she went to see what Michael wanted Dewie to tell her.

"Janie."

Cold like old bones. Trapped, frozen inside the earth. What did that Indian ghost want with her? She couldn't rescue an Indian from below the ground. That was silly.

She watched the nurses hook lots of tubes and machines up to her arm, neck and head. Dewie. Dewie must have hurt her. Dewie must have done this to her. But, but—what about—her kids? She woke Latasha up before she left and told her to watch Shontell. But, but—now she remembered hearing Latasha scream. They must have followed her to the empty house.

"Janie. I need your life, Janie. Your death will end your fears and pain. Soon you and your troubles will be over. Do not worry anymore."

Ice clutched Janie's heart with fingers cold as a snow-covered grave.

What happened to Latasha and Shontell?

Where are my babies?

13

II

St. Louis Abused Women's Shelter (secret location)

"I'm worried about her, Sara," Marilyn Patterson said. Her headache hammered a spike through the top of her skull. "She should be back here by now."

Sara finished marking the last entry in the account book, slammed it shut and ran her fingers through her elfin-cut short hair. "Do you know where we could lay our hands on a cheap used PC? One Wal-Mart special and I wouldn't have to stay here until after midnight once a week keeping the records straight enough to qualify for United Way funding."

"Don't you care, Sara?"

The other woman rolled her eyes toward the ceiling. "Lord, give me strength. Marilyn, we have been down this road a zillion times. You cannot worry your head off about every single resident, especially Janie. She'll come back when she comes back, just like always."

Marilyn walked across the cluttered office, turned and strode back to the desk. "She's moved back into that house. I know it."

"So? She always pops up here again after Michael practices karate on her, if that's what happens. With Janie, who knows for sure?"

Marilyn kept pacing. "I shouldn't have let her go."

"Like, just how were you supposed to stop her? She's twenty-three even if she looks twelve and acts five. This is where abused women come when they want to, right?" Sara slid the ledger book into its place in a desk drawer, stood up and stretched. "When they want to leave, they leave."

Marilyn collapsed into the lumpy, overstuffed armchair. "Why do some of them go back, Sara? We change their bandages, feed them hot chicken soup and give them counseling. We take them to sign up for TANF, SSI, General Relief, Energy Assistance, Food Stamps, Medicaid—you name it."

"So what do you want, a medal from the Goddess?"

"I want to think we're really doing something. We find them jobs and apartments. We drive them to safe houses in Kansas City and Chicago. We send them to GED classes. We help them sue for child support and file for divorce. Then some return to the same asshole who broke their jaw and punctured their lungs with a steak knife."

"Hey, divorce is just a piece of paper," Sara said. "I get pissed at myself for it, but my heart still goes pitter-pat every time my ex calls me. After they take the big step of coming here, some of these women find they really miss the guy. They're too scared to be on their own or it's too peaceful or they miss the adrenaline rush of the constant fighting and danger. Or maybe they still feel responsible for the poor baby. After all, they married the dude, so there must have been love there once. You need a vacation."

Marilyn laughed a hiccup of a laugh. "Where would I go? I don't have any money."

"So stay home and watch Oprah. Chill out."

"I wish I could."

"Believe it or not, the shelter won't fall apart without you. Get a life."

Marilyn glanced at her watch. "It's a quarter after two. She can't be with a friend this late."

Sara sighed. "Thanks to you, Janie and the kids get checks and Latasha's in school and Shontell's in Head Start preschool. Both girls are up on their shots and they have clothes. You've made Janie's life better. But she isn't going to leave Michael or his family behind, not permanently. Get used to it. And maybe she shouldn't. He does seem to give her some stability."

Marilyn closed her eyes. She felt so tired, so drained. Her muscles ached. Her blood pumped sluggishly, choked with the dull pain of too much missed sleep over too many nights. She couldn't keep track of the hours she spent at the shelter even though she was only paid for twenty-four a week, and that at only a small fraction over the minimum wage.

"Sara, what're you saying?"

"It's obvious, isn't it? Janie's using us. We're her free hotel when she needs a break from home."

"Janie doesn't think that hard."

"Don't underestimate her. Just because she sounds like a kid when she talks and can't read doesn't mean she's innocent. She lies. She goes over to that house when she says she's visiting a friend. That's probably where she and the kids are right now even though she said she was only going to stop by to ask about her big checks. That was two days ago. She's probably out spending that money right now."

"She said she wanted to buy a house with it. And I believe her."

"Don't you think maybe she's learned how to manipulate people by now? Especially you?"

"Oh Sara."

"She doesn't do it in a mean way. She's like my five year old kid. When I catch him sneaking cookies in the kitchen he lies brazen as can be. Janie just doesn't want you to know she's doing something you don't approve of. Basically, she doesn't tell the truth so it won't upset you. Don't expect total honesty from someone who has nothing else to protect herself with but deceit."

Sara's son. Even lesbians had children. This unwanted reminder of her friend's fertility coated Marilyn's mouth with scorched lead.

Sara put her hand on Marilyn's shoulder. "I've got to run. Important meeting in the morning, can't be late. I'll be here tomorrow afternoon by four. You go home and catch a few Z's. And don't beat yourself up. The damage is just as real as when a man does it."

Marilyn squeezed Sara's hand briefly. She wasn't going to follow the advice, but she appreciated the concern.

"I'm going to heat a glass of herbal tea in the microwave," she said. "That'll calm my nerves."

"Then drive yourself home and sleep late in the morning. Don't even think of arriving here before noon. Everybody knows how many hours you put in."

Home? The overpriced apartment where she grew her houseplants? This was her home, God help her.

"You're not Janie's mother," Sara said.

"She tells me I love her like a mother."

"So stop fretting, Mama Hen. That girl has a remarkable ability to find people to help her out. Remember the first caseworker she had at the welfare office, the one who broke all the rules to send Janie's TANF checks out as soon as she could and put the kids on Medicaid so they could have a checkup right away?"

"That's true, isn't it?" Marilyn said. "Either you want to do everything you can to help her, or to take advantage of her."

"And plenty of people have done plenty of both."

Marilyn sighed. "I'm afraid there's been more take advantage than help. Or else the damage they've inflicted is worse than the good the rest of us can do."

"She could be worse off," Sara said. "There's lots of women locked up in institutions who went through only one tenth the punishment she admits to. And we just know what she tells us. She denies the rest, but she couldn't have gotten all those scars from falling out of a tree, no matter what she claims."

"Sure."

"So she comes in here, battered and crying, saying Michael beat her up, then after a few weeks she tells us it was a bad man on the street jumped her. And when her wounds are healed she'll claim nothing happened at all. So she copes by denying reality, just like all of us do. She always bounces back. She's still on her own, more or less in charge of her life for all she insists on screwing it up. She doesn't do as badly as lots of people with three times her smarts."

"But she's the one I always worry about."

Sara waived at the resident files stacked in boxes in the corner. "We've had women in here with college degrees, even money of their own, but they were as helpless as babies and wouldn't snap out of it until their guy almost killed them. Janie had the strength to leave home at fifteen when she was pregnant and survive."

Marilyn grinned. "Actually, I think Latasha handles things now. When she's learned more how to read and write, and add and subtract, I think she could manage a checking account for Janie. She could write them out and have Janie sign them."

"Don't let Tyrannosaurus Regina hear you're teaching a seven year old to pay bills. She'd have a hissy fit."

Marilyn smiled. "Just because Mildred's Executive Director doesn't mean she has to know everything."

"She sure doesn't," Sara said. "Or she'd tell us to get rid of the guns."

"Guns? What guns?"

"You don't know? As many hours as you spend here? Of course, you're really day staff."

Sara pulled open the bottom drawer of a banged up file cabinet they had scrounged free from a local insurance agency which thought its useful life over. She shuffled through a pile of old ledger books and thick stacks of paid bills wrapped with rubber bands, pulled a cardboard box from the rear and opened it.

Marilyn couldn't believe what she saw. Four handguns, and lots of loose cartridges scattered over the bottom. Several of the pistols were small, but one looked big enough to stop a horse.

"Where'd they come from?"

"Residents, where do you think? A couple of women couldn't have gotten past their husbands without one. Remember that Sadie Jones? She thought she was a cowboy herself. We couldn't let any of them keep the guns, and we didn't know what to do with them after we took them, so we just put them here."

"Lord, Sara."

"Hey, a lot of times I'm here late at night so I always figured, what the hell, you never know what might happen. Maybe one day, despite all our precautions, some outraged husband or boyfriend will find us. Or maybe some night we'll get a run of the mill thief. This isn't exactly the safest neighborhood in the city."

"But guns—I had no idea."

"My ex is a gun nut and some of it rubbed off. So every once in a while, when I'm alone, I take them out, clean and reload them." She grinned." Oh, I know it's outrageous and it's not in accordance with Mildred's philosophy of strict nonviolence, but I believe in protecting myself."

Marilyn pressed her mouth into a sour expression to keep from speaking her mind. She didn't want to hurt Sara, who obviously derived some sicko thrill from the weapons beyond a sense of security, but her first duty was to Mildred, who had founded the shelter as a way to help women counteract male violence.

Marilyn chewed over the situation as Sara placed the box back inside the file cabinet. When skeptics asked Mildred theoretical questions about whether she would allow men to rape and kill her grandchildren, she answered with cold glares and elegant sniffs implying, of course, no proper lady or gentleman allowed themselves or their loved ones to be in such situations to begin with.

Coming from a working class and therefore much less sheltered background, Marilyn understood this attitude wasn't realistic. Violent people could strike anyone. But guns weren't practical for self-defense since they escalated confrontations into unnecessary violence. Besides, any bloodshed at the shelter and they would have to call the police. That would place the shelter's address on public record, and they couldn't afford to relocate.

So Marilyn would have to tell Mildred she discovered the box while searching for something in the file cabinet. Current staff and volunteers could simply disavow all knowledge and blame past workers. The shelter had a high turnover. Not many women could take the emotional stress for long.

Sara picked up her purse. "Come on, Marilyn, let's walk each other out to our cars."

Marilyn shook her head and checked her watch again. Almost three o'clock. Sara was right. If Janie's wasn't there by then, she wasn't coming back that night. Maybe not ever, not even to pick up their few clothes left upstairs. With Janie, who could know for sure?

"I haven't had that cup of herbal tea I promised myself."

"You need to sleep."

Marilyn heard a noise, jumped in her chair. "Who's there?"

"It's only big old me." Betty Silver trudged through the door and plopped herself down in the second armchair. "I hate to disturb you guys when it's so late, but I couldn't sleep."

"Do you need to talk?" Marilyn asked.

"No. I mean yes, but I really feel guilty bothering you so much. This isn't exactly my regular time to see you, but everything bothers me. I'm scared of little noises. I keep thinking Terry is going to find me and shoot me. He's looking for me, you know, I'm sure he is. He has this weird mystical idea about the importance of being married and his honor. If he knew I was so close to our house he'd—"

"He won't find you here," Marilyn said in a soothing voice. "You know how careful we are."

"But he's so close, and he can be so sneaky."

"Didn't you say he's a gun freak?" Marilyn gave Sara a sig-

21

nificant glance. See what kind of people like guns?

"Worships them, but you know the funny part? With everybody else but me, he's a sweet guy. He wouldn't hurt nobody unless he had to. Then he might do anything. He's got some strange shit in his head. He needs your counseling a lot more than me. Like, he believes serial killers are cool and admires outlaws, but he doesn't want to do anything like that himself. He just wants to come home from work, drink beer while he watches movies on TV, then beat the shit out of me before we fuck."

"You're safe here," Marilyn said. "I promise."

After Marilyn helped Betty back upstairs to bed, Sara stood up. "This time I'm leaving for sure. Go home soon, all right?"

Marilyn nodded, making a promise as empty as her womb, as faithless as her heart, as bottomless as her life. Her apartment, which took so much of her hard earned money, did not draw her.

Some of her sadness must have showed through her voice or her eyes, for Sara gave her a long hug. "What I'm about to say is horribly politically incorrect. It also offends my newborn dyke's soul to its womanist core and you'll probably never forgive me, but it's the truth. Girl, you need a man."

Marilyn gasped as though punched in the stomach and stared at her friend. She sputtered, then she and Sara broke into loud laughter.

III

Sawbuck Trailer Court, Jefferson County

choir began singing "Rock of Ages."

Judith Braxton dragged herself to the edge of waking.

She had just been dreaming about taking Janie to church, back when Janie was still a child. Back when she was proud to sit between her mother and father in the pew listening to the gospel preached, and singing her own words to the hymns. Back when she still said goodnight prayers on her knees before going to bed and talked about Jesus as though he were her closest friend. Jesus liked her yellow dress better than the blue one. Jesus told her to be good to Mommy today. The memory brought tears to Judith's eyes.

The ring tone tore at Judith's heart.

Cleft for me...

Through the haze of nearly two bottles of red wine she realized she lay across half the couch. Willie Lee snored at the other end. A black and white movie flickered on the TV.

Judith had been proud that, despite all Janie's limitations, she was bringing the child up as a good Christian. She may not be able to prevent other children from making fun of Janie. She couldn't buy Janie many toys or the special counseling and therapy the schools wanted her to have. And she couldn't stop Willie Lee from punishing Janie. But she could give Janie faith, and that was her obligation. Many parents with lots more money failed to meet their children's spiritual needs. After Janie died, Judith once believed, she would go to Heaven. That comfort was taken from Judith long ago.

Let the water and the blood...

One Sunday afternoon after her thirteenth birthday, Janie announced Jesus wasn't her friend anymore, so she wasn't going to church ever again. When Judith and Willie Lee tried to take her the next Sunday, she screamed and pitched a fit so hard they finally admitted they couldn't force her short of locking her in chains.

Some children could be reasoned with. They did what their parents wanted if only to keep peace in the household or avoid punishment. But not Janie. She was in her own little world. Willie Lee punished her, but that only raised the decibel level, as Judith could have told him if he had asked, which of course he never had because of course he knew his chastisements of Janie never worked but of course that never stopped him.

Save from wrath and make me pure.

Judith sat up slowly and swigged a belt of wine. Thinking about her daughter always made he reach for the bottle, an action as automatic as bowing her head to pray when the preacher raised his hand.

Judith had known all day something was going to happen. Women's intuition. Willie Lee made fun of it, said if women wanted to be as good as men they had to give up their intuition and think only with their brains, as men did. When they were younger she'd talked back when he said stuff like that, but that just made him angry, sometimes sent him right over the edge. Willie Lee had a lot of good points in spite of himself, but patience was not one of them. And raising Janie would have taxed the limits of Job. She shuddered. The Bible said God didn't give a person more burdens than they could carry, but Judith had long ago accepted neither she nor Willie Lee possessed the strength to shoulder the load of a child like Janie.

Willie Lee kept on snoring.

All for sin could not atone...

It hadn't just been Janie's retardation although, the Good Lord knew, that was difficult enough. The child had been so willful and cantankerous. Because she was so dumb she didn't understand what she was not capable of. Through church and Bible study groups, Judith had met many retarded children who were as sweet, gentle and obedient as could be, but Janie had the devil in her.

Helpless, look to thee for grace...

Willie Lee snorted, harrumphed, but continued to doze. Judith knew in her heart the call was about Janie. That's why she was afraid to answer. That's why she kept waiting for the person on the other end to give up.

She suddenly wished she'd drunk so much wine she couldn't wake up for a brass band. She wanted to ignore the phone. She wanted to stare at this old movie and cheer on the dead actors as they learned how much they loved each other despite all their arguments and misunderstandings. She wished she were at an old-fashioned revival tent meeting, with singing and mad shouting and people filled with the Holy Spirit speaking in tongues as they rolled and thrashed on the ground. Once she'd been to see those folks in the South handled poison snakes without fear.

When mine eyes shall close in death...

No matter how much Judith tried to put Janie behind her, leaving Janie to wallow in the filth she had chosen over God and her family, the girl kept invading Judith's existence and ripping her heart to tatters. Janie was her only child, the fruit of Judith's husband's seed in her womb and, for all the pain she caused, Judith couldn't cut Janie totally out of her life, even when that seemed to be Janie's preference. The girl would disappear for months, even a year, at a time, with no visits or phone calls, then reappear again when least expected and least wanted.

When I soar to worlds unknown,
see thee on thy judgment throne...

Heart slamming against her chest so hard she thought it would wake the dead, or at least Willie Lee, she picked up the phone and fumbled to press the green button. "Praise the Lord."

"I'm Jim Williams," a strange man said. "A social worker at Holy Virgin Mother of God Hospital in St. Louis. I'm sorry to disturb you so late, but it's important."

"What's happened to Janie this time?"

CHAPTER TWO

I

Corner of Ashland and Greer (several hours earlier)

D ewie's pants were bunched on the floor around his ankles. He reached into a pocket and pulled out his lead pipe.

Janie was crying and whimpering, holding her hands across her scrawny pussy like it mattered now if he saw her naked. Blood trickled from between her fingers. Now she'd been had by a real man.

The Indian chief pounded Dewie's mind, demanding the sacrifice continue.

Kneeling over her, Dewie raised the lead pipe high, then brought it down on the side of Janie's head as hard as he could.

The thwacking sound and the solid thump of impact felt even better than coming. That showed the little bitch. She wouldn't mouth off to him again.

The Indian seeped into Dewie's nostrils like smoke. Dewie inhaled deeply, a powerful rush zapping his brain. He dropped the pipe, took out his switchblade and flicked it open.

That's right.

The sound came from inside Dewie's own head. The chief's spirit was getting close to Dewie's soul. Dewie knew when it reached his heart, he would be transformed into the most powerful human being who ever lived.

Complete the sacrifice.

Dewie smiled and raised his hand. She wouldn't even know when he cut her heart out.

The back door creaked. "Mama? Are you in there?"

The kids! Those two little bitty bitches.

"Mama, where are you? It's late. I got scared knowing you're out here in this dirty old house. Shontell's crying. Let's go back."

Dewie's hand hovered in midair.

Latasha screamed. Dewie whirled about. The girl ran through the door, pulling her little sister behind her.

Dewie started to run after them then stumbled to the floor, feet caught in his pants. He picked himself up, pulling his pants back on, tried to rush after the girls again, but stood still. He couldn't move. The power of the Indian spirit burst full force into his body like a bullet train, paralyzing him. His skin thickened and hardened. His muscles bunched into tight steel cables and his bones set like concrete. His heart crystallized to diamond. The process shot explosions through his mind like underground nuclear blasts, shaking him to the core of his soul.

Compared to that, the finest crack was boring. His joints ached, the world spun about him and his bones shrieked.

Now you are heavier than lead, stronger than steel, harder than bullet proof glass, thicker than marble. But my spirit cannot enter you entirely because the sacrifice was not complete. You are stronger, but not yet all-powerful. Thicker and tougher, but not yet immortal.

Still dizzy and dazed, Dewie looked down at Janie's skinny little body lying limp on the floor. He groped for the door, then squeezed through the loose boards covering it, his heart beating a wild bass line. He looked quickly around him, but didn't see those girls. Where'd they go? He had to find them, stop them. Had to, before the police caught him and threw him in jail with Michael.

He ran through the alley. The back of his house was dark and quiet. He circled quickly to the front. He ran down the street for several blocks without seeing any sign of them. He turned and sprinted back the other way, tore up and down the sidewalks, looking under hedges and bushes.

When he heard the sirens he returned to the condemned house. Standing with some neighbors, he watched the paramedics carry Janie out on a stretcher. Then he went home.

His body ached from taking in the Indian's power. It was still changing. He wanted to crash, but he had important business to finish first. The Indian said the sacrifice wasn't over. Janie was still alive. He was the Indian Chief's new Eagle Warrior, but he needed help—those girls would lie on him to the police, he knew it. He had to stop them. Fast. There was only one person he could talk to.

He slammed the bedroom door open, rushed inside and shook her shoulder.

"Mama, Mama."

II

Goodfellow to Delmar

Latasha and Shontell jumped behind a big tree in the front yard of the house by the bus stop. The street light threw down a white glare. Keeping her younger sister between her knees, Latasha crouched low and leaned her head to the side to peep around the trunk. She could watch for the bus while hiding from Dewie.

Where was he? Where was the bus? What if Dewie found them before the next one came?

When Latasha saw Mama on the floor with no pants on, Latasha knew she had been Doing It. Mama did not like and feared Dewie. Although she Did It with lots of men, she wouldn't with him. Dewie must have Forced her. That's why he was kneeling beside her with his hand raised to cut her with a switchblade.

There was blood smeared on her mother's white thighs and her face looked like she was asleep, but more than asleep. A length of broken lead pipe lay on the bare floor. Dewie must have hit Mama on the head with it. That's why she looked so sick. Maybe she was dead.

Latasha forgot everything and screamed. Shontell didn't understand, but she screamed too.

When Dewie whirled around, his face looked really strange, way more than when he got mad. In Dewie's eyes Latasha saw deep snow, like they wanted to suck her inside where she would stay frozen, a solid block of dead ice, forever.

Although it cut her heart to leave Mama, in one split second she realized she could do nothing to help. She had to escape or Dewie would kill her and Shontell. Nails and splinters tore her arm when she squeezed through the loose boards nailed across the back door. Dragging her crying sister behind her, she ran down the alley as fast as she could.

"Shut up, stupid," she shouted at Shontell. "Do you want Uncle Dewie to hurt you too?"

Shontell's shorter legs couldn't move as fast as hers, but Latasha didn't let go of her sister's hand. Sweat slicked their palms, but their fingers clenched tightly together.

Latasha didn't stop to ask for help. It was late, and besides, most people in the neighborhood would recognize a little white girl with a black sister, and they knew better than to cross Odelia. Everybody in the area feared Odelia Sykes and her two sons. Michael was a gangster and Dewie a wild man idiot who'd be dangerous if he had half an imagination. No one would risk helping her and Shontell when Odelia might order her sons to burn down their house some night.

So Latasha's only thought was to sprint so hard and so fast Dewie couldn't catch them. In the moment between picking up one foot and putting it back down, a plan popped into her mind.

When they reached the street she pulled Shontell across without stopping to look for traffic. She risked a fast glance behind her. No Dewie. Yet. Although gasping for air, cold pain ripping her lungs, she pulled at Shontell. "Come on, we can't stop here."

"Where?"

"To the bus stop. Come on!"

Latasha ran down more alleys, cut through yards and crossed more streets, before they reached the nearest stop, on Goodfellow Avenue. And hid behind the tree.

Latasha was still panting when she spotted the high headlights and large, dark square silhouette of the Metro bus coming up on them like a jungle animal. She rushed to the curb. The bus pulled, hissing, to a stop in front of them. She took a giant step up then leaned down, caught Shontell's wrist and jerked.

"Jump, little girl," she said. "I can't lift you like Mama does."

The driver gave them a dubious look as Latasha ran their monthly bus passes through the fare machine. Latasha kept them around her neck on a plastic cord so Mama wouldn't lose them. He must wonder why a little white girl was in this neighborhood at all, with an even smaller black girl, and why they weren't with a grownup, especially so late at night.

They sat down and Latasha tried to think of a plan. Where could they go? What could they do?

Call the police?

Women at the shelter said the cops refused to arrest their husbands for battering them. Latasha had heard many black people complain about the way the police treated all of them, not just the gangbangers who deserved what they got. But the police never helped Mama either, although she was white. When bad men Forced her and beat her up, the police got there at the end, but they never prevented the violence. Why didn't they catch the wicked men and lock them up in jail forever? On TV the police always arrested the evil dudes in half an hour or an hour.

Most importantly, Mama had told Latasha never to talk to a policeman because he might take her and Shontell away from Mama and put them in Foster's Home. Latasha and Mama used to live in Foster's Home. Her mother told Latasha it was terrible. In one, Mr. and Mrs. Foster made her work real hard cleaning up the house, then wouldn't let her eat anything but leftovers. In another one, Mr. Foster Forced her. When Mrs. Foster learned that, she belted Janie in the mouth and kicked her out.

Latasha was in Foster's Home at the same time because the state took her away from Mama when she was born. After Mama turned eighteen she went to court and signed lots of papers to get Latasha back, but she was always afraid the judge would say she was an unfit mother again and steal Latasha and Shontell away from her.

Latasha didn't remember Foster's Home because she was just a baby then, but she didn't want to go back there. Now she was old enough Mr. and Mrs. Foster might make her work hard all day instead of sending her to school. Maybe Mr. Foster would Force her.

So she couldn't call the police. No way in LA.

Grandmama and Grandpapa Braxton lived far away, out near the country. Latasha didn't like to go there. Grandmama and Grandpapa also thought Mama was an unfit mother and Latasha and Shontell should be sent to Foster's Home. They didn't like Latasha because she was a child of sin and they didn't like Shontell because Michael was her father and they didn't like black people. Also, Grandpapa might want to punish them, like he did when Mama was a little girl. Latasha was afraid of that. Mama often scolded them, but never hit them harder than a swat on their butts.

What could she and Shontell do? Where could they go? It was way after midnight and they didn't have any money. Maybe Dewie was following them. He could be driving that car right behind the bus, just waiting for them to get off so he could kill them. He'd looked ready to tear them both to pieces.

"I want to go home," Shontell said.

"Shhhh, we can't go back there."

"Why not?"

"You saw how mean Uncle Dewie looked. Didn't you see Mama lying on the floor? Your Uncle Dewie hurt her real bad. He wanted to kill us too. You understand?"

Shontell nodded her head.

"Good. If we go back there we'll die. And I ain't dying yet for nobody."

"Where's Mama?" Shontell asked.

"She'll find us later."

The bus slowed as an ambulance, lights flashing and siren blaring, passed.

Latasha stared, feeling sick, knowing Mama was inside it.

Did that at least mean she was still alive? Would they ever see her again?

Maybe Odelia would want to keep Shontell, because she was blood kin and got a big SSI check because she was stupid like Mama. Mama also got an SSI check, because she was so dumb. She got money for Latasha too, but just a small TANF check. Latasha couldn't get a big check because she was smart, not stupid like Mama and Shontell. Latasha didn't understand why the government paid stupid people big checks and smart people small checks. She wasn't smart enough to figure that out.

Of course she could work if she were grown up, but she was only seven now, and nobody could hire her until she was sixteen, so what did it matter if she wasn't disabled like Shontell? She wasn't supposed to have a job, she was supposed to go to school.

Odelia wouldn't want Latasha, since her daddy was white and she was smart and got only the small check. Everybody at that house hated her. Everybody except Michael hated Mama and Shontell, but even Michael hated Latasha, because he wasn't her father. He played with Shontell, tickling and teasing her, but he just ignored Latasha, unless he was mad and yelled at her to get her little white ass out of his face.

Latasha wouldn't let Shontell stay at Odelia's house even if that family treated her nicely and spent her money on clothes and toys for her. Latasha would miss Shontell too much.

Just like she already missed Mama.

If she lost both Mama and Shontell she would start crying and maybe never stop.

Latasha wanted to cry now, but that might make the bus driver angry. Maybe he would call the police and the judge would take her and Shontell away. She didn't want that, so she refused to let her heart feel lonely and sad.

Would they ever go back to Odelia's house? She didn't care. She didn't want to live there. She liked it when Mama rented her own apartment, even if Michael and other boyfriends often slept over. At least then she and Shontell had their own beds pushed in corners, their dresses hung in a closet and their underwear and play clothes neatly folded in a small chest of drawers. They had toys, and Latasha had books. Lots of books then, because she loved to read, and when they were in a store she always begged her mother to buy her a book and Mama always did if she had the money because she was so proud to have a daughter so smart she liked to read.

Ever since Michael went to jail, all they had in Odelia's house was the floor. They slept in their clothes. Their toys were stolen and given to Shontell's cousins, Boo and Punkin. Pages were ripped out of Latasha's books. One morning she woke up to find all her shirts and pants pulled out of her backpack and stuffed into the toilet.

Right now, Latasha and Shontell had the clothes they were wearing and Latasha's purse, which she always kept with her, even when she slept, because its contents were too precious to risk losing or having someone steal them from her. The blue ribbon she won two months ago in a school spelling bee. The makeup kit her mother bought her at Wal-Mart just last week. And the snapshot Marilyn took of them in the shelter at Latasha's birthday party five months ago. The picture showed just the three of them, together: Mama, Latasha and Shontell—without any men to Force her mother or beat her up or make her daughters run away on a bus while she rode off in an ambulance.

A funny lump swelled in Latasha's throat. She couldn't swallow and felt even more like crying, but jammed the tears back into her eyes.

Shontell still carried Andy the stuffed brown dog clenched in her hand. Latasha felt proud of her for hanging on to Andy during their run from Dewie. Mama first bought Andy for Latasha when she took Latasha away from Foster's Home. Latasha had hugged Andy to her breast every night as she slept. She cried into Andy's brown fur every time she saw something bad happen to Mama. She wailed whenever Mama held him up to her nose, said, "Peeeeeeyuuu, Andy stinks to high Heaven," and threw him into a washing machine at the laundromat.

One night over a year ago Shontell grabbed Andy from Latasha's arms and refused to give him back. By then Andy's fur was matted and ragged, the stuffing was flat and loose and the bead of his left eye had fallen out. Latasha still loved the little dog, but she had recognized now Shontell loved him more.

Latasha taught Shontell to carry Andy everywhere she went when they were at Odelia's, because nothing was safe there. Her little sister was stupid like Mama but, also like Mama, she held on to what she loved.

"DeBaliviere parking garage," the driver called out. "This is the end of the line, ladies."

Latasha looked around and realized they were the last passengers.

"This is the last bus of the night on this route, girls. Do you two know where you're going?"

Latasha slowly shook her head.

"I was afraid of that. Where's your mama?"

"I don't know."

"That's what I figured. You kids just sit right there until I get back. You hear me?"

Latasha nodded. The driver stepped out of the bus and closed the front door behind him.

He was going to go call the police. They would come and take her and Shontell away from Mama and send them to Foster's Home.

"Come on." She pulled Shontell off the seat and along behind. She knew she didn't have to wait for the driver to open the back door. She'd seen passengers get off buses without the driver's permission by shoving open the two panels.

Latasha pushed hard with her free hand. The door gave way an inch, then pushed back. She threw her shoulder against it and dragged Shontell through. They ran around to the rear of the bus. She quickly looked in both directions down the big, wide street. The nearest headlights seemed far enough away, so she and Shontell scampered across.

The outside air was colder now after the heat inside the bus, and Latasha felt like she was running away from the condemned house all over again. She looked around for Dewie. Maybe he had followed the bus and they were running right to him.

Dodging gas pumps, they scurried to the alley behind the BP station. Behind them, the bus driver shouted, "Hey! You girls stop. Where you all going?"

They sped along the broken blacktop strewn with loose gravel, broken glass and soggy newspapers, past smelly dumpsters filled to overflowing with black plastic bags. Dogs had scattered chicken bones, used tissues, beer cans and corn flake boxes across the alley.

They reached the next street, turned a left around a thick evergreen bush, ran to the end of that block, cut across that street and into the alley running between the two rows of houses.

Latasha couldn't see or hear the bus driver.

They stood with their rear ends braced against a telephone pole, hands on their knees, gasping for air. When the pains stopped stabbing her sides like daggers and her head no longer felt dizzy, Latasha looked around. They were in a dark patch under a broken street lamp, between two bright lights glaring down over garbage dumpsters. Probably nobody would come this way until morning.

She didn't know where they were, but she could find her way back to that big street. It was an important street. She remembered often going up and down it on the bus with her mother.

If they didn't know where they were, then nobody could find them, not Dewie or the bus driver. If they were quiet and stayed hidden away like two tiny little mice, then nobody would call the police on them.

She realized she had to take a leak.

"You got to go potty?" she asked Shontell.

The little girl nodded. Latasha felt nervous about pissing outside, but neither one of them could hold it all night. They tugged their sweat pants down, then squatted by the side of a garbage dumpster, hidden in its shadow.

"You be careful," she told her sister. "Don't you pee on your pants. "She watched carefully to make certain Shontell didn't. The warm liquid hissed and smoked on the cold asphalt. Latasha wiped them both with a tissue from her purse.

The cold wind blew harder. Latasha zipped up the front of Shontell's pink sweat shirt and then her own blue one. It was spring, one of the in-between times of year. The days were almost as hot as summer, but the nights were almost as cold as winter. She was glad Mama insisted they sleep in warm clothes. Latasha had wanted to change to her denim cutoffs and Metallica t-shirt.

She crawled under a large bush by the alley, its branches green with budding leaves. She sat in the middle, leaning her back against the main trunk as carefully as she could so the branches didn't poke her, then sat Shontell down on the ground between her open legs, hugging her sister from behind.

Where could they go? Not to the police or Grandmama and

Grandpapa Braxton. Strangers were out of the question, because who would help two little girls they didn't know? They would die if they returned to Odelia's house. Latasha had no doubt in her head Dewie would kill them if he saw them again.

Latasha knew only one place they could go. One place where she felt safe from everybody at Odelia's house. One place where the people liked her and Shontell. One place a lot nicer than Foster's Home.

The shelter.

That's where Mama took them every time she got real angry with Michael and decided she was sick and tired of him. They'd just left the shelter a couple of days ago and still had clothes there.

The people who worked there, like Marilyn and Sara, tried hard to help Mama. They didn't want her to ever go back to Odelia's house again, but Mama always did because, she told Latasha, she had a hard head. Always did, always would. She might be stupid but she knew what she wanted, and not Mommy or Daddy or Marilyn or Odelia or Michael or anybody else could tell her what to do if she thought different.

"We're staying here until the sun comes up," Latasha said. "You understand?"

"I want to go home," Shontell said.

"We can't go home. We ain't got no home. You remember running away from your Uncle Dewie?"

Shontell nodded.

"He wants to kill us. Uncle Dewie hurt Mama real bad. I think he killed her. You understand? We maybe ain't got no Mama no more. If we go back to Odelia's house Uncle Dewie will kill us too. You want him to carve you up like a turkey?"

"No!"

"Then we got to stay here the rest of the night. Then we'll go back to the shelter. We had real beds and everybody was nice to us and to Mama too."

"Marilyn."

"That's right, that's where our friend Marilyn is. We got to find her or Dewie will kill us or the cops will take us away and put us in Foster's Home. I don't never want to go back there. We'd never see each other again. You want that?"

Shontell flipped her head back and forth like a dog shaking off water. "I want candy."

"We don't have any candy. Mama had all the money in her shoe, and now she's hurt real bad and maybe dead, so we don't have money to buy candy with. So you just don't think about it now, okay? In a few hours we'll go back to the shelter and they'll give us lots of food."

"I want to go now."

"We can't. If the cops see two little girls walking alone when it's dark they'll pick us up and take us to Foster's Home."

"I'm hungry."

Latasha tickled her sister along her tummy. "We don't have no food, so we can't be hungry, right?" She prodded Shontell until the girl had to giggle. "See? You don't feel hungry here, you just feel like laughing."

Latasha wrapped both Shontell's arms around Andy and folded her arms across Shontell's chest. "Little girl, you just close your eyes and hush up."

CHAPTER THREE

I

St. Louis Abused Women's Shelter (secret location)

"May I speak to someone regarding one of your residents?" A man.

Adrenaline jolted Marilyn awake. The shelter gave this unlisted number out only rarely. Some residents did need to speak to their husbands or partners about family or other business, but those men weren't supposed to call so late. This had to be bad news.

"What do you want?" She realized she sounded like Ms. Super Ballbreaking Bitch but didn't care.

"Is this the St. Louis Abused Women's Shelter?"

"First, you tell me who you are and what you want."

"My name's Jim Williams. I'm a social worker at Holy Virgin Mother of God Hospital and—"

"Oh Lord. Is this about Janie?"

He paused. "How did you know too? So this is the shelter?"

"Yes, yes, of course. And only Janie would have a social worker calling about her at four in the morning."

"So you do know Janie Braxton?"

"What's happened this time? How serious is it?"

"Very bad, I'm afraid." He gave her a brief description of the medical case, then said, "She's holding steady out of danger for now, but she could still go either way. She might wake up, she might slide into an irreversible coma. We've done everything we know how to treat her. All we can do at this point is monitor her condition and try to prevent complications."

"How'd you know to call here?"

"The police found the shelter's name and phone number on a piece of paper in her pocket. They want to help, but they don't have much to go on. If Janie wakes up, she'll be disoriented, and she could slip right back under. We were hoping to have someone here she knows, someone she'll talk to."

"I'll be there as fast as I can."

"What's your name? I have to leave it at the front desk. Janie's under a police protection order, so officially she isn't even here. That's what we'll tell any stranger who asks for her."

"Marilyn Patterson. Mr. Williams, thank you very much for calling. I'm sorry I barked at you."

"No problemo. I understand you have to be suspicious of men. And please, call me Jim."

"What about her kids? Are they all right?" Marilyn asked.

"Children?"

"Janie has two daughters, Latasha and Shontell, seven and four years old. What about them? Where are they?"

"We don't know anything about any children," Jim said. "Janie came in an ambulance, alone. I'll check with the police before you arrive."

"Please do. Thank you." Marilyn hung up.

Where were Latasha and Shontell?

II

Dreamspace

Janie watched as nurses wheeled her into a big room, then hooked her to an IV and to beeping machines. They pressed buttons on what they called the monitor and again checked her temperature, blood pressure and heart beat.

Bored, Janie wandered down the hallway and peeked into other rooms. The patients were asleep, dark shapes on the beds, some with arms or legs in casts raised up with wires.

"Janie."

That ghost was pestering her again. What was wrong with him? She had better things to do than play with a dead Indian who made her think of snow so deep even Eskimos would freeze in it. She had to find her babies. Did Dewie hurt Latasha and Shontell too?

Floating in the air like a speck of dust, Janie drifted out of the hospital. It was dark except for the bright lights over the sliding door entrance to the Emergency Room. Janie saw other big brick buildings nearby. One of them was Barnes, a real big and famous hospital. Another was Children's, where she sometimes took Latasha and Shontell for emergencies, even though they got their shots at Cardinal Glennon Children's Hospital. Marilyn taught her how to take the Grand Avenue bus to Cardinal Glennon.

The wind blew Janie like a kite over the dark trees of Forest Park. Trailing behind her like a kite's tail was a glowing silver string. It was attached to her chest and led back to her body still in the hospital. No matter where she went, she could follow the line back to her body.

She flew over more buildings and streets, then looked down and spotted her daughters under a bush.

"Latasha! Shontell!" Janie shouted. "Look up here at Mama. What're you two doing there in that dirty alley?"

They didn't pay her any mind at all. They could be such bad little girls, pretending they didn't hear her when they didn't want to. Especially Latasha. That child had a head near about as hard as her mama's. "You listen to me, I ain't playing! You look up here and talk to me."

They remained inside the branches, getting the seats of their sweat pants dirty from sitting on the damp ground.

"You leave that alley right now and get your little asses home to bed, before the dogs and rats bite you."

"They can't hear you," the Indian ghost said.

"Go away," Janie told him.

"We are in Dreamspace. Your people call it the spirit world or the astral dimension."

"Leave me alone!"

"I've been trapped in the Dirtworld part of Dreamspace for many years. I want to live again. I miss eating and sleeping. I miss wearing the finest leather clothes and copper jewelry. I

miss planting my seed in women. Above all, I miss command-
ing my people. I miss wielding the power of life and death. Your
sacrifice will free me."

Janie didn't know what that Indian was talking about and
didn't care. She just kept watching her children, her two babies playing a game she didn't like at all. She shouted at them
but they didn't respond. She could see and hear them, just as
though she was there with them but she couldn't touch them.
She couldn't make them see or hear her either, or react to her
in any way. Just like watching a movie in a theater when she
screamed out to the hero that the rich businessman was really a
bad guy who wanted to kill him and shouted to the pretty lady
not to go into the park with that handsome young man because
he'd already raped and murdered two other girls. But the actors
on the screen never listened to Janie, and now neither did her
daughters.

Wait a minute. How could she be watching them in an alley
when she was lying in a hospital room, hurt real bad in the head
and hooked up to lots of machines? Something very strange was
going on.

She looked down at the Indian ghost.

III

Holy Virgin Mother of God Medical Center

Jim Williams welcomed Marilyn into his office with a
grave handshake. He was in his early twenties—a baby—
and handsome, with straight blond hair and deep set blue

eyes that sparkled with a vivid, warm light.

He brought her a Styrofoam cup of coffee, then sat down beside her in the other chair in front of his desk. Did he understand how much she appreciated that? Marilyn always felt self-conscious on the client side of desks, even when she was just opening a checking account. She was used to being the one in charge of the interview.

"Are you new at this job?" she asked.

"Oh no. I've worked at Holy Virgin Mother for three years and put in two years at the welfare office before that. I couldn't take the mess the state bureaucracy's in. And even though I don't expect to get rich, I want more than what the state of Missouri pays. Besides, I wanted to be a social worker, not a caseworker."

"Oh. I thought you were right out of school." She smiled. "Why're you here working so late?"

He waved his hand. "The ER nurses know to call me when there's a case needing special attention. Janie won't even be in my alphabetical breakdown, but the other social worker won't care who started the paperwork."

Needing caffeine, Marilyn gulped the hot coffee. "I'm impressed. Still dedicated after five years. How long can you keep it up before you burn out?"

He waved his hand again, smiled. "I can always sell houses at my dad's real estate agency. But, really, I like to help people."

"I want to see Janie."

"Let me apologize first. The doctors tell me now if she does wake up she probably won't even be rational, so there really isn't anything you can do. I'm sorry I disturbed you."

"I'm glad you did. I was worried about her. At least now I know where she is and that she's getting the best care available.

That she's alive."

"Let's hope she stays that way. The prognosis is not good. Come on."

He led her past the nurse's duty station into the dark confines of the Neurological ICU. It was lit by the pulsing green lights of the monitors and was still except for the soft hissing of breathing machines. Marilyn shuddered.

Jim switched on the track light over Janie's bed, turning the rheostat until the soft dimness wouldn't disturb the other patients.

Bands of tension tightened around Marilyn's skull. Janie lay on her back, dwarfed by the surrounding machines, lost underneath the thick covers, tiny and frail, a wounded faun. The bandages couldn't disguise the size of the swollen lump on the left side of her head. Although much of her scalp had been shaved, some strands of hair lay in a tangle across a face that looked as devoid of personality and life as a department store dress dummy, as though her soul had flown far away, leaving behind only a shell.

Dizzy, Marilyn grabbed Jim's elbow." My God."

"Are you all right?"

"I can't stand seeing her like this."

Marilyn wanted to pick her up and cradle her in her arms, sing lullabies while rocking her to sleep. Did Janie's mother ever sing to her? Did Judith ever look down at her sleeping little girl, as Marilyn was doing now, and love her with her whole heart?

Or did Judith hate Janie because she was stupid? That's what Janie told Marilyn. Yet Marilyn knew she had to weigh everything Janie said. Janie did lie when it suited her. And because she was limited, even when she thought she was telling the truth it was only the portions she could understand and remember.

Why did Marilyn try so hard with Janie? Why did she let herself care more than was healthy for her own peace of mind and heart?

She knew of worse cases. Janie was retarded, but she functioned better than some people who scored much higher on intelligence tests. She often lost apartments, but some women couldn't or wouldn't even look for them on their own. Janie couldn't read, but she saved an envelope from Social Security, compared the return address on it to those on letters she received in the mail, and so knew whenever she had a new notice regarding her or Shontell's SSI checks. She either took it to Marilyn to read for her or went straight to the Social Security office. Marilyn knew women who could read but just didn't bother. They simply ignored their important letters until their checks were stopped.

Was it Janie's unusual mixture of vulnerability and gutsy independence that drew Marilyn against her better judgment? She was both a child and an old woman who had seen more of the bad side of life in her twenty-three years than most people even knew existed. She was irresponsible, but she did her best to raise her children. She was weak but tough. Small in body but big in heart. She had been beaten and raped more times than she could count, but she always bounced back, and horny as ever.

Could she recover from such a head wound?

Back in Jim's upholstered armchair, Marilyn held another cup of coffee and took deep breaths. When she first came in she had acted the older, more experienced social worker and treated Jim like an overenthusiastic youngster. She had to laugh at herself. She sure blew that image.

"I know it's hard," Jim said. "After two years at the welfare office I thought I'd seen everything, but working in a hospital is different because they're severely injured or sick. It took me months to get used to it, and then I think I am only because I didn't know the people before they came in. It must be worse to see somebody in a hospital bed when you've known them as a whole, healthy person."

"What did you find out about her daughters?"

"The police don't have them. They found Janie in an old house condemned when the people were busted for selling drugs. It's lucky she had her I.D. and the phone numbers of your shelter and her parents in her pocket."

"Where was this old house?"

Jim consulted the folder on his desk. "The corner of Ashland and Greer. Do you know the area?"

"That'd be only a short way from Odelia Sykes' house."

"Who's she?"

"Odelia's son, Michael Grimes, is the younger girl's father. At least, that's what Janie says, and he acknowledges paternity, so that right there makes him more responsible than many young men today. Unfortunately, that's as good as he gets. Burglary, car theft, selling crack—you name it, he's probably done it. Right now he's in jail for assaulting an elderly woman. Janie likes to think she's his main squeeze, but I think he keeps her around to beat up on, screw when it's convenient and pass to his buddies when they want a white girl."

"You're joking."

"I suspect he would've kicked her out for good a long time ago except for Shontell. Apparently he does dote on the little girl, even though he ignores Janie's other daughter, Latasha. But according to Janie he's never hurt either one of them, so he could be worse."

Jim shook his head. "That's what I hear every day—it could be worse."

"Odelia's a real piece of work herself. A friend of mine in the police looked up her jacket for me once. She's been arrested as a pickpocket prostitute. She would pull her customer's wallet out of his pocket while she was distracting him with a blow job in his car, then open the door and rush out before he could zip up his pants. Janie told me Odelia tried to force her to do it, but she refused. According to Janie, Odelia owes MasterCard, Visa, Macy's and I don't know how many other stores close to forty thousand dollars. She got approved for a bunch of credit cards when her husband was working. After they split up, she charged them to the limit and didn't make any more payments. The companies couldn't do anything to her because by that time her only official income was TANF.

"And creditors can't garnish or attach welfare checks. Convenient."

"She gets SSI for another son, Dewie. He's retarded too. Not as much as Janie, but he's also a little nuts. Janie told me every month, right after the checks came out, Odelia used to call Social Security and claim she hadn't received Dewie's check, even though she had. Then she would even go in there and get emergency advances. That went on for about six months before the Treasury Department caught up with her, and even yet, she's stalling collection of the overpayment by refusing to admit it, and they're real slow about processing her appeals. When Janie's living there, she demands most of Janie's SSI check for expenses."

"Just the lady I need as my financial advisor."

"Janie left our shelter two days ago with both kids, saying she was going to visit a friend, then stop by Odelia's for her Zebley class action back pay."

"So the children are probably safe at Odelia's?"

"If you call that safe."

"So what should we do? Janie won't be able to take care of them for a long time, if ever. Odelia's the one girl's grandmother, but she doesn't exactly sound like a wholesome influence. What about Janie's mother and father?"

Marilyn sighed. "Janie never got along with them, and maybe they deserve that. But it must be hard trying to cope with a child who pops in and out of their lives at random, when they know she's shacking up with a black gangster."

"Are they suitable?"

"I don't know. Janie told me they hated her kids, but then Janie tells me all kinds of wild stories, and later denies she ever said them. I never know what to believe about her, except she's had a hard life, and I want to help her."

"I thought I'd left messes like this behind when I resigned from Family Services."

"When Janie was fifteen and pregnant, she had a big argument with her mother. Judith either kicked Janie out or Janie was so outraged she left on her own. She threw some clothes into a grocery bag, took several dollars out of her mother's purse and hitched a ride into St. Louis. She must have scraped along by trading sex for food and shelter, at least until she got too big in the belly. The state put her and the baby into foster homes, but when she turned eighteen she found out how to sue them for custody and got Latasha turned back over to her."

"I thought you said she can't read."

"Janie always manages to find someone to help her. She got steered to a good lawyer at Legal Services."

"Can you keep the kids in the shelter?

Marilyn shook her head. "Not without their mother. We're not equipped to be full-time babysitters. We're not licensed childcare providers"

"Is there anyone else?"

"Not that I know of. Janie does have girlfriends, but I doubt any of them would be willing to raise two kids not their own."

"Any other relatives?"

"Shontell probably has lots more on her father's side. If there are any respectable ones, they keep their distance from Odelia."

Jim gave a long whistle. "So it looks like state custody and foster homes."

"It's a shame. If those kids're split up that'll be hard on them, especially with losing their mother too. Shontell's a real sweet child, very loving, but she's slow too. Biracial retarded children are difficult to place."

"Did you say Janie's due a big Zebley check? We have a memo on that. The Supreme Court ordered Social Security to reexamine all the children it had denied for years back, and apply easier to meet disability standards. We're supposed to watch out for disabled children who might be eligible for SSI."

"Janie was turned down the first time her mother applied for her. Months ago they went back and reopened that application, and now they owe her a lot of money. The checks were supposed to arrive at Odelia's any day. That's why Janie left the shelter, to go look for them in Odelia's mail, and maybe she found them. I don't know how much they are, but they're certainly enough for somebody to try to kill her for them. Maybe somebody in the neighborhood did. Maybe it was even somebody at Odelia's."

"Sounds all too plausible to me. The police found money in her shoe, but only a few dollars." Jim looked down at his watch. "It's late. We better get some sleep."

"I'm going over to Odelia's house. I want those kids. And maybe Odelia will know something about the Zebley checks and what happened to Janie."

"You plan to go now?"

"Why not? It's too late for bed."

"The sun isn't even up yet," Jim said.

"I can't think about anything else until I know the children are all right."

She began to leave and was surprised to see him reach for his jacket. "What're you doing?"

"Coming with you."

"Why?"

"In case you need some help."

"You don't have to, you know."

"Hey," he said. "It's my job."

"They let you leave the hospital to make field contacts?"

"I don't clock in until eight anyway." He waved his hand. "It's not my workload either, but it's my job."

She didn't know why he was going out of his way, but she would be safer with him along than by herself. "If you insist."

CHAPTER FOUR

I

Highway 44

"Damn fool girl never had the sense God gave a turkey," Willie Lee said as he drove their `94 Honda Passport SUV to the hospital. "Living with colored and white trash in the city. Doing drugs. I never did understand her, never in my whole life."

Judith turned the heater up a notch. "It's not her fault she wasn't born right in the head. If you don't have the brainpower you just can't use it, that's all."

"Don't hand me that bull hockey. Janie turned out just plain bad. I don't deny nothing I ever did. I had to punish her, because she didn't understand as fast as other kids. People got mistaken ideas. They think retarded people are children because they don't act like grown folks. But Janie never was a proper child, was she?"

"No," Judith said, "she never was. But she's hurt real bad now. We got to perform our Christian duty. God saw fit to appoint us Janie's parents. That didn't make neither one of us happy, that's for sure, but we can't let her lie up there, her head bashed in, all by her lonesome."

"Why not? She's been in the hospital plenty times when nobody saw fit to call us. Why's this any different?"

Despite the few hours of sleep and the coffee they'd drank before setting out, Willie Lee was still drunk. Judith closed her eyes a moment and felt the world spin. She was still drunk too. She pulled the visor down to block the glare of the rising sun.

"Mr. Williams told me she might die. Even if she does pull through she might just hang on in a coma, or be down so bad she'll have to stay in an institution."

"Can't say I'm surprised. Living in the city with maniacs and perverts, it's a wonder she wasn't mugged to death years ago. Who do you think's going to pay for this? Not you and me."

"Medicaid, I suppose. Mr. Williams said the police found her card in her pocket, so there's no problem with her hospital bill."

"Didn't we try to raise her up right? Didn't we try our level best to teach her right from wrong, to bring her to God? She wasn't like other people because she never was innocent. She was stupid, but not stupid in a way either of us could understand."

"Nothing penetrated into her skull she didn't want to, that's for sure."

"You remember how many nights I stayed up late praying on her? I read the Bible and studied, but never found nothing in there on how to bring up a child without the mentation required to learn the Ten Commandments. I couldn't see no other way than physical punishment for her."

"You just got angry a lot, Willie Lee. Don't drag the Good Book into it."

"Woman, I know how miserable I failed. Thinking about my own baby daughter in that big city whoring with colored, even bringing a half-breed little girl into the world—"

"Shontell's a sweet child."

"Yeah, she's sweet, and so cute. Everybody's supposed to love bastards nowadays. Janie our daughter's a slut and it makes me sick. I blame myself, but I don't know what I could've done different, except punish her worser than I did, and folks nowadays say that ain't right neither. We're supposed to talk to children, make them understand. But how do you explain to a retarded child when she don't even want to listen?"

"Janie was a heavy burden on both of us."

"Janie was God's greatest trial of us. All my grownup life the Lord's been testing me. I thought I passed the final exam when I escaped alive from that hellhole Korea. I thought he was forging me in fire all those years we spent scuffling, when I was hiring myself out as a pair of hands for farm labor, fixing flat tires in gas stations, operating a splicer machine, welding, washing dishes—all the time getting laid off and moving on, laid off and moving on."

"It was tough, but we're tough kinds of folks."

"But wherever we went, didn't I always preach at night and on Sundays? I spread the Word. And I thought God was tempting me with the whiskey, when I'd leave you and drink until my last dime was gone."

"We've been through a lot, Willie Lee."

"The day I learned you was pregnant, even though you were thirty-five, I was happy as all get out. I prayed to the Lord to thank Him for finally blessing us with a child. I was working steady then at that cement plant in Memphis, and I thought our sorrows were over. When I saw that little baby girl just taken out of you I thought I'd never seen anybody so beautiful, not even you on the day we married up. I thought she was a gift from Heaven, like manna fallen on us out of the sky."

"She was a baby angel," Judith said.

"I thought our troubles and tribulations were finally over at last. I thought I could lay down my burden and rest in the peace of Jesus. That I'd finally feel at ease in my heart.

"That the fire burning in there for as long as I could remember would finally go out, quenched in the pure, cool spring water of loving that little girl. I thought life didn't have nothing sweeter than that. You remember those times, when she was still so young we didn't know there was something wrong with her?"

"I'll never forget how happy we were then."

"I didn't drink a drop, didn't even think about whiskey. I could preach all night if my congregation didn't walk out on me, then go to work the next morning feeling strong as a bull in the springtime."

"Keep your eyes on the road. You almost hit that pickup."

"When'd it go wrong? When she was two years old and still not speaking? When she finally did, and I wished she'd shut up again? Because she didn't have nothing to say but back talk, heathenish speech. That child I loved so much, like I would've died for her, like I would've killed my best friend for her, like I saw the light of Jesus shining in her eyes every time she smiled at me, suddenly became the biggest trial of my life."

"For both of us."

"I discovered the Lord wasn't half done testing me. I was just beginning to learn how bitter the ashes of life can taste. I never expected my kid to be a genius—but not even normal? And a wicked, ornery, contrary not normal."

"If you don't want to go to that hospital you just pull over and walk back home and let me go on alone."

"You're right, it's our Christian duty. We failed in raising her, so we're bounden to do this. But it'd been better if I'd killed her the day we learned she was simple."

"Willie Lee!" Shock jolted Judith. Her husband had a terrible temper, but she couldn't remember ever before hearing him say anything so downright evil.

"Ain't it the truth? Her soul would have risen to Heaven free of wickedness, hardheaded but pure. Now, she's no better than a prostitute. I wish I could say different, but you know and I know it's true. If she ain't been living a sinful life, I don't know what sin is."

II

Ashland Avenue

Dewie shook his mother's shoulder.

After the Indian had started talking to him, Dewie slowly began to realize he had been mistreated. He felt the anger and frustration he'd been ignoring. He began to understand he deserved more—lots more.

Dewie had never thought much about it before, but in the back of his mind he knew nobody paid him the proper attention.

Nobody expected anything from him. His gang, the Ashland Rocks, was really just a few guys who knew each other from the neighborhood who cruised the streets in a pack, hanging together because it was more fun, and safer, to have friends.

Even his own people abused him. His older brother Michael had always made him cry by picking fights that of course Dewie always lost because he was younger and smaller. Mama laughed at him and put him down. Even now, even though he was a man, she was his payee up over his SSI check. Dewie hated to have to beg her on the first of every month to give him some of his own money. But if he didn't fuss and fight she would spend it all on herself. That wasn't right, for a mother to do her son that way.

The chief promised Dewie everything he wanted—money, gold chains, a Mercedes, fancy clothes, unlimited drugs and sexy women. Most importantly, he promised Dewie power. Respect.

Dewie wanted everything the chief promised. The wealth. Every fox he saw. He wanted everyone to fear and obey him.

Especially his mother and Michael. That would be the sweetest triumph, forcing Michael to kiss his ass.

Dewie would show them all.

However, the Indian chief told Dewie he couldn't have money, drugs, sex and power for free. He had to invite the chief's spirit into himself. That would make Dewie stronger than he could imagine, but there was a price. Someone had to pay.

Someone had to sacrifice. Magic wasn't cheap or easy. It took blood.

The Indian demanded Janie's.

He wanted to eat her soul somehow, to feed on her energy. Dewie didn't understand that part. He couldn't see how Janie could have that many spirit calories, but he didn't care. He would enjoy sacrificing Janie to the Indian just for the hell of it.

Dewie had wanted to put it to Janie ever since she first came to live with his family, but Michael wouldn't let Dewie screw her without paying the same twenty-five bucks Michael was charging his partners. Pay cash for a used up dirty hole like her? She wasn't worth it, Dewie told Michael. He ought to let Dewie have her for free one night just because he was Michael's little brother. But Dewie didn't have jungle fever - he wouldn't shell out good money for an ugly tramp just because she was white.

She was nothing but a skinny little cracker troublemaker. He had always resented she got her SSI check herself when he had to have his mother controlling his money for him. But he had never liked those Social Security peoples either.

He had never understood why Michael kept Janie around. Fuck her once or twice, pass her on to his buddies, okay. Let her and those two little bitches her daughters live in the house—hell fucking no. Michael wouldn't let anybody but him beat her up, and even though his tail was now in jail, nobody dared touch her in front of Mama.

Janie was waiting for the big-time bucks Social Security owed her from some court case. When Mama told Janie she'd have to give her most of that check, Janie told Mama she was going to buy herself a house with the money and if Mama didn't like it she could kiss Janie's little white ass. Mama screamed and hollered something fierce, and that's why Janie returned to the shelter. She came back only to ask if the check had arrived in the mail yet.

Dewie hated Janie's guts for always running off to that shelter place after she and Michael had a big fight. Maybe Michael didn't respect Dewie, but Michael was still his older brother.

Dewie didn't like Janie telling lies on Michael behind his back, especially now when Michael wasn't around to take care of business himself. He didn't beat her up so bad. Janie hadn't known then what a real ass-whupping was.

She did now.

Dewie took a deep breath. He felt stronger than ever, more powerful than anybody. He was going to fuck the world.

But Janie's daughters broke in during the sacrifice. Dewie hadn't killed Janie. He hadn't completed the ritual, and now she was in a hospital. What could he do?

As he was trying to wake Mama, the Indian spoke.

Leave Janie to me. Her daughters disturbed the door between our worlds at a crucial moment. The connection between you and I is stronger than ever, but the door is closed more tightly than before. To open it again will require even more power, more sacrifice. Now you will need virgin blood on your hands to make you totally invincible. The small ones are virgins. They interrupted the sacred sacrifice, so their hearts must be cut out also. That is now your task.

"What about Janie?"

She is in my domain now. I will deal with her. After you kill the girls you will be immortal like me.

"Where are they? I'll go right now."

I am still trapped in Dirtworld. That means I cannot interfere directly where you are. I can influence people. I can take advantage of sacrifices. I can take on flesh if I have the strength. But I may not myself directly strike down a living creature. I can see the girls, but I cannot give you directions you would understand. You must find the virgins yourself. When their location is in your mind, the circuit of power will be complete, and I will be able to partially manifest my power in your world. But to make that happen, you must know where they are. After that, to attain immortality, you must complete the sacrifice.

Mama's eyes finally opened.

"I got to talk to you, Mama," Dewie said.

She grunted and snorted, then wrenched herself out of the bed and pulled her house coat on. They went to sit in the living room.

"Mama, I got to tell you about this dead Indian chief. I met him in a dream, and then I saw him whenever I smoked whack or crack. And now he talks to me whenever he wants to."

Mama started to push herself up.

"Where you going to?" Dewie asked.

"Child, you done gone crazy again. You get me up in the

65

middle of the night for this bug-eyed shit? I thought I'd heard a commotion outside. What'd you do now?"

"That's what I"m fitting to tell you about. Just listen. A long time ago, before white or black folks came here, this Indian chief was the big king. He had Eagle Warriors that wiped out everybody else's armies. He controlled hundreds of villages up and down the Mississippi and other rivers. He got lots of loot."

"Dewie—"

"Goddammit, Mama, just hold tight and pay attention. I thought I was crazy again too at first, but I'm not. This Indian dude had all the women he wanted. Food, clothes, copper plates and shell necklaces—he was rich. And with one word he could order anybody's death. He had power, Mama. The people worshiped him as a god, the younger brother of the sun."

"Dewie, what's all this foolish talk got to do with them sirens woke me up?"

"The chief's going to rule again, inside me, Mama—me, Dewie Grimes. He promised. When his spirit power and magic's all the way inside me, I'll have my own empire. I'll be a god."

"That's real nice, Dewie. But tell me what's happened. Why ain't Janie and the kids out here sleeping on this couch?"

Dewie told her about meeting Janie in that old house on the corner.

His mother leaned back in her place on the sofa, where the springs were so bent to her shape nobody else could sit there in comfort. "So that's what this fuss is about. That girl just got herself took to the hospital again, that's all. We have to shut her trap, make sure she knows she's one dead slut if she talks. She ain't got no money or insurance, so of course they hauled her to Regency."

Mama dialed the number and asked for the Emergency Room.

"Hello," she said. "I was calling about my daughter-in-law, Janie Braxton. She was hurt real bad and taken away in an ambulance about an hour ago. How is she doing?"

Mama listened for a few minutes, then hung up. "That's funny. She's not there. Maybe they was too busy. I'll try Holy Virgin."

But Janie was not at Holy Virgin. Or Barnes-Jewish or SLUCare.

"That's mighty strange," Mama told Dewie. "I can't find her."

"Latasha and Shontell saw me, Mama. Them nosy brats came in right after I hit Janie. Then they screamed and ran out the door. I tried to catch them, but they got away."

"Can't you do nothing right? You sure they saw you?"

"Yes Mama."

"You know what that means. They talk to the police, they could get you put you away. They the only ones seen you?"

"Yes Mama."

"You sure about that?"

"It was real late. Nobody else was out."

"Where'd them girls go?"

"How'd I know that?"

"Then what the hell you doing here? Find them. Shontell's too young and slow to be dangerous. She couldn't tell nobody what she seen even if she understood it. But that Latasha, she old enough. She's white and Janie's white. The cops would love to throw a black man in jail for even touching her, and Latasha's mean and evil enough to try to make you die in the chair. She's just a little white bitch and if you half the man I hope you are you'll know what to do when you find her."

"Shontell too."

"She won't be a problem."

"They both saw me. Latasha and Shontell."

"She's your own niece, Dewie."

"Janie fucked a thousand black dudes before she got pregnant with that baby. Just because Shontell's black don't make her blood kin to us."

"If Michael heard you say that - -."

"Michael's in jail!" Dewie stood up. "Michael ain't the man of this house no more, you hear me, Mama? I am! What makes Michael so great? Just because he's got friends he sells drugs to? Just because he can steal a car if the keys are still in the ignition? Just because he can beat up old ladies?"

"Dewie—"

"That don't mean shit, Mama. I'm going to show you I'm ten times—a hundred times—more a man than Michael."

Dewie picked up the DVR/TIVO/VCR/CD combo set. "You think Michael's so great just because he bought you this three thousand dollar video machine? The hell with Michael! I'll buy you one twice as good and ten times more expensive. I don't care shit what Michael bought you."

Dewie gave the entertainment set a karate chop. The hard plastic and thin metal cover split in two down the middle, spilling out its twisted guts.

"You sure have gone crazy again, child."

"You watch, Mama. I'll buy you everything you want, everything you need. You forget about Michael. Michael's history. Just like everything he bought you."

Dewie raised his foot. "You think Michael's a good son just because he gave you this umpteen thousand dollar high def digital big screen plasma stereo TV? I say shit!"

Dewie kicked in the screen. The shattering glass flew across the room, covering the carpet. He smashed the top of it with one blow, then lifted the two halves and smashed them down on the floor until nothing was left but a jumble of glass, fake-wood plastic, wires, pieces of crumpled metal and tiny electrical parts.

His mother stared at the wreckage. She looked up at Dewie and said, "Son, you feel that strongly about something, nobody can stand in your way. You just keep me in touch."

"That's all I wanted to hear," Dewie said. "You're going to be so proud of me, Mama, I swear to God. This little mess ain't nothing. Anybody could've done that they get as angry you make me feel when you stick up for Michael. Killing those little girls is going to make me real strong, Mama, stronger than any man ever lived."

Odelia watched her younger son return to his room to change clothes and call his friends for help, then shook her head.

Thousands of dollars worth of video equipment was now strewn over her living room carpet. She'd have to keep Tiffany and Yolanda home from school to clean up the mess.

She was too excited to go back to bed. She set out several pieces of white scrap paper, a Bic pen and a welfare form Janie had signed. Janie couldn't write anything else, but she signed her name with a child's clearly formed, rounded penmanship. Odelia practiced Janie's signature a hundred times before she felt confident she could copy it perfectly.

Janie's Zebley checks lay in the top, locked, shelf of Odelia's dresser drawer, nestled under her socks and hose. Odelia had been thinking about the best way to handle them ever since they arrived in the mail, one last Saturday and another one Tuesday, an hour before Janie arrived to ask about them. If they were ordinary checks the Indian who ran the candy store down the block would cash them for her. But these were too large for him. However, she felt certain Abdul, the Arab who ran K & B Package Liquors on Dr. Martin Luther King Drive, would cash them if his cut was high enough.

Abdul knew Janie lived with Odelia. He'd often bought TVs, stereos, CD players and DVRs from Michael without asking where they came from. He wouldn't accept an obvious forgery, but why shouldn't he take signatures that looked real? Especially if Odelia told him Janie had been hurt in an accident and admitted to the hospital after she signed the checks but before she could deposit them at the bank?

Odelia added up the two checks. $15,678.42.

Odelia couldn't calculate how much would remain if Abdul held back ten or twenty percent, but it was still a lot of money. She could buy a new TV and DVR to replace what Dewie just demolished, a new living room suite and a new bedroom suite, and maybe new high def TVs for the girls to watch in their own bedrooms, and still have enough left for several trips to the Galleria shopping mall.

$15,678.42.

The government owed her that anyway. When she asked Social Security about receiving Zebley money for Dewie, she was told he wasn't due any. He was approved for SSI the first time she applied for him, and the big Zebley checks were only going to children who had originally been turned down. Odelia told the worker Dewie had been just as disabled since he was born, so they ought to pay her starting with his birth. But the woman told Odelia she couldn't receive any money for Dewie for any time before she signed an application. Maybe that was the law, but that didn't make it right.

$15,678.42.

No way in hell that fool-headed little white country girl would know what to do with so much money.

III

Dreamspace

"What did you do to my children?" Janie shouted down to the ghost staring up at her from below the ground.

"Nothing."

"Why won't they talk to me? I want them out of that alley. It's not safe."

"We are in the spirit world."

"Who are you? What's happening?" Janie knew she must be asleep back at the hospital. "I'm dreaming."

The Indian spread his arms. His hair was cut very strange. The sides were shaved like with a Mohawk, but the top locks were long and the front and back portions were twisted together as though in ponytails with their folds held in place with long white knitting needle pins Janie somehow knew were human bone. His long leather robe was decorated with polished shells, not beads. Around his neck hung a plate of shiny copper. Copper spools dangled from his ear lobes. His white headdress shown with a light like dawn passing through smog. The red circles tattooed on his cheeks glowed like evil mouths.

"This is Dreamspace, but you are not dreaming. Your air-soul has left your mud-body." He extended his hand. Tattooed in the middle of his palm was a picture of an eye, a single tear-drop falling from the corner.

"Come with me. I will show you the city where I am king, where I am God. Where I am Sun of Suns."

The ghost's deep voice sounded like Daddy's when Janie was a little girl. She had to obey. She slipped her hand in his. He pulled Janie down into swirling colors, then flew her through underground caverns. That strange silver string attached to her belly button trailed behind, keeping her connected to her body. Bats whirled and chirruped at her. Winged snakes shot through the air. Slugs, fat and slimy, crawled over the rocks. Grisly reptile monsters crouched in dark caves, their long tongues slithering out to catch Janie like a frog a mosquito. The boulders glowed with the light of hot, bright fires.

Janie was in Hell.

She learned about Hell when she went to church as a little girl. Now she was seeing it. Coal-black demons with wings and pointed tails boiled people in cauldrons. Men, women and children screamed and begged for mercy as steaming water eternally scalded their skin and cooked their flesh. The air smelled evil. That must be the sulfur and brimstone preachers screamed about. One demon wore a necklace of human heads, the brains still alive, the eyes glaring at Janie in anguish, tongues curling.

The ghost dragged Janie past those pits to an abandoned Indian city. The many rows of huts were dilapidated, the grass roofs rotted, the wooden walls sagging. White grubs squirmed through the big clay bowls of dried corn kernels covered with green mold. Flies buzzed about the meat of hunted animals hung out to dry in the sun. Folded clothes and blankets were mildewed and moth eaten. A dog lay with its bowels spilled out beside it and its neck crudely hacked as if someone had tried to chop off its head with a blunt knife.

In the middle was a large hill with strangely steep sides and a temple erected on its flat top. The big mound was surrounded by a circle of tall sticks with skulls jammed on their pointed ends.

"This is my city, the City of the Sun. In Peopleland you now call it Cahokia."

That was a town across the Mississippi River in Illinois, close to East St. Louis. "Where did everybody go?"

Then Janie saw the women lying on benches and floor mats in the huts throughout the village, as far as she could see.

Thousands, maybe trillions of women, young girls and very young girls, some even as small as Shontell. Most were naked and on their backs with their arms crossed over their breasts. They all had big holes in the middle of their chests.

"They don't have any hearts!" Janie said.

"They don't need them."

"What happened?"

"Their energy is in my soul, as yours soon will be."

"What do you mean?" Janie asked.

"I live on through their life force. I am immortal because these females, all virgins, gave their lives to me. You are also a sacrifice to me. When you die, your energy will be mine. You will remain here, with these other beauties, to serve me, and I will rule again in Peoplerealm. A new Eagle Warrior is eager to champion my cause, to obey my commands in exchange for infinite power."

"What are you talking about?"

"My Eagle Warrior will sacrifice your two daughters and you will die. That will complete my transformation. I will again rule Peoplerealm. Not just a portion of it this time, but all of it. All the people on this entire planet."

"You're crazy."

"Among the Great People, after an important chief died, his wives and servants always volunteered to be executed so they could remain together in Deathrealm. When a god such as I died, many young girls were also sent to accompany him. They fought for the honor of joining Sun of Suns in eternal glory."

"I won't."

"I will break your spirit. You will see how powerful I am and how small and weak you are. I will smash your soul between the boulders of those two truths."

"Let me out of here. Take me back to the hospital."

"I will grant you a glimpse of the splendor and glory that was mine in the past. You will learn my story, how good I was, how noble was my desire to free Elder Brother from his degrading descent into Dirtworld every night. And you will see your own life. You will remember what you have deliberately forgotten, so you will understand how helpless you are to resist me. You have always been a sacrifice, and so you will remain for eternity."

"No. I don't care what you say."

"You will see, and it will destroy you."

SUN OF SUNS ONE

City of the Sun, Year 486 after the birth of the Great Temple (1386 AD)

The ghost flew Janie to the Temple on top of the high dirt mound. Janie sat beside him in a big room that looked like a church, Indian-style. The walls were covered with hangings of rotted furs and faded, coarse and torn fabric. Pieces of broken pottery were scattered over the splintered floor. There was a pile of old boards on one side.

At the far end were three other piles, one of stone in the middle and the other two of wood. The pieces looked like long broken boards, but had several holes in them connected by deep, sloping grooves. They were stained with splashes of a peculiar dark brown color and smelled like rotten meat.

Janie shivered as that creepy gray mist smoked into the air. Suddenly the abandoned temple was new again. The ghost looked like a real, living person. Other weird Indian dudes were crowded into the church. But these pictures were wavery, fuzzy at the edges, and Janie realized they were not happening now. The dead Indian was showing her his past, like on TV.

Then she was inside the head of that Indian from many years ago. Through his ghost's magic, she lived inside his brain. As she watched, she read his mind. She saw what he saw, heard what he heard, knew what he knew and felt what he felt...

Sun of Suns prostrated himself before the altar of the Sacred Flame. Surrounded by twelve fire pots molded in the images of the bird, fish and animal totems of the clans of the Great People, he lay with his forehead and arms pressed flat against the fabrics of woven reeds covering the hard wooden floor. He lay with his head toward the horizon where Elder Brother Sun was reborn every morning. The priests chanted a song asking the spirits for guidance and requesting Elder Brother's help.

For the last four days, each corresponding to one of the four sacred directions, Sun of Suns had not eaten, slept or touched a woman. He had remained in his sweat lodge, coming out only to sip cool water and perform his sacred duty as the sun's younger brother, leading the ceremonies at the birth and death of each day.

Now it was the evening of the fourth and final day of his Vision Quest. Elder Brother had just dropped off the cliff of Peoplerealm, once again eaten by Dirtworld. Sun of Suns still wore his ceremonial outfit, his brilliant white swan feather headdress, copper ear spools and chest plate, deerskin robes embroidered with river pearls and a necklace of ocean pearls, grizzly bear claws and shark teeth. He had partaken of the sacred white drink three times and vomited three times. He would lie before the sacred fire until he understood the meaning of his shaken spirit.

Sun of Suns' skin rippled as fear cold as snow squeezed his heart. He had not gone on such a quest as this since reaching manhood. Learning the secrets of the spirits was the duty of the priests; but only he could solve the mystery of the sadness that had eaten his heart several moons ago. Since that time, food had tasted like wood. Watching his warriors play chunkey in the plaza was a dull pastime. He took no pleasure from the plump, big breasted women dragged from captured villages. They could not even stiffen his staff. Only contemplating the severed heads of his fallen enemies staked on the poles of the palisades surrounding the Great Temple Mound gave him any satisfaction. Yet that also intensified his sadness, for he felt an omen of death, of the displeasure of the gods and the downfall of the City of the Sun.

Sun of Sun's soul ached with the agony Elder Brother suffered. Every morning, Elder Brother struggled to free himself from the clutches of Grandmother Earth, escaping Dirtworld to ride swiftly across Skyworld all day, only to fall off the cliff again at the beginning of night.

His heart also grieved for the Great People. Farmers carefully tended the fields of maize, beans and squash, but each harvest yielded less than the one before, as every year less rain fell from Skyworld. Hunters prowled the woods but found little game. Although his fearless Eagle Warriors overpowered many villages to take their jars of dry maize, they never captured enough. Every day, many dead stinker laborers, stricken from hunger and disease, were burned in the death mounds.

Sun of Suns could no longer bear the burden of this pain. Elder Brother gave the Great People their life. Elder Brother daily suffered and died, and still the Great People perished faster than they were born.

The highest ranking noble suns surrounded Sun of Suns, silently waiting for his quest to end, for him to discover the root of his dissatisfaction, to issue new commands to control and benefit the Great People who lived in and near the City of the Sun.

But no spirits visited him that night.

By dawn he was desperate for guidance, yet had no answers. The ancestors had abandoned him, and he could wait no longer. It was time to conduct the ceremony to welcome the new day's birth of Elder Brother. To sing songs of power to aid Elder Brother as he struggled to free himself from Grandmother Earth's embrace.

Maybe that was why Grandmother refused to give birth to enough maize to feed the Great People. She was angry because every morning they helped Elder Brother escape her womb. But the Great People needed the light of Elder Brother's fire to warm the world. If Elder Brother failed to run across the sky each day, the Great People would freeze in a darkness of everlasting snow.

Yet the Great People could not risk incurring Grandmother's disfavor, for they also could not live without maize. The City of the Sun would die. The Great People would return to the days of their grandfathers' grandfathers, when only a few families lived together in one place, and they survived or perished day by day, killing animals in the forest, pulling fish from the rivers and gathering nuts and fruits.

No Sun of Suns to rule over them. No suns to organize their daily tasks and distribute food. No priests to tend the sacred fires and intercede on their behalf with the spirits. No warriors to protect them. Without farmers who grew more maize than their own families required, there could be no craftspeople to fashion beautiful clothes and jewelry, no potters skilled at molding jugs and clay figurines, no healers with time and knowledge to search for and use the herbs that cured illness.

The Great People lived between Skyworld and Dirtworld, between Elder Brother Sun and Grandmother Earth. The Great People needed both.

What could he do?

Sun of Suns suddenly conceived an idea so vast and mighty it must have come from the gods, although Sun of Suns had not felt or even seen the spirit who had just visited him.

Suppose Elder Brother circled Skyworld along the horizon, just above Peoplerealm? Not up and down across Skyworld, never sinking into Dirtworld, but always flying just over it? Warming Grandmother Earth, but never again falling off the cliff into her embrace?

If Elder Brother ran such a trail through Skyworld he would not rise high. He would not look down on the Great People from the highest of heights at the middle of each day, but he also would not die at the end of every day and spend each night struggling for rebirth. This could only please Elder Brother. Grandmother would not have her fiery lover inside her womb again, but she would always have him close by her side, warming her and quickening her seed.

With both Elder Brother and Grandmother so happy, the Great People would prosper. There would be no dark nights again, no more snow and ice covering Grandmother for two or three moons.

The farmers could raise two crops of maize every year instead of one. The Great People would grow fat and happy.

Sun of Suns would be hailed as a mighty hero of the Great People. He would be called the greatest Sun who ever lived, even more important than the ancestor who began raising the Temple Mound. In Deathrealm he would listen to the Great People sing praises to his name for as long as the City of the Sun endured.

But how could Sun of Suns rescue Elder Brother? Such a feat would not be simple or easy. As he thought, arrows of ice pierced his heart. He shivered as though swimming naked in the Father of Waters in the middle of the Moon of Deep Snow. His air-soul felt as though torn to shreds by animal spirits.

Grandmother Earth would not easily accept such a tremendous change. Grandmother would demand Sun of Suns himself descend to Dirtworld to free Elder Brother. Grandmother would require many sacrifices. Much blood must sink into the soil. And not just any blood, but powerful blood. Magic blood.

Virgin blood.

CHAPTER FIVE

I

Ashland Avenue

"Say, Turk, brother, yo, you up? This it, man." Dewie held the cordless phone to his ear as he pulled on his Nike's

"You know what time it is?" Turk asked in a fast, squeaky voice. "Man, I've been smoking rocks all night with my lady—you dig? We out now, so it's crashing time soon's this movie on Cinemax over."

"We winning the world today, dude. I mean everything."

"What're you talking about?"

"This the day we strike for blood," Dewie said. "This be the day we seize the power. We got to do one little thing and then we'll be on top of the world, and I mean the whole world. This is it, I'm telling you."

"You crazy, man."

"Turk, you hang with me and you'll have everything you want. The finest flake from Peru? Just snap your fingers. A Rolls

Royce? Just say the word. Beautiful pussy? You won't have to do nothing because they'll be fighting over who'll jump your bones next. Fucking A."

"What kind of shit you been smoking?"

"This ain't no drug talking," Dewie said. "This is real and it's a steal. I'm not like you think I am no more. I ain't just no Ashland rock like you no more, I'm a boulder. That's my new name—Boulder."

"Go to sleep, Dewie. You strung out."

"Turk, this is a done deal. Just one job I need help with. Janie's little girls run off a few hours ago. She dumped them here, and they just up and left. I don't like them little bitches neither, man, but my mama, she's responsible for them."

"What you want me for? They ain't my goddamn problem. Hunt them down yourself."

"Turk, you're looking at this from the wrong angle, dude. We're partners. I'd help you out any day. You know that. We're blood brothers."

His story did sound lame. Nobody'd call in his buddies just to search out two lost little girls.

"Listen," he said, "there's a lot going down here. Janie's supposed to get some big government check from Social Security on account of being so slow, and Mama's going to make Janie give her a big chunk of it. We're talking thousands of dollars, not no chump change. But if Janie thinks my mother did something to her babies, then she won't give Mama shit."

"Where they at?" Turk asked.

"If I knew that, I'd just run go get them. But they can't be too far away, so they can't be too hard to find. How many white girls you see in this neighborhood with little black sisters?"

"I hardly ever see any white girls around here period."

"So we drive around until we find them, that's all. If we help Mama, she'll give us a cut of Janie's check."

"You calling a gang action? You checked with Marko, Dewie? He's our number one man. What's he think of this?"

"Hell, you have to ask Marko's permission to take a crap? We're all partners together, we can do what we want. He don't like it, he can go fuck himself."

"Is that really Dewie Grimes talking that talk?"

"I'm walking the walk too, brother, and he who isn't with me is against me. You best believe what I say. Remember I'm telling you that straight up from the beginning. I'll be seen in fifteen."

Dewie called the other Ashland Rocks, Andre Miller and Lorenzo Fair, shouting into their answering machines until he woke somebody at their cribs. Like Turk, they didn't believe what he said about his new destiny but were going along with him to find Latasha and Shontell for a split of Janie's money. Dewie didn't tell them about the sacrifice because they wouldn't want to help him kill two little girls. They all had babies themselves—nobody in the Rocks had trouble attracting women except Dewie.

They wouldn't back out when they learned what Dewie had done to Janie. Turk and Lorenzo once raped a fifty-year-old woman in a church, then stole all the money from the donation plates. Janie was an adult and white, and so ought to know better than to hang around dangerous dudes even if she was slow. Besides, nobody liked her anyway. It'd be different if they did, but they didn't.

They for sure wouldn't split once the sacrifices were completed. They wouldn't dare.

Dewie thought about calling Marko, giving him a fair chance to join up, then decided not to. Marko could have joined the Crips, but he wouldn't take second place. He would rather be undisputed general of the Ashland Rocks than a lieutenant in the Crip army. He just would not take orders. He was boss or he was out.

Dewie organizing the Rocks himself? Marko wouldn't like that. He might command the others not to help Dewie. He might try to stop Dewie because finding the girls hadn't been his idea.

Dewie opened and closed his fingers, feeling the strength and power pulsating inside his bones and muscles. How much strength? How much power? He ached to find out.

If he tried to stop Dewie, Marko would be the first to learn the Ashland Rocks now had a Boulder.

II

Ashland Avenue

As Marilyn drove, Jim tried to look at her without her noticing his attention. He didn't want her to know—yet that she was one of the most beautiful women he had ever met. Of course, he thought that about every woman he fell in love with, at least while he was still in love. Until they left him, or he caught them dating another man, or something happened to break them up.

He wasn't like all those men who didn't want to settle down, who deliberately strung a woman along with promises of commitment and marriage until they tired of her and wanted a new body in bed. He wanted intimacy. He wanted commitment. His love was real.

But the women left him. He fell out of love only when he had to, because the lady was already gone. His heart had been broken so many times it must look like a jigsaw puzzle, carved up by scar tissue.

Every lonely night Jim asked himself what he did to drive them away. He didn't have bad breath. He didn't beat them up. He didn't even make them sleep on the wet spot. Why did he keep on subconsciously choosing the wrong women?

Marilyn didn't seem a likely candidate to fulfill his romantic dreams. She was not only African-American, she was older than him. Not that she looked it. She had a trim body and high, large breasts that any twenty year old would envy. Her face didn't have any lines or wrinkles. The only sign of her age was the aura of confidence she projected. Confidence and concern.

She wasn't afraid to show how much she cared about this Janie Braxton.

That attracted him because he too wanted to do his best for his clients. He often worked late at night to stay caught up with the paperwork that never stopped multiplying, processing claims for Medicaid, Medicare and private insurance as quickly as possible so his clients' medical care wouldn't be interrupted.

If they were on SSI and going to stay in the hospital a long time he had to rush certain forms to Social Security right away so their checks wouldn't be stopped for not having the papers in on time. The other workers didn't make that effort. They just did what they could reasonably accomplish in eight hours, then went home.

They told him he cared too much. But patients' children needed temporary housing. Bosses had to be notified if the employee couldn't call in themselves or the patient wouldn't have a job when they recovered. Crime victims had to be told of the state's compensation fund.

Then, just when he thought he couldn't accomplish any more, someone like Janie came along demanding more time and energy than ten other patients combined.

He had never gone out to somebody's home before. He'd never risked a physical confrontation. He was only doing it now because he was attracted to Marilyn and this client was special to her.

"This is the address." Marilyn parked her Civic across the street.

The house surprised Jim. It didn't look like the home of someone reputed to have bilked credit card companies and the government out of numerous thousands of dollars. A medium-sized brick bungalow, it needed new gutters, a roof job and tuck-pointing. The once-white paint on the wood trim was peeling off in gray strips. Only a few patches of grass and dandelions grew in the front yard.

"So this is where the infamous Odelia Sykes and her trigger happy sons live," he said.

"You don't have to go with me, you know."

"I've come this far, haven't I? It's my professional duty."

"I doubt your supervisor would agree."

"So it's not in my official job description. So Janie's not even in my assigned workload. So it's still night. So what?"

"So let's go."

After a few minutes of Marilyn knocking, a sullen teenaged

girl pulled the door open a crack and stared at them with a just woken up face. "What you all want?"

"Is Odelia Sykes at home?" Marilyn asked.

"Who are you?"

"Tell her I'm here about Janie Braxton. It's very important."

The girl slammed the door. They heard her yell out, "Mama! Some people here about Janie. A white dude and a black lady."

A moment later a heavyset women jerked the door open. Her figure reminded Jim of the dancing hippos in a Disney cartoon. She wore black stretch pants that emphasized her thick thighs. Her stomach strained the elastic band in front and her bottom pushed the seat far out to the rear. Her hair was done up in an elaborate coiffure with half of the intricately intertwined braids dyed gold. He didn't know much about women's hair styling in general or black women's in particular, but Odelia's doo must have taken someone hours to arrange.

"Who are you and what do you want?" she said.

"Ms. Sykes, I'm Marilyn Patterson from the Abused Women's Shelter and this is Jim Williams from Holy Virgin Hospital. Several days ago Janie Braxton left our shelter with her two daughters to come here. Now she's seriously injured. We're just trying to find out if the girls are all right."

"What about them?"

"Are they here? Can I see them?"

"They aren't in this house, and Janie hasn't come by lately for weeks. Now I don't know neither one of you from the Vice President of Iraq, so just scoot your asses the hell off my property. Don't neither one of you two fools ought to be out knocking on somebody's door this early in the morning."

"Please, Ms. Sykes. I know Janie came here, and with Latasha and Shontell."

"I ain't seen nothing of them, and I say good riddance. I took good care of her, and them kids too. She tells lies on me, but I swear on the Bible I done right. If my son Michael wasn't that poor little girl's rightful blood father I wouldn't allow that white harlot into my house. He's in jail right now because she begged him to steal more money to buy her drugs."

"Ms. Sykes—"

"That's all Janie good for, fucking anything with a dick and smoking crack. My boy ain't perfect, I won't lie and pretend he is, but she made him go wronger. Since Michael was put in jail, she been twitching her little honky twat up under my younger boy Dewie's nose, teasing him with it, even knowing he can't think straight. She nothing but white trash."

"Did her checks come, Ms. Sykes? She told me she gave Social Security this address for the mail."

"I done told you once, I ain't telling you again. They ain't here and her checks ain't here neither. So you all just take yourselves away before I call the police. Being social workers don't give you the right to be public nuisances trespassing on property where you ain't wanted."

"Ms. Sykes, please help us, for the sake of your own granddaughter. I'm sure Janie was coming here."

"Well then she never made it. You find Shontell, you send my grandbaby on over here and I will take care of her better than her mother ever did. You can keep that Latasha. That child think she too smart to be around folks like us. Michael sure in hell isn't her father, so I don't have to pretend I love her, because I sure as hell don't."

Odelia stepped out onto the small concrete porch. Jim

moved back, but Marilyn didn't budge.

"But, please," Marilyn said. "Let us know if those checks come, or least send them back to Social Security."

"You people, you think you can run folks's lives for them, like they too stupid to know what's good for them, like you understand they minds better than they do they own selves. You think you could tell Janie what to do, where to live, to stay away from my boy. Who was too good for her. Who treated that little tramp better than any other man she spread her skinny little legs for, better than she deserved."

Jim wanted to run back to the car, but Marilyn wasn't moving, so neither was he. Would he still have his job after his boss learned he'd been arrested?

"She's cheated on my boy with every lowdown black man in North St. Louis," Odelia said. "She likes men folks and she wouldn't let you keep her away from them. She said you all were nothing but bulldagger dykes who wanted to get into her pants your own damn selves. Now what did I just tell you? Get the hell away from my house or I'll run your asses into jail."

"We're leaving, Ms. Sykes," Marilyn said. "I just want you to promise me you'll call if you learn anything about the children. They're missing. If you don't know where they are, who does?"

Odelia shouted into the house. "Dewie! Boy, get your ass out here right now. I want these folks gone."

A young man in bluejeans, a Bulls jacket and a Nelson Mandela t-shirt swaggered out as Odelia huffily stepped back inside. He was short, with thick muscles bunched underneath his sweats.

"You stop bothering my mama!" His voice was so loud and powerful it pushed Jim back against the wrought iron rail. This time, Marilyn did not hold her ground.

"We're leaving, I said we're leaving. Take it easy." No longer fearless.

"You stop bothering my mama!" Dewie said. "You all get the hell out of here and stay away. You ever come here again I'll knock your fucking heads off."

"Just take it easy."

Jim started down the steps with Marilyn behind him. Dewie followed them from the porch to the street and across to the car. There was something about him that struck Jim as unnatural. He seemed too solid. He moved like a walking statue, stiff and lumbering, but with a frightening anger and ferocity.

Jim and Marilyn hurried into the Civic. As Marilyn fumbled through her purse for the keys, Dewie slapped the fender with the flat of his hand. Jim would have sworn the car shifted slightly.

"And you tell that whore Janie if I ever see her again I'll fuck her so hard what's left of her brains'll rattle around inside her skull bone." He hit the fender again, and this time Jim was sure he pushed the Civic several inches to the side.

But that was impossible.

Marilyn ground the ignition, put the car in gear and peeled away.

III

Delmar Boulevard

L atasha awoke to a car revving its clattering engine, over and over, machine gun spurts popping out its tailpipe in what she called car farts. Her muscles jerked. Her mind was as gray as the early morning twilight. Dew had seeped through the seat of her sweat pants to dampen her bottom with cold. Chills vibrated through her bones.

She cuffed Shontell on the head. "Come on, little girl. I'm hungry. We stay here any longer somebody'll see us and call the Po-leece. You want to go to jail?"

Hand in hand, Latasha and Shontell retraced the route they ran the night before back to the big street.

Odelia lived in North St. Louis. They had come from that direction on the bus last night, so the other side of the street must be south. The shelter was on the near South Side of St. Louis, but this did not look like the right area to start heading farther south. The shelter was somewhere close to Grand Avenue, which was a very long street that ran north and south through the middle of St. Louis. How could they find it? Latasha remembered when they went to the shelter or to Cardinal Glennon Hospital from Odelia's house they always went into the city. Into the city was east, wasn't it? She was pretty sure of that. And where was east?

Of course. The sun rose in the east. She led Shontell toward the dawn.

"We'll just keep walking," she said. "If we walk far enough, we've got to find Grand. I know it's in front of us somewhere. We just got to keep walking, that's all. Maybe it's a long way, but we'll be safe there with Marilyn and Sara. They'll feed us and let us sleep in a bed. So don't you start crying, you hear me, or I'll beat your tail end."

Latasha knew they made an unusual pair. She was used to people staring at a white and black girl together who were too different in ages to be just friends. Latasha didn't like to tell strangers she and Shontell were sisters because most of the white people and lots of the black ones made a face. They didn't like Mama having both kinds of kids.

A yellow school bus loaded with shouting children passed by them. Latasha would miss an arithmetic test. Ms. Davis, her teacher, and Mr. Tolliver, the principal, would be mad at her tomorrow because nobody would call in for her today. They'd want a note, which Mama couldn't write even when she wasn't beat up.

Latasha pushed the problem out of her mind. When they reached the shelter Marilyn would call the school and explain and make everything all right. When they reached the shelter Marilyn would make everything all right.

She hoped that would be soon because she was terribly hungry. Last night at Odelia's she'd eaten only mashed potatoes and green beans for dinner because, Odelia said, she had not defrosted enough pork chops for them because she hadn't known they were staying over another night. Yolanda cooked, and she gave Latasha and Shontell only the scrapings from the bowls of vegetables. Latasha hadn't eaten a full meal since lunch at school. Her belly gurgled.

When they reached the shelter, Marilyn would feed them. Marilyn would make everything all right.

IV

Ashland Avenue Neighborhood

After making those motherfucking social workers run away, Dewie walked to Lorenzo's crib. Then Lorenzo drove his mother's `95 Olds Delta 88 to Turk's house.

At Andre's apartment building Marko swaggered out the door before Dewie, Turk and Lorenzo crossed the street. Andre was right behind him, giving Dewie an uncomfortable, apologetic look. "I had to phone Marko, Dewie, man, when you calling the Rocks together. He's our leader."

They met in the small patch of front yard. Dewie smiled. He should have brought Michael's .45 revolver. His switchblade wouldn't be enough. But maybe he didn't need any weapons. He was Boulder now. The Indian had promised he was the weapon.

Marko cut Dewie with half-closed eyes like a rattler psyching out a toad.

"Dewie Grimes, my man," he said. "My main, number one man. Calling on the Rocks without checking with me. I don't believe this is happening. If you wanted the Rocks to help you, Dewie, why didn't you ask for a consultation with me first? Why call all the others but cut me out? So what if those little girls're lost? Who gives a good goddamn anyway besides their mama, who's the worse fuck I ever had?"

Dewie smirked. "I wouldn't touch Janie if she paid me a

thousand dollars. And I hate them kids."

"There's no mutinies allowed in the Rocks," Marko said.

"You done lost the last election. You ain't the Prez no more, so I don't have to kiss your ass."

"You always been a fuckup, Dewie. What you trying here? You too shy even to rap with bitches. Any twelve year old can hit on hoes better than you. You one of them stone fools we laugh about straight out of the `News of the Weird' newspaper column. If you wrote a holdup note the bank teller couldn't read it. If you did grab some money from the bank you'd run outside and couldn't remember where you parked your getaway car."

"You want to stay on, Marko, you number two man for sure. That's fair enough."

"Hell, even your own brother thinks you're a moron. When Michael asked me to let you join the Rocks I only agreed because you'd be another pair of fists or a finger on the trigger in a fight, and we're small. You good for laughs, but nothing else."

Dewie hesitated. Every word Marko spoke was true. What kind of shit was he trying to pull here? Dewie felt stronger thanks to the Indian, but maybe he'd just gone crazy again. Maybe the chief was only another psycho-hallucination and Marko was going to kill him. But he'd gone too far to stop now.

"You're history, Marko. You just ain't hip to it yet."

"You're an ungrateful motherfucker. Without me and Michael you ain't worth dog shit. When we all stop running the streets you'll live on your government check, watching the tube all night, growing fatter and stupider every day."

"You just wondering where I got the balls to challenge the late, great Marko."

Andre, Lorenzo and Turk stepped back, looking uneasily at

both Marko and Dewie, but especially to Dewie. They understood he had changed. They sensed he truly was not just a Rock any longer, that he was Boulder.

Marko's gold chains flashed in the morning sunlight, setting off the gold tooth in the front of his mouth with the shape of a star cut in it. He took off his black broad-billed cap and wiped his forehead with it, a pitcher on the mound at Busch Stadium showing his disgust with a blind umpire's call. He slowly nodded his head toward the other three, sharing the pathetic joke he thought Dewie was making of himself. They acknowledged his attention with small gestures but didn't commit themselves.

Dewie didn't need to prove himself with Marko. If Marko would just leave, Dewie'd let him go. If Marko would be his assistant, Dewie would agree. Marko was an old buddy. He didn't want to fight him.

Marko spit on the ground. "Sucker. And you say you got the power."

"That's right," Dewie said.

"Your Daddy thought he had the power too, until your mama told him once a month wasn't enough."

"At least my Daddy weren't no trick."

Marko stepped directly into Dewie's face. "You limp dick cock sucking gorilla-nosed son of a bitch, I'll bust your head so hard you'll—"

Dewie slammed his right fist into Marko's belly. A small whoof blew out Marko's mouth and his face faded to gray. He swayed back and forth, eyes closed, gasping for air in short, shallow puffs but stayed on his feet.

Dewie closed his eyes and inhaled. The Indian chief's strength surged in his veins, coursed through his blood. His muscles were steel now, not flesh; his bones granite, his blood ice.

He laid a left hook on the side of Marko's head. Marko staggered several steps then fell like a bag of cement. His skull thunked the ground. Blood trickled from his ear.

Andre knelt and examined him. "He dead, brothers. Dewie killed Marko with two punches. Jesus H. Christ."

They stared at him with awe and fear. Although still surprised and shocked by what he'd just done, Dewie liked that look.

"You guys are the Rocks," Dewie said. "I'm Boulder. Anybody have a problem with that? Say it now, because this is just beginning. I'm going to end up the big chief of the world. You stay Rocks. Won't nothing stop us from having anything we want. Anything. Everything. You think I'm tripping, you look at Marko. Anybody want out?"

Andre, Turk and Lorenzo looked at each other. Lorenzo said, "I believe you, Dewie. I ain't never seen nothing like that. Just put him down and out forever with two punches. I believe you, Dewie. Goddamn and motherfucker, I believe you."

Dewie looked at Turk and Andre.

"I'm in," Turk said, then pointed to Marko's body. "What'll we do with him? There'll be cops here in a minute."

You and Lorenzo dump that trash someplace where nobody saw this happen. Pick him up like he's just hurt and you're taking him to the hospital."

He had to be careful. He still didn't know how strong he was, maybe he couldn't catch bullets like Superman. He couldn't leave Marko lying in the yard when maybe a neighbor on their way to work had seen him punch the dude. Not that anybody would want to interfere with a gang. And two young guys having a short, quiet fight—only two quick punches—was hardly worth noticing anyway. The neighbors wouldn't even think, without the body as evidence, Marko was dead. After all, there had been no knives or guns, only fists.

Just Dewie's bare hands.

He stared at Andre. "Well?"

"I'm with you, Dewie. You're our leader now. We can all see that. Dewie, we're—"

Dewie slapped him across the mouth, not hard enough to injure him but enough to rock him back.

"Get this straight," Dewie said. "From now on, you all call me Boulder."

Andre wiped the blood off with the back of his hand. "I've got that—Boulder."

"I'll tell you all this, even though you won't understand it yet. Them two little girls is part of this. Don't ask me how or why. Just find them. After we get our hands on them we'll be the most powerful gang in the world. We'll laugh at the Crips, the Bloods, the Marauders, the Mafia—hell, we'll control the United States Army. My blood's strong now, but it has to be stronger. The old Indian chief needs those little girls to finish what he started, to make me like I am. They interrupted me last night. That's why we have to find them."

"What're you going to do with them?" Lorenzo asked.

Dewie reached out, grabbed Lorenzo by his Lakers jacket and pulled him to his chest, then lifted him off the ground.

"That's between me and the old Indian," Dewie said. "All you got to do is ride around in that old piece looking for them. And when you find them you call my mama and you hold them until I get there. Is that clear?"

"Hell, I was just asking."

Dewie reacted to this with a face that felt like stone, like those old presidents carved on some mountain he remembered seeing in a picture at school. "You said you was with me."

"I am, Dew—Boulder. I am, I am."

"Then don't ask no more stupid-ass questions. You obey me—or else."

The Rocks looked at each other. They didn't have to ask, or else what? They saw Marko lying in the grass, brains dripping out his ear.

V

Corner of Delmar and Kingshighway

As they walked Shontell kept slowing down. Latasha had to drag her along like a pull toy, which soon made Latasha's arm ache. How much farther could Grand be? Although she felt as though they had been hiking all day the sun was only a little higher in the sky.

When they spotted a major intersection with a stoplight Latasha ran ahead to try to read the street sign. If only this was Grand.

As Shontell toddled to catch up with her, wobbling to the side with every step, Latasha bent her head as far back as it would go, straining her neck, and sounded out the letters on the sign.

UNION BL

Although she could not pronounce it all she knew that first

letter, U, certainly did not make a `gr' sound. She clutched Shontell's hand. "Come on, little girl. This ain't it yet."

"I want to go home. I want Mama."

"We got to walk a little farther first."

Several blocks later was an even bigger intersection, and the Taco Bell and Burger King looked familiar. Latasha was sure she had eaten with Mama at that Rally's Drive In.

This must be Grand.

But when she looked up the street name had too many letters in it.

KINGSHIGHWAY BL

That was an important street. She heard people mention it a lot. But it wasn't Grand, and the shelter was close to Grand.

How much farther? How many more blocks?

She slumped against the signpost, backbone pressing the hard metal. She felt so tired but she didn't dare board another bus. Maybe the same driver would see them and call the police. Maybe all the drivers were on the lookout for them. Maybe the bus wouldn't go right. Some of them didn't drive straight down important streets. They made funny twists and turns. If you didn't know which bus to take you could wind up a long way away from where you wanted to go. That happened to Mama at least once a month.

If she felt this worn out already, Shontell must be exhausted. Her four year old legs weren't as long or as strong as Latasha's. She couldn't even ride a bicycle yet.

Latasha couldn't remember being so hungry since she was real little like Shontell, before she learned to hide fifty or sixty dollars out of Mama's purse every month right after she cashed the checks. Her mother never missed it and when they ran out of food late in the month Latasha could pull out a five or a ten dollar bill and they went to the store and bought sandwiches and candy.

But Latasha hadn't planned for an emergency to happen while they went to visit Odelia so the thirty-five dollars she had stashed for the end of this month was tucked away in her bag at the shelter. Why was she so stupid? Why didn't she always keep a ten dollar bill hidden in the lining of her purse for just in case?

"Come on," Latasha told Shontell.

Shontell always obeyed Latasha because her big sister was the adult who took care of her. She didn't understand why big grownups said Latasha was a child. Latasha was the smartest person in the world and taller than Shontell. Even if she was not as tall as the really old people, she was obviously a grownup.

Latasha took her into Burger King's potty to pee and wash. Latasha had to hold Shontell up to the sink.

"I've got a plan," Latasha said.

She took Shontell's now clean hand and led her straight into the dining room. The hamburger smell was so thick it made Shontell's empty tummy hurt. They approached an elderly woman sipping a cup of coffee.

"Please, lady," Latasha said. "Can you spare us some change to buy food?"

Without turning her eyes in their direction the woman hissed. "Scat, you two, before I give you a whipping."

Latasha led Shontell toward two men sitting at a corner table smoking cigarettes. Shontell spied several uneaten biscuits left among the waxed food wrappers scattered over their table.

"Please, sirs, can you spare some food for my sister and

me?"

They both wore the same navy blue work uniforms. The one telling a funny story in a loud voice stopped speaking and looked at them. "Fred, you know something's wrong with this country when little kids got to go begging for food."

"Where's your mama at?" Fred asked.

"She's home real sick," Latasha said. "She hurts too much to do anything and we ain't got no food in the house. Please, sir."

"Go head on, Fred," the first man said. "Give them those sausage biscuits. You done finished eating all you're going to."

Fred handed over the biscuit that he had taken only one bite out of. "Your mama ought to be horsewhipped," he said. "I don't care how sick she is, this ain't hygienic, little children eating food with my spit on it."

Latasha grabbed the first biscuit and was reaching for the second when a woman in a brown uniform rushed over.

"What're you little brats doing? We don't allow panhandling in here. What kind of place do you think this is? You give that right back and get the hell out of here."

Latasha grabbed Shontell's hand with her free one and they ran out the door. As they hurried through the parking lot back to the sidewalk, they passed by the men's table. The first man looked out the window, smiled and winked at Latasha. She raised her hand, sausage biscuit still clutched in it. Shontell thought that was funny so she waved bye bye to the man too.

Back on the street corner, Latasha tore the biscuit in two, catching the crumbs in the waxed paper, and gave half to Shontell. They gobbled the food down in seconds then licked the grease from their fingers.

Although still extremely hungry, Shontell felt better. Latasha made a good plan. Shontell sure was glad her sister was the smartest person in the world. Just like Mama was the most loving mother in the world. Having Mama and Latasha as her family made Shontell the luckiest little girl in the world. When the traffic signal's white WALK light flashed on, she and Latasha crossed the street and kept heading east.

VI

Dreamspace

66 Now you see I was a great chief," Sun of Suns told Janie.
They were back in the present time, in the ruined temple.

Janie wanted to cry, she felt so helpless, but her ghost eyes shed no tears.

"I was absolute ruler of tens of thousands of people. I reigned over the largest city and kingdom north of the Rio Grande River. I nearly rearranged the very cosmos. You are only a miserable little retarded girl. You cannot resist me."

Janie folded her arms across her chest. "You can't make me do anything. You can't kill me, can you?"

"I could, but then I could not use your energy. Your life must end on the material plane, in Peoplerealm, or I cannot capture your power for myself. That is the nature of sacrifice. I may not kill you directly for my own benefit."

"I don't understand."

"But I can sap your will to live. That is what I am doing now."

"I'm hurt and I'm in the hospital, but I've gone to the hospital lots of times before. The doctors and nurses always make me all better again."

"Your mud-body stupidly clings to life, but after you lose all hope it will let go and you will die. You are the weakest of the weak, the poorest of the poor, the stupidest of the stupid. You are a lamb in a forest of lions, a minnow in an ocean of sharks. You were born to be killed and eaten. You are destined to be a sacrifice to the powerful."

Janie screeched, then flew through the walls of the temple like a real ghost. She rushed away from the dead Indian and his dead city, zooming back through the huge caves and underground caverns, through darkness lit by devil fires.

Flaming crosses inside burning circles swirled around her. Men in deer, snake and fox head masks danced on the cavern floors. Rattlesnakes slithered between the dry bones of skeletons. Arrows with a point at each end shot across in front of her. Skulls with big, sharp teeth snapped their huge jaws at her. Hands with no arms clutched with bony fingers. Giant birds with snake scales poked their pointed beaks at her.

She again remembered the pictures of hellfire and damnation preachers had frightened her with. When she was a little girl she dreamed about Hell every night. She imagined a demon shoved a sharpened wood skewer through her asshole until the point emerged from her mouth, then turned her over a fire, roasting her like a hot dog on a stick.

Janie didn't understand eternity, but she knew it was a very long time and wanted no part of it.

She was a terrible sinner, she learned in church. She lied. She touched herself in the nasty place. She threw rocks at other children. Worst of all, she wished Daddy would die so he would stop punishing her. God would never forgive that sin.

Janie prayed for forgiveness, but she kept being a bad girl, so Daddy had to go on punishing her. And every time he did she hated him and wanted him to die even though he was doing it because he wanted to save her from Hell. She learned in school parents disciplined their children because they loved them and wanted them to grow up to be good people. All her teachers said that. The school principal said that. All the grownups in Sunday School said that.

She was a bad girl because she wouldn't stop doing bad things. That was the right way to escape Daddy's punishment. She was stupid, but she understood that.

It broke Janie's heart to sit in church and hear the preacher rail against sin when she knew she was the biggest sinner in the whole entire congregation because she prayed God would strike Daddy dead for trying to help her grow up into a good person. That's why she had to stop going. She was doomed already, damned to Hell.

But she wasn't dead yet so she sure didn't plan on staying in Hell now.

Dragons shot fire at her from their gaping throats. Alligators swarmed through a slimy swamp. Angry hornets chased her, trying to sting her, but Janie was so frightened she flew faster than the buzzing insects.

She looked behind her once, but instead of the dead Indian she saw her father, a giant, rushing toward her.

"No!" she screamed, and closed her eyes.

When she opened them, she saw a faded green car with her real Mommy and Daddy sitting inside.

"Help me," she said. "Mommy, make this bad dream go

away. When I was a little girl you hugged me and kissed me and told me those monsters in my nightmares wouldn't bite me, but this Indian ghost wants to hurt me real bad, worse than anybody ever done to me before. He wants to kill me and steal my soul. He wants to cut out my heart and keep me down in Hell with those Indian ladies with holes in their chests even though I sure ain't no virgin, I was never a real virgin because as long as I can remember I lusted in my heart for boys and you told me Jesus said thinking about Doing It is just as evil as Doing It.

"I'm real sorry I made you and Daddy so angry so many times but I don't want that Indian to eat my soul. Mommy, he wants to chew me up and swallow me down so I won't never be me again. I'm a bad little girl and when I die I'm going to burn in fire and brimstone, but I sure don't want no dead Indian chomping down on me like I'm a piece of pie. I'll give him a bellyache like he ain't never had. I'll make him so sick he'll puke me up. I won't stay inside no old Indian so cold I get frostbit thinking about him."

"Don't forget your daughters," the dead Indian said.

Janie had not escaped. She was still trapped.

"I will return to Peoplerealm," he said. Your daughters are virgins. Your death and their sacrifice will give me the power I need. I will greet Elder Brother again. I will rule!"

Janie suddenly understood. This ghost wanted Dewie to kill Latasha and Shontell!

"Help, Mommy and Daddy," she cried. "Protect my babies. Please don't let anybody hurt them. I'm sorry I'm not the good little girl you wanted. But please—take care of my babies."

But Mommy and Daddy didn't hear her any more than Latasha and Shontell had.

CHAPTER SIX

I

Holy Virgin Mother of God Medical Center

Jim's hands shook as he picked up his handset and punched a button. He slammed the phone down. "Look at me," he said. "I'm still shaking. I was more scared than I thought, and that was a lot."

Marilyn smiled, amused despite her own fear. "It's over and done with," she said.

His voice still trembling, he said, "I'm just not used to threats."

"I hope not."

"I know social work can be dangerous, but working here at the hospital, I've gotten used to people who were too sick or injured to try to hurt me if they wanted. At Family Services we had guards in the building."

"I'll do it." Marilyn picked up his phone and dialed.

"Social Security," a voice said a moment later. "How can I help you?"

"Hello," Marilyn said. "May I speak to Ms. Stapleton?"

"Just a moment."

Another voice on the line: a young, flighty white woman. "This is Ms. Stapleton."

"Are you Janie Braxton's worker?"

"I'm the claims representative who had her Zebley case. Why? Who are you?"

Marilyn explained the situation to Ms. Stapleton, who said, "Oh no! That poor little girl. What kind of monster would do such a thing?"

Marilyn realized she had found someone else who would go out of their way to help Janie. "The police are still investigating. I called to ask about her Zebley checks."

"Now she'll have to have a representative payee for them," Ms. Stapleton said. "And she has a daughter on SSI too, doesn't she? Who will do it?"

"I hadn't thought about that," Marilyn said.

"Janie told me she didn't want any of those people where she was living to get the money for her. Janie didn't trust any of them, so that's why I decided to go ahead and pay her the checks directly, despite the psychologist saying she needed a payee."

"Janie's parents are supposed to be on their way to the hospital now. We'll talk to them and see what they think. Have you sent out her Zebley checks yet?

Sure. I didn't let them get backed up with the rest of our

work. She ought to have them by now."

"How much?"

Ms. Stapleton hesitated. "You said you're from that shelter?"

"That's right. I wouldn't ask, but the hospital social worker and I went over to see Odelia Sykes earlier this morning. She denies the checks have come yet."

"I verified that my inputs took, so for sure they were mailed. Unless the Post Office lost them, she should have received them two or three days ago."

"What address did you use?"

"The one on Ashland. Janie told me she would meet the mailman. Look, I'm not allowed to tell you how much the checks were, but it's a lot. They're worth searching for. She's the only one who can legally cash them, so if you find them and she can't sign her name, bring them in here and I'll reissue them to whoever becomes her payee. Ask for me, and I'll make sure it's done as soon as possible."

"Thank you."

"It sounds like she got the checks, cashed them and somebody beat her up, then stole the money off her. I hope they catch the guy and string him up by the balls."

Jim's intercom beeped as soon as Marilyn hung up. He snapped out, "Yes?"

"This is the front desk, Mr. Williams. That couple you told me to look out for are here, asking about that patient."

"Please send them right up." Jim's nerves were on edge. This case was getting to him and it wasn't even his. How did he get into this mess?

He looked at Marilyn and, heart gulping, remembered. Why did he have to play the cowardly lion when he tried to call Social Security? He didn't want to look weak in front of her.

"Marilyn, would you mind sitting in the lounge down the hall for a while?" he said. "Hospital policy. You shouldn't be in here while I interview them."

"Of course. I need a cup of coffee."

Her sad, serene, mature beauty fascinated him. Her face and body had a timeless loveliness. The confident way she held her shoulders back attracted him—proud and comfortable with herself, not needing to prove a thing to anybody and all the more desirable for that.

The thought of knowing such a strong woman intimately both frightened and fascinated him. To win and hold her love was a daunting, but worthwhile, challenge. How could he make her see him in a romantic light?

Minutes later, a nurse ushered the Braxtons into his office. They looked stern and severe, Puritans. Judith's hair was actually in a beehive, the gray showing through the tint job. Her eyes were strong but sad. Willie Lee had the tank-wide abdomen and redwood-thick thighs of the old-time wrestler Dick the Bruiser.

Both appeared better than seventy, though Judith at least had to be much younger. But tough. They looked like two outcroppings of rock on a hillside, rough and hard.

Raising a retarded child without assistance was not easy for well educated parents in their twenties. She must have been a caution to these two.

Jim stood and shook their hands.

"Thank you for coming," he said. "I know this is hard on you, but—"

"Just let us see our little girl and we'll go away without bothering you any more," Willie Lee said.

"Hush," Judith told him.

"But that's what we came for, isn't it? To see Janie lying in the bed she made for herself?"

"Let the man talk," Judith said. "He has to do his job."

Jim smelled the stale alcohol on both their breaths. Alcoholics were the worst kind to deal with, at the welfare office or the hospital. He would rather talk to the insane, the retarded, the deaf, the drug addicted, the hostile and the foreigners who spoke no English, anybody rather than alcoholics, especially when they were still drunk.

As well as he could Jim started to describe what happened to Janie and what her medical condition was, based on the latest information he had from the Neuro ICU.

"Look, I didn't come here for all this malarkey," Mr. Braxton said. "Let's just get on with it, all right? She's our daughter, yes, but we can't afford to pay you anything, so we're not going to sign any papers. She's our daughter but we only saw her and the children at her convenience, which wasn't any too often. We couldn't control her even when she was a little bitty thing so we sure couldn't after she got old enough to run off and be a whore."

"Mr. Braxton—"

"I know what you're thinking. You sit there well- scrubbed and concerned with your fancy dancy education looking at us like we're a couple of backwoods holy rollers. I didn't abuse her no matter what she says. Sure, I tried to put the fear of God into her. Sure I spanked her, sure I took my belt to her. You would've too. But all I wanted was to prevent this, Mister Whatever-your-

111

name-is."

"Williams."

"I knew we wouldn't always be there to take care of her. And there's lots of people like to take advantage of kids like her. I know how things stand. Women are natural born whores, Mister, and that's the simple truth of it. Lots of people think men's desires are stronger because we can't control them and that's true in a way, but women burn too. They're just slyer about it than us. They know how to trade it off to us in return for something."

"Please, Mr. Braxton, I—"

"I don't know if you're married or not, Mister, but that's what marriage is all about. There's love, sure. I love Judith and she loves me. But I ain't fooled. If she didn't tie herself down to one man for security and because she's a good Christian, she could be slipping in and out of a thousand beds. That's just how every woman is."

Jim tried not to let his face show how appalled he felt. "I'm sure you must be upset, but—"

"Janie's retarded, so she's not naturally smart enough to control her desires the way most women do, to cleave to one man like the Bible says, so she wouldn't have the temptation of becoming a whore. That's what I tried to prevent, by teaching her the only way I know how."

"You talk too much," Judith said.

"I failed, Mister. I readily acknowledge that. Never in my worst nightmares, though, did I think she'd wind up screwing every black buck in sight for miles around, even having a baby by one. She turned her back on her own kind and now one of them blacks has showed just how much he appreciated it. I'm sorry, I'm real sorry, but goddamn it, I tried. I tried like hell."

Jim punched the intercom number of the nurse's duty station at the Neuro ICU. "This is Jim Williams in Social Work. Is Janie Braxton's EEG done yet? Her parents are here and want to see her."

He set the phone down and turned to Willie Lee and Judith. "They've finished her tests for now. We can go right up. She's in a coma and can't hear you, so please speak quietly. We don't want disturb the other patients."

It was no good trying to shut Willie Lee up when he went off on one of his tirades. He could preach for hours without rest. He could yell at this young man all morning and not run down. Sometimes he embarrassed Judith.

This worker did think he was superior to them, though, and that hurt her, but she was too proud to show it. She was also too proud to act as ashamed as she felt listening to her husband rant.

She learned a long time ago no matter how poor you were in money you could still have pride. Poor but proud was better than rich and ashamed. She wouldn't mind trying out rich and proud, but that didn't seem too likely an occurrence for the future since it hadn't happened yet, so she'd settle for poor but proud.

Much about Willie Lee made her proud. He was strong, a hard worker and good provider. He was faithful to her. He had chosen her as his woman and he kept himself her man. Other women tempted him but he knew they were whores from the Devil and wanted nothing to do with them. He was a righteous man. The bottle was his weakness but he kept it under control.

He never let it get the better of him. Not anymore.

He could be hard, even cruel by the lights of some folks. Some people would say he had abused Janie. But everything Willie Lee did to Janie, he did in faith, to teach her right from wrong, to lead her onto the path of righteousness, to save her soul.

His anger could and did boil over into violence. He had slugged Judith at least a hundred or more times. He had occasionally beaten her badly. The first time, after less than six months of marriage, she ran home to her parents. Her mother met her in the doorway with a .12 gauge shotgun.

"Stop right there." She leveled the gun at Judith's chest. "I'm your mother and I love you to high Heaven, but I'd rather see my daughter dead than an adulterating whore. And that's what you'd be if you walk out on your husband. Baby, when you said 'I do for better and worse,' them words meant something. For worse sometimes means for worse, sometimes for real bad worse. He's your husband and your cross and you belong in his house, in his bed, and you better haul yourself back over there real fast like. You bring him and a ham over next month for Thanksgiving."

Judith learned. Her place was by Willie Lee's side. There must be better men, but she knew of many worse.

The corridors reeked of hospital smells: disinfectant, cleaning chemicals, blood, puke, urine and medicine. Judith grew dizzy. Such bright fluorescent lights and brilliant walls. So much gleam of stainless steel and polished chrome.

Judith thought Mr. Williams was leading them to the wrong bed. A small lump lay underneath the white blankets. An IV was hooked to a skinny arm and wires and electrodes to other parts of the child's body. The head was shaved almost bald, what Judith could see of it underneath the huge lump of bandages. And there was a steel tube poking out of this person's skull and more tubes and wiring hooking them up to more machines that beeped and blipped and pulsed around them.

Judith had to stare directly into the slack, bleary, almost dead face before she realized that this was, indeed, Janie. Her daughter. Her own long lost, now wounded child.

Judith fainted.

II

Dreamtime

Wanting to cry because Mommy and Daddy wouldn't listen to her, Janie bowed her head and closed her eyes. When she opened them she was back in the broken down Indian temple.

"Your parents won't help you," the dead Indian said.

Janie sat up straight. "Mommy and Daddy love me. They always tried to make me be a good girl." She folded her arms across her chest. "It's my fault I'm an evil sinner."

"You must see and learn the truth for the truth will destroy you. I have searched your mind for everything you have deliberately forgotten. I will dredge up the sorrows and tears you don't want to remember. You can recall so little anyway, your lack of brainpower allows you to lock away much pain. The secret places of your heart are filled with the memories of your suffering. You will relive them. Then you will want to die."

Janie felt goosebumps and again saw the gray mist. The ghost was showing her another story.

When the foggy smoke cleared, Janie looked down on a little girl playing in a big back yard behind a small, yellow house. She wore dirty, worn-out overalls with iron-on patches holding the seat and knees together. The ends of her pants did not reach far enough to cover her bare ankles. Mommy had tied her brown hair in pigtails that fell flat on the sides of her head like deflated balloons. Her white cotton t-shirt tightly hugged her shoulders and chest and was smudged with dirt. She had left her plastic thongs near the house so she could run barefoot through the grass.

Janie lost herself inside the little girl just like she did before, into the Indian.

The yard was rough, chunky with rocks, partly-filled holes and patches of bare soil packed too tight for grass to grow through. Daddy said there was still broken glass, so she should wear her thongs all the time, but when the leaves of grass tickled her naked skin she forgot Daddy's orders.

On the other side of the yard was Mr. Peabody's field. Janie was not supposed to go there, especially now, because the corn had grown taller than her. Daddy said every darned row of corn looked like every other darned row of corn, so if she went into the field she would never find her way out. She would be lost in the corn forever, just like being damned to Hell.

Clutching her doll Suzy, Janie scampered to the rear of the yard. Large honeysuckle bushes offered cool shade and secret hiding places where nobody could find her. She would stay there with Suzy forever and ever.

Suzy had been Janie's best friend since she was a baby.

Janie vaguely remembered Suzy used to look like an angel. She wore a fresh, crisp white dress and had beautiful, clean wavy blond hair. She used to have two blue eyes that looked straight ahead in a funny way when Janie turned Suzy's head from side to side. Suzy also used to have a right arm and a left foot.

That was before a bad man sneaked into Janie's bedroom at night while she was sleeping and punished Suzy by gouging out her left eye with the edge of a spoon. He cut off Suzy's left foot with a big kitchen knife and pulled out Suzy's arm.

Janie didn't know why the bad man did those things. Suzy must have been a very naughty little girl to be punished so much. Suzy must have been even more wicked than Janie. Only sinful little girls were punished. Janie loved Suzy, so she hoped her dolly would learn to be a good girl, so she wouldn't be punished again. Janie hoped Suzy was not evil enough to want the bad man who punished her to die.

Because then God himself would have to punish Suzy. God would damn Suzy's immortal soul to Hell forever, because that's what happened to sinful little girls who refused to be good, and wished the bad man who punished them would drop dead. They suffered everlasting torment.

But Janie thought Suzy must be a nice baby when she was punished. Suzy wouldn't cry or scream or fight or kick or scratch or bite. She would take her punishment like a good girl. She didn't hate Daddy. She didn't wish Daddy would die. Janie was proud of Suzy.

Daddy wasn't proud of Janie, would never be proud of her even if she was a good little girl. Because even if she was the best little girl in the world Janie would still be stupid. She could not be normal like Mommy and Daddy wanted so they would never be proud of Janie no matter how good she was.

She crawled through the curtain of honeysuckle vines with their green leaves and slim, yellow flowers with a drop of sweet juice inside. She pressed through the tangle of branches and sticks poking at her eyes until she sat next to the main trunk.

She delighted in the cool shade, in the electric feel of the bush, its growing, pulsating life surrounding her, its sap flowing through every root and branch, its leaves quivering with delight, flowers shining with a glory like the streets of gold in Heaven.

Birds sang and in the distance Mr. Peabody's tractor thrummed. Her heart felt light as the dew, without a care or worry, as open and boundless as the fuzzy white clouds drifting through the blue sky above.

She raised Suzy to her face and kissed the doll on her dirty plastic lips, smooching her with a loud smacking sound. "I love you, Suzy," she said. "I love you, I love you, I love you."

She hugged the doll to her breast and sang. Nobody except Suzy understood Janie's songs.

"Jesus loves Suzy this I know cause in the midnight hour your cheating heart...mmmmmummmmmummmmm...don't come home rock of aces past I told you so...."

"Janie!" Mommy called out. "Janie! Where are you? You come home right now, Janie."

Janie stopped singing and knelt close to the ground underneath the bush, not moving a muscle. Mommy and Daddy never played with her. They said they were too old, because they had her late in life. That's what they said. Janie was stupid but she understood being old meant you didn't play games.

"You said she was right here in the yard." Daddy.

"I looked just a few minutes ago. There're her thongs in the grass."

"Great. So she's wandering barefoot again like some heathen."

"Let's hope she's past the stage of taking off all her clothes."

"So help me I'll tan her hide so hard it'll turn into leather."

Janie was an accident. That's what another little girl at school told her parents meant when they said they had a baby late in life when they were too old to play. She didn't know how Mommy and Daddy could have a baby by accident. Did a big stork leave her on their doorstep because it had the wrong address? Did she really belong to some other Mommy and Daddy who were young and liked to play games? Who wanted her?

"Janie!" Mommy called out. "You come home right now, young lady. You hear me? Don't make me come after you."

"If I have to go looking for you you'll be sorry," Daddy yelled. "You'll be in big trouble."

Janie hugged Suzy to her chest and hummed. She didn't hear Mommy and Daddy. She heard only the birds, the tractor and the squeak of Suzy's plastic body when Janie squeezed her.

"She's probably in the cornfield."

"She knows better than that. She knows how I'd punish her if we ever catch her there. She could be lost until Mr. Peabody ran over her with his thrasher."

"Don't say things like that."

"It's true," Daddy said. "Maybe it'd be for the best. We'd certainly have more peace."

Mommy's voice burned like a don't touch cast iron skillet on a lit burner. "I said stop it."

"You're afraid of the truth, Judith. We're not getting any younger, but that child's like a baby. Worse than a baby, because she can't be shut up in a playpen anymore. You're going to wear yourself out caring for her just when you ought to take it easy, only cooking and gardening. I put in more overtime at the plant than the young guys. Everybody thinks I'm crazy. I go out and preach every chance I get whether I feel the Holy Ghost within me or not. If I don't feel the Lord speaking through me I go through the motions, God forgive me, just so I can pass the collection plate anyway. She's a burden, Judith."

"Janie! Janie!" Mommy shouted.

Janie heard, but ignored them. Maybe she was stupid because she was an accident, a baby Mommy and Daddy didn't want.

"If she's in the cornfield she had to go through the bushes. We can see if she broke through someplace."

"Look! In the shadows! There she is!"

Mommy lifted some of the front branches and Daddy grabbed her arm just above her elbow in a rock-hard grip and dragged her out, still clutching Suzy to her chest.

"So there you are," Mommy said. "What's wrong with you, child? Didn't you hear us calling you?"

"She heard all right," Daddy said in the grim voice that Janie knew meant more punishment. "She was being bad again, weren't you, Janie?"

Janie stared at the grass. She watched a big black ant crawl along the brown dirt.

"You got the Devil inside you," Daddy said. "What makes you act like this?"

"We were going to give you a nice surprise," Mommy said. "Your father woke up early so he could take us all the way to the shopping mall to buy you new school clothes. I thought you'd want to look nice and pretty like the other girls do. Your father's very tired from working overtime last night and he has to clock in again at three. But he woke up early this morning just to be nice to you, and this is how you show your appreciation."

Janie hugged Suzy and looked down at the ants in the grass. She was so stupid. She didn't know what to say to show how sorry she was, to make Daddy stop being so angry, to prevent her punishment. She was just too stupid to know the proper words to say. Somehow, she was always wrong.

"Pretending you're still a baby and can't talk won't help you," Daddy said.

Janie paid no more attention to the tears streaming down her face than Daddy did. Crying just proved she was still a baby. She was so stupid she didn't even know how to act like right.

"You come inside with me right now."

Not letting go of her arm, Daddy dragged her inside and down the hallway to her bedroom. Janie knew what to expect when he slammed the door shut behind him and sat on the side of her bed. Her tears and screams never stopped him, but she couldn't stop the tears and screams.

Daddy pulled his belt from his pants, unsnapped her overalls, pulled them and her panties down to her ankles, laid her belly across his lap and strapped her as hard as he could.

"Why don't you ever learn, Janie?" he asked, panting, as he whaled away at her bare bottom. "How many times do I have to punish you before it sinks into your thick skull? You must learn to be good. You are the cross Jesus gave me to bear, the life in my Christian hands. I want you to go to Heaven, Janie. I want you to learn to be good so you'll be saved."

Blood trickled down Janie's bare legs, but Daddy didn't

stop spanking her.

Inside Janie's heart, a fire burned like a trick birthday cake candle, blowing out each time Daddy hit her, then re-lighting itself.

III

Corner of Delmar and Walton

Lorenzo and Turk took Marko's body away in Lorenzo's mother's car to throw it in a garbage dumpster in another neighborhood. Then they would cruise up and down the streets, going west from Dewie's crib, to look for the girls. Dewie told Andre he would ride with him in Andre's '96 Mercury Marquis.

"Errr, Boulder, you got any cash on you?" Andre asked.

"What you talking about?"

"I'm broke, and this car's almost out of gas. It's past Empty."

Dewie thought for a moment. He only had a little change at home on his dresser. His mother probably had some money, but he didn't want to ask her. For this important mission she would give it to him, but she would rag him about it, making him feel small, depending on his mama for gas money even if it maybe came from his own SSI check. The chief of the world couldn't live off his mama.

"Andre, my man," Dewie said, "Did I or did I not say there was a new order in this city?"

"You sure did, Boulder." Andre learned fast.

"But does anybody know about it yet?"

"I don't see how," Andre said. Slow. Cautious.

"That's right, they don't. Because I've been head of the Rocks only five minutes. That's long enough to be a secret chief. I think it's time everybody started learning who's in charge. You agree?"

"I sure do, Boulder. What're you going to do?"

"You got enough fumes in the tank to reach the Stroll?"

"What for you want to go over there?"

"I asked you a question, Andre. You need another lesson already?"

"I'll try, Boulder." He turned on the ignition.

The hoes might be gone, but maybe one or two were still out, looking to turn one last trick. It was worth a try. Maybe some were starting the new day.

Dewie spotted her sitting at the bus stop. She wore a black jump suit with net-mesh shoulders. "Turn left at the light and park," he said.

This fat bitch wouldn't board any bus until she was ready to return home. She was probably out this early because it would take her all day to find a man hard up enough to pay twenty-five dollars for a date with her. She looked about forty-five and must have weighed over two hundred pounds. Dewie liked women with big breasts and asses, but this one, filthy dirty with the touch of a hundred thousand men, made his flesh crawl. She probably had AIDS, the clap, syph, herpes, crabs, fungus and ten or twenty other sex diseases.

Andre pulled around the corner and over to the curb.

"Stay here ready to roll." Dewie said, then slammed the door behind him.

The whore looked him over. She apparently didn't like what she saw because she turned her face back toward the street. That suited Dewie just fine. He didn't want to be mistaken for a dude lame enough to actually want to fuck this bitch for free, let alone pay good money for her.

They were alone on this section of the street. Just behind them was an empty lot of broken bricks and glass. Next to that was the big empty building used to house The Metro Clinic. Dewie remembered his mother taking him to see shrink doctors in there.

He stood in front of her. "Ten percent."

"What the hell you talking about, boy?"

"I ain't no boy, and I ain't fucking around. I'll be reasonable though. Everybody's got to hustle for their money. All I want is my fair share—ten percent. You get to keep ninety." He held out his hand, palm up. "Now."

"I'll give you ten percent of your mama's pussy."

"You ain't heard yet, bitch, but there's a new day a dawning. Boulder's day. My day. I'm Boulder. I'm taking over everything. You, the other whores, the dope, the rackets—everything. Ten percent. Maybe your favorite peanut dick white tricks ain't been by here yet, but they will be. I want it in advance." He moved his palm up and down. "Now. I know you got some cash, because you ain't trash."

"I don't play these games, motherfucker. My old man's the only guy I give my money to, and you ain't him. I was working the Stroll before you was born, so you and your friend just go pick on some little girl your own age and leave real business to the grownups."

"I'll be fair about this," Dewie said. "What'll you make today, a hundred dollars?"

She snorted.

"Fifty, then. I'll still take ten. That'll pay your ten percent up through tomorrow."

The whore stood, looked up and down the street, and began to walk away. Dewie grabbed her shoulder.

"Don't ask for more trouble than you can handle," she said.

"I can handle you."

"You armed? What you got on you? I don't see no gun. You got a knife?"

"I'm Boulder. All I need is these." He held up his hands.

She showed him her switchblade, using her large black purse to shield it from the passing cars. "Touch me again and I'll slit you open."

Dewie hesitated. Could he take on a knife? That wasn't like hitting Marko. Knives were cold steel that could slice through his flesh. But he needed her money and she would be gone before he could take out his own knife.

"I want my ten percent now," Dewie said.

She jammed the point at his face. Dewie backed away then swung around and grabbed her shoulder again. She shoved the knife toward his gut but he blocked it with the palm of his hand. The blade twisted to the side.

Still holding her shoulder he seized the blade, gripped it tightly and bent his wrist up, snapping it off. The streetwalker stared at the broken knife in Dewie's uncut hand, then dropped the handle.

Dewie gripped her shoulder more tightly and, too late, she started to scream.

He squeezed her shoulder, snapping her collar bone, and

she stopped struggling. Dewie circled his arm around her as though she were his favorite girlfriend and put his fingers on the back of her neck. He crunched the vertebrae until sure she was dead.

As though they were lovers, he held her up as he walked back to the car.

Dewie slid her into the back seat and climbed in with her. "What're you waiting for?" he told Andre. "Move it."

After searching her purse and shoes, he found her cash inside the huge cup of her black lace bra. Thirty dollars. Enough to fill the tank.

"You stupid whore," he said to the corpse. "All I asked for was ten. You made me kill you over twenty fucking dollars."

IV

Dreamspace

"Now you realize how much your parents hate you," the dead Indian told Janie.

Once again she was back in the ruined temple in the city in Hell.

"Your father beat you senseless. You were only a burden to them. They didn't want you. You shouldn't have been born. You have no reason to live. Give up. Die."

"But I don't want to."

"You are a victim. Just like these long dead virgins of my people, you were born to suffer much and die early. You were created to take the blows of those older, bigger, stronger and smarter than you. You have been used and abused your entire life. Nobody loves you. Nobody cares about you. Nobody respects you. You will perish alone, unwanted and unmourned, and then you will serve me in Dirtworld."

Janie sobbed, face in her arms, wracked with coughs from deep in her chest. Then she looked up. "I'm going to get my money from Social Security. I'm going to buy a house for me and my babies. So there—I have lots to live for."

"Look, listen and learn."

The temple walls again dissolved into freezing, gray mist.

Janie was looking into a liquor store. The Arab man behind the counter led Odelia into the back room. Odelia handed the man a letter sized piece of paper and two small ones.

"You can see it with your own eyes," Odelia said. "The signatures are identical. Janie signed these checks yesterday afternoon, then didn't know where to cash them because she doesn't have a bank account. She left them with me for safekeeping and it's a good thing too, because she was hurt last night and now she's in the hospital. She won't come out for a long time so she really needs this money. The police took all her ID. I've got her two little girls with me, and one of them isn't right in the head herself. They need food and clothes."

The man cupped his chin with his hand. "I don't know. Fifteen thousand dollars is a lot of money. What if the Treasury Department won't let the checks go through?"

"How could they not pay you? The signatures are good. Look, you can see—she signed this form from Welfare. She signed the checks. They're the same."

"It's still a lot of money. What if you don't give any of it to her and she tells the government she didn't cash them? Maybe she signed them, but I won't know where the money goes after I give it to you."

"She's practically my daughter-in-law, Abdul. You know that. You've seen my son Michael and me in here with her before, when she cashed checks. You know she lives with me, her and her children. One of them's my little grandbaby. I wouldn't do anything to hurt family."

Abdul still shook his head.

Odelia leaned close to him. "She's hurt real bad, Abdul. Head injury. Real bad. I wouldn't be surprised if she's out cold for the rest of her life. Even if she gets over it, she's got brain damage, and you know Janie only had half a brain to start with. She won't even remember these checks, let alone know what happened to them. But she'll probably die, Abdul. I'm sorry to say that but it's true. She hasn't even told the police who did it to her, so she for sure isn't thinking about any checks."

Abdul continued to rub his cheek. "It would be hard. To raise that much cash I'll have to go see some people I know, and they won't help out for free. They'll be taking a risk too."

"Think of those two poor little girls," Odelia said. "They need shoes and jackets. Janie never did buy enough things for them. And if she does die, she's going to need burying. She never thought to buy life insurance or a burial contract. Where'll the money come from? I can't afford it."

"Twenty percent. That's my check cashing fee."

"Ten percent."

"Fifteen."

"That'll work."

"I'll start calling my friends now. You come back tomorrow afternoon this same time."

Odelia put the two small pieces of paper into a light brown envelope, stuffed it deep into her purse and left.

Janie suddenly realized they had been talking about her big SSI Zebley checks. But they was for her and Latasha and Shontell, so they wouldn't have to live with Odelia. So no man would ever kick Janie out again. She could let who she wanted stay with her, then boot his ass out if he didn't act right. That money was for her and her babies. She never signed those checks. Odelia told her they never came.

Odelia had no right!

"Lied to, stolen from, cheated on," the Indian said. "Everybody you've ever known has mistreated you. If you recover you'll just find someone else who will beat you up, torture and then kill you. Die now."

"No!" Janie screamed, her throat thickening. She tried to slap Odelia, to grab her purse and take the checks out, but Odelia didn't feel her presence.

Nobody heard her. Nobody saw her. Nobody felt her. She might as well be dead. She was already some weird kind of ghost. Frustration choked Janie's heart. She longed for the release of tears, but her spirit eyes remained dry.

V

Holy Virgin Mother of God Medical Center

While Jim was busy with Judith and Willie Lee Braxton in the Neuro ICU, Marilyn used his office phone. "Barb, hi, how's it going?" she said. "This is

Marilyn from the Women's Shelter."

"You must have another child for me to drag through the system." Barb was a social worker at the Child Welfare section of The Missouri Division of Family Services.

"I don't know yet." Marilyn briefly explained the situation. "So it looks like Odelia probably has the checks. She probably has the kids too, we just don't know for sure."

"Well if she does, what do you want me to do?"

"Get them out," Marilyn said.

"Why? I thought you said one of them is her grandchild."

"That's right. Her father is in jail, but Odelia is his mother."

"Then she's a close relative and the one with physical custody. Is she abusing them?"

"I don't know." That sounded lame. She had to make Barb understand how important this case was. "I haven't seen them, but I'm worried. Maybe they're lost somewhere."

"I need something specific, Marilyn. Have you ever seen Odelia hit them? Do they have bruises? Are they dirty or starving?"

"This all just happened last night. I went over there early this morning and she refused to talk. She just said she didn't have the kids or the checks. I bet she's lying."

"What if she is? She has no legal obligation to tell you anything. You're just an outsider trying to butt in on her family's business, and I can't take the children away from her without evidence they're in danger. What about this Janie's parents?"

Marilyn shuddered. She'd overheard Willie Lee even in the waiting area.

"They were relatively old when they had Janie, and they're still very bitter about her. I don't think they want the responsibility of raising two more little girls, one of them slow like Janie and black to boot."

"Jesus, the things you see on this job. Makes you want to renounce the human race, doesn't it? All these people having babies they won't take care of."

Marilyn's womb clenched. "What can you do?"

"I'll check this morning's intake to see if there's a report already. If not, I'll send out an investigator. It's not supposed to take more than twenty-four hours, but we're backed up on non-emergency leads."

"Thanks, Barb, I really appreciate it. I'll check in with you later, see what you've found out."

"Wait until after lunch, when we slow down a little."

Marilyn then called the homeless women and children's shelters. Children's and Cardinal Glennon hospitals. No luck. Nobody had heard of or seen Latasha and Shontell.

Marilyn phoned Latasha's school. Neither Janie nor Odelia were very responsible about making sure Latasha attended, but the child knew which bus to take and where to catch it from the house on Ashland, and she fed and dressed herself and caught it on time.

Today, however, she was marked down as absent with no phone call to excuse her. Marilyn explained what happened to Latasha's mother to the attendance secretary and the woman asked no more questions.

Of course it could be Latasha was at Odelia's house but, knowing how badly injured her mother was, didn't feel up to sitting in a classroom.

Maybe both girls were hiding in a ditch. Or dead.

SUN OF SUNS TWO

Temple of the Sun

"You will never buy your house," the dead Indian said. "Odelia will steal the money from your children."

They were back in the broken-down temple.

"I always knew she was a crook," Janie said. "That's why I wouldn't let her get my check for me like she wanted."

"You will never spend that money because you are worthless," he said. "I will continue my history. You will know how old and powerful I am. I want you to understand I am invincible."

Cold and gray mist again swept Janie into a movie of the past.

Sun of Suns determined to enter Dirtworld and rescue Elder Brother would require the sacrifice of fifty-two fifty-two virgins—the sacred number times itself. He instructed the chiefs of his Eagle Warriors to demand a tribute of virgins from the

villages under the City of the Sun's protection, as they collect-
ed the yearly corn and beans. Those village heads who resisted
were killed, and twice as many unopened girls were taken from
their villages.

Builders erected large thatched roof huts with no walls at
the Great Mound's palisades for the captives. The girls were giv-
en handfuls of firewood and meager rations of corn and squash.

The Great People living in the City of the Sun speculated
about the large number of new prisoners, especially because all
of them were young females. Most people wanted strong adult
male stinker slaves to clear fields, plant corn and haul dirt to
raise more burial mounds. But the city's unmarried young men
eyed the latest captives avidly. Many of them were desirable, so
the men could understand Sun of Suns collecting some to warm
his bed although he already had numerous wives. But why so
many? Surely one man, even the Sun's younger brother, could
not plow them all. Perhaps he would distribute the extras to the
warriors, craftsmen and traders who had earned merit in Sun
of Sun's service. Yet some of the girls were barely old enough to
walk. What use could Sun of Suns have for them?

It was soon obvious Sun of Suns was collecting virgins. Before the girls were allowed into the shelter inside the palisades
a female sun and a priest closely examined the clefts between
their legs. Those with open holes were not allowed inside. That
explained why so many were so young.

The Eagle Warriors guarded the compound diligently, never allowing any young man inside to try his skill with the maidens. Nor were any of the Eagle Warriors themselves allowed
that privilege. All had been warned if any of them were caught
copulating with a captive, his head and penis would be chopped

off. The threat of having no head or penis in Deathrealm so horrified them that so far only one warrior had disobeyed. His head was now set on top of a wooden stake of the palisades wall with his staff jammed into his mouth.

The rumor Sun of Suns planned a great sacrifice spread quickly through the Great People, but many scoffed. Human sacrifices were sometimes necessary, but rarely and only for good reason. When an important chieftain died it was an honor for his wives and servants to eat enough tobacco to pass out, then be strangled by relatives so they could continue to serve their leader in Deathrealm. When the gods showed their displeasure with the Great People by striking the Temple of the Sun with lightning, babies had to be thrown into a bonfire. Lesser misfortunes called for voluntary sacrifices, sometimes of young women. Priests determined the specifics from dreams and signs.

The Mexica Tenochca Aztecs in their city on a lake to the far south continuously cut out the hearts of captives. They believed the sun needed such sacrifices every day to shine and give life to the land, but the Great People knew the sun needed only their daily songs and dances.

Besides, nobody had ever heard of anyone sacrificing so many virgins at one time. True, many in the city and outlying villages were hungry. The corn crop was smaller every year. The rabbits, squirrels, raccoons and deer had moved far away from the arrows of the hunters. The fish in the Father of Waters grew smaller and fewer. But how would killing so many young girls from the other villages help?

If Sun of Suns wanted to weaken the other villages he should execute boys, the future warriors. When the few remaining males reached manhood they would each have two or three wives. That would keep them busy hunting by day and plowing at night. They would be too tired and content to make war on the City of the Sun.

Still, for whatever reason, Sun of Suns was gathering virgins. The far sighted and quick witted with virgin daughters sent those girls away from the city to visit members of their clans in distant villages. Soon, the only naked children running through the dusty streets and splashing in the creeks were male.

As the Great People speculated, argued and repeated rumors, the bands of warriors continued to bring many head of young girls to the City of the Sun. The shelter was a muddy, crowded mess. The girls had few clothes and not enough pots or wood to cook the little food given them. They were dirty, sick and lice-infested. The stench of their sweat and excrement was uncivilized. The little ones cried without ceasing.

The ceremony to rescue Elder Brother from the nightly embrace of Grandmother Earth began immediately after sunset. Sun of Suns sat again in the middle of the Sacred Circle, before the altar, surrounded by the everlasting flames burning in the twelve fire pots. Deer and buffalo hides covered the wooden walls of the temple. Their red and black painted designs danced in the flickering light.

Sun of Suns wore his largest white swan feather headdress and held the green stone ax. He would not eat, sleep or touch a woman until the sacrifice was complete, for to accomplish his mission in Dirtworld he had to be pure.

Three priests worked at the same time. Because the Temple contained only one stone altar designed for human sacrifice, with holes and sloping gutters to drain off the blood and other fluids, Sun of Suns had ordered two others erected. They were wooden but they served.

Eagle Warriors carried each girl to an altar. Many of the girls cried, some screamed. Some accepted their fate with the heart of warriors, not allowing themselves to show fear.

With black obsidian knives priests quickly sliced through the small breastbones then cut out the hearts underneath. They raised each tiny heart in their cupped hands and sang a short song to the spirits. Warriors carried the bodies to a special mound.

Beside the altars, the hearts piled up.

"Stop that!"

Sun of Suns looked up to see High Priest holding the arm of a young priest about to cut the heart out of a girl of no more than three winters. Sun of Suns knew High Priest would come after hearing of the sacrifices and was only surprised it had taken so long.

The younger priest looked at Sun of Suns, who motioned for him to continue.

"No!" High Priest turned to Sun of Suns. "What is the meaning of this outrage? This is murder. Sacrilege."

Only High Priest could dare to address Sun of Suns in such a manner. As High Priest it was his duty to speak directly with the gods. Still, High Priest was a wrinkled fool. Sun of Suns did not expect him to understand the sacred quest into Dirtworld to rescue Elder Brother.

"Why!" High Priest asked.

"Our people are suffering because Elder Brother must sink into the embrace of Grandmother Earth every evening."

"Our ceremony calls him back every morning. Elder Brother is always reborn."

"As his younger brother it is my duty to aid him."

"He needs only the prayers and dances you lead at the birth and death of every day. What are you planning?"

"I will go in spirit to Dirtworld while Elder Brother is lying in Grandmother's embrace. I must set him on a new path through Skyworld." Sun of Suns pointed toward the sky and circled his arm around to indicate the entire horizon. "Elder Brother wants to live forever in Skyworld. As long as he follows such a trail he will not fall off the cliff."

"Madness," High Priest said. "An evil star spirit planted this idea into your heart. You would destroy the harmony of the worlds. It is our duty to maintain the balance, not destroy it. And why the sacrifice of so many young girls? You are stealing the wives of the future. Who will cook? Weave the cloth? Warm the beds of the Eagle Warriors? Who will bear the next crop of children? What do you gain from killing them?"

"I dare not enter Dirtworld unaided. The spirit energy of their souls will go with me to protect me. It will take great strength to carry Elder Brother to a new path in Skyworld."

"This scheme was sent to you by an enemy demon and it will be your death. These girls are not volunteers gladly giving their lives for the welfare of all. This terrible slaughter will be the destruction of the Great People."

"What do you care about females?" Sun of Suns pointed to High Priest's dangling penis, its head cut in two since he was a little boy. "Your staff is split to give you the power to speak with the gods. You know the spirit strength of those who have never felt the touch of another's sex. When Elder Brother lives in Skyworld forever all people will have more corn than they can eat.

They will be happy."

"I cannot allow you to upset the harmony of the three worlds. The gods will destroy us if we permit this."

Sun of Suns motioned one of the Eagle Warriors escorting the girls to approach. "Kill High Priest."

After the warrior carried off the body of High Priest and his blood was washed away with water, sand and leaves, Sun of Suns took large gulps of the white drink and vomited into the clay bowl he kept at his side. The death of High Priest was no small matter. He wished it could have been avoided, but it could not, so he had to purify himself.

The ritual continued the next day, then for three more nights and days. The last girl died just after the sunset ceremony of the fourth evening. The sacrifices had taken exactly four days, the holy number. An auspicious omen.

The shelter behind the palisades was converted into a large pyre. As all the Great People of the City of the Sun watched, warriors stacked the wooden poles which had held the roof then shoved in the dry grass and reeds that had thatched it. They threw on the girls' meager belongings, their cloaks, skirts, tools and pots. At the same time, warriors at a distant burial mound commanded stinker slaves to cover the naked, heartless bodies with baskets of dirt.

The bonfire was lit with a torch in each of the four sacred directions. When the fire was burning throughout the pyre the warriors threw on the hearts of the virgin girls. Some were beginning to rot, already smelling of death; others were still wet and dripping red.

Seeing this, the Great People quickly returned to their huts and blocked their doors with hides to keep out the roiling smoke.

Their bellies heaved at the stench of burning human flesh. Their spirits quaked as they wondered what disaster would befall the city for this great slaughter. They feared the wrath of the spirits of the dead girls—the vengeance of the virgins.

In the temple, Sun of Suns drank more of the white drink. When he finished vomiting, he ate many jimson weed seeds. He swallowed enough tobacco to put him into the Sleep of Feeling No Pain and lay down in the center of the sacred circle, before the altar, on prepared deerskins. Around him priests chanted as they would continuously while he journeyed, to guard him from evil spirits.

He was greatly tired from his four nights and days with no food and no sleep. His flesh and bones felt light, as though he could stretch out wings and fly into Skyworld like his cousins Eagle and Hawk. But his blood flowed heavy, slow and sluggish, like a stream clogged with clay mud. Shapes and colors wiggled and thrust through the air. He saw them even when he closed his eyes. Inside his head huge spaces opened like the vastness of the prairie on the opposite side of the Father of Waters that stretched for many days of travel. His heart pounded with the fast rhythm of Maize Dance drummers.

Many animals ran and danced and swayed and flickered by him so fast he could hardly follow what he saw. The chanting of the priests sounded far away.

Spirits visited Sun of Suns. Some bowed with respect but others laughed at him and still others attacked him with flaming arrows. Walking skeletons stared at him with empty eye sockets glowing of star-fire. Huge beasts, monsters and serpents crouched outside the circle, but none could harm him while he stayed within.

Virgin Blood

The angry dead returned from Deathrealm. His slain ene-mies visited him as silent specters. Men with their heads cut off, their arms and legs broken, their chests punctured with arrows and ripped with spears and axes. Women defiled, their throats and breasts slashed. Children with battered skulls.

A hole opened in the forest floor. Sun of Suns looked down, but it was so deep he could see no bottom. This was his path to Dirtworld, where he must go to rescue Elder Brother from the embrace of Grandmother Earth. If he had the courage.

He tried to climb down the sides, but they were damp and slippery. He fell.

Into the dark.

CHAPTER SEVEN

I

The Schnucks Supermarket on Kingshighway

Dewie kept losing the cell phones his mama gave him, so he had to call her from a supermarket pay phone

"Lorenzo's on the other line," she said. "I'll transfer him to you."

"We've been up and down every street from Goodfellow to Skinker two or three times," Lorenzo said. "We haven't seen them."

"Head over to Grand and Chouteau, work your way south and keep your eyes open wide as Clyde. I think that damned shelter is around there someplace."

"I'll watch out for where beat-up broads are going."

"If you think you found it, check it out, but don't let them see you. Then call in. Got that?"

"We're on our way, Boulder."

"That's what I want to be hearing."

II

Many streets of St. Louis

As they drove up and down North St. Louis in her Civic Marilyn said, "I swear I don't know what else to do."

"You're sure you called everybody?" Jim asked.

"They ran away and they're lost. I just know it."

"You worry a lot, don't you?"

"So everybody tells me."

Jim shrugged. "Since they're not anywhere else they should or could be, they're most likely with Odelia. You're probably wasting your gas for nothing. They'll turn up."

"If they're with Odelia that still makes me worry."

"I heard that."

She smiled. He was picking up speech patterns from his clients. "But I don't believe it. If Dewie did that to Janie, the kids wouldn't stay around. It'd be too dangerous for them."

"First of all, you don't know Dewie did it. There's no shortage of guys low enough, especially if she was carrying that wad of Zebley money. Besides, even if you're right, that doesn't mean they're in danger too. Most hardened criminals think they're too tough to beat up on little kids. Except for some psychos, it's mostly their own parents who hurt them. Whoever did that to Janie probably doesn't pay the slightest attention to children."

"I know, I know. You make sense, Jim, but I've been working with Janie so long—"

"You've lost your objectivity."

She grinned. "I'm not being professional, you mean?"

"Is this what they taught you in all those social work class-es?"

"Of course not. I know, everybody says the only way to survive is to harden yourself. But if we don't care, then what're we doing this for? It's sure not the money."

"Beats the hell out of me," Jim said. "My father's a real estate broker in Rockhill, near Chicago. Really brings in the bucks. He thinks I'm crazy to be a social worker, wanted to send me to law school. Sometimes I still think I should try for that."

Marilyn drove slowly, continuously glancing up and down the sidewalks, searching for two little girls together. One tall white girl with a short black one would stand out. "You're not happy at the hospital?"

"I'm not satisfied. I'm twenty-five. This is fine now, but I'll need more money later, for a wife, some kids, a house in the suburbs, all that good stuff. Can't be done on my salary."

"Lots of men make less than you."

"Also, I want more satisfaction from my job. I don't have the clients long enough to make any real difference in their lives. All I really do is facilitate paperwork and hold the hands of upset relatives. What about you? Does the shelter pay you enough?"

Marilyn laughed. "Let's just say it's a good thing I don't want to support a wife and kids in the suburbs. I scuffle for freelance counseling work to cover my rent and buy groceries, but it's not easy. Not many whites want to take their problems to a black woman who doesn't even have her own office, and middle class African-Americans might talk about how proud of their racial heritage they are, but when they need a counselor they usually hire a white one. Poor African-Americans are the clients I like best, but they're the least likely to continue past two sessions or even to pay for those. I'm looking for a full-time job but finding social service positions is tough."

"Working at the shelter must at least give you a lot of satis-faction."

"Yes, but it's still frustrating," Marilyn said. "We try to teach the women new skills, to screen the men they date, to turn down the assholes and to assert themselves. I'm sure it helps a lot of them. I'm sure we've saved lives. But it's so hard to really know. I often wonder how many of our past residents are back with their old abusing partners or new ones, or dead. We don't have the resources to keep track."

Jim shook his head. "I've never understood. Why do so many women go for the mean ones? Even if the guy is nice at first, why do they stick with him after he's beaten them up? I look around, I see lots of nice guys who can't find girlfriends. They don't have tons of money or sports cars, but they're decent and concerned. Yet as soon as they start to fall in love with a woman, she senses it and drops them."

"You sound frustrated yourself."

Jim laughed. "Okay, I admit it, I can't hang on to women. I'm too nice, as I've been told at least ten or twenty times. I'm so nice I'm boring. They don't deserve a decent guy like me. They want me as a friend. When they're drunk late at night they'll call me up to bitch and moan about Harry the Jerk they left me for. How he just stood them up for the third time or he's making it with his sales manager or he just moved back in with his wife or he just gave her a black eye. But when Harry the Jerk calls, they jump. They want my shoulder to cry on but in bed they want Harry the Jerk's bod."

Blood flushed Marilyn's face. "I—I don't usually hear that

side." She gave an embarrassed laugh. "Working at the shelter, I've gotten too used to thinking of men as gorillas who ought to be locked up in cages."

"Some men are. But some women encourage their behavior. I always tell myself, the next one I start getting serious with, I'll try acting kind of tough. I don't mean violent, but I'll pretend I don't care about her, like I'm doing her a favor by taking her to baseball games, letting her cook me quiche and allowing her to enjoy my body."

"Oh, wow—so what happens?"

He forced a smile. "I never do it. At first, I feel I ought to be polite. Then, as soon as I do start to care about her, she becomes too important to me to take a chance on losing her. I don't want to risk her anger so I never argue. How could I disagree with the woman I'm madly in love with, who I want to spend my whole life with, the future mother of my children, the woman of my dreams? When I'm in that state I want to win her love with my own. I want to convince her by showing her how much I care."

"And that's when you lose her."

"To Harry the Jerk."

Marilyn shook her head. Jim's confession depressed her, she didn't know why. She also didn't know what to say, so she returned to what preoccupied her mind. "I think I've crossed the line of professionalism in Janie's case because she doesn't just leave and never come back, not even sending us a postcard. She comes back. And back. Even when she stays away from Michael for six months or so she finds another lousy boyfriend, or else she'll be hurt on the street." Marilyn sighed. "African-American women in the city aren't safe, but a white gal stands out as a target automatically. If she's not with a man some black dude will hit on her. Some guys will attack her just because of what she is. It's not right, but some African-American folks react that way."

Jim sighed. "Hate breeds hate, doesn't it? It's amazing any of us can stand each other."

Startled, Marilyn turned around to stare at him. "You are nice."

Jim fell back against the seat, clutching his chest. "Oh no, my heart's breaking. She thinks I'm a nice guy. Next she'll tell me she wants to be just friends. I'll never have a chance with her."

Surprising herself, she slapped him on the knee.

"Okay, okay," Jim said. "I'll stop. I knew I already lost my chance with you when I told you about myself."

"Why do you think that?" Marilyn asked.

"You know my weakness. You were falling madly in love with me but now you've stopped because you think I'm just another nice guy."

"While what I really want is to throw myself at the feet of a real man who'll rearrange my face. Puh-leeze."

"Are you married?" Jim said. "I should have asked that before I said anything."

"Divorced."

"I'm sorry."

"Not your fault," Marilyn said.

"Any kids?"

Marilyn tried to shake her head but her neck felt like rock. The womb between her legs opened to a vast, empty pit.

"Goddammit! Where are they?" Marilyn jammed the accelerator down. "I'm going back to Ashland. Let's ask Odelia's mail carrier if they remember delivering Janie's Zebley checks."

CHAPTER EIGHT

I

The Schnucks Supermarket on Natural Bridge

"You haven't found them little girls yet?"

"No, Mama."

"Damn it, Dewie, what's taking you so long?"

Dewie was Boulder to his gang. Soon he would be Boulder to the world. But to Mama, he was still the same old Dewie. She loved Michael. She treated Dewie like week-old garbage.

"I think they're at the shelter," Dewie said.

"With that stuck-up bitch come by here this morning?"

"I'll teach her a lesson, Mama. She'll be sorry. Soon's I find those girls everything's going to change. You'll see. It already has."

"What're you talking about now, Dewie?"

Just like he was still a little kid. He slammed the phone down.

149

"Get moving," he told Andre as he jumped into the car.

"Where to?"

"Just drive, motherfucker."

As they approached the corner of Enright and North Sarah, Dewie said, "Park the car."

"What you fitting to do?"

"I need to talk to those dudes."

"Them three waiting for their supplier? Boulder, man, don't you see them purple scarves and headbands? They Marauders. They don't want us walking on their turf."

"Time they learned it ain't their turf no more. Besides, how far you think we're going on the thirty bucks from that whore? We already used up half a tank and we still ain't found no trace of them little girls."

"They ain't going to tell you nothing."

"I ain't going to ask them to."

The three Marauders looked him over carefully as he approached. "Something I can do for you, brother?" one asked.

"Tell Rashaun I want my ten percent."

"You better move along, little dude. We don't know no Rashaun."

"Everybody knows Rashaun heads up the Marauders. You all wearing Marauders headbands, Marauder colors. Tell Rashaun I need the money now."

"You better move your ass down the street before it gets kicked in."

"You bloods look like you ready to take a delivery. You must have some cash on you. I'll take five hundred for now. I'll pick up the rest later from Rashaun."

Tense and alert, the three young men slowly spread out and

moved closer to Dewie, the talker directly in front, the other two edging toward him from each side.

"Who the fuck are you?" the talker asked.

"Yeah, we ain't been introduced yet. I'm Boulder. Tell everyone else. I'm taking over."

"Taking over what?"

Dewie acted surprised. "Everything, of course. I get ten percent off the top of all action."

"You one crazy motherfucker, that's what you are."

Dewie held out his hand. "Give me five hundred dollars or whatever you boys got on you. That's a fair deal."

"Get the fuck out of my face."

The talker turned and began to walk away. The other two followed, but more slowly, covering their partner's back, waiting to see how Dewie would react.

Dewie began to wonder himself. These gangbangers had to be packing. Could he knock them all out before they shot him?

He grabbed the one on the right by the collar of his athletic jacket. He was going for the revolver at his waist when Dewie punched his stomach in, fist slamming through to smash the man's backbone. Dewie let go, and the body dropped to the sidewalk. Both of the others drew their pistols and fired. Dewie grabbed the talker's arm and snapped it in two with one jerk of his wrist, then cut off the man's scream with a blow to his throat.

The third one stared at Dewie, then down at his two dead friends. He dropped his gun and ran away.

"Tell Rashaun I want my ten percent," Dewie shouted to his back. "Tell him I'm coming after it soon as I take care of some personal business."

Dewie took the cash he found on both bodies and returned to Andre's car.

"Jesus Christ, I don't believe it," Andre said. "I don't fucking believe it."

Dewie threw the money on the seat beside him. "We'll leave the trash on the sidewalk. Come on, let's get out of here."

Andre peeled rubber, turned left onto the next street and sped away.

"Look at what they did to my Bulls jacket, Andre." Dewie stuck a finger in a black edged hole with plastic filler leaking out of it. "Look what those motherfuckers did."

"Boulder," Andre said. "I see five bullet holes in your clothes, but none in you. Why aren't you dead? You ain't even bleeding."

"They must've just missed me, dude." Dewie threw a short jab. "I was lucky."

II

Dreamtime

Janie stared at the two piles of long broken boards in the Indian temple and the collapsed heap of stone carved in similar shapes. She now realized they had been the altars where the priests murdered those girls. Sparks of anger flickered inside her bones.

"So you killed a lot of girls," Janie said. "You don't scare me. You're just another big bully."

"You have been the target of bullies all your life," the ghost said. "Everyone abused you. Even when you were a child, the

152

other children hated you."

"Did not."

"Watch."

The cold gray mist crept up Janie's backbone. The tumbled down walls dissolved into the painted cinder blocks of a grade school cafeteria.

Janie sat down beside her friend Sally. "You didn't wait for me in line," she said.

"You never wait for me."

"I do too."

Another girl, Ruth, who had long, beautiful blond hair, sat on Sally's other side. "No you don't, Janie. You forget about her."

Sally was the tallest and fattest girl in their class. She also had breasts already, which Janie thought was funny. She didn't understand why so many boys teased Sally about them and why so many girls talked as though that meant Sally was a bad girl who did nasty things with boys. Janie and Sally didn't have many other friends so they often sat together. But sometimes Sally tried to talk to somebody else, such as Ruth.

Janie decided to ignore both of them. She hummed as she opened her brown lunch sack and pulled out the peanut butter and jelly sandwich Mommy made for her.

"What'd you get on the arithmetic test, Sally?" Ruth asked.

"B minus." Sally was tall and fat but she was normal in the head, not stupid like Janie.

Ruth leaned across Sally's tray. "What'd you get, Janie? Another F, I bet."

"I did not."

"Did too," Ruth said.

"Did not."

That wasn't a lie. Janie got a D minus and was proud of herself for not failing. It was hard, but she was starting to memorize her numbers and how to add some of them up. Two plus two equaled four. She remembered that.

"I got an A minus," Ruth said.

Janie hated Ruth. She was a genius, but even the other geniuses didn't like her because she was so stuck up. She liked to show off and brag. When the other geniuses wouldn't let Ruth stay with them she would sit next to anybody just so she wouldn't have to eat lunch by herself. That's the only reason she would go near Sally or Janie.

"So who cares?" Janie tore open her bag of potato chips.

As usual, she couldn't eat them all and gave the rest to Sally so she would have room for the Oreo cookies Mommy always packed. She separated the two halves of the first Oreo carefully, leaving the white icing on one half, then scraped it off with her front bottom teeth and licked the remainder from the hard chocolate.

"Eeeeeewwww, gross," Ruth said. "Janie, you're such a pig."

"I am not."

"We're in the sixth grade now. You shouldn't eat cookies that way. It's disgusting."

"I don't care." Janie said. "I'll do what I want."

"God, Janie, you're so immature," Sally said. "We all know you're a retard, but you don't have to act like a baby too."

"I am not either."

"I bet you wet your bed and have to wear diapers at night," Ruth said. "I bet you still sleep in a crib."

154

"I do not! I sleep in a bed with Suzy."

"Who's Suzy?" Sally asked.

"My dolly."

"You still play with dolls?" Sally laughed, blowing air out her lips. "You are a baby."

"I am not!"

"She only said she sleeps with the doll," Ruth said. "Maybe they get it on."

The two girls giggled uncontrollably at this but Janie didn't understand the joke.

"You have a Barbie doll in your room," she said to Sally.

"At least Barbie is grown up. Besides, I just keep her on a shelf along with the other toys I've outgrown. I don't play with her."

"Or sleep with her," Ruth said.

Before Janie could say anything else a boy made a farting noise next to her ear. He and his friends laughed as they carried their trays away.

Janie pretended she didn't hear. They were bad boys.

Another boy flicked her earlobe.

Janie stood right up, turned and swung a punch at him. It missed his face and barely grazed his arm.

He staggered back in mock alarm, holding the spot Janie hit. "She touched me, guys. Janie Braxton touched me. She gave me cooties. I'm going to die."

"Eeeeeewwwwww," another boy said. "Janie has cooties."

The boys took up the chant. "Janie has cooties, Janie has cooties." Even Sally and Ruth sang along, completing Janie's shame.

Inside Janie's chest something flared, as when Daddy tossed

kerosene on a campfire. She dumped her potato chips into Sally's hair and threw a crust of peanut butter and jelly sandwich at one of the boys. She pointed at them the way she had often seen Daddy and other preachers in church jab their fingers at people.

"You're bad sinners!" she shouted as hard as she could. "You're mean and wicked and evil. I hope you die and go to Hell and suffer and burn forever and ever and ever."

The cafeteria vanished and once again Janie sat beside the Indian ghost in the ruins of his old temple. She jumped up and poked her finger in his face.

"You're mean and wicked and evil!" she shouted. "I hope you burn forever and ever and ever!"

III

Pete's Shur-Save Market, corner of Page and Union

"I just talked to the mailman," Mama told Dewie on the phone. "That Ms. Patterson bitch asked him if he delivered Janie's Zebley checks already."

"I'll make her sorry she done that, Mama. Real sorry."

"That hincty hole probably fixing to steal Janie's money for her own self. You better stop her, Dewie."

"I will, Mama. She ain't going to bother neither you nor me again."

"She went heading down Page just a few minutes ago. You hurry, you can see her coming."

"I'll watch out for her, Mama. She going to find out who's boss in this here city. In this here universe."

IV

Corner of Grand and Grandel Square

Latasha leaned against a big brick building. Where was the shelter? They were closer to it but how could they find it? They couldn't walk over the entire city.

"Now that we're on Grand, what're we going to do, Shontell?"

If only they could call the shelter. But Latasha had forgotten the special, private direct line number. As soon as she thought about it again, now relaxed, it popped into her mind. She repeated it several times out loud so it wouldn't squirm out again.

"It's no use," she said, shoulders slumping. "We can't call from here. Mama had the cell phone, if she even remembered to pay the last bill." She took Shontell's hand and they trudged down the street. Then to her amazement, she spotted a pay phone set just inside the mouth of a small alleyway by the empty Woolworth's store. She ran to it, picked up the receiver and—set it back down. "We still need a quarter," she told her little sister. "You ever beg for money?"

Most of the people Latasha asked ignored her. Others criticized her and her parents. A few made rude remarks.

She stepped in front of a well-dressed white lady strolling along the sidewalk in high heels. She obviously had lots of money.

"Can you spare a quarter?" Latasha held out her hand.

"Little tramp. Go panhandle someplace else."

The tone of the woman's voice spit on Latasha. She sagged

against the building.

"Pretty lady," Shontell said.

"She just insulted me," Latasha said. Her leg muscles felt dead. Cramps pinched her sides and gravel coated her throat. "How come you call her pretty?"

She pushed her sister on the shoulder. Lightly once, then harder, then with all her might, knocking the smaller girl against the brick wall.

"What's wrong with you, Shontell? How come you don't have any sense? Even Mama understands when people hate her. You act like everybody loves you."

Shontell didn't say a word. Latasha felt guilty, but that made her angrier. She slammed her fist into Shontell's stomach.

"We're hungry, little girl. I'm tired, and mad, and you want to talk about that stingy bitch like she's a pretty lady. She's ugly as sin. She wouldn't even give us a quarter so I could call the shelter. How far do you want to walk before you die?"

"Oh," Shontell said, on the brink of tears.

"What do you think about Dewie, huh? He Forced and beat up Mama and wanted to hurt us, but I bet you still love him, don't you?"

"I love Uncle Dewie," Shontell said.

"You're a damn fool. What about Odelia? You love her too, even though she hates you and me? We go hungry even when Boo and everybody else gets lots of food. And Grandmama and Grandpapa Braxton? You love them? Grandpapa Braxton calls you a halfbreed, you know that? He's ashamed his granddaughter's a little pickaninny. Grandmama's scared of you and me both. Neither one of them likes us."

"We go to Grandpapa and Grandmama's house?"

Latasha pinched her sister on the arm until she started wailing.

"Hell no. I don't want to stay in that white trash trailer court. And they don't want us neither. Shontell, don't nobody love you and me except Mama and Marilyn. But you love everybody. You make me sick."

A man passing by slowed and looked at them. Latasha immediately asked, "Hey, mister, can you give me a quarter?"

The man paused, so Latasha felt certain he was going to refuse. Or ask them what they wanted it for. Or give them a lecture about how children shouldn't panhandle, how bad things could happen to little girls who talked to strangers. But none of those people had handed her and Latasha any change.

"I'll be glad to help you two lovely young ladies," he finally said, a smile in his voice. "As long as you're not going to spend it foolishly."

"No, sir, I just want to make a call." Latasha pointed to the pay phone.

"You'll need two quarters." He was a young white dude, dressed in a blue dress shirt, nicely pressed slacks and highly polished shoes. He reached into his pocket and handed Latasha the coins. She ran to the phone, picked up the receiver, pushed the coin into the slot, waited for the dial tone, pressed the correct buttons and listened eagerly as the phone rang.

And rang.

By the fourth ring she almost hung up, but then she heard Sara's voice. "Hello—"

"Sara, it's Latasha! Me and Shontell are in big trouble. We saw Mama murdered last night. Come pick us up quick! Dewie's still after us. We saw him. I—"

"I'm sorry nobody is available to take your call right now," Sara's voice continued. But if you'll please leave your name and number, someone will get back to you shortly."

Latasha slammed the receiver down. "Son of a bitch!"

"Trouble?" the man asked in a gentle voice.

"The goddamn answering machine is on. They're probably eating their fucking lunch." She stuck her fingers into the coin box. "It didn't even give me back your quarters."

Latasha suddenly realized she had thought the man had left, and felt ashamed for using such language in front of a stranger. Mama sometimes talked like that, and everybody at Odelia's house talked like that, but Latasha knew most white adults didn't want children to say those words. She didn't want to sound like the people at Odelia's house and didn't want this man to think she was a bad girl. But she felt so hot, so tired, so hungry, so thirsty and so afraid—if she were alone she would cry.

"Where do you want to go so desperately?" he asked.

"Cardinal Glennon Hospital." The words came out of Latasha's mouth before she thought about them. As she spoke, she remembered the shelter was near Cardinal Glennon. That's where Mama got off the bus when she went to the shelter. But where would they catch it?

The nice guy pointed to the street. "Just take the Grand bus. It runs straight down to Cardinal Glennon. Do you need more money? I can give you enough. You don't need a transfer."

"We have passes. I'm just not sure how to get on the right bus."

"There're no wrong ones here, only the Grand. Come on, I'll show you where to wait."

V

Intersection of Union and Page

Marilyn barely noticed the other cars in the traffic streaming through the clogged streets. She drove on automatic pilot, searching the sidewalks. She talked out loud to organize her thoughts. "I bet Odelia's already cashed the checks, or plans to."

"You don't know that," Jim said. "Maybe she gave Janie the checks, Janie cashed them, then got rolled by some guy after she left the check cashing joint."

"No, she was too close to Odelia's house. If some man had followed her from a business district he wouldn't have waited that long to take her money. Dewie must be involved."

"What can we do?" Jim asked.

"My top priority is to find Latasha and Shontell. Their lives come first. The money's not important except for them, although I'd hate to see Odelia get away with stealing it."

"She won't."

Marilyn gave him a brief smile. "That's right, keep up my spirits. I need encouragement."

Jim raised his hand like a minister. "Be of good cheer, my child. All is well."

Marilyn stopped for a red light at the intersection of Page and Union. She didn't see Dewie until he jumped in front of her car.

"Bitch!" he shouted. "I told you to mind your own damn

business. My mama told you to mind your own damn business. You got no right to be talking to our mailman."

"Run the light," Jim said in a breathless voice. "Hurry."

"I can't hit him."

"Just floor it. He'll get out of the way. Come on, he probably has a gun."

"I don't need no goddamn piece, motherfucker," Dewie shouted.

"My God, we're going to die." Jim pushed back in his seat, crouching down.

"Where're Latasha and Shontell, Dewie?" Marilyn asked.

Palm on the left front fender, Dewie approached Marilyn's window.

"Now!" Jim shouted. "Marilyn, floor it now!"

Jim's panic spread to her. This might be a busy street corner in the middle of the day but people had been killed in more unlikely places and times. In the heat of the moment many men had killed in front of crowds of people. Prosecuting Attorneys easily convicted them, but their victims were still dead.

She floored it.

The front wheels spun.

Marilyn pressed the accelerator all the way down. The high pitched squeal drilled her ears. She smelled the corrosive odor of burnt rubber. The engine roared and shuddered, shaking the car's frame. Smoke escaped from the edge of the hood. She pounded the steering wheel.

Dewie still stood just to the left side of the Civic, his hand over the rim of the headlight base.

"You ain't going nowhere, bitch."

He banged the left side of the Civic with the flat of his right hand. The metallic plastic crumpled and the headlight cover burst out in a spray of plastic shards. The left front tire exploded, the sudden tilt forcing Marilyn's face down. Her forehead banged the horn, blurting out a sharp honk.

"My God, what's happening?" Jim said.

"You're hiding those girls," Dewie said. "You're messing in our business. You got no right,"

"I don't have Latasha and Shontell," Marilyn shouted through the window. "I think your mother does."

Dewie hit the front of the car. The frame crumpled. The struts screamed. Antifreeze spurted from the crushed radiator grill. He struck it again. There was a loud metallic popping sound and the screaming engine fell silent.

The light turned green. The drivers in the cars behind them honked.

Dewie bent down and leaned his face through her window until his beard stubble almost scraped her cheek. "I want them children, you crazy uppity black whore. They're my little nieces, my mama's grandchildren. We're family. We got more right to them than anybody."

"Not if you're the one who assaulted Janie."

"You got no proof of nothing. You got no right to be poking your nose into our asses."

"Janie and those kids were residents of my shelter. They're under my protection."

"That was yesterday's news. I tell you something. I'm going to find your shelter where you're hiding my nieces and I'm going to tear it apart, piece by piece, just like your car."

He kicked the rear left tire. It blew out. Now the entire car was leaning to the driver's side. Jim had to hang on to his shoulder strap to avoid sliding into her lap.

"After what you did to Janie you ought to go to jail. You ought to have bamboo spikes driven up your fingernails."

Dewie slammed both hands on the back of the car. The right rear tire popped. The entire lift gate wrinkled, the safety glass of the windshield cracking and curving out in a clinging sheet of broken pieces, like crumpled foil. The exhaust pipe and muffler clanged to the concrete.

"You're awful bloodthirsty for such a high and mighty hincty educated cunt. When I find those childrens at your shelter, I got a job to do with them. I won't tell you what it is, but it won't be nice. I'll let you watch, though."

"You'd do that to them, your own nieces, like you did Janie?"

"Woman, you crazier than I thought. Janie ain't worth the paper I wipe my ass with. I wouldn't touch her with my dick if she paid me a thousand dollars. And I sure wouldn't touch no little girl like that." He tore the rear bumper off and waved it at her. "I'm a man's man, and I like my women large and round. Your tits and ass aren't big enough, but at least you fill out your pants. I'll give you a taste of a real man. That's why I'm letting you live now. You and your chickenshit little white boyfriend." Dewie laughed. "His face turns any whiter he's going to be a ghost."

Marilyn and Jim ducked low as Dewie pounded on the roof. The other windows and the corner frame supports accordioned down. Dewie lifted his right hand, screamed, "Hiiiaaaaaaa!" like Bruce Lee delivering a death blow and karate chopped the right front side of the car. The last of the tires burst. Stray pieces of broken car clanked to the street.

"I could crush you both in here like I was one of them wrecking machines in junkyards, turning cars into little steel cubes," Dewie said. "But it's too early. I want you around when I find them little girls at your shelter. I want you to know what it's like to feel a boulder jammed up between them fancy legs of yours."

Dewie ran across the intersection and leapt into a car. Just as it took off he shouted, "This ain't over, bitch."

Only the door on Jim's side, with a great screeching and straining of twisted metal, could be pushed open. Marilyn and Jim climbed out of it, avoiding the shards of broken glass, and collapsed, gasping, to the sidewalk.

"What'll we do now?" Jim asked.

"Take the bus."

VI

Corner of Grand and Washington

Lorenzo turned the CD player's volume up to the max.

"I don't even know what them little girls look like." Turk pulled a drumstick from the box of Church's fried chicken in his lap. "I only seen them one time, when I was over at Michael's crib one day, and I sure didn't pay them no mind. Kids're like roaches. Every house you go, there's some crawling around."

"It's as simple as vanilla and chocolate. One's white and one's black."

"So damn what? Lots of people black, lots of people white."

"Lots of people brown too."

"Deep, Lorenzo, deep. You know where Dewie's getting that

Boulder shit from? I don't know what the fuck it's all about."

"How in hell could I?" Lorenzo said. "But when I seen him kill Marko like that, I knew my life had changed. I was either in the big time or deep shit."

"It was cold, what he done. Cold. Marko was always good to him."

"You missing my point, Turk. Dewie ain't human no more. No ordinary motherfucker could've done what we seen him do. Arnold Schwarzenegger, maybe, but plain old crazy Dewie Grimes? No damn way. The son of a bitch is raving, with all that shit about an old Indian, but hell, it worked, didn't it? That's all that counts."

"Scared my piss purple," Turk said.

"Me too. If he could do that to Marko, he could do you or me the same way. That's why I aim to call him Boulder from here on in just like he wants. And whatever Boulder tells Lorenzo to do, that's what Lorenzo is doing, because, Turk baby, my mama didn't raise no fool. And maybe he's going to do all that other crazy shit he talked. Maybe he will be king of the world, and we'll be his big cheeses, his vice kings. Sounds good to me."

As they drove south down Grand, toward the old Woolworth's, Turk almost spilled his fried chicken to the floor. "Look over there. That them?"

"I ain't sure," Lorenzo said. "Hell, I never paid no attention to them little bitty kids neither."

"I think it's them."

"Can't be them," Lorenzo said. "There's a white dude with them must be the white girl's father."

"But why would they have a little black girl too?"

"Maybe he married a sister the second time around."

"That don't sound right."

"Jungle fever," Lorenzo said. "Some white guys know black is beautiful."

"People cross the line on their first marriage, when they young and so in love they don't care how stupid they are. Not on the second one, when they're cautious."

"How the hell would you know?" Lorenzo asked.

"My brother Greg married a white bitch. She busted his balls for seven years before he finally dumped her. You can bet his next wife was black. He told me all about it."

"I'll follow that bus. We got to check them out."

Sun of Suns Three

Dirtworld

"You cannot resist me," the Indian said. "I am more powerful than you can imagine. I have survived what no other mortal could. After you learn how strong my spirit is you will understand you are less than nothing."

Ice chilled Janie's spine. She rubbed her eyes to keep out the gray mist, but the temple walls again flickered then vanished like a turned-off TV.

Sun of Suns spun through darkness. Dizziness twisted his skull and he saw only blurs of colors. As the strength of the jimson weed seeds increased he lost the sense of his mud-body until the thin line of moon thread was all that connected his air-soul to the body he had left behind.

As his ties to his mud-body loosened, loud and jumbled thumping sounds attacked his ears—drummers pounding animal hides and hollow logs out of time and syncopation, each to a different beat.

How could Sun of Suns find Elder Brother? Dirtworld was

169

Skyworld at night without moon or stars, a never-ending empty blackness.

Maybe that was why Grandmother lusted for Elder Brother, so his burning radiance would shine through her cold, dark void. But Elder Brother had already fallen off the cliff at the edge of the world. Where was his light? Had Grandmother's womb-darkness extinguished it? Maybe it was rekindled at the dawn of each new day like the cooking fires of the Great People, banked to coals every evening and prodded to life every morning.

Finally, in the distance, a glimmering.

Elder Brother?

Sun of Suns pictured himself as the great bird man spirit guide, spread his arms out as wings and flew like an eagle through the darkness toward the light.

As he drew near the flames, an ancient crone appeared before him. The hag wore only a necklace of human skulls. Scraps of snowy fur matted her cleft. She danced, shaking the long, dry dugs that hung to her waist and waved a broom with only six reeds still tied to the end of the stick. In her other hand she held an ear of maize.

Grandmother Earth.

"I've come to rescue Elder Brother," Sun of Suns said.

She laughed, displaying the one yellow tooth in her black gums. "Foolish man. The Sun, the Earth—we are not your playthings. Your Elder Brother does not need your aid."

"I have come to return Elder Brother to Skyworld for all time, to free him from the pain of death and rebirth, to drag him from your wrinkled embrace and forever abolish night and winter."

"All who die in me are born anew," Grandmother Earth said. "Your elder brother will live again as long as the ancient balance is maintained. Move the sun, disrupt the established harmony of the cosmos and you destroy your Great People."

"You cannot stop me."

"I have no need to try." The woman of many winters cackled. "Others here wish to greet you, Sun of Suns."

Many spirits of women and young girls, some small children, appeared. As they approached, the hectic thumping sounds grew louder. Sun of Suns realized it was the beating of their hearts. Grandmother Earth laughed with the maniacal glee of a person with a wandering soul.

The pounding of the spirit hearts merged into one head-splitting beat. What did these demon girls want with him?

Suddenly Sun of Suns understood. He panicked like an unarmed child facing an angry mother bear and fled upward through the blackness, following his moon thread, anxious to escape Dirtworld and return to his mud-body.

But of course the girls could not hurt him. They were spirits, but only small, young girls. They had been weak in life and now were helpless in death. They were many, but he was a man. He was the sun's younger brother.

It was now simply time to return to Peopleland and rejoin his air-soul to his bones.

The girls dared not fight him...so why were a couple of them grabbing his moon thread?

Sun of Suns tried to pull his spirit link from their grasps, but they held on tightly. As he flew toward Peopleland he had to haul them with him and their weight slowed him down, allowing several more of the maidens to catch up with him. They also grabbed the silver line, holding back his ascent. Soon, even the tiniest spirits—the children barely walking when Sun of Suns ordered their hearts cut out—grasped the glowing string of his mortal life in their pudgy fists.

He struggled, but his already exhausted spirit muscles could not lift him and the spirits of all fifty-two fifty-two virgins. The power of the jimson weed seeds seeped from him and he began to sink. The maiden souls dragged him down farther and deeper into Dirtworld. Finally he plummeted through Dirtworld like a rock thrown off a cliff.

When he reached the farthest length of his moon thread it snapped. Its glowing light vanished the instant it broke. Far above him in front of the altar, Sun of Sun's mortal mud-body lay dead.

Sun of Suns was trapped in Dirtworld.

CHAPTER NINE

I

Holy Virgin Mother of God Medical Center

Jim's arms trembled as he lowered himself into his armchair, his face pale.

"Are you going to be all right?" Marilyn asked.

"A nurse gave me a sedative."

The hospital's air conditioning hit Marilyn with oppressive cold. What had happened back there? The strongest weightlifter in the world couldn't demolish a car with bare fists.

"We ought to call the police," Jim said.

"Nobody would believe it. I don't believe it. You don't believe it. Only my car believes it, and it's not talking."

"Lots of people saw Dewie."

"Who? What are their names and addresses? Try to find them."

"There's the car itself."

"So a gang wrecked it with sledgehammers. The police will probably ticket me for blocking traffic." Her shoulders slumped. "I left the license plates on. The city will send me a bill for the tow charge."

"No human being can do that," Jim said.

"But Dewie did. A maniac as strong as the Incredible Hulk hates my guts and wants to destroy the shelter. Great."

"So where does that leave us?" Jim asked.

"I'm more worried than ever about Latasha and Shontell. If they really were at his mother's he wouldn't accuse me of hiding them. So at least we learned something useful. He's after them too, and for what reason?—I don't even what to think."

"Why should he want to hurt the girls? None of this makes sense."

"So? That won't help those kids."

Marilyn again called all the agencies and shelters, hoping they now had Latasha and Shontell in their custody. After an hour of fruitless inquiries she phoned her friend Barb at the Division of Children's Services.

"Hi, any news for me?"

"Nobody's brought the children in or reported them to us," Barb said.

"What about the investigation?"

"I've ordered one, but it won't happen today. There's no evidence children in Odelia's custody are in danger."

"So it has to go through channels."

"Look, I know things aren't pretty at your shelter either, but if you could see some of the cases we have...We fall farther behind every day. Toddlers left alone and hungry while mothers spend all their money on drugs and booze. Parents beating their kids. So we take them and hand them over to Grandma, who's thirty-seven and just settled down herself. Now she has to raise her grandkids while their mother is off partying."

"I know, Barb. Thanks a lot. I owe you."

"I'll remember you said that."

Marilyn called the Child Abuse-Neglect desk of the St. Louis Police Bureau of Investigation. No Latasha or Shontell.

"Jim, I know this isn't your problem, and it's not fair of me to ask you, but—"

He lifted his head. "Ask away. I already told you I'm a pushover for a beautiful woman I care about."

Better let that pass. "Can I borrow your car? I swear I won't let Dewie wreck it."

"How could you stop him? Look, Janie is my client—"

"No she's not."

"All right, she's not officially in my workload, but she's in my hospital. So that makes it my problem. Kind of, so—yes. As long as I go with you."

"I don't want you hurt."

"By you or by Dewie?"

"Let's go. I can't let him find those children before I do."

"Just hold on a moment while I tell my supervisor I'm too sick to stay at work today. It's not really a lie."

"Go home and rest," Marilyn said.

"Sitting next to you will be the best medicine."

Marilyn rolled her eyes. "Oh, please." But as she spoke, she smiled.

II

Dreamtime

" Now you see it took the might of fifty-two fifty-two virgin souls to stop me," the dead Indian said. "You are just one weak little child. You have made getting beaten up and raped your life's career. It's the only thing you know how to do."

"No!" Janie hated this ghost devil from Hell. He just kept saying she was a worthless piece of shit. She'd known that since she was a little girl. Ever since she thought bad things about what boys and men had between their legs, wondering how good their wee wees would feel inside hers. That was nasty and evil.

But she didn't care what other people thought. If they didn't like her they could fuck themselves, that's what she always said. And this stupid dead Indian could kiss her butt too.

She was stupid. She was short. She was skinny. She was ugly. But some man always wanted inside her pants.

"I showed you how your father beat you and the other children picked on you. Your only friend was your doll. Do you remember these things now?"

"Yes." Janie wished she could forget them again. "But not everybody hurt me. Uncle Tommy and Aunt Marge, they treated me awful nice. They let me stay at their house when Mommy went with Daddy preaching on long revival crusades. I got to play games with my cousins, Sammy and Denise. Only sometimes they wanted to play Monopoly and I think they cheated. I couldn't count my money so they handled it for me and read the cards, and I always lost. But I was older than them, so Uncle Tommy and Aunt Marge let me stay up late to watch movies on TV. I was a big girl, fifteen."

"Who is Latasha's father?" the dead Indian asked.

"A bad man," Janie said. "He forced me when I didn't know nothing."

"What was his name?"

"I don't know and I don't care. Mommy told me he died of a heart attack."

"But you don't remember his name?"

"No. He was a bad man." Janie turned her face away from the ghost, feeling in her eyes more tears she could not cry out.

Icy gray mist swirled, sucking Janie into it.

She watched a young girl start to climb into the back of Uncle Tommy's faded yellow Pontiac.

"The front seat, Janie," Uncle Tommy said. "Sit up here with me."

Uncle Tommy worked at Home Depot. He always smelled of fresh lumber, paint and varnish. When he made bookcases, birdhouses and wooden window shades in his basement workshop the whine of his don't-touch saw howled through the house.

That night when the news came on at the end of the movie, Uncle Tommy had said he was starving and told Janie she could ride with him to McDonald's. He insisted Aunt Marge go to bed because she was exhausted. But Janie was young, she couldn't be tired yet and must be hungry for a Big Mac.

Janie felt sleepy, but she liked to eat at McDonald's and staying up later than Aunt Marge made her feel grown up, so of course she went with Uncle Tommy.

On the way home Uncle Tommy drove down a small road that dead-ended in the country near lots of trees.

"It's so peaceful here," Uncle Tommy said. "I wanted to show you my favorite place. You can almost forget we're close to the city."

In the small patch of forest darkness crouched, waiting to leap on her like a cat ambushing a mouse.

"I could stay here all night," Uncle Tommy said.

"Our hamburgers are getting cold."

"Do you have a boyfriend?" Uncle Tommy asked.

"No."

"I'm surprised. Don't you like boys?"

At night in bed Janie thought about boys and men she knew, imagining them in bed with her. She did nasty, evil things with her fingers between her legs. She didn't know why that felt so good when it was so sinful, but she couldn't stop.

"Daddy told me once, "Any boy I find tomcatting around here because he thinks you'd be easy, I'll shoot his ass full of buckshot.'"

"My brother can be mean," Uncle Tommy said in a low voice. He slid his arm around Janie's shoulders, just as she had seen boys do with other girls at the movie theater.

"I want a boyfriend," she said. "But the guys at school, they just ignore me or tease me. They don't ask me out because I'm so stupid and ugly."

"That's a shame. You're certainly not ugly."

"Anyway, Daddy says if a boy ever talks nice to me, I'm supposed to run away, because he's only got one thing on his mind. Mommy says Daddy knows what he's talking about. But I don't."

"I think you do, Janie. You're not a child. Deep down, you know."

"Daddy says good girls don't let nothing nasty happen to them before they're hitched up. He says no boy will ever love me, because I'm of sub, sub...subnormal intellect."

Uncle Tommy edged closer along the seat toward her. "Don't take my brother too seriously, Janie. He's been hurt himself."

"But it's true," Janie said. "No boy likes me. No boy ever liked me. No boy ever will like me."

"Your Daddy is really a nice man deep inside," Uncle Tommy said. "I bet you didn't know that, did you?"

Janie liked the feeling of Uncle Tommy near her, the way he hugged her hard. He really liked her. "Daddy wants to make me grow up into a good girl who'll go to Heaven when I die."

"But your daddy used to be more than that. It's hard to believe, knowing him now, but he used to be happy."

"What do you mean?"

"When we was growing up he was always smiling and grinning like a fool. He was so good-natured folks made fun of him, but he was too easygoing to care. Know what changed him around? A woman. What else? It's always you ladies ruin us men."

Uncle Tommy had a funny look in his eyes. "When your daddy was in Korea he fell in love with a native prostitute. He'd rather die than admit it now, but when he returned home from the Army he told me the story. His heart was still so broken it had near about collapsed. He still had her picture then, before his feelings changed from hurt to hate. She was a real beauty. I could see how any man could lose his love to her even if she was a heathen slope, even if she didn't know ten words of English that could decently be spoken inside a church."

Uncle Tommy reached over with his other hand and started rubbing Janie's leg, which thrilled and frightened her. Maybe she just didn't understand, like so many things. After all, Uncle Tommy was a born-again Christian just like Daddy, although he didn't preach like Daddy did. He went every Sunday to hellfire church.

"Sure, he met her inside a whorehouse," Uncle Tommy said. "And sure he knew all whores are damned to Hell. But he was easygoing then, like I said, and he realized lots of women did things in war, just to survive, that they'd never do in normal times. Either that, or his love just plain blinded him. She convinced him she hated working as a prostitute, she wanted him to take her away from that terrible life. She loved and wanted to marry him. She wanted to live with him in America. She would convert to Jesus and be baptized. She would love him forever. She would be glad to have only one man in her bed for the rest of her life."

"She wanted to be a good girl," Janie said.

"That's right. So he promised to marry her. But of course she had a family. Her mother and father had died in the war, killed by one side or the other. That left her the only support of two younger brothers and a younger sister. She said she could leave them behind on their own but not without money, or her younger sister would have to work in the cat house even though she was only fourteen. Willie Lee's fiancée couldn't allow that so she couldn't marry Willie Lee until he gave her enough money to fix them up."

Uncle Tommy started breathing fast. His fingers crept up the legs of Janie's shorts, stroking the inside of her thighs.

"Most men would have dumped her, but Willie Lee handed over his entire savings. Since he didn't gamble or drink much then or go with whores regular like other soldiers did, he still had most of his pay, but it wasn't enough. Her younger brothers and sister needed food, a house, clothes and school books."

Uncle Tommy's arm tightened on her shoulders.

"Janie," he said. "You make me lose control."

"But what happened next?" Janie asked.

"I can't stop it. Help me, Janie. Stop me." He started to kiss her, pressing his mouth against hers.

Janie didn't know what to do. She wanted a nice man to hold her close and make her laugh, but he was Uncle Tommy. He was married to Aunt Marge. This was sinful. Janie was sinful too but she didn't like Uncle Tommy licking her throat.

"Stop it!" She tried to push him away, but he was too strong. His arm held her against his chest. "You're scaring me, Uncle Tommy."

"Janie, you make me lose control. Help me."

Uncle Tommy tried to stick his tongue in her mouth, but she turned her face away. His hand rubbed up and down her legs faster and harder. He reached inside her Miss Piggy t-shirt and squeezed her little titties. Janie wondered why. All the boys at school laughed at her because they liked girls with big boobs.

Then Uncle Tommy's hand fumbled at the waistband of her shorts, yanked them. Janie squirmed and twisted. She tried to kick him, but her foot slammed the underside of the dashboard. He dug his fingernails into her shoulders.

"Stop it, Janie," he said. "Don't make this hard on yourself."

Maybe she could escape if she turned the handle and ran outside, but where would she go? She would be lost in the dark woods. She would starve to death under the trees. Janie screamed, a mewling wail cut off by his sharp slap across her mouth.

"You're too old for that. I'm sorry, I shouldn't have smacked you. I know what my brother's like and I'm sorry he hurts you and I'm sorry I hurt you. But you just shut up now or I'll tell your father how you made me do this. He'll kill you, Janie. I know my brother has a terrible temper. He'd kill you if he learned his daughter seduced her own uncle."

Janie whimpered far deep in her throat like a dog hit by a car but didn't scream. Uncle Tommy was right. Daddy would kill her if he knew how sinful she was being.

Uncle Tommy pulled her shorts and panties down her legs and forced himself between her naked thighs. Her heart pounded the top of her head. Janie gasped with pain and felt something break within her as Uncle Tommy's thing jammed inside. Cramps swept through her belly. His body jerked against her. A high-pitched whine drilled out from deep inside her chest.

Uncle Tommy let go and Janie fell back to the car seat. She looked down at herself. The smears of dark blood on her thighs made her scream again.

"Shut up, Janie," Uncle Tommy said in a tired voice. "That's natural because it was your first time. A woman always hurts then, but after that she craves it. I swear, I didn't know you'd never done it before. I figured by now you'd gone into the woods with some guy or other."

"Daddy would kill me, kill him."

"The boys in your neighborhood must be damn fools. Here." He reached behind to the back seat and handed her a rag that smelled of motor oil. "Wipe yourself off with that and pull your pants on. Your Aunt Marge will be wondering what's kept us so long."

He zipped up, scooted over to the driver's seat and they sped off. As Janie wiped herself he said, "Now, Janie, you aren't going to do anything real real stupid like tell somebody about this, are you?"

"Daddy'd kill me, he knew I sinned so bad."

"That's right, he would. You're no rocket scientist but you know what's good for you, don't you?"

She nodded her head.

"You understand you're the one'd be hurt if you tried to tell anybody. It's time you learned how things be, Janie. You're old enough, no matter what grade of school you're in or what your IQ is. We menfolks, we try to be strong about sex. I've held my-self back from you many times. But you women tempt us. You don't even have to try."

"I didn't do nothing."

Uncle Tommy drove home in silence for a while, then said, "Want to hear the rest about your daddy?"

Janie wiped her eyes with the bottom of her t-shirt. Her stomach still hurt and she wanted to pee so badly she thought she would burst. Suddenly she suddenly felt real old and grownup. Uncle Tommy was telling her a secret Daddy didn't want her to know. Uncle Tommy was saying he was sorry for what he done.

She nodded.

"Well, Willie Lee wrote home and asked our parents for money. They didn't understand, but they had saved a lot during World War Two and business was still pretty good. I was near-ly out of high school then and working at a gas station. They prayed over it, then sent Willie Lee four thousand dollars. All the money they owned that wasn't tied up in the farm.

"Willie Lee gave the four grand to that Korean gal just before he had to ship out to Okinawa. They were going to be married the day after, but she didn't show up at the chaplain's office. When he went looking for her at the whorehouse he discovered she'd packed her bags and left. Nobody knew where she went or they wouldn't tell him. He never saw her again.

Uncle Tommy stared at Janie. "Your daddy thought he was going to share his life with an exotic creature who had a loveliness that put all the girls in our hometown to shame. He thought he was going to have his back massaged every night. He thought she would be meek and passive and love her man with her entire heart the way American women don't. For that he was ready to sweat himself to the bone for the rest of his life, to give her the clothes and jewels and nice house and car she wanted and provide for her entire family. Instead, he gave our parents' entire life savings to a slant-eyed prostitute. Ever since then, he hasn't been his old smiling self. That shows what you women can do to us men."

Uncle Tommy nodded, thought to himself a moment, then added, "No, he was his old self again after you were born. When you were a baby he was full of joy and love again. I wish you could remember how he acted when you were a tiny thing, before anybody suspected you were retarded. He was so proud of you. The first two years after you were born, he was the happiest man on God's green Earth."

Janie took lots of aspirins and Tylenol every day until her tummy stopped aching. Back in her own house and bed, after a long time, Janie again rubbed herself between her legs. She was afraid it wouldn't feel as good but, instead, it felt better. The bad man was right. It hurt a woman only the first time. After that, she liked it.

Now Janie was a woman. Even though the bad man had frightened and hurt her she felt proud he wanted her. She was stupid and ugly, but one man had lusted after her. Even if he was a bad man. Even if Janie was sinful and evil for letting him. Thinking about sinning made her insides warm, wet and gushy.

She started having horrible nightmares of burning in a bonfire like a witch. Almost every night she woke up sweating hard even though the room wasn't hot. She couldn't go back to sleep until she hugged her dolly Suzy close to her chest.

Forgetting she was a woman now, Janie sang to Suzy. "I saw the light...no more darkness in a material world...now I'm so happy...like a virgin."

III

Corner of Grand and Park

"This is it, cuz," Turk said. "Boulder is going to reward us for real." His teeth tore the last hunk of greasy white meat off a chicken back. He swallowed, then licked the grease off his fingers.

"You sure it's them?" Lorenzo asked.

"Got to be. How many other white and black girls walking together around this city?"

"Could be lots. This ain't the old days."

"Fucking integration shit. I don't even like white people."

185

"You fucked Janie," Lorenzo said.

"I couldn't tell Michael I didn't want her," Turk said.

"Bullshit. Your eyes was lit up for three days after, you was so proud of yourself."

"Shut the fuck up and drive."

"They're getting off right in front of Cardinal Glennon Hospital. They're just sick."

"Little kids don't take themselves to a hospital."

"Maybe their mother's a fat lazy bitch like my baby's mama. Sleeps all day, don't do shit except watch Oprah. Then she's got the welfare office after me for child support, like I have a job or something. Like she really takes care of the kid anyway."

"Slow down, man, you're driving past them."

"I can't park in the middle of the damn street."

Turk kept watching. "They ain't going into the hospital, they're crossing Grand. We got to stop this heap."

They found an empty spot several streets down and several blocks west of Grand, the opposite direction the girls had headed in. Lorenzo and Turk ran to the front of Cardinal Glennon. They waited for a break in the traffic, sprinted across Grand, then jogged east.

The first block was empty, just the back side of Incarnate Word Hospital. They trotted on until they got to an area where there were a few houses in between a lot of vacant lots. Weeds grew tall through cracks in the sidewalk. The soles of their Nike's crunched broken glass.

"Man, this is a creepy area," Lorenzo said. "You could build four new houses for every one already here. This must be what they call urban renewal."

"Who gives a damn? You see those little girls?"

186

They kept running until they spotted the two children turning right down a side street. When they were still half a block behind the two girls, the white one turned her head and spotted them. Holding the black girl's hand, she sprinted down the sidewalk.

"That's it," Turk said. "She knows we're after her."

"Maybe she's just scared."

He and Lorenzo almost caught up with the girls when they ran to an elderly black woman hobbling down the sidewalk, a cane in one hand and a plastic bag of groceries in the other.

"Grandmama," the white girl cried out. "Help us, please. Those two big men are chasing us."

Both girls clung to the old woman's long gray skirt and cried.

Turk and Lorenzo stopped.

"Excuse me, ma'am," Lorenzo said, polite and as slick as curl relaxer. "But are these two little children really your grandbabies?"

From behind her thick bifocals the woman gave them a cold, sharp stare. In a harsh voice she shouted, "What for you want to know?"

"Well, uh, they was throwing rocks at my car."

"Was they? I'll see about that." She grabbed the white girl by her ear. "That true, what he said?"

"No, Grandmama."

"I'll learn you to lie to me. I'll whip you right good when we get inside."

"Then, you do know them?" Turk said.

"Why you think I don't know my own kinfolks? What's wrong with you?"

"They really are your grandbabies?" Lorenzo asked.

The old woman put her hand on the white girl's head. "You think just because she's white she can't belong to me? Get your funky-assed self out of my face. Her mama had her when her mama was real young, with a white boy. But later she married my youngest son and they had this here little girl." She placed her palm on the black child's shoulder. "If my son loves a white stepdaughter, I do too, even if she's not a blood relation. And what business is it of yours?"

"They threw rocks at my car."

"Two big strong men ought to have better things to do than go running after little girls. Get the hell out of here before I call the police. You look to me like a goddamned gang."

Turk and Lorenzo turned to each other and shrugged.

"Must not be them," Lorenzo whispered.

"I don't know," Turk said.

"Come on, let's go."

In Turk's bones he was sure those two little girls had never laid eyes on that old woman in their lives before two minutes ago. But what could he do if she was covering for them? And maybe it was true. Why kill the old bitch if these were the wrong children? Boulder didn't want just any pair of white and black girls. He wanted Latasha and Shontell.

"All right. I guess it can't be them." Turk turned and started back to the car with Lorenzo.

Then, reluctant to just walk away, Turk swung his head back around to give those kids one last look.

CHAPTER TEN

I

Dreamspace

Holding her arms across her eyes, not looking and not caring, Janie staggered away from the ghost. Uncle Tommy was the bad man. Uncle Tommy raped her. Uncle Tommy was Latasha's father, because she didn't do it with no other guy until after she knew she was already pregnant. She stumbled through the rotted slats of the temple wall and stepped outside. Maybe she ought to die, she was so stupid.

The dead Indian stepped on the silver rope that followed her every place. "Do you want to see your children?"

Janie stopped. She had to, though nothing else he could have said would have mattered to her.

"You can talk to them, touch them," he said. "I will send you to them."

"Why? I thought you wanted me to die."

"Seeing your children will hurt you. You will want to die."

"No way. I love them. They make me happy."

"Maybe you don't make them happy. Maybe they hate you."

"You're lying. You're a bad ghost."

"I will show you. My power is now linked to Dewie and your daughters, so I can send you to Peopleland, but only close to them. Do you really want that?"

"Yes!"

A blizzard blew through the hole she had made in the wall. The snow-filled wind carried her high into a gray fog.

Suddenly Janie slammed into a solid, hard wall. What happened? She opened her eyes, blinked and saw her daughters. She didn't know why they were clinging to the legs of that old lady. She didn't know why they looked at her with such fear—but of course they were shocked to see her right now. All this surprised Janie too.

"Latasha! Shontell!" she cried out, her voice sounding strangely harsh and deep inside her throat. "I finally found you."

She was so glad! She loved them so much! No matter what happened to her, she didn't care as long as Latasha and Shontell were safe. She could be beaten, robbed, raped, starved, tortured—it didn't matter, not as long as nobody hurt her babies. Love for them gripped her heart and she rushed toward them with outstretched arms.

Latasha and Shontell screamed and ran away.

"Where're you going?" Janie shouted at them. Why were they acting like that? "Don't leave me."

The girls rushed down a broken-brick walkway to the front door of a rickety frame house sided with red shingle. Their feet thundered on the wooden porch, knocking loose powdered flakes of gray paint. Latasha pounded on the front door.

"Latasha. Shontell. What's wrong with you?"

Her children were running away from her. Her daughters, the only two people in the world she loved. They hated and rejected her. She would trade the whole world for Latasha and Shontell, but they acted as though she was threatening them. She wanted to cry with frustration and heartache.

Latasha shouted, "Help! Somebody help us, please! A man's attacking us. Please let us in! Somebody help us."

The old woman hobbled toward Janie, cane held high. "You leave them little girls alone! I'm going to whup your tail, then call the police."

A young black man who looked vaguely familiar to Janie ran up to her and grabbed her elbow. "What's wrong with you? Why you think it's them?"

What was going on? She just wanted her babies. She wanted to hug and kiss her daughters and show them all the love she felt inside her like a golden ocean of fire, burning only for them. Her life, her body, her soul—all for them.

She jumped up onto the porch, but before she could bend down to embrace her girls the door opened. Latasha sped through the gap, dragging Shontell behind her. Janie tried to follow, but the young white man slammed the door in her face.

"What do you want?" he asked through the door.

"My babies! Latasha! Shontell!"

"You leave them girls alone you rotten son of a bitch!" The old lady slammed her cane down on Janie's head.

Janie sank again into the chill, gray mist.

"I told you your children hate you," the Indian said. "They are afraid you will hurt them like your father hurt you. They are

191

afraid you will drive them away from you like your mother did to you. They are afraid you will kill them like you cut up your doll Suzy."

II

Compton, near Park

Turk staggered, dizzy with a sudden sharp pain in his skull. What happened? Just a moment ago he had been standing on the sidewalk looking at the two girls and their grandmother. Now he was on the porch of a house, head aching, staring at a door that had a big sign on it, with a picture of a guy pointing a gun directly at him.

FORGET THE DOG—BEWARE OF OWNER

Then the door flew open and a white dude with longish brown hair was really pointing a revolver in his face. What the fuck?

"Take it easy. Take it easy, everybody," Lorenzo shouted as he grabbed Turk's arm. "You okay, man?"

"I think so. What's going on?"

"I'm going to beat the living shit out of you, you big motherfucker." The grandmother swung her heavy wooden cane at his head.

Lorenzo blocked it with his arm. "Take it easy, old woman, we ain't done nothing."

"I asked you what you wanted," the man with the gun said.

"If you don't tell me fast I'm going to drill you both for trespassing."

Lorenzo held up his hands. "Please, everybody, calm down. There's no cause for alarm, no need for violence. My friend got carried away, that's all."

"Why'd them two little girls run into my house? Why're you guys chasing them?"

"You remember my grandbabies, Terry," the old woman said. "These cats say my little girls threw rocks at their car. I don't believe it."

Lorenzo kept his arms raised. "Look, we were wrong. We're real sorry. Okay?"

Terry's gun didn't waver. "Get the hell off my property."

"We're real sorry we scared your grandchildren, ma'am." He shook Turk's arm. "Aren't you, Turk? You're real sorry, aren't you, man?"

Still dazed, Turk shook his head. "Sure am—real sorry. I don't know what came over me."

"Come on, let's stop bothering these good people." Lorenzo appealed to the white dude and the old woman. "See how sickly he looks? I better drive him to the clinic. Sometimes he has seizures. And he didn't take his medicine this morning. He didn't mean no harm. We're real sorry. Come on, Turk. Take it easy, man."

The old lady shouted, "And don't come back here. When I was a young gal, the boys knew how to dress sharp. They had too much pride to walk around like you two, looking like something the cat dragged in, with pants falling down and your undies showing like you just begging the faggots to stick their things up your stinky asses."

193

As they walked back to the car Lorenzo asked, "What is wrong with you? Why'd you act like a crazy motherfucker?"

"What'd I do? I don't remember. I feel like when Benny Dobson and I fought each other with bricks in the fifth grade."

"You shouted out them little girls were Latasha and Shontell and ran after them like you wanted to kill them and eat them up right there, just like a wild animal. You scared me, man."

"Jesus, I don't remember a goddamned thing."

"You're one lucky dude, I tell you," Lorenzo said. "That white son of a bitch was dying for an excuse to blow your head off. If you'd gone one more inch, if that old lady hadn't whacked you upside your head with her stick, you'd be one dead homey."

"What'd the girls say when I shouted those names?"

"They just screamed and ran for the house."

"So maybe that means that was them. Maybe the white man and the old lady were lying."

"Shit, I'd've run too, you come after me like that. It don't mean crap."

Turk shrugged. "I guess you're right, but, damn, I sure wish I could remember."

III

Virgin Mother of God Medical Center

"Wait a minute." Marilyn grabbed Jim's arm as they were on their way out of his office. "I just remembered I haven't called in to the shelter yet. Mildred'll be furious. She's my boss, the director."

"Go ahead while I talk to my boss. I'll be back in a minute."

Marilyn picked up Jim's desk phone. She also wanted to report the secret cache of guns in the file cabinet. She hated to betray Sara's confidence, but her obligation to Mildred was more important. Besides, Marilyn agreed with Mildred: good people didn't need to own guns.

Marilyn couldn't forget the many pistols she'd seen men carry when she was growing up in the projects, and the shots that often woke her in the night. She recalled the faces of the men and boys she'd known who were now dead, killed by their 'black brothers' during drunken arguments in taverns, over accusations of cheating during crap games and by jealous husbands. That didn't even count the organized gang and drug slayings. She also remembered the many who now languished in jail, out of sight and mind of society, because they had used a gun to kill or wound someone.

Yes, Marilyn hated guns.

Someone finally picked up the phone at the shelter. "Hello."

"Mildred, it's me, Marilyn."

"Where are you? What's wrong?"

"I'm at the hospital. It's been a long night—day."

Marilyn explained the situation about Janie and her children, but Mildred insisted she report to work immediately anyway. Mildred was a combination of upper class New England puritan sternness with the thick skin of a radical who had organized strikes and demonstrations in the face of scabs, death threats and jail terms. Marilyn hated to be on her bad side.

"Dear, I realize you take these things very personally," Mildred said. "I remember what you told me of your own situation, so I realize these children are an issue close to your heart, and

I respect that. But you have to learn where to draw the line. I want you in here as soon as possible. Betty Silver feels rejected because you missed your morning appointment with her."

"I'll talk to her. But there's also something else I have to tell you now."

"Later, child—when you arrive." Mildred hung up.

A sharp nail drilled the top of Marilyn's skull, signaling the beginning of another headache. Her doctor told her they weren't technically migraines, but migraine wannabes were bad enough.

"Are you all right?" Jim asked, holding her shoulders.

"I, sure, I—" She must have dozed off for a moment. She slept so little last night, and not enough every night before that for as long as she could remember.

"You sure? I came back in here and you looked sick." He felt her forehead. "You don't have a temperature. Let me ask one of the nurses to check you out."

Marilyn shook her head and stood up. "I'm fine, just a little tired from last night. That's all."

"You're sure?"

"Come on, let's get a move on."

Job or no job, Mildred and Betty Silver would just have to wait until Marilyn found those kids.

IV

Compton, near Park

After Dewie's friends left Latasha heard the man at the door say, "I didn't know you had grandchildren, Mrs. Addie."

"Terry, thank you so much. I never seen them two little girls before, but I couldn't let those hoodlums have them, could I?"

"What happened?"

"They look like such sweet things, and were so scared of those two boys chasing them, so I just had to help out. They called me grandmama just as iffen I was, so I played along. Tickled me, and sure shook up them gangsters."

"Sure did."

"How's Betty? How come I don't never see her in her garden no more?"

"She's working a lot these days, Mrs. Addie. When she's home, she's tired and sleeps."

"I'm glad somebody still has a job. I never seen such hard times since I was a little girl. Okay, I'll go. You'll call the police now, I reckon. Such cute little girls."

"I won't let anything happen to them, Mrs. Addie. You're very brave."

"If I'd hit him again, I'd've smashed his skull, I surely would have."

The man didn't put his gun down until after he closed and locked the door.

Latasha suddenly realized she had rushed into the house of

a stranger. He had saved her and Shontell from those friends of Dewie, but now he had them trapped. What was he like?

The living room was old but fixed up neatly, with lace curtains over the windows and pretty knickknacks on the mantel over the fireplace. He had a wife—her play grandmother had asked about a Betty. She was at work.

But although the room showed a woman's touch, Latasha didn't think any woman had lived there for a while. Dust covered the screen of the portable TV. Beer cans and hamburger wrappers littered the coffee table. A piece of pizza with gray mold lay on the floor at her feet.

The man pulled a cigarette from the pack in his shirt pocket and lit it with a Bic. "Why'd you girls run in here?"

"I didn't want that man to catch us," Latasha said. "I'm sorry we bothered you. We'll leave now."

"Just hold on a minute, young lady. What's your name? I'm Terry Silver."

"Latasha. And this is my baby sister Shontell."

"Pleased to meet you both." He sat down on the sofa and shoved several empty Burger King cartons onto the floor to make room for them. "Come on, I ain't going to bite you."

His clear brown eyes sparkled. He wore clean slacks and a yellow sports shirt. He combed his hair straight back, which made his forehead look wide, like he was smarter than he acted. He wasn't handsome but he seemed nice enough.

He turned off the soccer game on TV. "You must have quite a story."

"Look, we'd really better go," Latasha said.

"Now what if them two guys are waiting for you outside? They might still suspicion you're the ones they're after. There can't be too many white and black sisters in this city, not with the older one playing hooky on a school day." He grinned. "You are the ones they're after, aren't you?"

Latasha slowly nodded. No point denying it. He knew they weren't Mrs. Addie's grandchildren.

"Why are they chasing after you?"

"I don't know."

"You must have some idea," he said. "You have valuable jewels on you? Cocaine? You witness a murder?"

Voice trembling, Latasha said, "No."

"Oh, don't mind me. I've just seen lots of movies. I can watch them on cable all day and all night. I would, too, if I didn't have to go to work. I got lots of time since my wife up and left me. All I got to do now is go to work, drink beer and watch movies. You like movies?"

Latasha nodded.

"You're real smart, aren't you?"

Latasha shook her head.

"I think you must be. You called Mrs. Addie grandmama. That took real quick thinking. I couldn't've done it. Not now, and for sure not when I was a little kid. I was a dumbshit. Your little sister talk?"

"She's shy and kind of slow."

"Look, I don't mean no harm. If you really got to go—but I like you two. And I'm lonely, what with my wife leaving me. You guys look hungry. I've got sodie pop in the ice box and a big bag of White Castles I just brought home. I always buy more than I eat, they look so good when my belly's empty. I don't want them to go to waste. Come on, I'd love to hear why those guys were after you. It's like a real life adventure movie."

Latasha's stomach rumbled. In the excitement of being chased by Dewie's friends she had nearly forgotten she was near starvation.

"Thank you, sir."

He went into the kitchen and returned a minute later with the food. "Call me Terry. We're friends, aren't we?"

Latasha studied him as he shoved a can of Mountain Dew into her hand. His eyes and face smiled, but he moved in a jerky, kind of awkward manner. He probably didn't want to hurt her and Shontell—in some way he might even like them. But did she really trust him? She didn't know. Anyway, she was too hungry to worry.

"Excuse the mess." The man shoved more burger wrappers off the table and put down the White Castle bag. "Like I said, my wife's been gone. She's the housekeeper, not me."

"We don't mind," Latasha said. Terry's house looked cleaner than Odelia's usually was, except when Odelia grew disgusted by the filth and made Yolanda, Tiffany and Mama clean.

Latasha tore into the bag and began gobbling down the White Castles, barely chewing. Oozing delicious grease, the meat, buns, onions and pickles slid down her throat.

Terry, slowly chewing a burger himself, turned on the TV and let Shontell play with the remote control until she flicked to a station showing a kick-boxing movie.

Latasha pondered their situation as she ate. They had to reach the shelter but they still didn't know how to find it. They couldn't just wander the streets. They might never stumble on the right block. Dewie and his friends might spot them again or another bad person might kidnap them. Latasha knew from the things that happened to her mother the streets were dangerous.

Some men would even Force little kids the same way they did her mother. Mama warned her to always be careful.

But right now she and Shontell were safe. They didn't have to run, didn't have to fear every car, every person on the street. They had food and drink. They had air conditioning. Latasha's tired muscles relaxed. It felt good to just sit and watch Jean Claude Van Damme in action.

V

Streets of St. Louis

Jim drove his red Camaro up and down, back and forth across North St. Louis and the near South Side. Marilyn felt conspicuous in the bright red sports car. "I bet you bought this just to attract women."

"It didn't work. They look at the car instead of me."

Such sadness in his voice. Such a puppy love crush he had on her...

She didn't want to think about it. As she scanned the sidewalks Marilyn kept wondering how Dewie smashed her car with his bare hands. If he wanted to tear down the shelter what could stop him?

And he said his strength would increase if he hurt the children.

Dewie's threats suddenly seemed more than the boasts of a teenage hoodlum howling his frustration at society. Maybe they were a warning to the world. If so, then finding Latasha and Shontell before Dewie was now more important than saving their lives, no matter how much those lives mattered to her.

Everybody's life might be at risk.

Marilyn shuddered, then shook her head. Wait a minute. Dewie take over the world? That was comic book stuff.

But he had destroyed her automobile. Marilyn couldn't know his true strength. Did Dewie?

Either way, she had to find the girls.

"Where would you go if you were a bright seven-year-old who saw something bad done to your mother by a man you were staying with?" she asked Jim.

"That's simple," Jim said. "To the police."

"For all the years you can remember you've been raised with people who hate the police."

"You mean the old thing about how blacks don't like pigs?"

"It's more complicated than that. African-Americans call the police more than white folks do—when they're having a baby and can't afford an ambulance or to report a rival gang leader is selling drugs. But they're also more afraid than your average middle class white that the police might turn on them."

"But Latasha—"

"Doesn't want to go back into a foster home. She spent nearly her first three years in one. I don't think it was a problem, but Latasha loves her family and doesn't want to be separated from Janie or her sister. She knows some people think Janie's not a fit mother because she's slow. But to Latasha Janie is Mama, and she forgives everything. In a foster home she'd be alone. She might have more clothes and regular meals, but not as much love."

"So she might not call the police because she's afraid they'd take her and Shontell away from Janie."

"Now you've got it."

"So where would they go?"

Marilyn's headache throbbed. "That's what I asked you." For a moment she felt the answer was obvious, on the tip of the tongue of her mind. But then her headache flared and she lost it.

It was wrong to neglect her duties at the shelter, but Latasha and Shontell were her responsibility too. If not hers, then whose? The Division of Children's Services? They needed to know the children's whereabouts before they could even send an investigator. Odelia Sykes? Willie Lee and Judith Braxton? No, Marilyn was the only one besides Janie who cared about those girls.

If Janie died or couldn't function outside an institution, Marilyn could adopt them.

She tried to drive the thought from her head but it wouldn't leave. For a frightening moment she wished Janie dead or totally disabled. She wished Odelia dead or disgraced or jailed and Janie's parents dead or disallowed. Then Latasha and Shontell would be hers.

All hers.

Her children.

Guilt gnawed her heart with rusty teeth. She didn't want anyone else harmed but if, at the end, she wound up with the girls....

She had to ride these streets until she found them. It would hurt her dearly if Mildred fired her, but if something bad happened to Latasha and Shontell the pain would be too unbearably deep to live with.

VI

Dreamtime

Janie collapsed to the grimy floor of the ancient temple and curled into a ball, moaning and mewling like an orphaned puppy.

"Your daughters hate you," the Indian said. "They know you're a bad mother. They know you're going to hurt them, just like your mother hurt you."

"No," Janie said. "That was Daddy. You showed me. Daddy hit me. Daddy made me bleed. Daddy burned me with an iron. Not Mommy. Mommy was good, just like me. I love my babies just like Mommy loved me."

She began to shiver even as she hugged her knees close to her chest. Even though she squinched hard, a cloud of gray mist surrounded her.

When she opened her eyes Janie was watching "GHOST WORLD" on cable TV with Mommy. Daddy was away preaching at a church in the Missouri Bootheel.

Janie said, "When I stayed with him and Aunt Marge, Uncle Tommy stuck his thing up me."

"Don't tell stories like that, Janie. It's not nice."

"It's not no story."

"It's very bad to say such wicked things. Please be quiet."

"He poked his thing inside me, Mommy. It hurt a lot."

Mommy slapped the arm of her chair. "Janie, you know truth from stories. When you make up stories you have to say that, like this movie. You know it's not real, the people are just actors. It's fun to watch, but it'd be bad for the movie people to tell us it was true when it's not."

"But he did so, Mommy. Sometimes I forget, but then I remember it were Uncle Tommy."

Mommy grabbed her shoulders and looked into her eyes. "What boy you been playing around with, Janie? Who put these sinful thoughts into your head?"

"Uncle Tommy did it so fast, I didn't understand."

"Stop these lies," Mommy said. "I'm warning you. Stop them right now."

"I think I'm pregnant, Mommy. I haven't dripped blood for three months, I throw up every morning and my tummy's stretched tight."

Mommy shook her, hard. "Whore! How dare you blame your Uncle Tommy who's been so good to you? No more lies—you understand?"

"But he—"

"What boy you let do it to you? You tell me now so I can call his parents and fix things before your father learns about this. How do you think he'll punish you?"

"Mommy—"

"You let some boy dip his wick in your wax, that's what you done. It's time we married you off. If you're old enough to use what's between your legs you're ready for some boy to support you."

"No boy ever touched me, only the bad man." Janie wailed at the top of her voice, crying now. "I never did nothing with no boy. Bad man Uncle Tommy jumped me like a bull on a heifer."

"You won't tell me what boy done it to you, then you gotta get an abortion. You understand, Janie? If you have a baby out of wedlock, you'll disgrace our family. And your father and I have too much to handle with you. We can't raise some bastard kid."

"Don't you hurt my baby, Mommy. I won't let you."

"You dare say one word to your father and he'll kill you. I'll take you to one of them clinics in St. Louis before he comes back home and nobody will never know nothing."

"Not my pretty little baby dolly, Mommy. Please no."

"Any baby you have will be stupid and mixed up as you, honey. It'd be a sin to bring it into this world."

Janie clutched her stomach and cried like she couldn't never stop.

Mommy slapped Janie again and again. Janie's head whipped side to side, Mommy's palm scalding her skin with red-hot shame, Satan's brand. Punishment for sin. She deserved it.

But not her baby. Blood burning, bone melting. Janie screamed a high-pitched never ending fiddle string scraping and sawing scorching her eardrums.

Save her baby.

Janie sat on her bed, fire tornado spinning round head, whirlwind lost souls in Perdition screeching. Hands cupping ears, fingernails gouging flesh, clawing skull. Nerves crackling, dynamite sizzling fuse blaring Fourth of July sparkler halos.

She had to protect her baby.

Wailing, listening, knowing, waiting...Mommy shuffling down hall to bedroom. Drunk again.

Janie, knowing without remembering deciding without thinking acting without planning.

She would never let anyone hurt her baby. Nobody. Not even Mommy.

Clothes into plastic grocery bags, shoes toothpaste hairbrush—not too much, don't want too big, too heavy.

Suzy? Where was Suzy? Remembering...bad man tore off Suzy's dress, ripped to rags, pulled her legs apart like chicken wishbone split Suzy down middle, thrown into garbage can. No more Suzy.

Now Janie had her baby to kiss and hug and sing to. She would protect her baby from the bad man in the city who wanted to abortion her and throw her into the garbage can. Janie would die first, before she let anybody hurt her baby doll.

Money from Mommy's purse to pocket. Outside hot red night, walking, whistling, thumbing...to big city Babylon, she evil pleasure pussy, fattening belly carrying bastard child of sin.

Her own beautiful little baby dolly she loved so much.

CHAPTER ELEVEN

I

Holy Virgin Mother of God Medical Center

Judith looked up from her purse-sized red Bible and leaned against the hard sofa back. She had been searching the gospel of Matthew for some verse, some saying of Jesus to comfort and guide her, but the tiny print was straining her eyes, making them itch and water.

The coat rack holding their jackets filled most of the small waiting room. The picture of Jesus on the wall was too ornate and garish, too vivid—too Catholic.

Willie Lee noticed where she was looking and said, "Janie even had to be contrary about the hospital, coming to a Popish one."

"They're giving her the best care they can. That's all that matters."

Willie Lee harrumphed, a clearing his throat sound, then

lapsed back into silence.

Judith went back to her Bible, searching in vain for the passage that would help her. It was there of course—The Good Book contained the answers to all life's questions, its problems and mysteries. But it was so long that, even after a lifetime of study, Judith couldn't find the selection she now needed with such desperation. She snapped the Bible shut.

"We have to talk about the future, Willie Lee."

He harrumphed again.

"You heard the doctor. Janie ain't going to be walking away from that bed. She might not even talk again. She might die. The longer she goes without coming to, the worse she gets. You saw her. It's as though she were already dead, even with her heart beating and her lungs breathing, because there's no soul in her body. It's as though she were already with the angels."

"That'll be the day," Willie Lee said. "She done committed every sin imaginable and probably some that a decent Christian woman such as yourself can't even think of."

"She never hurt nobody," Judith said softly. "Not intentionally. If she stayed away from us, I expect it's really us who drove her away."

"She didn't hurt me none by keeping her distance. I didn't like seeing my black grandchild, and the one ain't got no father at all so she lied about my brother that way, may he rest in peace."

Judith shut her eyes, clutched her Bible tight. "Willie Lee, I have prayed and sang in the choir and gone to meetings and shouted hallelujah and kept our house together and supported you while you was out preaching. But I look at my only child lying in there, with all them big machines around her, and I feel like somehow it's my fault. Like my entire life is nothing. I've read this Good Book for more years than I can remember and now I wonder whether I ever truly understood a blessed word in it."

"Don't be profane, Judith."

"I wasn't cussing. The words of The Bible are blessed, and nothing this side of Hell could make me doubt that. But I've started to wonder if I really understand them. That's all I said."

"All we did to that child was try our best to show her the way, to teach her how to behave right, to believe in God and Jesus, and not sin. We done our best."

She rubbed her eyes. "That's what frightens me so. Our best wasn't good enough, was it? Not near good enough. And now I begin to wonder if we aren't the ones headed for Hell instead of Janie." She tried to hide the tears in her eyes by rubbing them. "God gave her to us as a gift, but she was like the seed thrown onto rocky soil."

"You're just upset," Willie Lee said. "You don't remember how it really was at all. She wasn't no gift—she was a burden, a challenge. She wasn't even a sweet child like we've heard tell lots of retarded children are. She was a baby longer than most kids but when she learned to walk and talk she was incorrigible. She never minded a word we said, just wanted to go off and be by herself. Didn't ever get along—"

"We were afraid of her."

Willie Lee harrumphed again. "I tried to beat the evil out of her. I'm only sorry I didn't punish her enough, because look where she wound up. I knew she'd be a weak woman, too easily led astray. I knew if I didn't train her hard any slicker with a kind word could con her into his bed and out of her money. I

211

figured we wouldn't be around much after she grew up, so I had to instruct her quickly, while I could."

"And look how you did it."

"She didn't grasp words much. She only understood her body, so that's what I used to teach her. That's why I whipped her. Janie always pushed us to the limit. She didn't understand nothing, but when I said yes she said no. She wanted up down, black white and wrong right."

Judith folded her hands in her lap, composing herself. "All right, that's over and done with. What I meant was, what about those two grandchildren of ours?"

"Let them live with that black woman, Odelia something or other. Janie wanted to whore with that woman's son, so let them kids stay with her."

"But she's not a positive influence. She's not a good Christian like the nice colored people we see at revivals, doesn't even go to church according to Janie. She's lazy. She hates the girls. She don't feed them right. She don't stop the others in the house from picking on them."

"I'm tired, Judith. I've worked hard all my life. Janie about killed me when she was a little girl, and I'm over twenty years older than I was then. Don't ask this of me, Judith. Don't ask it of yourself. I'm sorry Janie's hurt, but I'm glad she won't be sinning no more."

"Those children need to learn about the Lord."

"That is not our burden. My only hope right now is Janie will recover just enough to repent, accept Jesus as her personal savior and be born again. Then I'll know I done my Christian duty and can go in peace to my eternal reward."

Without knowing why, Judith again started to cry.

II

Ashland Avenue

Odelia sat on the couch with the phone in her lap. "You make sure you get it all. I don't want my feet cut up."

"We ain't never going to find all these little bitty pieces of broken glass," Tiffany said over the whine of the vacuum cleaner. "What'd Dewie have to go crazy on us for? I wanted to watch All My Children."

"Hush up and work. You'd be in school now if I didn't need you here."

Dewie called five minutes later. "Any word from Turk and Lorenzo?"

"No, and I see you ain't done no better," Odelia said. "You got to find them childrens. They talk to the police first, you'll rot in jail the rest of your natural born life."

"That ain't the way it is anymore, Mama, I already done told you that. I hope the girls do go to the damn police. Then I'll find them."

"You get them first, boy." Odelia wished he would stop that crazy talk. She didn't want to have to try to take him to Metropolitan Crazy Hospital again, like the time he threatened her with a knife, ran off and didn't return home for three weeks. Said he'd been to California.

"Besides, Mama, them girls are in that shelter with that black bitch and her white boyfriend. It's a secret place. I called up their number in the phone book but the bitch answered wouldn't tell me nothing on account of I'm a man."

The idea hit Odelia so hard she wondered why she hadn't thought of it before. "That makes sense, Dewie. They won't tell you nothing because you might be one of the husbands put their wife in that shelter, looking for to beat her up more and drag her ass back home. But I'm a woman, they'll tell me. You hang on. I'll call them right now."

Odelia shouted at Tiffany, "Girl, bring me that phone book over here and a pen that writes. And turn off that vacuum. Hurry quick."

In a few moments a woman's voice said, "St. Louis Abused Women's Shelter. How may I help you?"

Odelia tried to make her voice sound upset. "My husband's been whomping on me something fierce. I got to leave before he kills me. All he does is drink and cuss and slam me against the wall, and I ain't done nothing wrong!"

In a sympathetic but businesslike tone the woman said, "Who are you, please?"

Odelia almost blurted out her own name, then said, "Scarlett Whitfield." It was the name she used to have the phone turned back on after Dewie ran up a $655 bill one month calling 900 numbers. She still had a phony state I.D. in that name.

"Are you in immediate danger, Ms. Whitfield?"

"I do believe I am. He ain't here right now because he walked down to the store to buy himself another bottle of that god awful whiskey he drinks, but he's coming right back. And he's mad as hell because I told him I can't stand it no more."

"Then our advice is to get right out. Your life comes first. Call the police if you need to, but get right out. Can you do that?"

"I believe so, yes. I'll just stuff some undies in my purse and go."

"Do you have any children, Ms. Whitfield?"

"Our daughter's grown up and moved out, thank the Lord for that. He didn't used to be this bad when we was younger, before he started drinking so much."

"Write this down." The woman gave Odelia an address that she recognized as being downtown, close to the projects.

"Is this where I'll be staying at?" Odelia asked. "I can't go nowhere else. My daughter's in California. My neighbors and church folks is all scared of him. Won't nobody take me in, I've already done asked them."

"This is our public office, but don't worry, Ms. Whitfield. Once I take you through our screening procedures—I'm Janet Drake by the way—someone will drive you to our shelter if we decide that's the best option for you."

"Where's that at? Is it a long way?"

"I'm sorry, but we don't give out the physical address of our shelter over the phone to anyone. That's how we make sure you'll be safe there."

"All right. I'll be there quick as I can. Thank you very much, Miss Drake."

"You're welcome, and good luck."

Odelia switched back to Dewie's line. "They want to interview me first, so I couldn't get it after all."

"But Mama, sure you can. Just go down there like the lady done told you."

"But I ain't no battered wife. I once broke a wine bottle upside your daddy's head when he started carrying on, and I whupped Mr. Sykes' ass once a month."

"Just go. Make them take you to the shelter and then you call me with the address."

"They won't believe me," Odelia said. "I don't think she trusted me over the phone, and I sure don't look like no battered wife."

"I can fix that, Mama."

"What you talking about, boy?"

"Don't worry. I won't really hurt you none."

"Dewie, what you thinking of?"

"I'll be right over, Mama."

III

Compton, near Park

As the afternoon dragged on, Terry Silver smoked cigarettes, drank beer, ate White Castle hamburgers, watched the kick-boxing movie and pondered why Fate sent these two strange little girls to his house.

It was a Sign. Terry Silver believed in omens and prophecies. Shit happened but you could smell it coming. Shit—as well as everything else—happened for a reason.

He didn't know how, but the two little girls were connected to his wife.

Betty never understood. She was just another silly, shallow woman who took things as they came, not caring, not believing, not thinking about the Great Plan of Life. Of course she went to church but that didn't count because all the sheep went to church. That's how they were trained to be sheep. Betty thought she really believed, but it didn't mean anything to her real life. And if what you believed didn't change the way you felt, thought

and acted, it was just words programmed into your skull by society's witch doctors.

Terry Silver had never been a sheep even if he was also never a wolf or a shark. He understood himself and his limits. He
didn't need to hurt anyone else, though he would if forced to—
he could never have a career as a bank robber or a serial kill-
er. He also knew he was not strong in the brains department.
He had enough, but he would never learn to program computers to steal a million dollars undetected or anything clever like
that. Besides, he didn't need a lot of money any more than he
needed to kill for the sake of violence. He would be content just
to thumb his nose at society while working, watching movies,
drinking beer and living simply with his wife.

Nothing wrong with that. If the universe didn't want people
to drink beer it wouldn't have created hops and all those micro-
scopic little buggies that excreted alcohol. If the universe didn't
want men to fuck women it wouldn't have given penises to the
males and holes to the females. He was simply carrying out the
Divine Plan.

He never hurt Betty, not really. Sometimes he hit her a little
harder than he intended because of how much beer he'd drunk,
but hell, why didn't she punch him back? He might enjoy that.
It would add real passion to their sex life. But she would never
understand. She always got so angry when he suggested it.

That was because Betty refused to accept the Divine Plan.
That's why she left him. But she should have known he couldn't
tolerate desertion. Marriage was a sacred institution. Terry believed in marriage, and he acted on his beliefs.

That was simple honor. A woman like Betty, who thought
only about furniture, soap operas and what she would buy with

his next paycheck, didn't grasp the importance of honor.

She would learn.

She had been gone two and a half weeks already. She wasn't with her parents or her brother or any of her friends. He'd watched all those houses until he was certain. But he would find her. These children were a Sign. If only he could find the connection.

He had to keep talking to the smart girl, trying to dig more information out of her.

"I bet your mama's real worried about you. Two pretty little girls like you, I'm sure she takes real good care of you."

"She's hurt right now," Latasha said.

"If she's sick, then you ought to head on home."

"I told you, we don't have a home."

"Then where do you stay?"

Latasha sipped at her can of soda. "With Shontell's grand-mama Odelia, or sometimes at another place."

She was cagey all right. What other place?"

"Just a place. We go there when some guy beats Mama up."

"That sounds terrible."

"It is, but the place is nice. They take care of us real good."

"Is that where you're heading back to?"

Latasha was quiet.

"Latasha?"

"I'm thinking."

"Well excuse me."

"I just mean, I don't know if I should tell you or not, because it's a secret place."

"Oh?"

"Because they take care of lots of women beaten up by their

husbands and boyfriends. See, they don't want anybody else to know where it is, because some of those men are real bad, and if they knew where the women ran away to, they'd come and make trouble."

Bingo. Terry set his beer down and took a puff on his cigarette to appear casual. These girls would lead him straight to Betty.

"That is a real secret place, Latasha. You're right to be careful. Is that where you want to go?"

"I think so."

Terry nodded. "Those two guys chasing you didn't want to return no boxes of Girl Scout cookies, did they? They the ones hurt your mama? Why did they want to hurt you too?"

"I don't know," Latasha said. "I'm scared."

"Now don't you worry none, little girl. I'd like to keep you with me for a long time, letting you eat my White Castles and drink my pop and watch movies on my TV, but I've got to go to work in about one more hour. The law wouldn't let me keep two little children who just ran in off the street like you did. Besides, you don't want to stay with me anyway, do you?"

"We don't know you, Terry."

"That's right, but I still want to help you. If that shelter is a safe place for you, that's where you should go. I'll take you there on my way to work. Do you know the address?"

Latasha shook her head. "It's a secret."

"I'm not asking you to tell it to me—of course not, I'm a man. But do you know the address?"

Latasha shook her head again.

"Do you know where it is?"

"Only sort of."

Damn. He didn't care how smart she was, he wouldn't let a little kid make a fool out of him. "But it must be around here someplace, because this is where you came. Would you know this shelter place if you saw it?"

"I think so."

Terry nodded. "Now we're getting somewhere. Do you know the phone number? You could call them and ask for directions, and I'll take you there." He held up his hand. "I already know what you're going to say and I won't let you off at the door. You can give me fake directions, let me drive around a little until I'm confused but you know how to walk back to the shelter after I drop you off. You'll be safe and I'll go to work knowing I did my good deed for the day."

"I don't know—"

"Look, it's going to be dark very soon," Terry said. "You can't walk around at random, just hoping you'll find it. And besides, you're about worn out already, aren't you? I saw that right off. Your baby sister's been napping for an hour. You've both walked a lot today, haven't you?"

Latasha nodded.

"And these streets aren't safe. Those two guys might still be waiting for you, and there's other evil men out there who'd like to kidnap little girls like you and your sister."

"Where's your phone?"

Terry handed it to her. When she pressed the buttons she made certain she held the handset so he couldn't see which numbers she dialed. Cute, kid.

"Hello? Is Marilyn there? Sara? This is Latasha - I'm okay. Shontell's here too, she's okay - We're at a house, in a man's house - I don't know, just some guy who helped us—

"That's why I called. I need you to tell me how to go to the shelter - I know—he understands. He says he'll just drop us off a few blocks away, so he won't see the place. He's okay. Wait for Mildred to bring the only car back from an errand so you can pick me up? How long? One and a half hours?"

"That's no good," Terry said quickly. "I have to be at work in an hour. And I can't leave you alone here in the house or let you wait outside. Something might happen before they arrived and I'd be responsible."

"You heard him," Latasha said. She listened, turned to Terry. "Where is this, so she can tell me how to go?"

"Compton Avenue, just down from Park. We're a little north of Highway 44."

She told that to Sara, "I'll remember. We'll be careful. Thanks." She hung up.

"You got it?" Terry asked. "You can direct me there?"

Latasha nodded.

"You are a smart one, all right. If I ever have a little girl I hope she's half as intelligent as you. Okay, drink another sodie while I finish this beer. We'll watch the end of this movie and then leave."

Terry believed in Signs.

IV

Dreamtime

Holding her face in her hands, Janie staggered out of the temple, not noticing the tilting beams she bumped against or the splinters that scratched her arms. Mommy hit her.

She stumbled through a dark hallway, groping until she reached the doorway, then lurched outside. Mommy wouldn't believe Uncle Tommy raped her. Mommy wanted to kill her baby. Mommy wanted her to have an abortion on Latasha.

The ghost said something in a voice like river ice cracking at midnight but Janie ignored him.

Suddenly there was no ground below her foot. She opened her eyes just in time to pull herself back from plummeting down the mound's long flight of stairs.

Fever chills shivered through her body. She had forgotten how high the mound was. From it she could see countless rows of ruined Indian houses and many more, though smaller, mounds. Beyond the ghost city were fields of corn, the stalks brown, the dry cobs unpicked.

"Your air-soul cannot die like your mud-body," the ghost said. "Falling here will not kill you. But when your heart no longer wants to go on, then your physical life is doomed. And why cling to it? Flesh is pain. To live is to suffer. Dying will free you from your anguish."

"I don't want to die."

"Why should you wish to live? In the twenty-three years

222

since your birth you have suffered more than most people in an entire lifetime. Did you ever wonder why you were so stupid when others were smart? Did you ever wonder why God punished you so?"

"I hate God," Janie said. "But my life is good. My family did lots of bad things to me, but I have friends. They like me."

"Who are your friends?"

"Marilyn takes care of me. I go to parties with Solange. We have lots of fun together."

"Friends betray you just like your family," the ghost said. "Solange betrayed you. Marilyn will betray you."

"No, not Marilyn. Not Solange."

A gray fog cold as a gravestone rose from the ground until it shrouded the ruined city and became the dark of night.

Janie and Solange were walking to Solange's apartment but were still a long way south of it.

"I'm going to kill that son of a bitch Darrell," Solange said. "I told him, 'Come pick us up at Shirlynne's party before one o'clock. Pick us up before one o'clock.' Now it's after two. Where is the motherfucker?"

A carload of drunken men passed by, honking the horn, hollering and whooping out the window.

"I wish Shirlynne didn't kick us out already," Janie said. "I don't like to walk outside this late at night."

"I heard that. But Shirlynne has to be at work early tomorrow. Not like you and me. We can sleep as late as our babies let us."

"I'm sure glad I don't got to have a job."

"I used to take orders at McDonald's, before I had Franklin and got on welfare. Girl, they want to work you near to death.

You got to smile and act all polite and nice to each and every single customer."

"I sure couldn't do that," Janie said. "I'm too mean."

Solange hooted. "Go on, girl. You ain't never hurt nobody. But your job's taking care of your children. That Shontell sure is a pretty baby. I hope my next one's a girl."

Janie had drunk more cans of beer than she could count and sucked on every joint passed her way. Her nerves twitched but she also felt fuzzy and good. The night was deliciously warm, the air thick as a sweater.

"She's a good little baby too," Janie said. "She don't hardly cry or nothing. She sure is fun to play with. I love to kiss her tummy and tickle her. She just laughs and laughs."

"Franklin's starting to talk and he don't want to shut up. He's going to be a bad little boy."

"I was a bad little girl."

Just as Janie and Solange reached the parking lot of the supermarket at Grand and Magnolia, the same car that had gone by earlier pulled up behind them.

"Hey!" a man called out. "You babes looking for a party?"

"Pretend you don't hear them," Solange whispered to Janie.

"We got the best party in town right here," another man shouted.

"Yeah, we got beer, lots of beer."

"Hey, Charlie, look—the little one's white."

"Boys, looks like we going to have a chocolate fudge sundae for dessert."

The car stopped and two white men jumped out. "You're going with us, ladies," one of them said, a short, thick man with long, wavy hair.

Solange pulled a switchblade out of her purse and waved it at them. "Get the hell out of here before I cut off your dinky little white peckers."

The two men came at Solange from opposite directions. The short one grabbed at her arms while she tried to slice the other in the stomach.

Janie tried to stay behind Solange, but it wasn't easy because she kept jumping around to avoid the two men. Janie tried to jump with her, but the world was spinning too fast. When two more burst out of the car Solange slashed wildly with her knife, then turned and sprinted across the street. Janie, shocked and fuddled, didn't move.

A tall, older man in an oily mechanic's uniform grabbed Janie, picked her up, swung her around and shoved her into the car. Janie was held across the laps of the men in the back seat. Janie kicked and squirmed, but she was too small and weak to break free from the arms tightened about her. Rough hands pawed her, squeezing her breasts and goosing her.

A pudgy man with a beard tried to kiss her on the lips. She spit on him and he slapped her. Someone shoved their thick dirty hand into Janie's mouth so she couldn't holler for help.

"This one's too small," a man said. "We ought to throw her back, wait until she grows up."

"This time of night, we got to take what we can find."

"I sure wanted a piece of that dark meat. Shame she got away."

They turned into Tower Grove Park and stopped. Then they tore off Janie's shirt, pulled down her pants and ripped her panties off. They carried her, still kicking and squirming, onto the grass underneath a tree and held her down.

225

Janie didn't know how many men raped her. Through the blur of beer and dope fogging her brain and dampening her nerves she felt their stiff flesh tear into her body with a force that made her gasp, a ripping pain that made her scream.

"Shut up!" One of the men pinning her arms slapped her across the mouth.

"What a baby," one of the others said.

"I told you all, she ain't even ripe yet."

Janie gagged, then vomited across herself and the men.

"This baby's already drunker than we are. Good thing we didn't give her no more beer. We'd be contributing to the delinquency of a minor."

"No minor ought to be out on the street this late."

Time passed in brief, dizzy, flashing moments. Harsh, jarring laughter rushed back and forth over her head. She kicked, she bit a finger, an arm. She tried to scream. She tore her hand free and belted a man in the eye as he was pressing his weight on top of her.

The stars swirled around her. She blacked out and came to, blacked out and came to, the intervals connected only by the thumping, tearing pain below her waist and the sick, desperate fear twisting her guts.

She woke up in the hospital, bandages wrapped around her head, more swaddling her groin front and back. She couldn't help the police. She'd been drunk and stoned. It had happened so fast she remembered only blurs of upside down faces, a red corduroy work shirt, black boots, a gold earring, curly black hair retreating from a bald spot, a thick hooked nose.

After she left the hospital she stayed for over a month with Michael's cousin's friend Kimberly. She helped cook and clean, but she wouldn't go out, especially wouldn't go grocery shopping at the store across from Tower Grove Park. She watched TV with Latasha and played with Shontell and Kimberly's twin baby girls.

Eventually, lying in the old, spare bed one night, Latasha sound asleep in her arms, Janie felt inside herself a tiny spark ignite a small flame, a birthday cake candle burning in the deep winter darkness of outer space. She put what happened out of her mind. She had survived.

Like a tape recorder starting slowly in mid-song, a short tune squeaked out of her mouth: "Bend me, shake me - she loves you yeah, yeah, yeah—"

The next morning, she returned to the house on Ashland to live with Michael.

Chapter Twelve

I

Ashland Avenue

The first blow knocked Odelia's head back. Her face swole up immediately and blood trickled down.

"Not so hard, goddammit!"

Dewie smiled, but too quickly, too apologetically. "Sorry, Mama."

"Sorry my black ass! You like this shit."

"You want to find that shelter or you want me to go to jail?"

"Put some bruises on my arms and shoulders," Odelia said.

Dewie worked her over more carefully, punching her upper arms and shoulder bones hard enough to show injury, she hoped, but not enough to hurt real bad. She hoped.

"Hit me once on the other side of my face, but don't knock me out. I ain't no motherfucking punching bag."

Dewie cocked his fist back.

"Hold on just a minute," Odelia said. "I don't want to fall

229

down." She sat on the sofa. "All right, now do your stuff."

The blow blinded her for a moment, jarring her brain. Lights flashed in a field of black. She shook her head. "Who do you think you are, Mohammed Ali? I told you, don't hurt me too damn rough."

"Mama, if I wanted to hurt you, you wouldn't have no skull left."

She examined her face in the mirror. "If this ain't good enough you can find that shelter your own damn self."

"Mama, you are now a for real battered woman."

She handed him her cellphone. "You stay right here and wait. Soon's I'm in the shelter I'll call you with the address. Andre, you watch and make sure he don't wander off."

"Yes, ma'am," Andre, who had watched everything without speaking a word, said.

As she started to leave she turned to Dewie. "Don't feel so damn proud of yourself, tough guy. I'm still your mama. I put pampers on your shitty little ass when you was a baby, and I'm still big enough and mean enough to whup your ass any time I want. Just because I let you do this, ain't nothing changed."

As he watched Mama go, Dewie felt the thick power, the hard armor, the solid strength inside him. He had enjoyed hitting her. Of course, she was his mother, she had raised him, and he loved her, and he owed her. But maybe she owed him something too, for all the times she made fun of him, put him down, bought Michael everything new and gave dumb, crazy Dewie the leftovers. Michael's used clothes. The food Michael left on his plate.

The hell nothing ain't changed.

II

Savoy Court Apartments

66 Sit down and relax." Marilyn disappeared into a back room. "I'll be out in a moment."

"I presume you're going to slip into something more comfortable," Jim called to her.

"Don't you wish."

The sofa was large and lumpy, made for comfort, not appearance. Across the back hung a rainbow colored, knitted wool rug. Plants filled Marilyn's apartment. Cacti on the dining room table. Philodendron sprawled over issues of JET on the coffee table. Shelf after shelf of red impatiens, purple and pink hydrangea, geraniums, coleus and many more he did not recognize moistened the air and scented the room with green.

"You should start a nursery," he said when she brought out a tray of tea things. What he really wanted was a good solid meal, but Marilyn was so obsessed with finding the children she had apparently forgotten about food.

"I couldn't do that," Marilyn said as she sat next to him and poured. She had changed into another professional woman's uniform, attractive but businesslike. Jim had hoped for something sexier.

"Why's that?"

"I like to be around people too much. I love plants, but they don't talk back."

"I knew you talked to your plants—that's why they grow so well." The tea smelled and looked strange. Jim took a sip to be polite. "Anyway, I only meant when you're burnt out on social work."

She shook her head. "I'll never burn out."

"Famous last words."

"I can't even imagine it. I worked too hard to get where I am. You're already looking ahead, though, aren't you? You need more money."

Jim shrugged, vaguely ashamed although she wasn't trying to guilt-trip him. "I'd like to marry a woman who made a hundred grand a year so I could afford to stay on at the hospital, but they want husbands who're even richer. Women hardly ever marry guys who make less money than they do. It's a law they passed in 1973."

Marilyn laughed. "Why'd you want to be a social worker in the first place? You could be selling upscale houses."

"I felt guilty. I wanted to help. And maybe I wanted to rebel against my father."

"Oh, Lord, we have to take too many psychiatry courses. We start to turn them on ourselves. Are you sorry? You'd probably have a lot of hot dates if you made big money."

Jim wanted to shake her, hold her. Is that all she thought he was after?

"I just don't feel all there with the women I take out." He shifted his weight, leaning back on the soft cushions. "I talk and laugh and enjoy myself. We flirt and exchange life stories and I fall in love and I let it show—and that's one weakness, I know. But my work also comes between us. I can't talk about my job to secretaries, law students or receptionists."

"I know what you mean."

"Sure. How do you tell a junior stockbroker or a dental hygienist about a woman whose two preschool children died in a fire because she left them alone to go out smoking crack with her boyfriend? Or the woman brought to the emergency room by her live-in lesbian lover who had just beaten her senseless? Or the man who keeps asking us to operate to remove the secret radio space aliens implanted in his brain?"

"Other people just can't understand," Marilyn said.

"I go to parties and feel like a dipshit while my middle class friends stand around and talk about stock options and legal briefs."

"What do you say?"

"Nothing about my work, not anymore. After I first started at the welfare office, I was at a party with a bunch of my college buddies. When we got drunk I told them about a woman I'd interviewed that week."

As he talked, Jim stared at Marilyn's legs sheathed in transparent hose, then at her face, a living embodiment of the shiny black African statues decorating her living room. He wanted to see those liquid black eyes from across a pillow, behind a wedding veil. He wanted to tell her that, but he couldn't let his desperate, lonely neediness scare her away too.

To cover the pause in his conversation, he sipped more tea. "That woman weighed about four hundred pounds, had ten kids, couldn't read or write and talked to me as though I were the idiot. They laughed about her all night. I did too. The next morning, laying in bed with my hangover, I felt guilty, as though I'd violated her privacy. She was a real person—however messed up and stupid...not a joke. But my buddies couldn't see that and neither do the women I go out. They're sincere, liberal and concerned, but too sheltered."

"Exactly." Hot ginseng tea warming her belly, shoes off, feet up and surrounded by her green babies, Marilyn relaxed. As the active ingredients of four Tylenol capsules circulated through her bloodstream the sharp pain released its grip on her skull. In the car she had thought of something important, something so obvious she ought to have seen it immediately, would have if she weren't so distracted by worry.

Where would two lost little girls running from a dangerous man go? What would Latasha think to do?

"What about you?" Jim asked. "Why're you a social worker?"

Marilyn closed her eyes and took a deep breath. "Because I couldn't do any other job, not and be happy. I'd rather not talk about it. It just brings up other memories."

"Forget I asked."

She laughed. "You are too accommodating. It's the same old story, just my variation on the theme. I married young and foolishly. He was handsome, tall and muscular, not to mention charming and sexy. He was going to revitalize the Civil Rights Movement and the Black Panthers, and start a free vaccination program for children. He was full of fire and piss, but one kept putting out the other—marching and picketing one week, then drinking every night the next. After we split up I worked as a secretary and went to night school until I earned my degree in social work."

"How'd you wind up at the shelter?" Jim asked.

"I suppose you could say it was personal."

"Oh. He beat you up." He suddenly stared down at his shoes. "I'm sorry, I shouldn't have said that."

"No, you shouldn't have, but it doesn't matter. Women being ashamed is part of the problem. So many stay in horrible marriages because they're too humiliated to admit they need help. I didn't want to either."

"But you were smart enough to get out."

Marilyn shook her head. "You might not be as sheltered as your middle class friends, but there's a lot you still don't know. He divorced me. I even contested it, though it cost me a lot in legal fees."

"Why?"

"I loved him."

"I guess I am stupid."

"Smart enough not to ask why he left me."

"I'm still wondering why you didn't leave him."

Don't cry, goddammit Her eyes blurred although she didn't want them to. Jim was only a friend, but she didn't want to drive him away.

Her womb contracted and released, spasm after uncontrollable spasm, her vagina vibrating in intense, warm, erotic yet painful, lonely orgasms of shame.

"He was right to beat me up."

That startled Jim. "I...err...thought that men weren't ever justified in hitting women, outside of self-defense. It just isn't right."

"That's the party line," Marilyn said. "I believe it, too, for the women I see every day who've been bruised, cut, shot and burnt because they were late cooking supper or the kid got a bad report card or they cheated on him with the entire Cardinal baseball team. Even when the anger is justified the violence isn't. Except for me. My husband never hit me until he found out I'd stopped taking the Pill."

"Just because you wanted a child?"

"No... We'd agreed to put off having children until we had more money, but he wanted babies too. It was because I'd been lying about taking the Pill for two years. Two years, Jim—but I wasn't pregnant. That hurt us both so much he had to hit me and I had to let him. After we fussed and fought about whose fault it was, we finally agreed to have the medical tests done. He had viable sperm coming out his ears. I was infertile...that's why he left me."

"I'm sorry."

"You didn't do it."

"Still, he had no right to leave you because you couldn't have children."

"Sure he did. He wanted them too, Jim, we both did, very badly. I still do. I would have left him if I'd found out it was him that was sterile. I wish I could leave me."

"Do you still love him?"

"No, so don't be jealous." Marilyn grinned at the expression on his face. "You're very obvious, you know."

"So I've probably made you reject me already, before I could even ask you to dinner."

"Jim," Marilyn said. "You're right. We haven't even eaten a meal together, but you already think you love me. Have you ever considered counseling?"

"I'm trying to slow my heart down, really. I'm just afraid that another man will win yours while I hesitate."

"Hey, give me enough time to make up my mind whether or not I'd accept a dinner date. Who knows, maybe I'm as bad as the other women. I say I want a nice guy but I'm not attracted to the nice guys who are attracted to me."

"So I'll be a mean son-of-a-bitch."

"You aren't the type," Marilyn said. "Besides, you can't really want a woman my age. Though, maybe I should take you to bed and find out why so many men prefer younger women."

"Have I even made a move on you yet? I know right now you're only thinking about Janie and her kids."

The shelter!

Marilyn threw the cup and saucer onto the coffee table and rushed to the phone in her kitchen. Sara picked it up on the third ring, thank God.

"Marilyn!" she said. "Where are you? Mildred's having kittens."

"Have you seen Latasha and Shontell, Janie Braxton's two little girls?"

"They're not here, but they called a while ago."

"My God, where are they?"

"Take it easy. I gave Latasha directions."

Sara explained to Marilyn, who then shouted to Jim: "Grab your jacket."

As they started to scramble, Marilyn looked into his warm, concerned eyes and knew he wanted to put his arms around her and comfort her. She wanted that too but couldn't let him. Besides, he couldn't help her. His hug wouldn't soothe her, couldn't vanquish her pain.

He was a nice man, a good man, maybe even a man she could love in time. But he was only a man. He could be the best and biggest lover in the world, but he could not expand her womb.

He wasn't a baby.

III

Holy Virgin Mother of God Medical Center

Judith poured through the four books by the Apostles all afternoon, then read Acts and the many epistles of Paul. Looking, searching, seeking—but not finding.

Judith thought about when Janie ran away. Only eight years ago, but it seemed like an event from before Columbus discovered America. Yet Janie couldn't be as old as twenty-three. Whenever Judith dreamed of Janie, she was always a little girl.

The relatives of other patients came and went. Willie Lee talked a long time to an obese, thickly sweating black man whose son had been shot in the head two days ago. Like Janie, he was still unconscious.

"Goddamn drugs," the man said. "All the kids think about these days is money and drugs, money for drugs. They don't care about nothing or nobody—God, they parents or theyselves. Just money and drugs. Sometimes I wish I never moved up here from Mississippi, but my cousin back home says kids're near about as bad down there as in St. Louis."

"City or country," Willie Lee said. "It doesn't matter to the Devil."

"I took my boys to church every Sunday. This one's the youngest. He used to love to hear the choir belt out them hymns, praising the Lord at the top of their voices. Now he's close to death and it's all on account of drugs."

"Our daughter used to worship with us too, until she fell away from the Lord and into a life of sin I'd be bitterly ashamed to tell you about. Last night she met up with a guy who wasn't satisfied taking what she gave away free to any man wanted it. He had to beat her head in too."

"It's a crying shame," the other father said. "Just when we're getting older and think they'll soon be out on their own, supporting themselves, letting us enjoy the rest of our lives— then come to find out, we got it even worser than when they was babies."

The other man paused, staring vacantly out into the Neuro ICU, then said, "The doctor tells me my boy probably won't never be back completely normal. He's thrown his whole life away. I'd give everything except my eternal soul to be seventeen years old again. But these kids, I swear, it seems they hate life. I don't know where that hate comes from. It drives them to that crack cocaine and where it starts, must be the Devil."

"That's right," Willie Lee said. "My girl and your boy, Satan dragged them both down."

When the man was leaving, Willie Lee shook his hand. "You have my sincerest sympathy."

"Thank you kindly, brother," the other man said. "May God have mercy on our childrens. Let us pray for them both."

After that, Willie Lee sat for hours without speaking or moving. Judith thought he was sleeping, but every time she glanced over at him his eyes were open.

At supper time she dragged him with her to the cafeteria, but she could only drink coffee and pick at a Jell-O salad, afraid something would happen to Janie while she was away.

After supper, Willie Lee paced back and forth like a prisoner locked in a jail cell.

"Judith, honey—"

"We're not going to have a drink."

"Just one or two, then we'll come back. We're not doing any good here. Nothing will happen while we're gone."

"You're a preacher," Judith said. "You remember that. It's human to have a weakness and we both drink too much. But you're going to stay here with me as long as you have to."

"She doesn't even know we've come. All she needs now is good doctors and nurses."

"Willie Lee Braxton, I have been your wife going on thirty years. It's been good and it's been hard, and mostly it's been good and hard, but I always stuck by you. I stayed with you when you punched me out. I stayed with you when you caned my daughter's back until she couldn't walk. I've kept my wedding vows like not many women do these days."

"I ain't never said a word against you. I wouldn't."

"Now it's time for you to just set yourself down and wait. The bottle will be there for both of us just like it's been for years, but we ain't leaving this hospital until this is finished. We ain't getting drunk again until our little girl either wakes up or dies. I know in my heart she's going to do one or the other before the sun rises again."

"The doctor said she could stay in one of them comas for years, like people in the newspaper."

"I vastly appreciate what these doctors are doing for Janie, but deep down, I perceive she's going to make her choice this very night. And, may God forgive me, I swear I don't know which one I really want."

"I do."

"I don't pretend to be strong or perfect or the best wife and mother, but I did my duty. I did it when I was glad and I did it when I wanted to kill you, Janie and myself."

"We all have our burdens. Janie was the biggest one God could have given us. She was a punishment against us."

"Then maybe we're still too sinful, for I don't see any two ways around this. It's our bounden duty to take them two little girls in and give them a home, at least until Janie's well enough to be a mother again."

"Then woman, you just go straight to Hell."

"You're a righteous man," Judith said. "I always honored you for that, and I thought you understood God never promised your lot would be easy."

"Not them two children. Not that bastard child of sin ain't got no father. Not a mixed-breed girl as retarded as her mother. That can't be God's purpose. We put up with Janie for twenty-three years, that's punishment enough."

"You can't quit the Lord, Willie Lee."

"We can't carry that cross. There's no way—just no way."

The freezing water of her husband's cold anger dashed against Judith's face.

"I'm reading the Good Book and praying on it," she said. "That's all I request of you. Pray on it, Willie Lee. God won't come down from the sky and tell us what's right and what's wrong, that's why he gave us a conscience. We've got to search our hearts."

Willie Lee pointed his finger, a stubby granite pillar aimed at her chest. "Judith, you've been a good wife and a good mother all these years. I know how hard you've worked. I know what's in your mind now, and it won't happen. Janie is gone from us and you can't bring her back by taking in those two worthless kids. You think we were too hard on Janie, and we can make it up to God for the way Janie turned out by raising her two children."

"You've got it backward."

"You're the one better start facing to the front. Janie left us of her own free will, because she chose sinning over God. She wasn't never too smart, but there's plenty even dumber than her who've accepted Jesus into their lives. That's what's important. Janie couldn't ever have learned to read, but she could've listened to the word of God—if she so pleased. She had ears, but she would not hear."

"Maybe we said it the wrong way for her to really understand."

Judith wanted to tell him the secret why Janie left that night, but she was too ashamed to confess the torture inside her heart for the last eight years. To think she'd wanted Janie to abort Latasha. It was a weight like to crush her soul.

"Janie is not our guilt, Judith. We tried as hard as we could. She turned away from the love of God. She chose her life. In a way, she chose this, her death. Raising them two grandkids won't redeem us, because we don't need saving. We believe. We're born-again."

"That doesn't mean we just coast along until we die."

"We don't have to prove anything to God or ourselves. Those children are not our responsibility."

Judith slammed her Bible shut. "Then whose are they?"

"That's in the hands of the Lord. I do know we're too old and weak to handle them. God asks the difficult, not the impossible."

"They're not monsters, Willie Lee. That Latasha, she's got brains enough for her and us and more leftover besides. The little one, she's slow, but she's real quiet and sweet. She's not contrary like Janie."

"Love them all you want, Judith. Send them presents at Christmas. But they will not live with us. I won't have it."

"Willie Lee—"

"I'll leave, Judith. You won't never hear nor see of me again, I swear as God is my witness. I'm dead on serious. I won't watch two more children slide into wickedness like their mother done."

IV

St. Louis Abused Women's Shelter (secret location)

The tall white lesbo with tattoos up and down her arms tapped the eraser of her pencil on the desk top as she shuffled through the many papers she had just filled out on Odelia.

"Everything appears in order, Ms. Whitfield. You can stay here at least tonight. Tomorrow morning when we have more time, we must discuss some other matters."

"Like what?" Goddamned bossy bulldagger bitch.

"Basically, your plans for the future. I realize you're upset and in shock—that's quite natural. But you must begin to make some decisions. Do you want to divorce your husband? Where do you want to live? What do you plan to do for money? Can you obtain employment in the near future? Would you benefit from some education or job skill training? And, certainly not least, how is your emotional state? You must see a counselor for an initial discussion. We have a very good one on staff, Marilyn

Patterson. You'll meet her later."

"I don't want no damn examination. I just want to get away from that motherfucker I married."

"Of course, Ms. Whitfield."

Butch kept her cool, showing her irritation and surprise only by blinking too much.

What did she expect, gratitude? She want Odelia to kiss her honky ass for the great favor of staying there one night, like it was the Ritz-Carlton instead of a dumpy old remodeled apartment building? Why should Odelia have to answer so many questions about her personal life? What was the bitch talking about, future plans and counseling? This place was as bad as the welfare office and Social Security. Be all up in your business before sending you a stinking little check every month.

"But everything costs money," the woman said. "We find economic necessity is the one thing that either prevents women from leaving their battering partner or forces them to return. It would be irresponsible of us not to look at the entire picture. We'll refer you to any services you need to become economically independent. And all our residents are required to take classes that teach them to improve their self esteem. That is absolutely vital. You must learn, to your very inside core, you are a worthwhile person. You don't deserve to be beaten. That's the bottom line."

"Thank you. Thank you Jesus. May I use your telephone in private for a moment? I left the house so fast, I forgot my cell phone."

"I can't tie up this line, but we have a pay phone out by the kitchen doorway. First, though, why don't you have Celia look at that cut over your eye? She's our volunteer R.N. We serve breakfast at seven o'clock. Nobody wants to have to come here, but since you are, we'll do our best to help you."

"You've already helped me more than you know."

SUN OF SUNS FOUR

Dreamtime

"I don't care about Solange." Janie threw a chunk of splintery wood at the collapsed altar. "She wasn't really my friend no way. I want to go back to my children."

"They hate and fear you," the Indian ghost said.

"Not me!"

"Life is hard and cruel for you." Icicles hung from his voice. "After you die, Dewie will be invincible. Already he is more powerful than he understands, just because he raped and almost killed you. He stole your life, your strength and your future. You have always been small, weak and stupid."

Janie fell to her knees. It was the truth. But she couldn't live without Latasha and Shontell.

"You're going to make me die here some way, ain't you? You're going to kill me because you're so old and strong. I hate you."

When you know just how powerful I am, you will understand you cannot resist. You must learn how I have been increasing my strength for over six hundred years."

Dark gray fog circled her. She didn't live through this movie, but watched its pictures while the Indian explained them.

"I hunted the spirits of the fifty-two fifty-two sacrifices through Dirtworld until I ate them all and absorbed their spiritual energy into my air-soul. You can see their dead husks throughout this city.

"After that, I fed on acts of violence and cruelty in Peopleland. I want to regain material life by possessing a body, so when I have felt strong enough, I have tried to escape Dirtworld. Over time, I have learned to transfer some of my power and energy. Soon I will totally possess Dewie.

"After the downfall of the City of the Sun the Great People scattered and reverted to the hunting and fishing ways of our ancestors. They stayed in little family groups and grew only small fields of maize. They did not build mounds or worship Elder Brother Sun.

"One of these groups, the Illini-wek, lived near the Father of Waters, what you call the Mississippi River. Their great war chief, Ouatoga, killed his sixteen year old daughter Laughing Moon for meeting at night with an enemy Osage warrior. Her father-shed blood, though no longer virgin, supplied me with the strength to possess a large eagle and transform it into a giant armored bird with huge claws and teeth. Every morning this Piasaw Bird swooped down on Ouatoga's people. It carried a man, woman or child off to a nearby cave and ate them. Arrows couldn't penetrate its hard scaly armor. Eventually, Ouatoga tricked me by sacrificing himself. His death provided his warriors the opportunity to shoot the Pi-a-saw Bird in the soft spot under each wing and the monster died from the poison on their copper arrowheads. I learned, and I ate Ouatoga's soul.

"In 1736 in the town of Kaskaskia, just a short way south of the City of the Sun, an Indian named Bear Claw eloped with a woman named Maria. When her father, a Frenchman named Bernard, caught up with the young couple, he and his friends tied the Indian to a log and drowned him in the river. Before he died, Bear Claw cursed Bernard and the entire town, swearing he and Maria would be reunited within a year.

"This violence and mutual hatred opened another gateway to Peopleland for me. Before the passing of twelve moons, Maria died of a broken heart and Bernard was killed in a duel. Kaskaskia took more time. The Mississippi River steadily eroded away at it. The flood of 1881 destroyed the original city and turned the surrounding area into an island. The flood of 1973 drove out all but a few of its remaining inhabitants. The flood of 1993 engulfed it entirely."

"As my price for making Bear Claw's curse a reality, I ate the souls of him, Bernard and Maria.

"In the early nineteenth century in Edwardsville Illinois a few miles north and east of the City of the Sun, I gained access to owners of the Three Mile House, a hotel, when they murdered a guest for his money. Before I was done, they had murdered both runaway slaves who sought sanctuary there, thinking it a stop on the underground railroad, and paying guests, thirteen people in all. I held the spirits prisoner. In the middle of the twentieth century, when a young family moved in and actually made friends with the resident ghosts, I frightened them away with evil manifestations.

In Alton Illinois where those Illini-wek people used to live, I sent a plague of smallpox to kill thousands of Confederate prisoners during the Civil War.

"Later in the nineteenth century a wealthy brewer named William Lemp built his family mansion on South 13th Street in St. Louis across the river from the City of the Sun. He located it over the largest natural cave formations below any city in America, which enabled me to use what I had learned to influence the family members.

"In 1904, William Lemp put a bullet in his temple. His daughter Else shot herself in 1920. William Jr. killed himself in the same fashion in 1922. In 1949 I ate the soul of the last of William's children when I persuaded Charles Lemp to put a gun to his head.

"By now, I knew enough about projecting my energy that I was able to retain a spirit link to the Lemp mansion. After someone bought the dilapidated building in 1975 and began remodeling it, I played experimental games with the workers and, later, with the staff and customers of the restaurant. I turned TVs on and off, opened and shut doors, lit candles, played notes on the piano, knocked wine glasses off tables and materialized strongly enough to give many people the impression they were being watched. I also made noises, such as the hooves of horses from the area where they were once tethered. When I focused my attention, I could make myself appear as a man for several seconds.

Janie remembered hearing people talk about the ghosts in that restaurant. She had never been stupid enough to believe such crazy stories.

"In 1915 I possessed my first body, a housewife named Pearl Curran who unknowingly opened herself up to me when she worked a Ouija board at a party. Because I was invited, I didn't need prior bloodshed, but could not commit violence. I remained because every taste of flesh-life gave me pleasure.

"Calling myself `Patience Worth,' I spoke through her, dictating to Mrs. Curran over four million words of stories, poems, inquiry answers and three novels, including one about the life of Christ, The Sorry Tale. Soon I was famous. It amused me, and I learned.

"In 1949, for the first time, I gained the power to successfully possess a person and cause evil even without prior bloodshed. A St. Louis woman gave her fourteen year old nephew a Ouija board and, once again, this opened a doorway for me between Dirtworld and Peopleland. At first I could only make the boy hear scratching sounds, but after the aunt died and I consumed her soul, the boy heard footsteps. Soon I took over the boy and entertained myself by levitating his bed and writing words on his skin in rashes. I gave him the supernatural strength to smash furniture. I drained the warmth from around him so his room remained unnaturally cold despite all attempts to heat it. He was taken to Alexian Brothers Hospital and the Catholic Church authorized the first exorcism in America in over 100 years.

"My possession of the boy later inspired an author to write a novel that was made into a movie. The fright and horror of its readers and viewers further strengthened me. THE EXORCIST opened in movie theaters in 1973, and that's where your father and mother went on their first date.

"I have been waiting for you a long time, Janie Elizabeth Braxton."

CHAPTER THIRTEEN

I

Compton near Park

In his bedroom, Terry strapped his shoulder holster on under his windbreaker. He decided to take his Smith and Wesson .38 caliber semiautomatic.

That Latasha was smart, but not even the smartest person in the world could alter Fate. The Divine Plan called for Terry to find Betty. That was why those girls pounded on his front door. It was no accident, no coincidence. It was a Sign. They were going to lead him straight to Betty. Terry believed in Signs.

Fate would not be denied.

Fate happened.

II

St. Louis Abused Women's Shelter (secret location)

Odelia found a huge white woman talking on the pay phone like a teenager.

"Mona, Betty here. Yeah, I'm fine. I finally left Terry, that spooky son of a bitch. You should see all the bruises he gave me, the motherfucker."

The bitch had a dumpy, flabby figure—at least three hundred pounds of disgusting, floppy, sagging flesh. Thin brown hair matted her scalp and she wore wire rim glasses.

"Oh, fine, fine," Humpty Dumpty said. "I've started taking GED classes so I can find a job. How're your kids?"

Jesus. And only one goddamn pay phone in the whole lousy joint. What a fucked up stink hole—cold, bitchy women in charge of stupid, putrid sheep without the guts to fight back.

Not one of her husbands ever laid a hand on Odelia more than once. She lived with Mr. Grimes her first husband for thirteen years, from when she left high school until she was pregnant with Dewie. That's probably why the boy acted such a fool. Those first few months after she finally left the bastard she never had enough to eat.

She'd always kept Mr. Grimes in his place, Mr. Sykes too. And the three or four cats she lived with in between marriages and all the men who followed her like hungry dogs whenever she let them have a whiff of it. Even Duke, the slick, high tone shit eating pimp who'd looked out for her when she was on the street corners. Even Duke, who taught her how to snatch billfolds while licking dicks in cars and how to get credit cards in fake names. Even Duke, who beat every pussy in his stable once a week so none of them would withhold any of their earnings. Even Duke, she didn't allow to lay a hand on her.

As she waited for the fat woman to finish yapping to her friend she looked at the women in the nearby lounge. Such a bunch of pitiful, droopy-chinned, teary-eyed, sorry-for-themselves pigs she had never seen in all her years. She didn't blame their husbands. If she was the man of one of these hangdog creepos she'd put a fist upside their head herself. Why didn't they fight back? They were losers and loved it.

As Odelia stood there, she noticed that dyke who interviewed her approach the old lady in charge and say something in a soft voice. She caught the words: "Janie...Latasha...Shontell."

Odelia moved as close as she could to the pair while still apparently waiting for the phone.

"You say they're on their way?" the old bitch asked.

"Latasha called while you were out. Then Marilyn called too. I wanted to tell you when you returned, but I had an interview."

"They may stay for the weekend, but someone must contact Children's Services first thing Monday morning. Make that clear to Marilyn when she arrives."

"Yes, Mildred."

"According to Marilyn, their mother is in the hospital. It's a very sad situation, but we're not a baby-sitting service. I tried to convince Marilyn, but she wouldn't listen."

"She cares a lot, Mildred."

"She's personally involved, that's the trouble. And she's

stubborn. When people like her are pulling in the same direction as you, you love them. When they pull against you, you want to crack their skulls open."

"Mildred, we all love Marilyn."

"We all depend on her too much. It makes her feel needed, but no matter how much she does she's not satisfied. Right now, it's time for me to retreat to my quiet little house and drink a hot brandy to steady my nerves. And to think, there was a time when I could stay up all night running off strike fliers or preparing food for breadlines."

"Don't worry, Mildred. Nothing's going to happen here tonight."

III

Dreamtime

"Of course you're stronger than me," Janie said. "Everybody's bigger and stronger than me. I'm just a stupid weak little girl. But I got my man Michael to protect me."

"Then why do you run to the shelter for abused women so often?"

"Bad men on the street jump me."

"When you go to the shelter, you always tell Marilyn Michael beat you up."

"Sometimes I get confused because Michael has to act mean to me. He really loves me but he can't show it, or other guys would think he's weak. When bad men on the street jump me, he tells people it was him, but it weren't. Not really."

"Marilyn doesn't believe that."

"See, if people start thinking Michael gone soft, then he got lots of trouble. If the other dope suppliers and gangsters ever think he's pussy whipped, especially by a skinny white girl like me, they'll move in on his business. He'd have to kill somebody, and he don't want that, not if he don't have to. So he has to make other people think he whips me. Even his own family, they think that. It took me a while to understand, on account of I'm slow."

"It's time for you to really understand."

The cold gray mist seized her. "No!" Janie screamed. "I won't watch. I won't, I won't...."

The last day of the month was Thursday. Michael left the house with several buddies and Janie didn't see him again that night. The next day, Friday the first, she received her and Shontell's SSI and Latasha's ADC checks. She cashed them at the nearby drugstore and hoped Michael would stay away the entire weekend.

Maybe he was driving across the country to pick up a shipment of white powder in New York City or Los Angeles, or pulling a burglary heist in Kansas City or Chicago, or cribbing with some young woman until they finished snorting all his coke or simply carousing with friends through St. Louis' after-hours joints. Or in jail. A hospital. The morgue.

She gave Odelia the three hundred dollars she demanded even though they lived in Michael's room and weren't allowed to eat much out of Odelia's refrigerator. Janie caught the bus to Wal-Mart and bought clothes and a winter jacket for Latasha and clothes and a large supply of Pampers for Shontell. She also added to the bills in the lining of Latasha's little pink backpack.

When the stack was thick enough to pay the first month's rent and deposit on an apartment, she would move herself and the children away from Ashland.

Michael arrived late that night while Janie, Odelia, Yolanda and Tiffany were watching DICK TRACY on cable. He still looked sharp in his brown leather suit but the pink shirt was wrinkled and his shiny black boots were scuffed. He smelled like an open bottle of Mad Dog 30-30.

He slammed the front door, grabbed Janie by the arm and dragged her to their room.

"Where's my money?" he shouted, throwing her onto the bed.

"What're you talking about?"

Whack! He slapped her across the cheek. Hard. Janie fell back.

The money, bitch. Hand it over."

"What—?"

Whack! again. Whack! Whack! Whack! Back and forth across her mouth he swept his hand. Her lip bled. Her face felt broken, smashed.

"My purse. Michael, please—"

He picked up her handbag, dumped it onto the bed, dug out the folded bills, counted them, then slapped her again.

"Where's the rest?"

"There ain't no—"

Whack! Whack!

"Bitch! You got almost thirteen hundred dollars today. You say only two hundred's left? Bullshit!"

"I give your mama three hundred on the rent. I bought clothes for the kids, and Pampers."

Whack! Whack! "You're lying, you goddamn skinny white whore. You give me more money or I'll bounce your ass onto that street so hard you'll break the goddamn concrete. Every black dude in the hood'll stick it to you."

"Michael—"

Whack!

In her crib in the corner, Shontell started crying.

"Now you woke her," Janie said. "Be quiet, little baby, it's all right." She started to move to pick her daughter up and comfort her, but Michael grabbed her shoulder and flung her down again.

"Let her cry! That's all you whores know how to do anyway. That little white bitch of yours is probably pretending to be asleep." Michael grabbed Latasha's arm and lifted her from the large easy chair where she lay curled up in blankets.

Janie leapt at him. "You leave her be!"

He pushed Janie back. "I ain't hurt her none—did I, `Tasha?"

"No, Michael."

"That's right. Now get your sorry little ass in the front room with the others until I'm gone."

Janie shoved at his chest. "I don't care none what you do to me, but you hurt either one of them kids, I'll cut your balls off. I don't care if I go to jail the rest of my life."

"Shut your mouth and give me some more fucking money."

"You got to leave us something for the month. Shontell's your own baby daughter. She needs Pampers. She's not two yet, she's still a baby, Michael. You can't leave her go without no Pampers."

"I'll do what I want. You take care of them kids. What else

you good for anyway? All you know how to do is open your legs and have babies. And you fuck like a snake. So don't pull no crap on me."

"I said I ain't got no more—"

Whack! Whack!

"You can't lie for shit."

He quickly checked out the rest of her purse and her piles of clothing, then turned to the children's things. That's when he noticed the rip in the lining of Latasha's backpack and found Janie's escape money.

"You goddamn thieving bitch! You come here, stay in my goddamn house, eat my goddamn food and then you hold out on me."

He punched her in the gut with his fist, knocked her in the head, the chest. Yanked off his leather belt, tore her shirt off and whipped the buckle across her back.

"You think you suddenly grow a brain?" he yelled. "You dare hold out on me? I'll learn you, girl. I'll learn you real good."

He hit her again and again with the belt. The buckle bit into her skin, gouging out chunks of flesh. The blood ran down her back, soaking her pants, the blanket and sheet.

Just like your daddy," Michael said. "I'll beat the living hell out of you just like your daddy done."

Janie screamed until her throat rasped so sore she could barely make a sound. Her shouting and Shontell's crying must have been heard around the block, but she knew nobody'd do nothing. His people in the front room hated her and the neighbors were too scared of Odelia and her sons to call the police.

Janie didn't want cops anyway. She was evil and wicked. She deserved the beating. In the last month she had screwed two other men. She even gave one of them fifty dollars. Michael sometimes let his friends have her for money, but he would hate to learn she wanted to fuck any man but him. And for her to pay another guy for sex—that would be a blow to Michael's manhood he would never forgive. He'd kill her if he knew.

So she deserved this whipping. She deserved more. Micheal was right, she wasn't good for anything, not even fucking. She enjoyed it, but she wasn't pretty. She didn't have large tits and a big ass. She was lucky to have a strong, handsome man like Michael.

Michael loved her. Yeah, he hit her a lot, took her money and left her alone for days while he slept with other women. But he always came back to her—that was the important thing. He never took any of the party hardy, fly girl freaks to his home, but he always returned there to Janie. And he didn't kick her out, although he could any time he wanted. She was his girlfriend and everybody knew it. And when she left him, grabbed the kids and ran to the shelter or a friend's house, he always took her back.

Lying in Michael's bed later that night, Latasha asleep beside her, the house hushed and still, Janie thought about Michael's hard, muscular body, how his sleek, brown skin gleamed with sweat when he made love to her. She adored his deep, husky voice when he told her how much he cherished and adored her, that he would always take care of her. She remembered twiddling the crinkly black hairs sprouting from his chest.

He was so passionate. He made her feel so soft and open and needed when he stroked her body, then entered. And when he came, a fire burned in her heart, melting her flesh into soft wax, making her nerves sing and thrum like electric guitar strings.

Despite her raw wounds, fire danced in Janie's flesh. It coursed through her blood like burning oil, warming and strengthening her. She would live through this pain, through all pain. As long as she had her children, she was happy. They were worth anything and everything she suffered.

She was stronger than Michael. She could take the beatings. For him, she could bear any torture or hardship. She needed some money for her babies. He could have the rest. As long as she had enough for Latasha and Shontell, Janie was satisfied.

Janie hugged Latasha and softly sang her favorite song: "Hush little baby, don't you cry, Jesus loves you...Papa don't preach in the midnight hour...it's like a prayer."

IV

St. Louis Abused Women's Shelter (secret location)

When the lard ball finally hung up the phone Odelia grabbed it before anyone else could butt in ahead of her and called the house. She told Dewie the address of the shelter then said in a harsh whisper, "Get your ass over here straight away. Those little girls're coming."

V

Ashland Avenue

Dewie slammed the phone down. "Let's roll."

Andre, Turk and Lorenzo tossed down their cards. Lorenzo pulled open the front door and stepped onto the porch.

Car headlights flipped on outside and guns opened fire. Blood sprayed out the holes in Lorenzo's back as he fell in jerky, spastic motions.

"Shit!" Andre dropped to the floor. "They got TEC-9s."

Turk flattened against the wall. "Must be Marauders. Dewie, the one you let get away this morning recognized you. They think it's payback time now."

Ambush. Dewie frowned. He was so close to the girls, to the sacrifices that would make him invulnerable. How could he die now? It wasn't fair. His Indian-strength couldn't protect him from high caliber bullets, could it?

Maybe. He'd killed Marko with two blows, stopped the whore's knife and dodged bullets to take out the first two Marauders. He totaled a car with his bare hands.

What couldn't he do? Time to find out.

Dewie stepped outside.

VI

Streets near St. Louis Abused Women's Shelter

As Terry drove around, the muffler of his old Buick LeSabre rattled, making Latasha want to scream.

As they had agreed, she deliberately gave him false directions, but kept him headed correctly overall. She hoped to confuse him by taking him two blocks past the nearest right turn, then having him double back again, but it made her head hurt because she didn't know the area. Once she had him drive south of Highway 44, then tried to take him back north As he drove along a street which did not have an overpass over the highway, Terry gave her a strange look.

"You sure you remember what they told you? Seems to me we're just going around in loopy circles."

"I was wrong a little bit," Latasha said.

"I have to be at work pretty soon. I can't drive over every street between here and downtown."

As they zoomed past the blocks lit by orange cones of streetlights, Latasha frantically tried to think of a plan. She didn't believe Terry wanted to hurt her or Shontell, but ever since they started talking about the shelter she had sensed something lurking inside him like a rattlesnake under a rock. He seemed too nice, too concerned about two little children he didn't know—too interested in the shelter.

Shontell whimpered and pressed her face against Latasha's sleeve until Latasha put her arm around the other girl's shoulders. What a pest. Shontell still clutched Andy tightly to her side.

At least her little sister was good for something. She would hold on to and protect the stuffed dog while Latasha tried to think how to reach the shelter without Terry learning its location.

He slowed at every intersection so Latasha could read the street signs. That was hard in the dark even when they weren't crumpled, defaced or missing.

"What street are you looking for?" Terry asked. "I know this entire area. I can go right to it. You don't have to tell me the exact block. Every street is plenty long. Even if I wanted to find this shelter place—and I don't have no reason to...it'd still be like looking for a speck of dust in a sandpile."

"I don't know how to say it. But I'll know it when I see it. I can read that good."

That was a small fib, but she didn't think Terry could know that. She was the top reader of her second grade class, but many St. Louis streets had funny names. However, when she saw it she did recognize the street:

HENRIETTA AV

"Look, I've got to get to work."

"We're real close," Latasha said. "We're so hot we're almost on fire."

Jim parked his car where Marilyn pointed, presumably several blocks from the shelter. "You sure you won't let me take you to the door?"

"Look," she said. "maybe it seems silly to you, but I just can't. That's the rule: No men. Not inside, not allowed to know our location."

"I understand, but look at this neighborhood." He waved his arm. "You could get mugged or raped just walking around the block."

"It's not too far away. I come here every day."

"I know I'm being insecure, but I don't want you to leave me."

"Jim, I'm sure you're harmless and wouldn't tell anyone else the address, but those women have suffered horrifying violence at the hands of men. They have a right to hide out from the entire male gender while they heal. You're nice, but you can't make up for the rest of your sex."

"I'm not talking about the shelter or the rule. I'm talking about Marilyn Patterson."

Marilyn leaned over, gave him a brief hug and a kiss on the cheek. "Don't wear your disappointment on your sleeve." She backed out of the car. "It doesn't go with the color of your eyes."

"Marilyn—"

"I'll see you again if you want. Maybe we'll have that dinner, okay?"

"When?"

"I'll call you at your office in an hour or so with a status report. If you really want to help me, straighten out Mr. and Mrs. Braxton."

He watched as she strolled quickly down the sidewalk, her shiny black pumps in vivid contrast to the broken, weed-choked and littered concrete paving. Her animated, polished style clashed with the surrounding squalor.

After she disappeared around a corner he leaned back in his Camaro. He would wait five minutes, drive around the block to make sure she wasn't being attacked, then return to the hospital.

Latasha let Terry pass Henrietta Avenue, then guided him back to it by going around several other blocks. Once on Henrietta she had him continue as she watched the house numbers for the correct address.

When he finally passed the shelter she almost didn't recognize it. From the outside at night in a car, it looked like just one more dirty red brick building in a line of dirty red brick buildings. But she saw the row of plants Marilyn kept along the upper window.

She almost gasped, but didn't. She had to act as though she still hadn't noticed anything.

She directed Terry to take several more turns, then drive until she was certain they were at the same block as the shelter, but on the street on the opposite side. As soon as Terry let her and Shontell out of the car, they could cut through a yard, cross the alley and knock on the shelter's rear door. Someone would let them into the kitchen.

"Park here," she said.

He slowed to a stop next to a fire hydrant. "This it?"

"Close enough. You go away now—okay, Mr. Silver? Thank you very much for the food and the ride."

"You're very welcome, little lady. You're sure one smart cookie. I enjoyed your company, I truly did."

Latasha straightened her purse strap around her shoulder and pulled her younger sister out of the car. Shontell had her finger in her mouth and refused to look at Terry. "Shontell thanks you too, even though she's too shy to say it."

"I understand. Good luck. I hope everything works out for you two."

She waved until she saw the red tail lights of his car turn

right at the first intersection. "Come on, Shontell. It's time for you and me to vamoose. You want to see Marilyn, don't you?"

Her finger still in her mouth, Shontell nodded.

"Good."

Latasha held her hand and led her to the side yard of the nearest two family flat. There was a chain link fence around it. Latasha could climb over it, but not with Shontell.

A long howl pierced the air, joined by yapping and barking from behind nearly every house on the block. Dogs.

Latasha didn't want no animal biting her or Shontell. She pulled roughly on Shontell's arm.

"Come on," she said. "We'll just have to walk around the block. Let's go before Terry maybe comes back and spies on us. He was nice to give us all those White Castle burgers, but I don't trust him anymore. He's a sneaky snake."

Just as he had with Marilyn a few minutes before, Jim stared after the two girls, silently watching their backs. They must be Janie's children. Marilyn said they'd found a ride. The smart one must have told the man to drop them off on this side of the block for the same reason Marilyn had refused to let him take her to the shelter's front door. She knew no man should know its location.

The noisy engine died suddenly rather than gradually fading away into the distance. Jim decided to wait a little bit longer.

Seconds later, movement on the fringe of his vision attracted his attention. A dark shadow crept along the sidewalk. When the two girls turned left at the corner, the hunched figure scuttled right after them.

Jim opened his car door and shut it quietly behind him.

Chapter Fourteen

I

St. Louis Abused Women's Shelter

Marilyn searched out Sara. "Are they here yet?"

"They'll show up," Sara said. "Settle down. Have you eaten? There're leftovers in the fridge."

"I'm not hungry. Did you hear what happened to Janie?"

"Only what you told Mildred. She's in bad shape?"

"She might be a vegetable for fifty years or she might not last the night."

"Jesus I'm sorry. I know how attached you were to her."

Marilyn laughed a bitter laugh. "I didn't realize just how much I did hope for her. And now it's over. Her past was lousy and one blow to the head has taken her future. I tried to give her a good life, Sara."

"I know. Some of these women just get under your skin more than others."

"I failed her."

"Hey, you're not her guardian angel. If anything, she failed herself."

"She would have known better if only I'd taken a little more time, tried harder to reach her."

Sara took her hands, looked into her eyes. "Don't let this break you," she said. "There're a lot more Janie's. They need you too. They all deserve your care. Don't lose your faith because of something beyond your control."

"But Janie tried so hard. That's why it's so difficult to accept. She had real spirit. She endured more than most of us will ever have to, but she always came back fighting."

"Nobody bats a thousand. You need to rest."

"I'm too keyed up. I'll wait in the office. I want to be by the phone in case the kids call."

Marilyn's headache was back. Her heartbeat throbbed against her skull and fireworks exploded between her ears. She held her head in her hands, closed her eyes and took deep breaths.

The doorbell rang. Marilyn ran to the peephole.

Latasha and Shontell.

II

Dreamspace

Michael too. Every scar on Janie's body shrieked. Tears swolled her eyes shut. Michael betrayed her like everybody else. Daddy. Uncle Tommy. Mommy. Solange. And—

Michael.

He beat her. She knew it, but she loved him so much she always forgot and forgave, until he beat her again.

Sobs racked her chest. She ought to die. She jumped off the top of the mound.

But the Indian was right, she couldn't die here like that, not so easy. Although it was a long fall the shining silver rope yanked her up just before she hit the ground. She set her feet down flat and ran away from the bad temple on top of the big mound, broke through the surrounding wall of high, rotted sticks topped with skulls and sprinted down rutted dirt streets. Past the ruined homes, broken down like the condemned house on the corner of Michael's street. Dirty, falling apart, stinking. Dangerous.

Filled with dead girls with holes in their chests, body after body of dead girls, dried blood splashed over their dark brown skin.

"Your daughters are at the shelter!" the ghost shouted from the top of the mound, "Now Dewie knows where they are. The circuit is complete. Now I can manifest my power in Peopleland again. I will surround your daughters with Hell. The sacrifice

271

will soon be completed. I am almost free!"

"Marilyn will stop him," Janie said. "Somebody's my real friend. Marilyn will help me. Marilyn will find my babies. So there!"

"Marilyn will betray you too—just like everybody else."

III

St. Louis Abused Women's Shelter

Marilyn hugged and kissed the girls with the passionate hunger of a lion devouring an antelope. "I've been looking all over St. Louis for you two. Where oh where have you been?"

Before Latasha could answer, the bell chimed again. Latasha jumped up. "I'll get it!"

"Wait," Marilyn cried out, but Latasha was already turning the knob.

A strange man barged in.

Marilyn stood up. "Who are you? You're at the wrong house. Get out of here before I call the police."

"It's Terry," Latasha said. Her voice drooped. "Oh, Marilyn, it's my fault. I'm sorry."

Terry pulled a pistol out and pointed it at Marilyn. "Where's my wife?"

Odelia was washing her hands in the downstairs bathroom when she heard the commotion. From the frightened screams and shouts, she thought maybe it was Dewie, but she had just called him only ten minutes before. He couldn't have driven across town that fast.

She stepped outside and saw all the noise was about a strange man at the front door holding a gun on that hincty bitch Marilyn Patterson. So many women in that place, some of them bigger and stronger than most men, yet all of them crying and running away like rabbits from one skinny dude with a popgun. Didn't none of those bitches have any guts? Even Latasha and Shontell, who must have also arrived while she was sitting on the can, had better sense than to be afraid of a runt like this cat.

Odelia strode down the hall determined to take care of business. He looked to be just the kind of cowardly sucker would shoot an unarmed woman or child. She couldn't let him cheat her son of his revenge against the Marilyn Oreo.

The female sumo wrestler who had tied up the pay phone was coming down the stairs. "Terry? Is that really you? You found me here?"

"Betty!" the man shouted. "Goddammit, you left me. Why'd you leave me?"

"You hit me, Terry. I couldn't take it anymore."

Terry aimed at the woman on the stairs. "You hurt me! You broke my heart! You're trying to destroy our marriage."

Terry fired two shots. The blasts filled the house, popping Odelia's ears. Splinters flew from the steps. Betty shrieked, turned and ran back up the stairs.

Before Terry could fire again, Odelia swung and knocked him down. Sprawled on the floor, he said, "Who are you, bitch?"

Not waiting for an answer, he pointed the gun at her. "You must be crazy."

Odelia grabbed his wrist and punched him in the mouth.

The bands of her rings hit bone. He cried out, and she grabbed the gun, then kneed him hard in the stomach and kicked him even harder in the balls.

"Who the hell are YOU, motherfucker?"

Marilyn gasped as the woman turned. Despite the nasty black eye and cut on her forehead she hadn't had this morning, she was obviously Odelia Sykes. "What're you doing here?"

Odelia pointed the gun at her and shouted to the entire building, "You can all come out now, children. The big bad wolf won't hurt you. But everybody stay away from me and keep your hands where I can see them. The party's already started, though the guest of honor hasn't arrived yet. That's my son Dewie, for those of you don't know."

She pointed the pistol at Latasha and Shontell. "And these girls are the maids of honor."

Jim was near the end of the block when he heard the shots. He sprinted as hard as he could toward the building the strange man had disappeared into. As he ran, he noticed a crinkly snapping noise, like static electricity. Chills froze his backbone and a gray fog suddenly condensed in the air.

But he didn't have time for a weather report. The shelter's front door was ajar. He hesitated a moment, then pictured Marilyn inside at the mercy of a gunman—and stepped in.

He immediately saw Odelia holding a pistol on Marilyn and two children, a strange man writhing in pain at her feet.

Odelia swung the pistol toward Jim.

"Another guest has arrived," she shouted. "We couldn't leave out Marilyn's honky boyfriend, Mr. Tiny Dick."

"Jim," Marilyn said. "Why? How'd you—"

Jim pointed to the man on the floor. "Right after I dropped you off I saw him sneaking behind the girls, so I followed him."

"You shouldn't have waited. I told you."

"I just wanted to make sure you'd be all right."

"Can the chatter." Odelia grinned at Jim. "Boy, after my son gets through with her, you're going to have to find you another sister to poke your little white wee wee into. After a real man's jumped her bones, she won't want nothing to do with you. She wouldn't even feel your stubby pecker inside her."

Jim took a fast step forward. Odelia pointed the pistol straight at his chest. "Don't even think about it, boy. You'd make my day. Ain't that what Big Harry Clint Eastwood says? Make my day."

She wouldn't shoot him, not in cold blood. Not in front of twenty witnesses. She wouldn't dare. Would she? His body weight shifted back and forth as he bunched his muscles to spring forward, then thought better of the idea. Caution, caution. Wait.

But Marilyn's life was in danger. If he didn't do something, Dewie was going to rape and probably kill her just as he had Janie Braxton. If Jim allowed that, he would be just as much a little dick coward as she taunted him. To hell with caution. Jim jumped at Odelia.

She shot him.

The bullet slammed into his right leg. Then the floor hit him in the head, his forehead and nose slamming varnished wood. Blood sprayed from his nostrils.

Agony pulsing in his right thigh and upper mouth, Jim tried to push himself up. Marilyn was grappling with Odelia, he had to help. He pulled himself forward, grabbed Odelia's ankle and wrenched it toward him. She fell back. Her head bounced on the carpeting with a muffled thump.

Marilyn leapt on top of Odelia, twisted the gun from the woman's grip, rolled off to the side, turned and pointed the pistol at her head. "Freeze."

The man on the floor rolled to his knees and tried to stand up.

Marilyn moved the gun barrel so it pointed directly at him. "You too."

The man groaned.

"Latasha, Shontell, go into the lounge," Marilyn shouted. "Stay with the others, away from these two. Sara, bring up the clothesline from the basement and tie them both up. Celia, take care of Jim. Maria, call 911. The police ought to be here any minute. They won't let anybody hurt us."

IV

St. Louis Abused Women's Shelter

The back of Odelia's mind opened up. It felt like drinking whiskey all night, sleeping a few hours, waking up with the shakes and drinking more. Just drinking and passing out for a week or two. She hadn't drunk a drop, but that's how her brain felt. Odelia started laughing so hard she didn't think she'd ever stop. Vast energy invaded her mind, expanded it like strong acid or E. She suddenly knew things she hadn't understood before. Like some dreams, when she realized something important was obviously true but when she woke up she couldn't remember it. Now she felt half asleep, yet fully alive.

"911 is busy," the Hispanic chick told Marilyn.

"That's impossible. Try it again."

"I've been trying," she said. "I can't get through."

"Call the police on a regular number," Marilyn said. "Mildred's going to kill me."

The douche bag punched at the phone some more. "All the numbers are busy. I can't get an operator either. Every number I dial is busy."

Odelia kept laughing. "You can't call out."

"What's going on?" Marilyn asked. "Did you cut the lines? Somebody get a cell phone."

"They won't work either."

"What're you talking about?"

Odelia couldn't stop laughing. This really was a good joke. The stuck-up bitch thought she was in control because she had a gun in her hands, though anybody could see she didn't know shit from shinola about using it. Odelia could grab it away from her without half trying, but why bother?

"Dewie's on his way. Nothing can stop him. Nobody can help you. Nobody can escape. Take a look outside."

Sara nervously turned the doorknob.

"Go on," Odelia said. "Open it."

"What's out there?" Sara asked.

"Don't worry, Dewie ain't here yet. When he arrives, he won't ring no doorbell. Just take a look."

"It must be a trick," Marilyn said. "Maybe somebody else is out there."

Sara looked through the peephole. "I don't see anything,

not even the street light. It's just blank."

Sara threw the door wide open, screamed.

Everybody looked outside, and screamed.

Odelia tried to laugh again, but she screamed too.

V

The door to Hell

Instead of the ugly four family flats across Henrietta Avenue, the doorway framed a deep, colorless nothing.

Then a cold gray mist, the ghost of early morning riverbank fog, swirled through emptiness. A hole like a cave entrance opened in the cloudy depths, widening and contracting with a seething, pulsing rhythm. Alive—a toothless, tongueless hungry mouth. A gullet with slimy, slippery walls.

A frosty dread chilled every female's vagina. The two men covered their genitals with their hands. Everybody clenched their anuses. The hole gaped open, revealing a bottomless throat.

In those depths, each of them saw their own vision of eternal pain and punishment.

Maria's teacher forced her to stand in front of her sixth grade class as rivulets of piss streamed down her legs.

Giant green slugs gang raped Sara, embracing every inch of her with their slimy bodies.

Betty Silver crawled on hands and knees, Terry riding her like a cowboy a horse, jabbing his sharp spurs into her ribs.

Terry Silver saw chaos at the heart of the universe, Fate

a Mississippi riverboat gambler dealing five card stud from a marked deck.

Jim staggered lost and alone through an Arctic wilderness of snow and ice.

Odelia wiggled naked in the Sahara desert surrounded by tiny pygmies who jabbed her with needle-sized spears.

Latasha and Shontell lay naked on a giant stone altar, their hands and feet bound. Wearing a magician's black robe, Dewie stood over them holding a gleaming black knife.

Marilyn hung alone in outer space. Helpless, she strangled on choked outrage and frustration.

Sara finally closed the door. Everyone stopped screaming, but continued to sob and weep.

"My boy Dewie's on his way," Odelia said. "That gun won't stop him. The police can't help you. The Indian chief won't let anybody in but Dewie, or any of you out, unless you want to jump down that hole."

Nobody did.

CHAPTER FIFTEEN

I

. Louis Abused Women's Shelter

At Marilyn's direction several women carried Odelia up-stairs to a bedroom and Terry into the kitchen, then trussed them up with clothesline, her to a bed and him to a leg of the Frigidaire. Marilyn then asked Maria to stand guard over Terry. She took a position just inside the kitchen doorway, obviously too nervous to stand any closer. Maybe that was safer anyway.

While they were doing that, Celia examined Jim. She said the bullet had torn Jim's thigh but missed the bone and the femoral artery. She applied a compress of ice cubes wrapped in a spare pillow case. Betty Silver, who hadn't been hit by either of the shots her husband fired at her, helped hold down Jim's arms and torso as Celia poured most of a bottle of hydrogen peroxide into and around his wound.

Marilyn flinched at his screams.

Then Sara, Betty and Marilyn opened the bottom drawer of the office file cabinet. Although Odelia had said guns couldn't hurt Dewie, and Marilyn had seen him destroy her Honda Civic just that morning, she remained convinced guns could protect her.

Guns could kill anybody. That was their horror and their glory. They were indeed the great equalizers of violence. Before guns, the weak had no weapon against the strong but their wits. In an open, fair fight a person with big muscles could be defeated only by someone with bigger muscles or greater skill. Guns allowed anyone to defend themselves—or to commit murder.

"We got any heavy tranks hidden away?" Celia came and asked Marilyn. "I passed out all the Valium, but some of our residents are still ready for rubber walls."

"We might all go loony tunes when Dewie arrives," Marilyn said. "What I've seen him do, you wouldn't believe." She stared at the four pistols in the box. Evil bluish steel and gleaming chrome. "The rest of you divide them up. All I know to do is point and pull the trigger."

"That's enough," Sara said.

Celia grabbed the smallest gun. "I'll take this .22 rimfire. I've had self-defense courses. I'm a pretty good shot with it." She gathered up a number of tiny bullets, loaded six into the revolver and slipped the rest into the pocket of her blouse.

"I'll keep my husband's gun," Betty Silver said. "He taught me how to shoot it."

"Give me the Smith and Wesson," Sara said. "Maria should have the other .32 revolver." She carefully loaded both of them and put the rest of the .32 caliber cartridges from the box into the front pocket of her bluejeans.

Then she picked up the last gun, the biggest one—a gleaming black, wickedly beautiful demon. She checked the magazine, found it fully loaded.

"This is one of those infamous plastic guns," she said. "A .40 caliber Glock 22. A couple of bullets from this baby will stop Dewie, Indian chief or no Indian chief. It holds fifteen or sixteen rounds. I forget which."

Carefully keeping the muzzle pointed away from them toward the outside wall, she drew the slide back, then forward, and cautiously held it out to Marilyn. "There you are, cocked and locked."

"That sounds obscene."

"It just means you're ready to go."

Marilyn pushed it away. "I've never even shot a gun before. You or Betty or Celia keep that monster. I'm scared of it."

"You're in charge," Sara said. "You're the only paid staff member here."

"It's past my scheduled hours. Anyway, Marilyn's going to fire me after all this is over."

"You're the boss, Marilyn, so you should have the biggest gun."

"What are we? Teenaged boys comparing dick sizes in the locker room? You guys have more experience than I do."

"We've shot more," Betty said. "But not with that size. We'll be more effective firing what we've practiced with."

Marilyn didn't want to shoot anybody. But Dewie was on his way, and he wanted to kill Latasha and Shontell for some crazy reason about an Indian chief. She wouldn't hesitate to pull the trigger on anybody who threatened those children.

She took the gun from Sara as though handling dynamite. "What do I do?"

"Aim for his stomach," Betty said. "There'll be a kickback you're not used to, but try not to let your hand jerk up. Hold your firing wrist down with your other hand like you've seen in movies. Your hand will probably still raise up a little bit. That's only natural because you don't have experience. But if you aim for his stomach, with any luck you'll hit his chest."

"He has a gang of friends. What if they all show up?"

"We'll shoot them," Sara said. She paused, smiled. "Mildred would definitely disapprove, but this might be fun."

Marilyn carefully examined the black pistol. It wasn't as heavy as she'd thought it'd be, maybe because it was plastic. "Where's the safety? I thought all guns had to have safeties."

Sara pointed to the small lever inside the trigger guard. "That's it."

"I don't understand."

"This gun's safety is part of the trigger mechanism. You don't have to think about it. Just don't stick your finger in there until you're ready to shoot."

"I don't even remember what Betty just told me. What do I do?"

"Just what you know, dear—point and shoot."

Holding her sister by the hand so she wouldn't wander into everybody's way, Latasha watched Marilyn and the others prepare for Dewie with a guilty conscience. She was to blame. She led Terry to the shelter, then opened the door for him. Dewie was on his way to kill her and Shontell. Because of her mistakes, everybody could die.

She should have known better than to come there. She should have taken Shontell away from Dewie to another city, another country. She didn't see Mama, so Mama must be dead. All because Latasha ran away.

After Sara, Celia and Betty left the office, Marilyn sat in the large, comfy armchair and motioned to Latasha and Shontell. It felt good to snuggle in Marilyn's lap, to wrap her arms around Marilyn's neck and press her face into Marilyn's shoulder while Marilyn held her tight.

"I missed you two so much," Marilyn said. "Where have you been? I was out looking for you all day, I swear."

Latasha briefly told Marilyn everything that had happened to them since last night.

Marilyn kissed them. "You're both so strong and brave. I never would've thought you could walk so far. My God, what you've been through."

"I'm real sorry." Latasha cried despite her efforts to scrunch back the tears. "I didn't mean to bring that Terry dude. He really did save us from Dewie's friends and he was nice and gave us hamburgers. I tried to keep him away, I really did."

"I know, baby. It's not your fault, don't worry. And Terry's not our real problem, is he? Dewie is."

"I'm so sorry about him too. If me and Shontell didn't run away from him last night, he wouldn't be coming here now. He's going to ruin the shelter, isn't he? He's going to hurt you and everybody, isn't he?"

"He's going to try, but we've got five guns. We'll stop him. And if you two hadn't run away last night he probably would've killed you then. I wouldn't want that, Latasha—not for anything, do you understand?"

Latasha nodded. She felt a little better.

Her face serious and stern, Marilyn looked directly into her eyes, "I'm proud of you, dear. But, Latasha, your job's not over yet. You've got to watch Shontell. I know she's a nuisance, but you keep her out of trouble. Okay?"

"Yes, Marilyn."

"From now on I want you both to stay upstairs. Hide under a bed or something. All right?"

"Okay."

Marilyn sniffed. "Lord, you stink. I wish I had time to give you both a bath and change your clothes."

"What happened to Mama?" Latasha asked. "Is she dead?"

Sadness thickened Marilyn's face. "I'd forgotten you didn't know." Her voice sounded as though she were about to cry too. "Dewie hurt her very badly. Shontell, are you listening? I want you to hear about your mother. She's still alive, but she's in the hospital."

"When will she get out?" Latasha asked.

"Honey, I know she's always come out before, lots of times, but last night Dewie hurt her worse than she's ever been hurt before. She probably won't come out for a very long time. She might have to live at the hospital, babies. She might be so sick she won't do anything but sleep for the rest of her life. The doctors don't know yet. It just all depends on how badly she's hurt deep inside her head and how much she wants to live. I know she does because she won't leave you kids behind if she can help it. Your mother's a fighter and she loves you both. But she is hurt really really bad."

"You mean she might die."

"Maybe. I wish I had better news for you."

"If Mama doesn't leave the hospital then where'll we live?"

Marilyn sighed. "That's a very good question and I need you to think about that for me, all right? Your mother's mother and father are at the hospital. Would you like to live with them?"

Latasha shook her head. "Grandpapa and Grandmama Braxton don't like me and Shontell because we were born in sin. That's what they told Mama."

"Do you have other relatives besides Odelia? Your mother had an uncle, but he died of a heart attack two years ago. What about his wife and their children? I've never heard Janie talk about her family. Do you two know any other Braxtons?"

Latasha shook her head. "I don't know where they live. We never met them."

"Maybe Shontell's father has some respectable uncles and aunts."

"Odelia said once that half her family won't talk to her, so maybe they are nice people. But they don't know me and Shontell. Anyway, I'm not blood kin to them. And Michael's the only one thinks Shontell is really his daughter. Dewie and Yolanda and Tiffany all say Shontell could be any black dude's child—I know that's a bad word, but that's what they say, because Mama slept with lots of black guys." She paused, then added, "Maybe it's true. Mama did that, and Shontell doesn't look anything like Michael. Marilyn, I don't want to go to Foster's Home. That's why I couldn't go to the police for help."

Marilyn squeezed them so tightly Latasha thought her ribs would crack. "You're both such adorable, lovable children. It's a sin there isn't somebody who'll take care of you."

Latasha kissed Marilyn on the cheek. "We want to stay with you."

"Oh, that'd make me so happy, you can't know how happy that would make me." Marilyn was crying now. "You'd be the best two little girls I could ever hope to have. But your family has to come first—you understand? If your grandparents want to take you, I can't stop them. I wouldn't, because they are your grandparents. They brought your mother into this world and that means something."

"I'd be scared of them," Latasha said. "They hurt Mama real bad when she was a little kid."

"This might be hard for you to understand, but you've got to try." Marilyn swiped at her tears with the back of her hand. "When people are cruel to other people like that it usually means they hurt deep inside themselves. And your grandparents are older now. Maybe they're not so harsh as they used to be. It wouldn't be easy for them either. It's difficult for people as old as they are to raise two little children. I don't think he would hit you." She wiped her eyes again, but that didn't stop the tears. "But if he ever does, you call me and I'll come snatch you both away. I'll take you to Mexico if I have to. Do you understand?"

Latasha nodded.

"I won't let anybody mistreat you and Shontell, I swear to God. And I promise on my grave that I won't let you two go into a stranger's house. I have a friend at Children's Services. I'm sure she'd expedite the paperwork to approve me as a foster parent and give me custody. Then I'll adopt you. What do you think of that?"

Latasha kissed her cheek again.

Marilyn tried to say something, but her hoarse voice choked in her throat.

Latasha thought Marilyn would never stop crying, but she

finally wiped her eyes and pushed them to the floor. "Now you two go run and hide just like I told you. I don't want to see you again until this is over. Don't come out until you know you're safe."

II

Ashland Avenue

Bullets shot past Dewie as he walked through the door, biting chips of crumbling brick out of the wall. Slugs kicked up clouds of dust in the yard. The loud, rapid cracks punched his ears. The Marauders were shadows standing behind pairs of headlights.

Andre and Turk took quick pot shots, put out one headlight and sent a dark silhouette falling to the sidewalk, screaming.

Bullets struck Dewie's chest, arms, legs and face. The feel of the lead slamming his body reminded him of mud ball fights.

He strode slowly, savoring the moment. He would show these Marauders. He would show Michael. He would show Mama, and all the gangs, teachers, cops, social workers and doctors. He wasn't crazy. He was in charge.

Nothing could stop him now.

"Ten percent," he shouted over the roar of the blazing guns. "That's all I asked. For that you killed my partner."

Then he was close enough to hear the Marauders.

"That motherfucker ought to be deader than hell."

"I don't like this, man."

"I told you all what he done to Deron and Tony. I warned

you, but you wouldn't believe me."

"I hit him, I know I hit him."

"He ain't real, bloods. He must be the Terminator."

Dewie grabbed a sawed off shotgun out of the hands of one Marauder and broke it in two.

"Mother—" the dead man said just before Dewie's fist slammed into his mouth, breaking his lower jaw, slamming his teeth into his tonsils. "Ummmmph," he gargled as he fell back.

Dewie grabbed his head and thomped his face onto the hood of the green Trans Am. It hit with a dull, liquid thud, then the Marauder slid motionless to the ground, leaving a trail of smeared blood.

The remaining Marauders ran for their cars. Doors slammed. Keys frantically ground ignitions while feet stomped gas pedals. Tires squealed.

The driver of the Trans Am was trying to start the engine while a tall Mr. T wannabe in the back seat shot at Dewie with a .38 revolver.

Dewie kicked in the right front tire and tore off the front door. He leaned inside, grabbed the yellow skinned dude with the purple bandanna by the shirt and punched in his chest. Dewie grabbed the shooter by the strands of his gold chains, gave them a half-twist, then pulled, slicing through the man's neck. His throat puked blood.

Andre and Turk stood in the middle of the street firing at the retreating Marauders. Those not in cars disappeared down alleys. "Come on," Dewie shouted to the two remaining Rocks. "Move your tails. We'll finish with them Marauders when I'm king."

After he sacrificed those little girls he would be totally invulnerable, totally free. With the Indian chief all the way inside him Dewie was going to be the biggest, meanest baddest motherfucker in the Valley of Death. He wouldn't be just Boulder no more.

He would be Mountain.

CHAPTER SIXTEEN

I

St. Louis Abused Women's Shelter

Shontell liked to sit in Marilyn's lap but she missed Mama. She hugged Andy to her chest as Latasha led her to the hallway bathroom. Why was everyone acting so scaredy? Where was Mama?

Latasha washed Shontell's face and hands. "Marilyn says we're funky as skunks," she said. "We can't take a bath yet, but we can be sort of clean. You got to go pee pee?"

Shontell shook her head.

Latasha started to wiggle down her sweat pants, then stopped. She pushed Shontell out the door. "Go on, we don't have to be together every single second. But you stay right there. You understand me?"

Shontell nodded.

"Don't move until I come out." Latasha slammed the door.

Shontell's belly growled. It had been a long time since she ate hamburgers at that nice man's house. What a lot of fun. She gobbled down as many White Castles and slurped as much Pepsi as she wanted without anybody scolding her or wiping her mouth off.

Warm, inviting smells floated to her from the kitchen. That was where they cooked the good food she ate when she was at the shelter. And she remembered if she stood near the refrigerator long enough, some nice lady would make a sandwich for her. She'd like a bologna sandwich and lemonade or a piece of leftover fried chicken. Maybe some nice lady was in there now.

Still clenching Andy's neck in her fist, Shontell peeked her head inside the door.

A man lay on the floor in front of the refrigerator. That was funny. Why didn't he sit on a chair? After a moment Shontell realized he was Terry, the nice man.

Maybe Terry would give her more White Castle burgers.

II

Dreamspace

Janie dropped to her knees, dizzy with weariness and heavy with despair. In a brief instant of blinking her eyes she was back inside the ruined temple on top of the mound with the Indian ghost.

She sat on the floor and let her head fall down as far as it would go. "Leave me alone."

"Flesh is weak, especially yours. Flesh feels pain." He

yanked on the silver string so hard that Janie felt her belly button pull out. "You are better off in your air-soul."

"I miss my body. I miss my children. I want to wake up and see my babies again."

"I will give you a body, a healthy body. And you will see your children."

"I want my body."

"Mud is mud. Do you want to see your daughters again?"

"You fooled me before. You made me look like some strange man so my children ran away from me. They thought I was going to hurt them. I may be a slow learner, but I learn. It just takes me longer."

"This time, you will look exactly like you. You will not look like a strange man."

"Don't you play no more awful tricks on my babies."

"You will look just like yourself. I promise."

III

St. Louis Abused Women's Shelter

Shontell blinked. The air chilled and Terry now looked misty and silvery, like the fog outside when the front door opened and she saw something that frightened her. The mist vanished and suddenly Terry was gone.

Mama was there.

"Baby!" Mama cried out, warmth and love in her voice. "My Shontell."

Shontell didn't move. She was glad to see Mama, but where

did Terry go? Something was very strange. She hugged Andy to her chest. The last time she saw Mama, she was scared and she and Latasha ran such a long way. She was very tired and out of breath and frightened.

Janie was so happy. "Come here and give me a kiss, honey. Mama missed you so much. I'm so glad you're here at the shelter. Did they take good care of you while I was in the hospital?"

Janie's crotch was sore and her swollen mouth hurt. She was out of the hospital, but must be still recovering. She tried to stand up, but for some reason couldn't scooch her feet up under her ass. She tried to raise her arms to reach out to her daughter but couldn't. The Indian had tied her ankles and wrists to a leg of the refrigerator.

"Come here, darling," she said. "It's so good to see you again. I had the strangest dream about this old Indian ghost."

Shontell didn't remember what she saw outside the front door, but it was scary and now that same empty color was inside Mama.

"Are you really my mama?" she asked.

"Why sure," Mama said. "Are you really Shontell Kendra Grimes? Is that really Andy the stuffed dog you're holding so tight? You're going to suffocate him to death."

It was Mama, because only Mama and Latasha knew Andy's name. Nobody else cared. Grandmama Odelia didn't know it. Aunt Yolanda and Aunt Tiffany didn't know it. Shontell told Marilyn Andy's name once, but Marilyn forgot by the next time Shontell wanted Marilyn to say hello to Andy.

"Mama! Mama!" Shontell ran and threw her arms around

her neck, kissing her cheek and neck and mouth.

"Oh, honey, I missed you so much. Get a knife so I can cut these ropes off, they're hurting Mama's wrists. I want to hug you back so bad."

Shontell looked around. Whether here in the shelter or at Odelia's house, when grownups saw her playing with knives they took them out of her hands and slapped her fingers. But Mama let her do things other big people didn't. Mama was a little girl like her, only taller.

Shontell stood on her toes, slid open a drawer and pulled out a big chopping knife.

"That's real good," Mama said. "Bring it over here."

Anxious to please her mother, Shontell ran as hard as she could, almost falling as she skidded over the smooth linoleum tiles.

"That's sure a big one," Mama said. "Can you go around me and slice the ropes between my wrists? I know you're not strong yet, but see if you can cut a few so it'll be looser. Don't chop Mama's wrist off, okay? Just push the blade back and forth, like a saw. You remember. You've seen Grandpapa Braxton do that to two by fours."

This was hard work, but real important. Shontell was doing it all by herself too, without Latasha bossing her around and acting smart. Latasha would be so jealous when Mama told everybody Shontell cut her loose.

She discovered if she held the sharp edge of the blade against the clothesline and leaned against it with all her weight and sawed the knife back and forth as hard as she could, she cut through the outside plastic. Then it was easy to slice the white ropy thread inside.

After she cut a few ropes like that, Mama started to wiggle her hands loose. "That's it, baby. Cut some more for Mama. You're such a big girl now, Shontell. Mama's real proud of you."

The paper towel dispenser was empty as usual. Latasha wiped her wet hands down the sides of her sweat pants and stepped out into the hallway. Where was Shontell? She was worse than a puppy, never minding and staying put when she was supposed to. Where did that girl go?

Latasha looked toward the front but saw only adults. Maybe her sister wandered into the kitchen looking for something to eat. The smells made Latasha's head float, and she realized she was hungry. She hoped Shontell had found someone to make a sandwich for her, because Latasha suddenly wanted one too. And an apple. And Frito's. She hurried to the door.

Latasha's mouth went dry and her heart dropped out of her chest when she saw Shontell holding a big knife on a patch of gray mist that looked like Mama but obviously was not. This strange glowing blur in Mama's shape was evil. It chilled Latasha's blood and scratched her deepest nerves. Latasha felt its hate in the pit of her belly.

She blinked and realized Terry was sitting there on the floor in front of Shontell. Terry Silver, tied up—but Shontell was cutting the ropes around his wrists.

"Shontell, get away from him!" Latasha rushed toward them. Run!"

IV

Dreamspace

The dead Indian yanked Janie from the body. Now she saw it was a man tied to a refrigerator and Shontell was cutting him loose. There shouldn't be a man in the shelter's kitchen. Janie watched Latasha, obviously frightened, speed toward the man. He was struggling with the ropes and in a moment would be free. If he was tied up and Latasha was scared of him, he must be a bad man. He must want to hurt Shontell. The Indian tricked her again.

Janie screamed.

V

St. Louis Abused Women's Shelter

Terry shook his head as though he were waking up from an afternoon nap. That stupid little black girl stood next to him holding a knife, a strange look on her face. A knife? And his wrists were almost loose.

"What're you doing?" Latasha screamed.

"Where's Mama?" Shontell was confused and hurt. She must have done something wrong. Now she saw Terry again instead of Mama. What happened?

Latasha grabbed her shoulder and pulled. "Come on."

Shontell refused to budge. Even for Latasha, the smartest person in the world, she wouldn't leave Mama. But where was Mama? Mama was right here, but now Terry was sitting on the floor by the refrigerator.

Latasha snatched Andy from the floor and threw him into the doorway.

How could Latasha be so mean? Shontell dropped the big knife and ran to save Andy before anybody stepped on him.

Terry slipped his hands from the cords. Before the girl could move, he crushed her to his chest with his left arm and grabbed the fallen knife with his right. He held the edge of the blade to Latasha's throat.

"Don't scream," he said. "You're a real smart kid, so don't be stupid now. Don't make me kill you."

Little black sister started crying, then scurried from the kitchen. Nothing he could do about that. He held Latasha in a viselike grip and cut the ropes tying his ankles to the refrigerator. "Don't try anything. I can kill you faster than they can rescue you."

Terry didn't understand why or how he had been given this opportunity to escape, but that wouldn't stop him from using it. It was Fate.

And nobody could stop Fate.

That neglectful black haired bitch who was supposed to be guarding him poked her head around the door. "Oh my God." She jumped in and raised the gun.

Terry crouched on one knee and held Latasha directly in front of him. He pricked her throat with the knife. Latasha flinched but knew better than to cry out or run away. Terry felt the frantic rabbit thumping of her heart against his ribs. He felt sorry for the girl and sure didn't want to hurt her. But now it was time to prove he wasn't one of the sheep, that he could break any and all of society's rules when necessary.

He held the knife in front of Latasha, showing her and that woman the drops of red blood clinging to the stainless steel tip.

"Don't make me cut her any deeper."

"Oh my God." The woman lowered her weapon.

"Keep your mouth shut and slide the gun over."

"Huh?"

Her eyes were glazed over. The stupid cow must be in shock. Her man should have horsewhipped her.

"Put the revolver on the floor and slide it to me."

"Mother of God, I can't do that."

Terry jerked Latasha up, exposing her throat, and made a slashing motion in front of it with the knife. "Sure you can. Come on, I don't have all night."

Hands trembling, she knelt down and almost slammed the gun onto the tiles.

"Watch it," Terry said. "Don't you know how to treat a gun with respect? Do you want it to go off?"

Lips moving in a silent mutter, she backed away from the gun on the floor.

"Didn't you hear me? Slide it over."

Her hand jerked forward, but the heavy metal weapon skidded to a halt just halfway to Terry.

"You idiot. Even my wife is smarter than you. Push it harder."

Her entire body vibrating, the woman crawled on her hands and knees to the gun. She reached for it with a hand shaking so badly Terry was afraid she might pull the trigger out of nervous tension.

She pushed at the gun with the flat of her palm as though batting an insistent kitten from her lap.

CHAPTER SEVENTEEN

I

Dreamspace

Still screaming, Janie looked on as Shontell ran away from the man and he grabbed Latasha and held a knife to her throat. She didn't know who the man was and she didn't understand what happened before or after she was inside his body, but she saw her babies in danger.

Latasha, her beautiful genius first daughter with a knife to her throat, blood dripping from the blade.

Screeching anger like a bird of fire, Janie flew high into the sky over the Indian city.

Rage.

The overpowering need to hit. Kick. Bite. Stab.

Hurt.

Janie sizzled and blazed with the intensity of a welding torch. She wanted to set the Indian on fire. She wanted to burn burn burn.

II

Holy Virgin Mother of God Medical Center

"Code Blue! Code Blue in Neuro ICU. Code Blue!" The words leapt from the overhead speakers.

Judith looked up from her Bible. She had been tuning out the constant pages for doctors so she could concentrate on the Word of God. But this announcement compelled her attention.

The machines surrounding Janie beeped and buzzed. The green lights had changed from a steady, continuous pulse to a frantic flashing.

Interns and nurses ran into the ICU. "Give me ten milligrams of diazepam, stat," the doctor said.

"The EEG says this is her second clonic stage grand mal seizure in the last four minutes," a nurse said. "The beta waves are pushing fifty cycles per second and are extremely spiked in the left temporal lobe."

Judith punched Willie Lee in the shoulder. He snorted, woke up. "What's going on?"

"Something's wrong with Janie. It looks real bad."

"What're they doing?"

"I don't know."

Judith closed the Bible and edged as close to her daughter as she could.

A doctor shouted at the others, "What're her vital signs?"

"BP 200."

"Pulse 100 and climbing."

"The seizures must be throwing the readings off. They're too high."

"Temperature is up to 102.3."

"What? Check it again, that's crazy."

"Now it's 102.5."

"She's burning up."

"Out of the way, lady." A doctor brushed past Judith.

She retreated a few steps but kept watching. She could barely see Janie through the crowd of white uniforms surrounding her. She was so tiny buried underneath those blankets. She had been so still, motionless for hours, but now was twitching and jerking as though shot with electricity. Judith watched as the doctor gave her an injection.

What was going on inside her little girl's body?

A woman shined a penlight into Janie's eyes. "Her pupils are nearly blown."

"Temperature's up to 104."

"Give her a Tylenol suppository and pack her in ice."

They gave Janie a second shot. They worked on her for twenty minutes while shouting at each other. Judith didn't understand most of what they said except that Janie was running a dangerously high fever and also having too many seizures and they didn't understand why.

"For God's sake, why isn't she responding to the diazepam? Give me 600 milligrams of Phenobarbital."

They injected Janie a third time. When the fever reached nearly 105 with a pulse rate over 130, they draped her in a cooling blanket.

Richard Stooker

III

St. Louis Abused Women's Shelter

Latasha stared at the gun spinning in wobbly circles as it approached over the green and yellow, scuffed floor tiles.

Deep in her heart she knew what she had to do, but it frightened her.

If she didn't do it, Terry would escape and maybe shoot Betty. Maybe he would kill other women at the shelter, maybe Marilyn. Maybe even Shontell.

If he hurt anybody, it would be Latasha's fault. She brought him to the shelter. She let him in. She failed to watch over Shontell right after Marilyn asked her to. She had already messed up three times. She couldn't do that again. If he got his hands on this gun everything he did with it to hurt people would be Latasha's fault. So she had to do it.

If she did it, Terry might kill her. She didn't want to die. So she couldn't think about it because then she might not do it.

Under the bright, bluish fluorescent overhead lights the steel was a dull, deadly gray. The metal scraped the floor with a sound that reminded Latasha of Yolanda's baby Boo pushing his plastic cars and trucks through the hall in Odelia's house.

Latasha held her breath, tried to relax. tried not to think. She watched, only watched. And waited.

The gun slid to a halt at least ten or twelve inches from Latasha's feet.

"Goddamn bitch," Terry muttered. He leaned forward and stretched his knife hand out toward the revolver.

306

The instant the blade left Latasha's throat and Terry's grip on her relaxed slightly she slammed her arm straight back as hard as she could. Her elbow hit the soft of his eyeball and the hard bony ridge over it.

Terry yelled. The grip of his left arm around her middle loosened more. Latasha lunged forward and grabbed the barrel of the revolver with both hands.

Terry reached out, captured her ankle and jerked at her. Latasha swung around while searching for the trigger. Holding this big hunk of heavy deadly metal, her hands never before felt so small, so childlike. How dare she even touch a real weapon? Not a plastic water gun or a cap pistol, but an actual killing machine.

Terry was pulling her to him. In just a second he would take the gun from her. Her tiny fingers found the huge trigger. She closed her eyes, tensed—and pulled.

The force of the recoil shocked her. Her hands and wrists hurt. The explosion of sound was the loudest noise she had ever heard. A shelf of glass bottles on the wall fell to the floor, the crash releasing the odors of mixed spices.

Terry's face was an empty mask as though he couldn't believe what Latasha had done. His mouth gaped open wide. He looked almost funny. Latasha waited for him to fall over.

But blood didn't spurt out a hole in his chest or stomach. He didn't grab his shoulder and stagger backward. Nothing happened like in the movies.

When he smiled at her with an ugly grimace, Latasha knew he wasn't dead.

She missed.

Terry yanked her arm and she almost dropped the gun. Now

he would escape and kill Marilyn and Betty and Maria and the other women and Shontell and Latasha too, because she tried to shoot him. This man would murder everybody and it was all her fault.

Latasha raised the gun again, but fell forward as he jerked her to him. As she stumbled, she shoved the barrel into his stomach.

She couldn't miss if she held the gun pointed against him, could she? She closed her eyes again and, flinching, pulled the trigger.

She didn't miss.

IV

Dreamspace

As flames rampaged through Janie the Indian spoke. She heard him as though he were right by her ear.

"You are not even a spark. You are not strong enough to bear this rage and torment. This temper tantrum will only consume your spirit, heart and energy. You are just a weak, helpless victim, hurt and betrayed by everyone you know. Remember my power, remember my strength. Remember the lives I have taken and the souls I have absorbed. You cannot stand before me. You are nothing."

Janie then felt the heat of her own blaze of anger as though tied to a stake in the middle of a bonfire. She turned frantically as though rolling on the ground, twisting and spinning to extinguish the fire consuming her body.

The flames bit her with jagged rows of furnace-hot teeth, grilling her flesh to charcoal black. A high pitched keening surged from her throat. She once knew a woman who had been badly burned in childhood. Her face was an ugly mass of scar tissue, oddly pink and rough. Only a few wisps of curly black hair clung to her bald, jagged scalp. No eyes. An open sore of a nose. Mouth a lipless gash splitting twisted flesh.

Janie would look like her, so gross no man would touch her.

"You are powerless," the ghost said.

Even through her rage Janie realized the Indian was right. She was young, small, ugly, stupid and weak. He was old, big, handsome, smart and strong. She couldn't hurt him.

Her spinning, which had fanned the flames higher at first, now blew them out. Tired, all hope lost, she slowly stopped rotating, winding to a gradual halt like the spinner arrow on a board game. Her fire died to a cold cinder.

The Indian ghost won. Janie had known he would. Janie always lost.

Just like the dead Indian said, Janie was born to suffer. A natural victim—beaten, raped, abused and murdered.

Weak and exhausted, she toppled over like a fallen top and plunged backward to the ground, into a mountain of snow. She sank through its freezing white until she came to a halt at the bottom.

Alone and chilled to the core, Janie closed her eyes and waited to die.

V

Holy Virgin Mother of God Medical Center

"Temperature's dropping," a nurse reported. "It's back down to 104."

"Finally," the doctor said. "I knew it was going to be a long night."

A cold presentment clouded Judith's mind, chilling her heart. Janie's death would be a stain on her conscience. She could never explain it to God, could never ask forgiveness for it. It was duty unfinished, love denied.

In that cold lonely moment she realized for the first time how proud she was of Janie, that her retarded daughter ran away from home, risked the streets of the evil big city to protect her unborn baby from the abortion Judith threatened to force on her.

Judith closed her eyes and prayed as she had never before in her life prayed.

For her daughter's life.

For her own redemption.

VI

Outside The St. Louis Abused Women's Shelter

When Dewie, Turk and Andre found Henrietta Avenue they drove the wrong way onto it and had to make a U turn. When they found the block containing the shelter, Andre stopped the car in the middle of the street and stared like a fool.

"What the fuck's wrong with you?" Dewie shouted. "There's an empty space right there, just across from the place. Park this sonuvabitch and let's go."

From the back seat Turk said, "Boulder, this is real wild."

As he backed into the space, Andre hit the front fender of the van behind. He turned off the ignition, grabbed the wheel with both hands and pressed his forehead to it. "What kind of shit's going down here?"

With a flick of his finger Dewie broke the glove compartment lid off. "Two big rocks begging to be broken into little bitty pebbles." He punched out the glass in his window. "I want to smash something RIGHT NOW!"

"I ain't going in there," Andre said, voice trembling. "Boulder, I ain't no pussy, you know I ain't. I wasn't scared of them Marauders, was I? I'll fight any people you want, but let me fight just people. Not ghosts."

"What the hell is wrong with you two?" Dewie asked.

Turk cowered in the back seat. "Hell's opened up, Boulder. How come you don't see? There's animals—lions and tigers, and gorillas, and giant snakes and piranha fish, and vultures.

311

They all in there waiting to eat me alive."

"My Daddy's in there," Andre said. "And my older brothers. All them's bigger and meaner than me. They all dead, but they all in there waiting. They fitting to whup me harder than they ever whupped me when I was a little kid—and never stop."

Dewie heard the Indian chief inside his mind and realized everything was all right. He didn't see anything because he was the only one the Indian wanted inside. Andre and Turk were his lieutenants, his rocks, but they were only human. The sacrifice of the two virgin girls would make Dewie far more than human. This was his job. His alone.

"You two stay here and wait for me." Dewie slammed the door behind him. "Won't nothing out here hurt you as long as you're loyal to me. Got that?"

Turk and Andre nodded with miserable faces.

"When I come back I'll be so strong won't nothing ever stop me. Nothing—not ever. When I come back, that's when the fun starts. What I done tonight to the Marauders won't be nothing compared to what happens next."

Backbone straight and head held high, Dewie marched to the entrance of the shelter, grabbed the knob and pulled the door off its hinges.

He stepped inside.

CHAPTER EIGHTEEN

I

Holy Virgin Mother of God Medical Center

The crisis over, the doctors and nurses returned to their ordinary duties. Janie was again motionless, unconscious and surrounded by blinking, blipping machinery. Judith understood now those fancy gadgets were only watching Janie. They monitored her heartbeat, blood pressure and other things the medical people understood and when they detected a problem they set off alarms that brought the hospital staff running.

But they weren't keeping Janie alive.

What was? God? The Devil? Probably Janie's sheer cussedness. It was just like her to hang on to life when everybody expected her to die, to make more work and more problems for people.

Willie Lee, now wide awake, squirmed in his seat.

"Stop fidgeting," Judith said. She tried once again to concentrate on her Bible, but the black letters blurred. Judith wiped her eyes and blew her nose. She closed The Holy Book and held it in her lap.

After a long silence she said, "I'm taking them."

"The hell you say."

"Don't start on me. It's our Christian duty. But things got to be different. There's discipline and there's overdoing it. We overdid it with Janie."

"I won't listen to this."

"You don't have to listen to nothing else because I got nothing else to say. I just wanted to tell you, is all."

"I'll leave you. I won't share my home with no little black girl and some unknown man's bastard daughter."

Judith didn't even look at him, just stared straight ahead. "Janie almost died just now. Maybe next time she will. There's something so strange going on inside our little girl that even the doctors don't understand it. She ran a fever on the brink of poaching her brain and that ain't supposed to happen the way she is now. She had out of control seizures for forty minutes. Her blood pressure was high enough like to give her a stroke. Her pulse was two hundred. Two hundred!"

Judith hit her Bible with the meat of a fist. "Something god awful bodacious is going on inside her, Willie Lee. Don't you feel it? It's like Good and Evil, God and Satan, are fighting over her soul. I'm afraid for her. Deathly afraid."

"Judith, why do you keep going back, reopening our wounds over and over again? The past is finished. She made her decision. She wouldn't accept our help when we offered it. She abandoned us, not the other way around. We've prayed over this. We prayed over her hundreds of nights."

"We didn't pray—we begged the Lord. We whined. We made excuses so we wouldn't have to look deep inside our hearts. Then we got drunk."

"There's no struggle over Janie's soul. I know where she's bound, the Devil won that fight a long time ago. I ask the Lord for forgiveness for being too easy on the girl. I should have taken her to church every Sunday morning even if I had to hog-tie her to the pew."

Some fumes in the air must be irritating Judith's eyes. They kept watering no matter how often she dabbed at them with her handkerchief.

"Seems to me you just overstepped your bounds, Willie Lee. We don't know all there is about why some folks go to Heaven and some to Hell. Only God decides on the soul."

"You know what I mean. Sinning sends souls to Hell and Janie's been sinning up a terrible storm. Those little girls are the fruit of her wickedness."

"They're our granddaughters. Whatever we think about Janie's behavior, they need a home. They need love and care just as much as any children. It's not their fault Janie didn't marry a nice man. Where else can they go? You want them growing up in Odelia Sykes' house where they won't never go to church? Where they'll learn everything the Devil wants them to know? Where we can't even imagine the horrors they'll suffer?"

"Let the state take them, put them into a foster home. They'll be better off if they forget their mother. Everybody'll be better off once they're gone away and forgotten, to some home don't mind taking in used children."

She slammed the Bible against her knee so hard the whap

sounded like a pistol shot.

"They're our blood. They're our kin. We can't turn our back on family. That isn't right."

"I told you, Judith—don't think I'm not serious. I can't raise no two little kids at my age and neither can you. I'll leave you first."

"Then go. Get the hell out away from us. I married a man always tried to do his Christian duty. I married a man looked after his kinfolks. I married a strong man with honor. I don't know who you are, but you ain't my husband, so you can just get out of my sight and don't come back."

II

St. Louis Abused Women's Shelter

That social worker Marilyn Snoopy Slut was dragging Latasha through a hallway when Dewie ripped the front door off. She stopped dead at the noise and stared at him. She had an arm around Latasha, who looked near ready to fall. She didn't even glance at him.

The bitch threw Latasha up onto the staircase. "Hurry!" she shouted. Latasha turned her head to give Dewie one thoughtful but angry, spunky look, then ran to the second floor.

"That's all right," Dewie called up the stairwell to her. "Latasha, you and Shontell wave bye bye to each other because your turn's coming."

The women in the living room screamed.

Dewie smiled.

"Yo! Hoes!" He picked up the lamp on the table next to the doorway and threw it against a silly picture of flowers, knocking it off the wall. They crashed to the floor in a mess of shattered glass and crumpled lampshade.

He was tripping. Anybody could pitch a lamp across a room and he wasn't just anybody no more, he was Boulder. He strode into the living room and karate chopped the old-fashioned kind of TV there.

With a loud bang it burst into crumpled pieces. Several women screeched as shards of flying glass cut their faces and arms. They scurried away from him.

"Don't nobody move," he shouted. "You all ain't going no place nohow."

A tubby bitch with stringy brown hair ran up close and pointed a little popgun at him. "Halt! Or I'll shoot."

"Hey, big fat mama, you got enough lard on you to satisfy three dudes. Good thing my pecker's big as four regular sized ones put together. But I don't care how horny you are, you got to wait your turn."

"I mean it—I'll shoot."

Smashing the TV was fun, but he'd done that before and his mama's TV was ten times as big. How could he show he was Boulder?

Dewie punched the wall, sending his fist clear through the double brick side of the building. Cool outside air drifted into the room.

Barrel Butt fired. His chest stung where the bullet struck him. When he didn't fall down bleeding, she fired again. And again.

Dewie reached out, took the gun from her and broke it with

a screeching pop. "Go fuck a fire hydrant."

He stared at all the women watching him with frantic eyes. "Listen up, bitches. We got all night, so it must be all right. I know you cunts take my meaning. I'm going to rape you all, but Marilyn comes first because she's got a big nose don't know enough not to stick it into other folks's business. So I got to stick something in her even bigger than her nose."

Their eyes moved. He turned and saw Marilyn holding a large automatic on him.

"I know you're impatient for a real man, baby," he said. "But you got to squeeze your knees until I'm ready for you."

He stood and smiled while she fired several times. He felt smarter, slicker, cooler than ever before in his life. A house full of bitches to play with and nobody could stop him. Fuck a duck. And tonight only the beginning. After sacrificing them two girls he would have the whole entire world to play games with. Yeah.

A voice from the second floor called down to him. "Dewie? That you, boy?"

"It's me, Mama. Why don't you have some fun too?"

"I'm all tied up, Dewie. They roped my hands to a bedpost. You haul ass up here straight away and cut me loose."

"In a few minutes, Mama. I'm having too good a time."

"What? You ungrateful little bastard. After I carried you for nine months? I ought've flushed you down the toilet like a kitten."

"I love you too, Mama."

He snatched the toady one's t-shirt and ripped it off, exposing her giant breasts inside a dingy white bra. She squinched her eyes shut as he squeezed a tit. "I'm looking forward to our time together, fatso. Everybody knows us blacks love to eat watermelon, and you got two big ones."

"Stop it, Dewie," Marilyn said. "You can't treat people like this."

Dewie shoved Mrs. King Kong to the side and pushed his face right up to Marilyn's. "Let's get one thing straight right now. I. Can. Do. Whatever. The. Hell. I. Want."

He lightly slapped her upside her head, knocking her against the wall, sending several more pictures falling to the floor. She tried to stand up straight, but winced and remained stooped forward.

"I promised you'd be first, and I aim to keep my promises. Hell, I'm near about ready for you. I ain't had no pussy since I raped Janie last night."

"I knew it was you," Marilyn said.

"And you know what else? She loved every second. She wiggled and squirmed like a dog in heat. She told me to stretch her, tear her, rupture her. She was screaming from the pain but she kept begging me for more. She told me I was five times bigger than Michael. She told me Michael never made her come. I was so far up her I made her gag. You believe that? Any man ever make you choke on his dick—from the inside?"

Marilyn didn't reply.

"I didn't think so," Dewie said. "Because ain't no man alive that big except me. And you know the best part? I wasn't even halfway in her. I didn't push all the way in because I would've split her wide open like breaking a wishbone. And you know what else?"

Silence.

"I was just a regular man then. That was even before the Indian chief started to possess me. Them two little girls interrupted us. That's why they got to die, so the chief can go completely inside me. Then won't be nothing I can't do, won't be nothing can hurt me. Nothing."

In a quiet voice Marilyn said, "I'll kill you before I let you hurt those children."

"Talk on, lady. Hot air cheap even these days. Your gun ain't no better than a toy. How you think you or anyone else going to stop me?"

"I'll kill you for what you did to Janie."

"She never had better. You'll find out when I stick it up you. You won't never know how you lived without it. Janie asked me to marry her, said she'd do anything for me if only I'd give her a good dicking every night."

"Marry you?"

"But I said, hell no, you crazy. You ugly, you skinny. I like my women big and beautiful, with tits out to here and a butt that don't never stop. You just a little girl ain't worth shit. Michael only kept you around so's he could show you off as his pet white girl. That's what he called you—his slave. He only fucked you when he felt sorry for you."

Marilyn fired her pistol again.

Dewie smashed the table by the door, then shouted upstairs, "Latasha and Shontell, your Uncle Dewie's coming after you real soon now. You can't run nowhere."

He tore the banister and railing from the staircase. "And you ladies hiding up there with them two little girls—you watch yourselves, you hear me? I know you're all lesbians. That's why your husbands hate you, you disgusting filthy bulldaggers. That's why you ran away here to live with a bunch of women. I need virgins, so put away your dildoes and vibrators. I catch any of you going at it with those girls I'll tear your tongues out by their roots then make you eat them."

"Go away and leave us alone."

A man's voice. Just then Dewie noticed the white dude lying on the couch, a belt around his upper thigh, a slight bullet wound below that. He eased on over.

"Well well well. If it ain't the dickless wonder boy, Marilyn the Big Nose's very own white fairy pussy."

"What do you want?"

"And I thought they didn't allow no men in here. Of course, you're not really a man, are you? So you must not count."

Dewie grabbed his crotch. "You want a piece of this too, you homo faggot? Maybe after I get done fucking all these cunts, I'll tear out whatever teeny tiny little dick and balls you got—just yank them like a dentist pulling a tooth, then I'll plunge in between your legs, ripping through your guts. Think you'd enjoy that, you fairy?"

"Go away."

Dewie slapped the dude on the chest. "Hell, you flatter than me. I don't never fuck a bitch ain't got no tits at all. Even Janie got little bitty ones. So you in luck tonight, pal—I won't fuck you last. I'll just fuck with you right now."

Dewie toyed with the belt buckle. "I could pop off this here belt and watch you bleed to death. What do you think of that?"

"You wouldn't."

"But I don't want you to die yet. First I'll tear the beating hearts out of them two little girls. Then I'll let you watch your girlfriend Marilyn fucking a real man. Then I'll give Watermelon Titties over there the ride of her dreams. Every woman here's going to walk bowlegged for the rest of her life."

Dewie grabbed the white dude's leg just below the knee. "But I don't want you to think I'm leaving you out." Dewie clenched his fingers, applying pressure in one fast, controlled grip. There was a loud snap like a broken branch.

The honky motherfucker rewarded him with a high, womanish scream. Dewie laughed and admired his work. The man's calf looked like a roll of play-doh squeezed in the middle. The flesh where Dewie's fingers had pressed was shrunken in. The bone had to be broken in two or three places. Maybe crushed.

Dewie was cooking. He rampaged through the room, picking up every chair, couch and table and smashing them on the floor. He ripped down the shelves of homemade pottery and knickknacks, shredded the brightly colored afghans on the back of the sofa, wrecked the paintings on the walls. He kicked the legs out from under the couch the white man lay on, pitching him forward onto the floor where he moaned in agony.

Served the son of a bitch right for snooping around Dewie's house.

"Dewie!" Mama shouted. "When you coming up here to untie me?"

"Pretty soon. I got more things to do."

"What the hell you talking about? You always was crazy, boy. Michael's the real man. I can depend on him. You always got underfoot in the goddamned way, crying and whining. You wet your bed until you were fourteen. What the hell's wrong with you, boy? Run on up here."

"Shut the fuck up, Mama."

"You rush up here and untie me and then I'll quiet myself down. You never did listen to your mama. Cutting up animals. Trying to smother Tiffany with a pillow when she was just a little baby. Mr. Sykes almost killed you that night. I should've let him. It took me and Michael two hours to calm him down."

"Be quiet, Mama, before I bust your mouth wide open."

Dewie marched into the small office off the hallway. He smashed the desk into firewood, knocked down the file cabinet and crumpled it into a ball of aluminum foil. He ripped the phone out, kicked apart the green easy chair.

Enlarged, framed photographs lined one wall. A young woman in real old pictures, with stocky, tough looking men. The same woman carrying a picket sign. The woman, older, having her hand shaken by Dr. Martin Luther King Jr. With many men and women Dewie didn't know and didn't want to.

He punched out the frames and ripped up the pictures, covering the worn carpeting with broken glass and confetti. Dewie turned the gray steel waste can upside down and squashed it flat with his foot.

He strode into the kitchen then halted, surprised to find a man lying there in a pool of blood.

"Why, you bitches ain't as goody goody as you make out. A man comes here and what do you do, you tie him up, then shoot the motherfucker. I swear, I'm doing the world a favor getting rid of you murderous whores. I bet you raped him first, didn't you? Probably pulled his pants down and bit off his dick. Poor damn son of a bitch."

Dewie slammed the refrigerator down onto the man's body, mashing it into a bloody pulp. The metal screamed as he ripped through the sides of the icebox. Bottles of mustard, relish and salad dressing broke open. Foil-wrapped packages fell out. A plastic Tupperware container spilled a soggy mess of green mold.

"You bitches can't even keep house."

"Dewie, you going to tear down this whole place before you set me loose?"

"Hold your water, Mama."

As he played, four women including Marilyn and Giant Jugs with a new pistol, kept him covered from a respectful, nervous distance but didn't shoot. The others huddled in small groups in the living room. Sometimes one screamed and ran for the front door, but she always stopped. They never turned the handle to escape, like they were more afraid of the outside than of him. Dewie realized the Indian chief was holding them prisoner with his magic.

He hadn't even worked up a sweat yet. He knocked a big chunk out of the interior wall separating the office and the hallway. Punching and kicking, he moved down its length until he had systematically destroyed the entire section. Now the hallway was strewn with torn pieces of drywall and jagged, splintered wood beams. Clouds of dust, mold and plaster filled the air. The joint looked like the rubble of a condemned house hit by a wrecking ball.

Dewie grinned at the women, flashing his shiny white teeth. "Don't go away, ladies. The fun ain't even started yet."

"Dewie, get your ass on up here."

He started to climb the stairs. "I'm coming, Mama. I'm coming."

III

Dreamspace

66 Wake up, Janie. For your daughters. For all of us."

"Huh." Janie's lips were so numb with cold she could hardly talk.

"You must go into a body in your world." The voice sounded like a choir of young girls, hundreds or millions, blended together.

"Leave me be." Still embedded in the giant snowdrift, Janie closed her eyes and tried to sleep again, to forget. Its freezing embrace caressed every inch of her skin. She sought the darkness and waited for death.

"You wanted to live. Now it is time."

"Go away and leave me alone. I hate you."

"If you abandon hope now Sun of Suns will devour your soul. We will all be doomed."

"So damn what?"

"Ask him again. Beg him for another chance to live inside flesh."

The Indian might make his voice sound beautiful, not evil, but Janie wouldn't be tricked again. When she was in high school a boy told her he could make sparks by swirling the soda in his glass around real fast with his straw. The whole cafeteria laughed at Janie when she said she wanted to see him do it. Everybody could fool her because she was such a dumbbell. She wanted to die. She was tired of everybody always laughing at her.

"You must listen," the Indian voice said.

"Go away."

"He's preparing to sacrifice your daughters. If his Eagle Warrior tears the hearts out of those two virgins, Sun of Suns will completely possess the man's body and soul. If Sun of Suns escapes from Grandmother Earth he will upset the ancient harmony of the cosmos. Chaos will destroy all the worlds. Not just yours, but Dreamspace, Skyworld and even Deathrealm."

"I don't understand," Janie said—but she opened her eyes.

As she blinked, the snow melted and the darkness lightened. She saw another Indian, a woman. Only, she was fuzzy and rippling because she kept changing. She was big and small, her hair was long and short, in bangs and braids and weird topknots and just straight, but always deep black. There was a big hole in the middle of her chest.

"Are you my friend?" Janie asked.

"We are your sisters. If you don't save your daughters you will join us."

She was only weak little retarded Janie Braxton. The Indian ghost was right, although she was too stubborn to admit it to him. Everybody took advantage of her. She knew it, but still always fell for the next sweet talking man who fucked her then fucked her over. Who beat her, raped her and robbed her. She was born a fool and grew up a fool. No matter how hard she tried, she would always be a fool.

"What can I do?"

"You must tell Sun of Suns you want a body again. We know what he will force you to suffer in his colossal arrogance and his desire to destroy your will to live. When you see what you will see, you will know what you must do. If you do not—" The Indian girl raised her many hands, palms flat and out.

"What does that mean?"

"Sun of Suns will win. He will return to Peopleland and thereby disrupt the universe."

"I don't understand."

"That is not important. Just be yourself, Janie Braxton."

"That's all I ever knowed who to be."

CHAPTER NINETEEN

I

St. Louis Abused Women's Shelter

Dewie kicked out boards and punched holes in the stairwell wall with every step. Why not?

But people were more entertaining. Bricks and furniture crumbled and broke apart. They didn't scream or plead. They didn't bleed. They couldn't feel his dick inside them.

All the upstairs doors were shut with no light shining under them. Dewie grinned. Everybody was trying to hide, but he would find those two girls no matter which bed they crouched under, which closet they huddled in. Even if they were on the roof. He'd just rip the place apart.

"That you, boy?" Odelia shouted from the nearest room.

Dewie kicked through the door. These shelter women could turn out the lights but they damn sure couldn't shut up his mama.

He flicked the switch. The room held four small beds with

wooden tables next to them. Although it was filled with scattered women's clothing and underthings, his mother was alone.

"I told you I was coming, Mama." Dewie snapped the clothesline holding her wrists to a wooden bedpost.

She massaged her arms from her fingertips to her elbows.

"You've been knocking the shit out of the place down there for over half an hour," she said. "What the hell's your problem, Dewie? Knowing your own mama up here, a prisoner, and you let me sit there on that dirty stinking sheet with my wrists rubbed raw and all swole up. You might be as strong as Superman but you act almost as retarded as Janie, and crazy too."

"Mama, you talking to the next king of the world, so you watch what the hell you say. You hear me talking to you?"

"Like you shouldn't ought to be talking to your mama."

Dewie squeezed one of the bed posts until the wood popped.

"I ain't no little kid no more," he said. I'm a full grown man. You don't tell me what to do, not no more. You got that?"

"You the orneriest child a mother ever done dropped. I swear, I wish Michael was out of jail so he could talk sense to you, keep you in line."

"Michael ain't never coming out." Dewie didn't care all these people heard their private family business. They'd soon be dead.

"He's kin, boy. Instead of wasting this place you ought to be tearing down your brother's jail."

"I done told you, I'm the next king of the world and I ain't letting Michael out. He going to rot in jail if he lucky. He not, I'll tear him apart piece by piece and feed his damn guts to piranhas."

Mama stood up and took a step toward him. "You're talking

about your own brother, Dewie. Michael always stuck up for you and took care of you. He kept the other boys from whaling the shit out of you every day after school. After you came home bawling your fool head off a few times, Michael found out who done it and stomped them."

"I don't care about all that old past shit."

"You're not hearing me, Dewie. Michael looked out for you. He rode you to school in his car every morning. He made sure your clothes looked sharp. He asked Marko to accept you into the Rocks even though you had a rep as a poor fighter."

"That's a motherfucking lie! I whupped every dude I ever fought."

"Only if they was three or four years younger than you. And Michael always held back a few lines of cocaine for you."

"Big deal. The bastard made thousands of dollars off that shit. He gave away more rocks to strangers at parties than he did to me."

"You got high off him every night. Nobody lets you deal—you just don't have no brains for it. Every time Marko advanced you some weight you just snorted it all up yourself or let some girl have it for talking nice to you. That ain't how dealers make a profit. If it hadn't been for Michael backing you, nobody would've ever let you have a quarter of a gram without cash up front. Michael loves you, Dewie. You're his only brother."

Like Michael really gave a shit about that.

"Michael wouldn't even let me shoot one of his guns."

"You might've blowed a hole in your head. He let you work out with his weights down the basement."

"So big fucking deal. What about Janie, huh? He turned her out to all his friends. Any black dude in the hood wanted a taste of white girl, Michael let him have her. But not me—why?"

"Hell, Dewie, you are retarded. Ain't you never figured out Michael loves that little white slut? Sure, he sold her to a few friends, but just because he scared they'd find out he soft on the skinny bitch. But he think she the mother of his baby, so no way he wants his own brother, right in the same house, chasing her little pussy, trying to get some honky leg behind his back."

"I don't care, I don't care. Michael didn't do shit for me. I'm glad he's in jail. He's going to die in jail."

"Dewie, I'm still your mama. You got to listen to what I say. He's your brother. You got to use this magic power in your hands to bust him out."

"That's how you always are, Mama—on Michael's side. You don't care nothing for me. Everything's Michael. Michael is the man of the house. Michael brings in the big time dope dealing money. Michael buys you gold jewelry and fancy clothes. Michael's always putting me down, but you don't care about that. Everybody wants to laugh at Dewie. Dewie the funny crazy retard."

"He only tells you things for your own good. He's older than you, so he thinks he ought to teach you what he knows, learn you right how to be a man. He knows you resent it, and that hurts him even though he won't ever show it. But he won't never stop trying, because he'll always be your big brother and he thinks he has to be your father too."

"Me, simple Dewie, hurt the great Michael Grimes, the cool, strong, handsome, smart and sexy Michael Grimes? The baddest motherfucking ass in St. Louis? No damn way."

"Chill, Dewie. You running that motor mouth of yours so hot ain't nothing coming out but funky farts."

Dewie got right in her face. "I'm going to kill Michael, Mama." His voice was low. "This morning you was thinking Dewie just acting the fool again, crazy talking about dead Indian chiefs. But I ain't playing. I'm taking over the whole damn world and ain't nothing nobody can do to stop me. You my mama, so I'm going to make you so rich you won't know how to spend the money, make what Michael gave you look like chump change. I'm going to give you more clothes than you can wear and more food than you can eat. You'll have slaves to dress you and clean your fancy mansion and drive your Rolls Royce limousine and lick your toilet clean. I'm going to—"

Then Dewie saw that Mama was near to crying. What the hell?

"Honey, listen to me a minute," she said. "Maybe I treated you bad when you was a little kid and maybe Michael sometimes teased you too much. But I love you, and Michael loves you. I want everything you talked about. I want it all and I'm proud you my son. But I won't enjoy all that gold and silver if I know you killed Michael. He my son too, Dewie. I love you both. When he slapped and pinched you behind my back, I always turned around and belted him, didn't I? Because I'm both you all's mama, and I don't want neither one of you dead, especially killed by the other."

Like she would be crying if Michael was the one fixing to stomp Dewie's butt into the ground.

Dewie slapped his mother, harder than he planned. She fell backward over the mussed up bed. The side of her face had black marks where his fingers struck her. She looked at him with frantic, frightened eyes.

"I hate Michael," Dewie said. I'm going to rip out his guts."

He turned to leave.

"Hold on, child," Mama said.

He wouldn't have listened except her voice suddenly sounded quiet and nice, not like he had ever heard his mother talk before. She was changed.

He turned back around to her. "What now?"

"Do what you want with that Latasha, but don't kill Shontell."

"It got to be done. Both of them—the Indian says so."

"You better listen to your mama instead of him. He don't mean you a bit of good, son. When he zapped this place, he opened up my head, because I'm connected to you. Now you got to listen, because I'm smarter than you and understand things you don't."

"I want all his power, Mama. I got a small piece of it already, but what you seen me do ain't nothing. I want to be king of the world. For that, I got to sacrifice both them girls, because that's what it'll take."

"After he all the way inside your body, where you think Dewie Grimes going to reside? You think he going to share all the good shit with you? I ain't begging you for Shontell's or Michael's sakes, I'm pleading with you for your own good, Dewie. That Indian going to eat your spirit and digest your soul."

Dewie couldn't believe it. Here he was, Boulder, almost Mountain, king of the entire world, and Mama was still trying to fuck things up for him. Just like she always done. But not this time.

"I hear any more, Mama," he said. "I'll kill you."

Dewie crashed back through the door into the hallway. Where were those two little brats? He was ready to tear their hearts out from their flat, skinny chests. He would kill both the children of the white bitch Michael loved more than his own brother.

II

St. Louis Abused Women's Shelter

When she heard Dewie leave his mother, Marilyn said, "I'm going up there. You guys wait here."

"You can't stop him," Betty said.

"I'd rather die trying than stand down here listening to him kill those girls. I might as well put a bullet in my own head. I have to shoot every last round just to know I tried."

"I'm going too," Maria said. "I'm the one let the other creep alone for a few minutes, so it's my fault that poor thing had to shoot him."

"Terry deserved it," Betty said. "I just wish I'd put that bullet in his heart instead of her. If it was anyone's fault, it's mine."

"Listen to us," Sara said with a forced laugh.

"You're right." Marilyn waved her gun. "None of this shit matters. If we don't stop him we're all dead anyway. Come on, let's go. Behind me."

Marilyn thought about the eight or nine cartridges remaining in the Glock's magazine. If she shot all but two...

Dewie'd said that once he killed the girls he would become invincible. Looking at the wreckage of the shelter, Marilyn couldn't afford to disbelieve him. Something evil and powerful was already inside the man. Whether the spirit of an ancient

Indian chief or not, Marilyn couldn't begin to guess, but obviously, from his obsession with the girls, he was not yet as strong as he could and wanted to be. Their bullets hadn't hurt him, but maybe a shotgun or a machine gun could still stop him. He was superhuman, but not yet immortal.

But what if that changed? An indestructible Dewie could take over the world just as he boasted. He could indulge his cruelty with total impunity. He would live out a sadistic sociopath's grandest fantasy.

Wasn't preventing such a catastrophe to the entire human race worth the lives of two children?

Marilyn worked out the rationale as she strode up the stairs, but in her guts she wanted to puke. She loved those girls like daughters. How could she kill them, even to save six billion other human beings? Even though—if she did not shoot them—Dewie would murder them moments later?

Jim bent his good leg at the knee, trying to set the bottom of his shoe flat on the floor. Pain shot through his body. He fought the urge to throw up. An older woman with a bandaged arm wiped his forehead with a wet rag.

"Take it easy," she said. "You don't want to open that blood clot."

"Help me," Jim said, gasping. He braced his hands and elbows on the floor, raised his head and tried to push himself up. Dizziness almost forced him back down.

"What're you doing? You stay right there until we can call 911 for an ambulance."

"Marilyn...needs...me."

"She's in better shape than you are." The woman took one

of his shoulders in her hands and tried to ease him back down, but Jim grabbed her neck, braced himself and, using her as a support, stood up wobbily, his weight on his good leg.

A short woman in a sweat suit gasped and ran over to him. "What're you doing? You stay right there."

"I've...got...to help Marilyn."

"Just like a man," she said, looking to the older woman for agreement. "If you're not beating us up, you're hurting yourself trying to protect us from another man."

"Just get me upstairs."

She hooked Jim's arm with hers. Another woman handed him a broomstick to use as a cane. His field of vision went dark as blood rushed from his head and he almost passed out, but he closed his eyes and fought the weakness and nausea.

The older woman nodded. "We can't escape anyway, so we might as well all be heroes. I'm tired of running away."

Without speaking, they slowly walked Jim up the stairs to the second floor.

In one bedroom Dewie found five women sitting together. A thin one with short, punk-cropped black hair sat in an armchair, legs crossed and smoking a cigarette. "Well big boy, it's about time you got here. I'm horny as hell, listening to you brag about raping us. I've searched through every bar and club in St. Louis for black studs with huge dicks. When you ram your tool up me, I better not be disappointed. And wear some studded leather wristbands."

Dewie turned his eyes away from her. What a weirdo douche bag. He crossed the hall to the last room left and kicked in the door. It landed on a bed as it fell, then clattered sideways to the floor. Two yelps sounded from underneath the mattress.

Dewie grabbed a leg of the frame and lifted the bed off the children. Lying on their stomachs on the bare wood floor with the dust and hair rabbits were the two girls. They still wore the same pink and blue sweat suits they had on the night before when they interrupted his rite to sacrifice Janie.

Latasha stared up at him. "I killed a man."

Dewie laughed. "Your mouth always was too damn smart. Now your scrawny little ass is going to get what's coming to you. And your baby sister too."

"She's your own niece."

"Like hell."

Dewie reached down, flipped them both onto their backs. Latasha glared at him with hateful eyes and tried to scoot away, but he grabbed her arm and slammed her back down onto the floor in front of him. She kicked at him, but he twisted her ankle until she gasped with pain.

Shontell just looked curious. "Hello, Uncle Dewie," she said.

Dewie flattened his palm and fingers to deliver the cutting blow. He barely noticed the many bullets striking him in the back, tearing yet more black-edged holes in his jacket and t-shirt. The flattened lumps of lead clattered onto the floor.

The little white bitch first. For sure, Latasha first.

Dewie raised his hand.

III

Dreamspace

Janie thought about the temple and was back there in an instant.

"I want to live," she told the Indian ghost. "I want back inside real flesh and blood."

"Your mud-body is used up, broken and unconscious. Your heart and brain can no longer hold you."

"Give me another body, any body," Janie said in a pleading voice. "Just like before."

"I tricked you then."

"I don't care. I hate this dream. I want to see my children again. I want to be with my babies."

"I will teach you how stupid you are. You will see your children." The Indian paused. "Are you sure you really want that?"

"Yes. I love them. I'd give anything to be with them again."

"I will send you to them."

"Yes yes!"

"I will send you into another's body. You will share his brain. Through his eyes, you will see your children."

"Yes!"

The Indian ghost lifted his big stone hammer higher than his head. The red tattoos on his cheeks glowed as though on fire. "You will be sorry you asked for this," he said. "It will hurt your heart more than any torture I could devise. You were born a victim, you will die a victim. Others have beaten you, raped you and stolen your money. I am the last and greatest of your abusers. I will murder your spirit. I will rape you until your heart splits open. I will steal what no human thief can—your eternal self."

"Just let me say good-bye to Latasha and Shontell."

"Say good-bye to your soul."

Chapter Twenty

I

St. Louis Abused Women's Shelter

Her pistol useless against Dewie, Marilyn forgot her plan to shoot the children before he could butcher them, dropped the gun and jumped onto Dewie's back. She circled both arms around his neck and tried to choke him.

Dewie shrugged her off, throwing Marilyn across the room onto a bed which collapsed underneath her. She fell, off-balance, and the hard headboard slammed the air from her lungs. She rolled onto the floor and struck her head on the bare wood, knocking her out.

II

St. Louis Abused Women's Shelter

D ewie turned. He'd get that nosy bitch now, smash her skull right while she lay there eyes fixed wide open like she already dead.

He ran toward Marilyn, but stopped when something soft and furry hit him in the cheek. What the hell?

He spotted that funky old stuffed animal Shontell always carried around laying on the floor near his feet. Shontell was hollering and Latasha was cutting her eyes at him so fierce like she wanted to butcher him like a hog. She'd thrown that rag-gedy-ass toy at him like it'd hurt even if he wasn't almost Superman.

She'd eat his balls raw if he let her. Maybe she did kill the dude in the kitchen. She was mean enough.

"You wait your turn, bitch," he told Marilyn. "You're for fun, and I got business to take care of first. I'm going to sacrifice this little white girl deserves to die no matter what, for the Indian King."

Dewie raised his hand. He wouldn't let nothing stop him now.

III

Dreamspace

J anie's babies, Latasha and Shontell, lay on the floor below her, their eyes wide open with fright. She saw the hand poised to strike them dead. She felt the super strength and power in this flesh.

She understood. The Indian ghost had fooled her into occupying Dewie's body while he killed her daughters. Although Janie could see and hear through his eyes and ears, Dewie was still in control. He didn't even feel her inside him. She couldn't stop him. His hand sacrificing her babies would feel like her hand.

The Indian girl who claimed to be her sister had lied to her, betrayed her. Just like Daddy. Mommy. Uncle Tommy. Solange. Michael. Everyone.

Janie tried to break contact, to fly away, but the Indian ghost kept her spirit locked inside Dewie. She couldn't stop him and her mind couldn't escape his brain. She would be an inside witness and participant to the murder of her own children.

IV

St. Louis Abused Women's Shelter

Marilyn groaned and rolled to her side. Her skull throbbed with the meanest headache of her life and her lip was split and bleeding. But Dewie was still after the girls.

She crawled toward the gun, reached out and grabbed it.

V

Dreamspace

Janie, fooled again. Janie the weirdo retard, always good for a laugh. Awake or dreaming, in her body or floating in spirit, she was a dumbbell idiot fathead fool. Raped, beaten and cheated. Always had been, always would be.

Now her children were about to die, murdered by the same man who punched a big hole in the side of her head. He would have knocked out her brains if she had any.

Heat flushed Janie's face. Her heart pounded in her ears like the thumping bass from a boom box.

Dewie was going to kill her daughters. Dewie was going to murder her babies. The Indian ghost was going to make Janie feel Dewie slaughtering Latasha and Shontell.

Janie's heart ran faster and louder like she used to pound her Grandma's old iron washtub with a stick in the back yard, hammering as loud and fast as she could until Grandma finally couldn't stand the noise any longer and ran out of the house to stop her.

Janie remembered everything the dead Indian had shown her of her life: every scolding, whipping and beating, every lie, blow, insult, threat and assault.

The spark in her heart flickered. The same fire that had always sustained her. When Daddy whipped her, when Uncle Tommy Forced her, when Mommy slapped her and tried to murder Latasha, when Solange let the bad men in Tower Grove Park capture her, when Michael beat her. Every time something bad happened she felt cold and empty, as though the fire had gone out, but she always relit it.

Now the flame appeared again, like flicking a Bic.

Then it grew, feeding on her hate and anger. It frightened her but, this time Janie couldn't put it out by swirling her spirit body because she was stuck inside Dewie. So the fire continued to burn and spread.

The coals of her heart flamed high like Daddy squirting starter fluid into a barbecue pit. Janie opened the valve of her rage, letting it pour out in a deluge she had never realized she was holding back. Intense wrath flooded her heart, stoking the fire to the intense heat of the sun.

Her heart burned like prairie wildfire. An oilfield inferno. A forest fire. A fireball. A giant incinerator.

The angry volcano inside Janie erupted. Melted rock and clouds of burnt ash exploded out the top of her head.

She saw only fire, an ocean and sky of yellow and scarlet flames. She heard only the loud booms of her heart like a cannon.

Every sermon she had ever heard promised her damnation if she dared to cuss, gamble, drink or defile her body with impure thoughts. Even as a little girl Janie knew she was damned. She was too stupid to be a good girl. She tried, but she couldn't learn how. She tried, but no matter what she did Daddy called her a little demon and punished her. She could never figure out how to be a saved Christian. She was too slow. She was locked out of Heaven. She already cussed, pitched pennies at school, stole sips of beer behind Daddy's back and polluted herself with unholy thoughts about men and boys and the wee wees between their legs.

Daddy tried to beat the Hell out of her, but he never succeeded—so Janie still had Hell and its wildfire inside her.

Now she let it burn free out of control.

VI

Holy Virgin Mother of God Medical Center

66 Code Blue in Neuro ICU. Code Blue!"

The words blaring from the loudspeaker wakened Judith from a fitful sleep. She clutched at her Bible as it slipped off her lap. Beside her, Willie Lee snorted.

The doctors and nurses came running. They shouted. They checked the machines. They gave Janie shots. They cursed.

"Temperature's 103.4 and rising. BP 200. Pulse rate 150."

"Why?" a doctor asked in frustration. "God Almighty, why?"

"Look at those seizures jerking her body."

"The EEG spikes are trying to jump off the graph."

"Hand me that 10 milligram diazepam stat."

Could they save her little girl? Janie's heart was going way too fast and her blood pressure was smashing her arteries. Doctors and nurses couldn't control what threatened her daughter because they didn't understand it any better than Judith.

She prayed to God, knowing that only He could save Janie.

But did God want to?

VII

Dreamspace

Every fireplace and campfire she had gazed into. The searing pain when Daddy pressed a hot clothes iron to her legs. The lit cigarette an old boyfriend held to her tummy.

The boy in one of her many foster homes who showed her how he liked to set fires. When he burned his arithmetic book in the bathtub, searing the white porcelain charcoal black and sending smoke and ash through the house, he told his parents Janie did it. They had the state take her back.

The way the flames danced when Michael made love to her by candle light.

When the Corbetts' house across the street burned down, red lights flashed and fire engines screeched. Janie watched from her front yard as huge clouds of black smoke billowed from the roof. Several times, when the wind shifted, she saw orange flames behind the smoke. Firemen broke out the windows and aimed a huge hose of streaming water into the house. It made her think of a giant man taking a piss and the idea excited her. Daddy smacked her in the mouth for laughing during a tragedy.

Watching a meteor shower, little stars torching through the night time sky. The exploding gas tanks of cars falling down cliffs on TV. Sparks flashing from underneath her heels when she stomped down on the little red rolls of tape used as cap pistol ammunition. Every Fourth of July huge fireworks burst overhead and bad boys scared her with cherry bombs.

Her heart hammered like drum inside her skull. The blood in her arteries boiled. Pink steam hissed out her nostrils.

Janie felt fragments of the Indian ghost's spirit power inside Dewie's body. Thick, heavy walls of solid rock. Dense, strong and tough. She smelled the Indian with her spirit nose, felt his hard, rocky granite texture with her spirit hands.

Releasing more molten lava from the depths of her volcanic wrath she breathed raging fire onto the huge boulder inside Dewie. Hotter than a crematorium, hot enough to incinerate men into a single ash, hot enough to melt every metal. Flames covered the rock, dancing and spiraling across its surface, licking it with sizzling tongues.

VIII

St. Louis Abused Women's Shelter

Dewie suddenly felt weak and nauseated, dizzy and hot in his head like with a spell of high blood pressure. Even bullets couldn't hurt him—how could he be sick? He closed his eyes and took a deep breath.

Marilyn saw Dewie stagger back a step. Bracing herself with her left hand, she forced herself upright despite the pain in her hip, back and her ribs. She raised the gun, holding her right wrist with her left hand.

But who should she fire at?

She pointed the barrel first at Dewie, then swung it around to Latasha, then back to Dewie.

Waste her final rounds on a bulletproof Dewie? Or grant the children a mercy killing to stop Dewie from taking over the world?

IX

Dreamspace

The Indian screamed with icy rage. He tried to pull Janie from Dewie's body by yanking on her silver thread but she dug her spirit fingers into Dewie's brain and held on tight.

With the flame of her agony she broiled the boulder of the Indian ghost's hardened spirit inside Dewie. It hissed as smoke curled off it. Bubbles popped over its surface like cheese on a pizza baking in the oven. It melted into greasy puddles that crackled like frying grease. Gray ash rose, was scattered in the wind.

The big rock was gone, leaving only a residue of slimy pitch.

X

St. Louis Abused Women's Shelter

Dewie felt the Indian chief's superhuman strength inside him melt like an ice cube in the August sun. His stomach dropped like unexpectedly stepping into a hole in the ground while running.

His arms and legs trembled. His flesh was bruised and aching, his muscles pulped and his ligaments stretched and torn. His entire body suffered the damage of the physical exertion and punishment he had absorbed, from destroying his mother's TV entertainment set that morning to demolishing the shelter a few minutes ago. He throbbed to the bone.

What should he do now? He hurt so badly and felt just as weak and helpless as any ordinary person. He wasn't Boulder, or a rock—not even a pebble. The loose, flimsy, open, normal vulnerable feeling of his skin frightened him. He wanted to turn and run back home.

But maybe this was a test of his worthiness. Maybe the Indian had to go all the way out before he could return all the way back in, after the sacrifice. Dewie no longer had the strength to simply plunge his hand into the children's chests, breaking through their breast bones and rib cages to pull out their hearts, but he still had his switchblade in his pants pocket. That would work.

Jim stood in the doorway leaning on Celia's shoulder and supporting himself with the broom. The agony in his leg made him bite his lip and dig his fingernails into the broom handle, but he had to stand by, ready to help Marilyn if he could.

Noticing Dewie's hesitation, Marilyn jumped between him and the children. She wanted their deaths quick and painless. That would be the final gift of love she would give them.

"Better you than Dewie," Latasha said, apparently understanding Marilyn's dilemma, miraculously forgiving her. "Please do it fast."

Marilyn steeled her determination, then pointed the gun at Shontell's head.

XI

Dreamspace

Haaving destroyed the dead Indian's power within Dewie, Janie found she could now control his body just as she had the first two people the ghost had sent her into. The Indian was still trying to tug her out of Dewie, back to Hell, but she refused to go. She couldn't leave Dewie with her babies.

She saw Marilyn jump in front of her. Saw Marilyn start to shoot Shontell.

Marilyn.

Janie's friend, betraying her too, about to murder Janie's daughters. Just like Solange and all her other smile-in-your-face back-stabbing so-called friends. Just like the Indian said she would. Even Marilyn.

A man shouted, "No! Don't!"

Janie jumped toward Marilyn.

XII

Outside The St. Louis Abused Women's Shelter

"Do you see what I see?" Turk asked.

"It's my father," Andre said. "And he's coming after me with the biggest ass-whupping strap ever." Andre jammed the key into the ignition. "He's crazy looking. Wild."

"It's a tiger the size of King Kong running for us. He just broke out of his cage. Whatever Dewie said would protect us is gone and that tiger is starving."

Andre pulled away from the curb, made a tight U turn that bounced him off a car parked across the street, straightened out and burnt rubber. Horns blared as he zoomed through an intersection.

"Look out where you're going!" Turk screamed.

"Ain't nothing worse than my Daddy," Andre shouted. "Nothing." Andre glanced back. "Holy Shit, my brothers're still gaining." He floored the accelerator.

Turk moaned. "That motherfucking crocodile's—move it!"

Frightened by the danger behind, Andre didn't notice until the last second Henrietta Avenue ended in a circle. He pushed down the brake pedal with both feet.

The tires screamed. He twisted the wheel, but the heavy

Marquis kept skidding, over the curb and through the steel mesh fence around a parking lot. It was still doing fifty when it hit the concrete pillars blocking the closed gate.

CHAPTER TWENTY-ONE

I

St. Louis Abused Women's Shelter

In that same split second Jim shouted, Marilyn realized she couldn't kill those children. Her womb clenched at the thought, sending shock waves of pain through her body, shaking her soul. She would save them or die trying.

"Watch out!" Latasha cried.

Dewie was jumping at her.

Marilyn turned and shot him twice, aiming at his stomach just as Betty told her. It was hopeless. He had survived so many bullets already, what damage could these last rounds do to him? But she had to try. He would have to kill her to reach the girls.

She dropped the gun and arched her fingers into claws. Maybe she could scratch out his eyes.

Dewie's face registered the same shocked surprise Marilyn felt when she saw the blood gushing from his chest. Two big spurts pumping out liquid red. Dewie's skin color faded to a light waxy yellow and he crumpled to the floor.

II

Dreamspace

As the bullets blasted into Dewie's chest, Janie let go of her hold on him. The Indian ghost was still pulling at her so she was jerked back into the underground caves as though attached to a rubber band. Still burning with rage as she whisked past the caverns, she torched every demon and monster inside them.

When she entered the Indian's city of death she set fire to the wood huts. The thatched roofs burned fast. The ceiling beams fell and the walls collapsed. Fire spread through the dry grass, leaves and debris scattered over the ground, consuming the stacks of kindling. The water stored in jugs blew open with blasts of steam. The racks of drying meat cooked, then blackened to cinder. The clay pots holding dried corn, nuts and vegetables burst open.

The dead Indian screamed and tried to stop her, but couldn't extinguish the bonfire of Janie's heart. He diverted the flow of the spirit city's Mississippi River and sprayed her with it, but Janie boiled the water into clouds of vapor before it could quench her flames.

The remaining devils and horrible creatures Janie had seen inside the Indian's caves attacked her. Shrieking and wailing, they rushed at her in a crowd. Their voices, threats and jokes sounded like the bad men who jumped her on the street near Tower Grover Park.

Hate shot from Janie's eyes as though from a flamethrower.

Large batwings flapping, the demons in front tried to retreat, but the weight of the ones behind pushed them into Janie's searing fire. They screamed and rolled on the ground but were devoured. When the ones in the rear saw what was happening they tried to run away, but Janie blocked their escape with a wall of fire. Their fur and skin ignited. Their flesh fell from their bodies and their blackened corpses melted into sizzling grease.

The burning oil of Janie's wrath spread throughout the caverns until it covered the entire floor of the Indian's Hell. Black smoke filled the space and the air shimmered with waves of rising heat.

Janie turned to the young girls with holes in their chest. She concentrated the heat of the flames on each, one by one, until their bodies crumbled to gray ash, cremated.

When she finished with the young girls, the entire city was burnt except the huge mound in the middle with the strange church on top of it.

"Not the Temple!" the ghost shouted.

The well of Janie's screaming fury was far from empty. The Indian had tricked her. Now she would destroy his home in Hell and leave him nothing.

The dry wood of the palisade poles caught fire easily, surrounding the mound with a circle of flame. The skulls on top of each stick were scorched, then burned. Like a dragon, Janie's breath torched the Indian church, blackening it to a cinder.

The Indian ghost screeched with a long, helpless, outraged wail.

Janie's entire body a blazing fireball, she burned the grass growing along the side of the large hill then vaporized the dirt just as she had the boulder inside Dewie's body. This was bigger, but that meant nothing to her. She burned and burned until nothing was left but a blackened hole like the remains of a campfire with the coals scraped out.

The Indian choked, coughed and wailed. "How could you do this? How could you destroy me? You are only a girl—a weak, stupid little girl!"

Janie didn't know and didn't care. She vaguely remembered someone was about to murder her children. The fire in her heart flared up again, but she had nothing else to set on fire. No other targets.

Except one.

III

St. Louis Abused Women's Shelter

Marilyn dropped the gun.

In relief, she half sat, half fell to the floor, nearly landing on Latasha. She bent over, hugged and kissed both girls. "Are you all right?"

Latasha nodded.

"Thank God you're both safe."

"How come Uncle Dewie's bleeding so bad?" Shontell asked. Then she ran across the room, pounced on her stuffed dog and hugged him to her chest.

Jim watched as the women crowded around Marilyn and fussed over the girls. Waves of pain washed through him. He wanted to throw up and faint, and badly needed to lie down. Glad the nightmare was over, he turned to make his way to the nearest bed. He found that Odelia was right behind him.

She drew a large pocketknife from her purse, flicked open the blade. "You killed my son, you goddamn bitch!" She charged into the room straight toward Marilyn.

Jim quickly shifted all his weight to his right foot, lifted the broom and swung the handle at Odelia's head. It rapped her across the bridge of her nose hard enough to make her miss a step, but she didn't stop.

Jim swung again, now falling forward to shove the point of the handle into the small of Odelia's back. This pushed him off balance, but as Jim fell he saw Betty and Sara start to move.

The blade cut Sara across her lower arm, then clattered to the floor as Betty tackled Odelia. Marilyn pulled the kids back out of the way.

Jim's injured leg slammed hard wood. Blood spurted from the gunshot wound.

Torment from the massive break swallowed him and he passed out.

IV

Holy Virgin Mother of God Medical Center

"BP reached the top of the monitor—the highest we can measure. She can't go on like this. Her head'll burst."

"Pulse rate 250. Her heart's going to fibrillate."

"Temperature 106.9."

"Nothing we do is even slowing down the seizures."

"What's happening to her, doctor?"

"You tell me and we'll both know. You tell me how to fix it and I will."

V

Dreamspace

Eyes ablaze, Janie turned to the Indian ghost.

"No!" he screamed.

His spirit tried to rise but was not as quick as Janie. She opened her mouth and vomited all the hate, anger, fear and resentment she carried inside her. She threw up every painful memory the Indian had made her think of again. She regurgitated every moment of torment, loneliness and suffering in her life. Every wound and every betrayal. Every insult and every blow. Every disappointment.

It burned him like acid, destroying his white feather headdress and his leather robes decorated with fancy sewing and seashells. It sizzled away the copper breastplate and ear spools. It etched off his tattoos. It ate him to his bones. They glowed red like logs in a fireplace then crumbled, leaving only a tiny, hovering speck of charred ash.

A thumping noise slammed Janie's ears. Clouds of glowing fireflies surrounded the tiny dot of the Indian. Janie understood she was watching the spirits of the young Indian girls capturing their murderer.

The loud booming was the beating of their hearts.

Holding the dead Indian in their midst, the young girls rose in a group until Janie could no longer see them.

Leaving Janie behind in the burnt out ruins, alone.

She turned around and saw the silver string that trailed behind her was burning too. It sizzled like a dynamite fuse, then flared in a bright explosion of light.

In that blinding lightning flash, Janie saw Daddy standing in front of her. Daddy looked right at her. He saw her too, but he was inside a deep, cold dark shadow.

In one blink of her eyes, her silver string vanished in a puff of black smoke and Daddy disappeared.

VI

Holy Virgin Mother of God Medical Center

Willie Lee took Judith's hand, jolting her.

She knew then there was no hope. She was not surprised when the spiked waves on Janie's EEG monitor flattened to a straight line, when her heart rate dropped from 275 to zero and her blood pressure went from 375 to nothing. Her temperature peaked at 107.3. Numbers Janie would not have understood plotted the end of her life. As a nurse pulled the sheet over Janie's face the doctor noted the exact time for the death certificate.

Willie Lee dropped Judith's hand, returned to the waiting area and stood with his face pressed to the wall, arms folded across his chest. Judith saw her husband's shoulders bunch and tremble. She realized he was sobbing. She'd never before seen Willie Lee cry.

After detaching all the monitors from her body and shoving the huge machinery to the side, the doctors and interns returned to their regular duties, leaving one nurse behind to clean the area. She told Judith she could sit beside Janie until someone from the morgue in the basement arrived to claim the body. In a case like this, with somebody so young, they would have to perform an autopsy.

Judith held her daughter's cooling hand and kissed her cheek. She wanted to start drinking wine and not stop until she fell down dead in a gutter. She wanted to die right away. She would ask one of these doctors for tranquilizers then swallow the entire prescription, joining her daughter in Hell.

Willie Lee was right on that score. If anybody Judith knew was going straight to Hell, it had to be Janie. She had sinned all her life. But Judith no longer cared, she wanted her daughter back. She wanted to join Janie. She missed her.

Judith would someday see Janie again. She was responsible in a way for Janie's death and was therefore destined for Hell herself.

SUN OF SUNS FIVE

Skyworld

Although trapped by his enemies, Sun of Suns' heart sang with joy as he ascended. He was leaving Dirtworld! He was escaping Grandmother Earth's muddy embrace. He would worship Elder Brother Sun again.

He had not seen Elder Brother for twelve fifty-two years. He had failed in his effort to save Elder Brother from the daily cycle of birth and death, but now he understood how foolish he had been when alive in Peopleland. He had not the strength to change Elder Brother's daily journey across the sky and back into Dirtworld. High Priest had been right, that was an impossible ambition. Even with the added power generated by the sacrifices of the fifty-two fifty-two maidens he had not been strong enough. Their spirits had simply weighed him down, trapping him in Dirtworld.

Now he was free.

Rising rapidly through Dirtworld, and Peopleland, and into Skyworld.

363

Elder Brother Sun shone directly above him. Elder Brother would surely appreciate and reward Sun of Suns for trying to help him. After so many years of separation Elder Brother would certainly be glad to greet his younger brother. This was truly a new dawn, a rebirth of life and joy.

Then Elder Brother's rays began scalding Sun of Suns like liquid fire.

Sun of Suns screamed. The farther up he went into Sky-world, the closer he rose toward Elder Brother, the more intense the searing pain tormenting him. He tried to escape, to return to Dirtworld and the dark safety inside Grandmother Earth, but the spirits of the fifty-two fifty-two virgins continued to surround him. They forced Sun of Suns to fly higher.

Into Elder Brother's scorching, burning welcome.

CHAPTER TWENTY-TWO

I

Holy Virgin Mother of God Medical Center

As a well-liked fellow hospital employee in severe condition, Jim received immediate attention from all available staff members in the Emergency Room.

Marilyn took quick advantage of their focus on Jim. Holding Latasha and Shontell's hands and still limping from the pain in her lower back, Marilyn pretended to walk them toward the waiting area, then quickly turned the corner to the elevator bank before the receptionist noticed them.

Their luck held when they reached the Neuro ICU for the floor nurse was in the rear of the station bent over a desk, not paying attention to the front. Marilyn whispered to both girls, "Remember what I said, you must be very quiet."

Marilyn found Judith Braxton sitting beside Janie's bed. "How is she?" Marilyn asked before she noticed the lack of machinery and IVs hooked up to Janie and realized what the answer must be.

Judith's red, puffy eyes burst into tears again but she smiled at the children. "Girls, say good-bye to your mother."

Marilyn lifted Latasha and Shontell so they could see Janie's face one last time.

"Mama!" Shontell squealed with delight so loudly Marilyn was afraid she would bring someone to check on the noise.

Her feet flat on the floor again, Shontell asked Marilyn, "Why's her head look so funny?"

Latasha punched her in the shoulder. "She's dead, stupid."

Shontell began to cry. Latasha then hugged her baby sister until the younger girl stopped.

Marilyn kissed Janie on the cheek and pulled the sheet back over her face. She extended her hand to Judith who was looking at her with a question mark on her face. "I'm Marilyn Patterson, from the women's shelter Janie went to."

Judith looked twenty years older than she had when Marilyn glimpsed her and her husband in the hallway early that morning. The lines of her face were etched deeper and her flesh sagged. Her eyes were pools of misery.

"Of course. Janie talked about you so many times. She said you were her best friend."

"I only wish that were true."

Judith knelt and hugged the girls. "It's so good to see you two are safe." She glanced up at Marilyn. "Were they at your shelter? I wish you'd brought them earlier."

"It's...a long story. They've been through a lot. They really need to go to bed, but they wanted to see how their mother was doing and I couldn't refuse. How long...?"

"Fifteen, twenty minutes, I don't know. Forever."

A hulking shadow stumbled from the adjoining waiting area. "Latasha? Shontell?" The deep husky voice of Willie Lee Braxton was a hoarse croak. "Is that you? Is that really you?"

"Grandpapa!" Shontell said in her high voice. She pulled her sweaty palm from Marilyn's hand and ran to him, then threw her arms around his leg. To Marilyn's amazement, Janie's father picked up the little girl, then hugged and kissed her.

"I'm so glad to see you, Shontell. Grandpapa's so glad to see you." He pressed her tightly to his chest.

Judith bent down and put her hands on Latasha's shoulders. "Don't you want to say hello to your grandfather?"

Latasha shook her head. "He hates us."

"Please, Latasha, for your mother's sake, say something to him. Give him a chance, dear. Please, give us both a chance."

Shontell still in his arms, Willie Lee stepped forward peering uncertainly into the dim light. "Is Latasha there too? Shontell, did you bring your big sister with you? I want to see both of you."

Latasha looked up at Marilyn.

Willie Lee's voice was scored by grief and tears. The Willie Lee Marilyn had heard this morning in Jim's office was a loud, closed-minded bigot. This Willie Lee was crushed by pain.

Marilyn did the hardest thing she had ever done in her life. She nodded to Latasha, dragged the girl forward, then released her hand and said, "Go on, baby. Go to your grandfather."

Two men in white uniforms rolled a gurney up to Marilyn and Judith from behind. "Excuse us, please."

Judith led Marilyn into the small waiting area. "It'll be a relief to leave this place," she said. "It feels like we've been here a hundred years."

Willie Lee sat on the armchair, both girls on his lap, Shontell's eyes closing as she started nodding off.

"I shot a man, Grandpapa," Latasha said.

"You did? A little girl like you?"

Latasha nodded.

"How?"

"With a gun of course." She showed him the dark stains on her sweat suit. "He bled on me."

Mr. and Mrs. Braxton looked at Marilyn. She nodded. "It's true. She was defending herself. She was defending all of us."

"He was a bad man," Latasha said. "I didn't want to kill him." She raised her chin and pointed to the nick on her throat. "See that? He was going to cut my throat. And he wanted to hurt Shontell and shoot Betty and Marilyn and Sara and my other friends."

"The police will want to question them both tomorrow," Marilyn said.

Willie Lee stared into Latasha's eyes. "If you know in your heart you had to do it, then you done right."

"My goodness, what has been happening to them?" Judith asked.

"We've been having a lot of adventures," Marilyn said. "I don't understand everything myself, but tomorrow I'll tell you what I can. Right now, I just want to ask you—who's going to take care of these two? Jim—Mr. Williams, the social worker you talked to this morning—told me you didn't want custody."

Willie Lee reared back. "Give these girls up? You'd have to kill me first, Miss Patterson. I haven't seen them for more than a month of blue moons since they was born because Janie hated to visit us. But now I got my arms around them, ain't nobody taking them away from me."

"I know what you're thinking, Miss Patterson," Judith said. "But believe me—"

"Let me tell it, Mother." Willie Lee stared at Marilyn. "Janie probably told you lots of bad things about me. I'm ashamed to admit it, but they're all true. I had a demon inside me I tried to beat out of her. It don't work that way, only I was too damn stubborn to stop. I was stupider than Janie ever could've thought to be. I didn't treat her right and that's the plain truth of it. It won't bring her back, but I am sorry."

He paused to give both girls another hug and to look at Latasha's face, which was raptly attentive.

"See, we stood out there and watched her die, Mother and me. Them doctors and nurses worked hard, they done what they could, but there was forces at work stronger than them. You're going to think this mighty strange, even crazy, but when she died, I saw a flash of bright light like the fire of the sun. It hurt my eyes and suddenly I just knew, deep in my heart, that Janie wasn't no sinner like I'd always thought. That no matter what she'd done in her life, all the things I'd thought were so bad, sin just didn't abide in her. I don't say I understand, but it was too powerful to argue with."

Judith was nodding.

"I felt as though God had abandoned me because of the way I treated Janie," Willie Lee said. "I was in the Valley of the Shadow of Death right out of the Twenty-Third Psalm. Yet Death itself didn't worry me. I was afeared of the darkness that was God's face turned away from me, of the emptiness of God's silence. I was alone with nothing to hurt me but my own soul and that frightened me more than any Devil I ever preached about. I realized I'd been in that deep midnight darkness near about all my adult life but was too much a damn fool to admit it. I thought I was thrown there by a heathen woman, but it was really my own fault. My hate, my anger, my frustration—even my lust for booze—dropped away from me like a set of clothes too wore out and stinking dirty to wear again. I was left naked."

Marilyn listened with surprised wonder.

"I was in Hell, Miss Patterson. You can keep your brimstone and sinners roasting over flames. I was in the real Hell—the shadow behind God. I was frozen there in solitary blackness until the voices of these two children called out to me. They just now led me out of that lonesome valley."

He hugged the girls close. "I was alone, and now I have them. They can't replace Janie, but I trust God will take care of her as though she were one of his angels because I see now that's what she was. I understand I just got to do right by these two little girls or when I die I'll stay in that valley forever, and my soul shivers at the thought. So all I can say is, you don't have to worry about no child abuse. May God strike me dead if I hurt them one little bit."

Latasha pulled a snapshot out of her purse and showed it to Willie Lee. "This was my last birthday party, Grandpapa. We were at the shelter. They baked me a cake."

A drill pierced Marilyn's skull. Her heart clenched. Her eggless ovaries ached. The small room was suddenly hot and stifling. She had to escape.

Marilyn turned for the door.

Judith grabbed her arm. "Thank you ever so much for all you've done to help them and Janie," she said. "I want you to know you'll be welcome any time you drive down to Jefferson County to visit us. I know the children will always be glad to see you and so will me and Willie Lee. It'll be crowded in our little trailer but with the Lord's help, we'll get by."

Marilyn opened her purse and handed Judith a brown envelope. "I'm sure Janie would want you to have these."

Judith looked inside the envelope and gasped. "But these are two checks for— over fifteen thousand dollars."

"It's her Zebley money, from that Social Security court case."

"I remember when they denied her the SSI. But these checks will have to be returned. They're made out to Janie. We can't cash them."

"Look on the backs."

Judith gasped again. "They're endorsed. Those're Janie's signatures all right. That's her penmanship exactly, those big curves and curlicues just like she was still in the third grade. Did Janie give these to you?"

"I found them in Odelia Sykes' purse when I was searching for other weapons."

"There's still a joint savings account me and Janie took out three-four years ago. Only two dollars in it, but it's open. I'll just write 'For Deposit Only' at the top. If there's a problem, one of the vice-presidents at our bank, he knows us and Janie. He goes to our church. He'll recognize Janie's signature because she's cashed her checks there before. He'll make sure this goes through."

"Obviously Janie signed them before Dewie attacked her. Or maybe he stole them from her, then gave them to Odelia to get them cashed."

"Who's Dewie?" Judith asked.

"Dewie Grimes, Michael's brother. He's the one who attacked Janie. Latasha and Shontell actually saw him right after he'd hit her. That's why they ran away. About twenty of us heard Dewie confess."

"My goodness. Has he been arrested?"

"He's dead."

"Is he the one Latasha shot?"

Marilyn smiled with a grim heart. "No, killing Dewie Grimes was my privilege. Mr. and Mrs. Braxton, it has been a very long day and an even longer night. I will explain everything I can to you tomorrow. Though there's a lot happened we don't understand. Right now, I think we all need to rest."

She stood up. She wanted to kiss Latasha and Shontell but both girls were sound asleep in their grandfather's arms. Shontell still hugged her little stuffed dog. Willie Lee's head was also falling back.

Marilyn couldn't stay any longer. She rushed away without another word. She groped through tear-clouded darkness to the elevators. She felt within herself the emptiness of her lifeless womb. She hadn't been so sad and lonely even after her husband Sam moved out. Like Willie Lee she trod alone through the shadow valley.

And it was truly Hell.

II

Holy Virgin Mother of God Medical Center

❝ Five minutes," the blond nurse told Marilyn. "He needs to rest and all those painkillers are going to knock him out real soon anyway."

Jim's leg was in traction, the entire calf in a cast, a thick roll of bandages around his thigh. He grinned when he saw her, then frowned.

"I'm sorry about the shelter. What're you going to do?"

"That's up to Mildred, but I'm sure we'll just move to a new location. She's not a quitter. I dread the job of putting our records back in order. That is, if I don't go to jail."

"It was self-defense."

"He didn't have a gun—I did. But the cops told me they've been finding dead bodies all day long. With witnesses describing a slim young black guy in a Bulls jacket and Nelson Mandela t-shirt. And all of them killed by blunt trauma, not bullets. So they understand how dangerous Dewie was even barehanded. Or I'd be arrested now."

"I'd be sorry if Dewie succeeded in destroying the shelter after all."

"It's a lot more than bricks and boards. I'm sorry you got hurt."

"Hey, it's my job."

Marilyn smiled. "Even though Janie wasn't in your official workload?"

Jim waved his hand. "Picky picky."

She sat down next to the bed. "How're you doing?"

"I'll recover. Though the doctor says he's never seen a fracture like it before. He's going to put my x-rays in a journal article, so they'll make medical history. I'll probably walk with a limp. That'll make it even easier for women to run away from me."

Marilyn took his hand. "Maybe you should let them chase you."

"That might be fun. I've never tried it, and with a crushed leg bone I won't be able to run away from them very fast."

"Maybe you won't want to. Do you still want to take me out to dinner? I could arrange to be available one evening after you're released, if I'm free on bail."

"You know, you're right—I do need counseling. Who could fall in love with you before dinner?"

"You certainly should at least wait until after the appetizers."

"If you really want to go."

"Let me chase you—all right? You're going to honor me by taking me out to dinner. We'll figure out where we want to go from there after desert."

Jim smiled and nodded, eyelids drooping.

Marilyn kissed his cheek.

Back in her apartment, she sipped a cup of herbal tea and hummed to herself as she watered her green babies.

Until she sniffed the gunpowder on her hands. She dropped her glass of tea and remembered how at the instant of his death she'd seen deep inside Dewey's eyes a look she recognized. She'd seen it often in her clients. Fear and pain. Dewey was another tortured soul she fail to save.

III

Deathspace

Janie wandered through the empty caverns of Hell until the giant spirit of an old woman appeared to her. She wore a necklace of skulls but no clothes to hide her wrinkled, sagging flesh. She held an ear of corn in one hand and with the other she shook a makeshift country broom in Janie's face.

"I'm sweeping you out of here, young lady," the old woman said, cackling. She swung the broom. "Fly away, little girl. Fly as high as you can."

Janie now remembered in this dream she could go anywhere she wanted. The dead Indian had pulled her down there but now he was gone. If he could go up, so could she, even though that silver string attached to her had burnt up.

Janie rose through the empty blackness until she found herself back in the hospital. She looked for her sleeping body but it was no longer in the big room. She was surprised to find it sleeping in a little box in the basement. No machinery or wires attached to her. Why weren't the pretty nurses looking after her? On the side of her head was drops of blood.

She finally found Latasha and Shontell sleeping in chairs beside Mommy and Daddy. She tried to say hello to them, but they still couldn't hear her. As Janie passed by Latasha stirred and Shontell smiled, but nobody woke up.

The sun was rising and the dawn was so beautiful Janie just had to go outside to watch it. She felt drawn to the immense spectacle of glowing, vibrant pink spread throughout the eastern sky. She wanted to fly nearer, to see the beauty close. She zoomed up.

She remembered hearing in school the sun was a long way away, farther than anybody could think about, but that didn't bother her. She didn't care what her teachers said. She wanted to see the sun.

She rose into the sky like a kite, then like an airplane into clear purple air. From above, the tops of the clouds looked like oceans of snow lit an intense, glowing yellow light. The sky over Janie blackened and the blue earth and clouds shrank but she saw only the wonder and majesty drawing her.

She heard music.

Dim at first, it gradually grew louder and clearer, powerfully throbbing. It was like no other music Janie had ever heard, but somehow it reminded her of her favorite hymn when she was little girl, The Ode to Joy.

Holy yet happy.

The closer Janie soared to the sun the brighter and more beautiful was its golden brilliance and the more powerfully it drew her, warming her. It ignited a flame inside her heart. A dazzling, burning light that matched the sun's.

Glory blazing inside her chest, Janie marveled the sun could love even her, Janie Elizabeth Braxton, who was so stupid, ugly, sinful and worthless. Her mouth opened and a tune left her throat.

To Janie's surprise and delight, although it was only a small melody sung in her own little voice, Janie's song joined and harmonized with the music resounding through the sky's choir of angel stars.

Dear Reader,

I hope you enjoyed reading Janie's story half as much as I enjoyed writing it.

If so, please leave a book review on Amazon and tell your horror-loving friends about it.

And sign up for my email newsletter so you get notified of new releases and special promotions:

http://forms.aweber.com/form/23/1283521023.htm

Thank you,
Rick Stooker

Email: rick@richardstooker.com

Blog: http://www.richardstooker.com/

Goodreads: http://www.goodreads.com/richardstooker

Facebook: http://www.facebook.com/richardstookerwrites

LinkedIn: http://www.linkedin.com/in/richardstooker/

P.S.

This is a note that relates only to the physical, paper, version of Virgin Blood.

I didn't plan to include so many pages in the back promoting my other books. A little of that is good, but I don't like having nearly 20 pages.

When I first put Virgin Blood on CreateSpace, I used Microsoft Word to lay it out. That works okay, but it doesn't look as good as a professionally published book. Plus, Word is extremely tough to work with, especially to create headers and footers.

So, I decided to re-do it, using Adobe InDesign, which is the professional desktop publishing program of choice. New York publishers use Adobe InDesign to lay out bestselling books.

What I didn't expect to happen, is that when I use Adobe InDesign, the book is published in a lot fewer pages. I'm not sure why that is, but it's happening.

The problem: my cover for the CreateSpace version is sized for 408 (total, counting front and back matter) pages. I cannot get the artist to change it, and would have to pay another artist.

So I decided to keep it at 408 pages total. That means I have a lot of pages at the end which are no longer needed for the actual novel.

Amazon does not allow that many empty pages.

And you, the reader, might not like it either.

Therefore, they have to be filled, with something.

Hence, I am putting in pages describing other books. I hope you don't mind.

If they interest you, check them out.

If they don't, that's all right. I appreciate you reading Virgin Blood.

Best,
Rick Stooker

Also published by In Dreams Extreme Press

The Chaos Formula

Richard Stooker

Can Jaxon Hampton love the Moon Queen enough to save Earth?

If Zeth, the servant of her enemies the Shadow Giants, defeats Jaxon in battle, the Shadow Giants unleash chaos on Earth and destroy humanity.

Every night Jaxon experiences vivid recurring dreams in which, 10,000 years ago, he escorts a beautiful woman through many dangers to the top of a cliff overlooking the Nile River.

How come his boss's daughter dreams the same story? And why does a strange man hypnotize Jaxon to take the young woman to a bluff overlooking the Mississippi River during the next full moon?

Jaxon works as head trader for a small money management business. His boss tells him she came up with a sure-fire trading system, the Chaos Formula. Her test account verifies a terrifyingly high number of winning trades.

Jaxon can't believe. Stock market results form a random, bell-shaped curve. Perhaps not a strictly normal distribution, but unpredictable.

Yet this ability of his boss to foretell stock market results constitutes just one sign of reality going haywire.

What compels Jaxon to spend his evenings staring up at the moon, even to the point he forces his girlfriend to leave him?

Every night, he dreams he wields a bronze sword ten thousand years in the past, at the mouth of the Nile River, long before the pyramids. He fights as a soldier for the king of a growing empire. The other soldiers call him Blood Reaper.

One night the king assigns him to take a young woman far upriver, for a sacrifice.

A strangely beautiful woman, despite her white skin, blue eyes, and gold hair.

She must travel to where bluffs overlook the Nile River, protected only by Jaxon -- against roving animals, wild people, and superstitious dirt farmers.

Jaxon does not understand why the sacrifice takes place so far from the temples, but he must obey his king. He figures a wealthy merchant wishes to sacrifice an ex-mistress to gain merit with the gods instead of just selling her to a brothel.

When she reveals her true identity as the Moon Queen herself, he does not believe . . . until he meets her ancient enemies the Shadow Giants.

How and why does his boss's daughter, Laura Ewing, dream the same story, only as the woman?

And how can he and Laura use her mother's Chaos Formula to win over five hundred dollars at a Mini-Bac table at the Lumiere Place Casino?

Why does Mr. bin Hasad, the small, dapper foreigner keep visiting Jaxon on his job even though he doesn't open up a trading account? And Jaxon can't remember what they discuss?

How did Jaxon's brother Keith buy the most evil book in the

world from Ken, the Romani and Bosnian refugee who runs the largest occult bookstore in the New World, when Keith claims he stops dealing drugs?

Why does someone calling himself Zeth kill young women and drain their blood into a crystal bowl to scry messages to and from the Shadow Giants?

Who lives? Who dies?

Do the Shadow Giants overwhelm life on Earth with chaos and destruction?

This paranormal fantasy adventure combines stories from ten thousand years ago -- a nitty gritty historical dark fantasy -- with a contemporary dark fantasy in the modern world. A form of urban fantasy as well.

Try out The Chaos Formula now.

Assassin Years

Melody Ryan

In October 1968, teenager Denise Reid falls asleep one evening just like every night. So does, in October, 2012, Taylor Williams, also 17 years old.

In the morning, they discover they exchanged personalities.

Denise wakes up in 2012, in Taylor's body. Taylor now occupies Denise's body and time.

Each must learn to cope with the forty-four year-switch. And each attends a presidential campaign speech central to a European billionaire's plot to destroy the United States.

His plan? Assassinate presidential candidate Richard Nixon in 1968 and President Obama, running for reelection, in 2012. Only Denise and Taylor stand between him and success, but how can two teenaged girls stop the armed killers?

To Denise, 2012 and cell phones, personal computers, and $6 per gallon gasoline come straight out of an episode of The Jetsons.

To Taylor, 1968 feels like a museum come to life. The pink Princess telephone won't work unless plugged into the wall. Typewriters. Clothes either too demure or too outlandish.

However, her high school teachers horrify Denise the worst. They criticize the United States more than the hippies of her time. Teachers! And the students agree!

But not all. Soon she meets Andre, who writes the blog the Voice of Young Black Republicans. She doesn't know a blog from Wi-Fi, but he answers her many questions. He takes her to a meeting of a conservative. He doesn't know an inner circle of the group, manipulated by an agent of the European billionaire, plans to meet President Obama's upcoming campaign speech with bullets instead of protest signs.

Taylor hates Denise's annoying boyfriend, but comes to rely on the hippie Georgie. He helps her find the ancient library book that promises to send her back to 2012.

Georgie also tells Taylor of the Black Cougars' plan -- also caused by manipulation by the European billionaire -- to assassinate Richard Nixon when he makes a campaign speech.

Taylor thinks it's not her problem until Georgie convinces her Nixon's death by assassination in 1968 would plunge the United States into violence and chaos . . . that would inevitably change 2012 as she (and we) know it.

Georgie proclaims himself a lover, not a fighter, and he won't stand by and watch his country overrun by hate.

And Taylor loves Georgie.

How can the two teenage girls, in shock from time travel lag, stop two presidential level assassinations separated by forty-four years?

And what happens when they must return to their own years?

In this teenage adventure fiction, two teenage girls battle ruthless men determined to carry out the crimes of two centuries. An unusual young adult time travel adventure and romance.

Two presidential level assassinations that don't occur in history as we now know it -- but young adult time travel political thriller, a powerful, wealthy man plans to change that. He hates history as we know it, because the United States remains strong.

Try out Assassin Years now.

The Pi-a-saw Bird

Richard Stooker

In 1673 the first European explorers to travel down the Mississippi River spot on the high, sheer bluffs the painting of a huge, winged monster. Where does it come from?

Why did somebody take the trouble and risk to paint it on the bluff face? The Indians told them the terrifying story of a man-eating dragon-like creature, and the brave chief who killed it.

This historical, Native American dragon fantasy short story previously published in FANTASTIC December 1975, and unavailable since then, until now.

We know dragon stories and legends from Europe and Asia go back thousands of years. Did some such creature prey on people just north of modern-day St. Louis? A dragon in North America?

The French explorers Pere Marquette and Joliet paddle their canoes down the Father of Waters, the first Europeans to journey through the middle of the newly discovered continent of North America.

They spot the painting.

Why did some unnamed Indian artist risk their life to create it? The perpendicular bluffs rise up from the river hundreds of feet high. Other Indians must have lowered the artist on a rope from the top, and the artist dangled above the rocks of the river shore as they worked.

Canoes of Indian warriors pass the explorers on the river.

As they pass the painting of the dragon-like, flying monster, they shoot arrows at the Indian dragon.

A certain loss of good arrows, because they break or bounce off the white limestone rock of the bluff and fall into the river.

What frightens the Indians so much?

1. The Behind the Scenes Story of "The Pi-a-saw Bird" by the author. It's normally spelled The Piasa Bird, in Alton Illinois where the painting is kept up on the bluffs.

Try out The Pi-a-saw Bird Now

The Copper Quarter

Richard Stooker

The friendly man shocks the bar by paying for everybody's drinks with a silver quarter. His ruthless killing in the street outside surprises nobody.

When private detective Crain Dalton seeks out the beautiful widow, he uncovers a plot to buy local elections with the only kind of money worth anything -- silver and gold, once again illegal to own.

Down the mean streets of the near-future, a man must go .

Welcome to the near-future of the United States:

Economic malaise and poverty and want for the vast majority of people.

Ecological decay.

Lots of paper money that buys nothing.

Criminal gangs and politicians cooperate to run the government, and split the swag.

Big cities deteriorating into hellholes.

A lot like the present, only worse . . .

Yet, as the world grows more and more amoral, Crain battles the powerful in defense of humanity dignity.

Until now, unavailable for over thirty years! The Copper Quarter originally appeared in the February 1979 issue of AMAZING.

Try out The Copper Quarter now